Betrayal

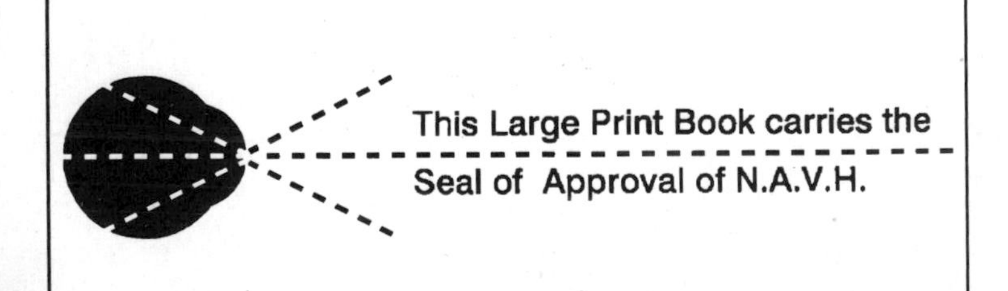
This Large Print Book carries the
Seal of Approval of N.A.V.H.

BETRAYAL

FERN MICHAELS

WHEELER PUBLISHING
A part of Gale, Cengage Learning

Detroit • New York • San Francisco • New Haven, Conn • Waterville, Maine • London

GALE
CENGAGE Learning™

Wheeler Publishing, a part of Gale, Cengage Learning.

Set in 16 pt. Plantin.

LIBRARY OF CONGRESS CATALOGING-IN-PUBLICATION DATA

Michaels, Fern.
Betrayal / by Fern Michaels.
p. cm. — (Wheeler Publishing large print hardcover)
ISBN-13: 978-1-4104-3581-1
ISBN-10: 1-4104-3581-4
1. Friendship—Fiction. 2. Revenge—Fiction. 3. Marriage—Fiction. 4. Large type books. I. Title.
PS3563.I27.B48 2011
813'.54—dc22 2011012033

Published in 2011 by arrangement with Zebra Books, an imprint of Kensington Publishing Corp.

Printed in the United States of America
1 2 3 4 5 6 7 15 14 13 12 11

Betrayal

Prologue

Alex Rocket's normally steady hand trembled as he punched the End button on the telephone and placed it on the butcher block island in the center of the kitchen. He glanced at the phone as though it were evil, a thing to fear, then scanned the room, reminiscing. So many happy moments had occurred in the cherry red and white haven. Kate's numerous recipes were created here. Some good, some not so good, but most of all, Alex recalled the happiness he always felt in the large, cheery kitchen. O'Keefe & Merritt retro red appliances, handmade oak cabinets, Kate's collection of pottery, some she'd made herself, and several small pots filled with fragrant herbs, dozens of cookbooks lining built-in shelves, all contributing to the kitchen's merry atmosphere.

The Ruffoni cookware Alex had purchased for Kate as a wedding gift still sparkled, bright and coppery, as it hung from the rack in the center of the kitchen. No diamonds and gold for Kate. A sad smile touched the corner of his mouth as he recalled asking Kate what she'd like for a wedding gift. She'd wanted Ruffoni cookware — copper and handmade in Italy. He scanned the contents of the kitchen as though he were in a museum. Each and every fork, knife, and spoon held a memory. Bowls, plates, and filet knives had all at one time or another played such an insignificant role in his everyday life that he never gave a thought to the object, other than its basic use. Now, however, all the inanimate objects in the kitchen held new meaning. With every fork, knife, and spoon he had shared a meal with Kate, maybe Gertie. Unbeknownst to Kate, he'd even spoon-fed a few of the pups from the everyday dishes. All of these memories cascaded through his mind like a waterfall. He couldn't stop them; he felt as though he would drown in the sheer abundance of them, there were so many. Most of his memories were good ones, too. If only he could turn back the clock to gentler times. Hell, if only he could turn the clock back one hour. A sudden sense of foreboding engulfed him like a shroud. As of that very hour, the hands of time swiftly changed the course of life as he knew it. From that second forward, life as he knew it would never be the same.

CHAPTER 1

Naples, Florida

"How can you possibly think of food at a time like this?" Emily asked Sara, her younger sister, as the older girl sat on top of her baby blue Samsonite, hoping the extra weight would make it easier to close. She had surprise presents for Uncle Alex and Aunt Kate inside that she didn't want Sara or her parents to see.

At twelve, Sara was fifty pounds heavier than Emily, who was already fifteen. Emily wished her sister wouldn't focus on food so much.

"Mommy says I'm healthy because I eat well. Daddy, too. So there." Sara struggled to push herself out of the child-sized rocking chair she'd had since she was three. She stood with the small chair still attached to her burgeoning hips.

"Here." Emily closed the locks on the luggage. "Let me help." In one swift motion,

Emily yanked the rocking chair from Sara's growing bottom.

"Ouch!" Sara yelled.

"You're way too big for that chair. You need an adult-sized chair now," Emily explained.

"No, I don't. You're just jealous." Sara smirked as she rubbed her hands up and down her backside.

Emily rolled her eyes and placed her luggage in the hall. "I can't imagine why you would say that. Listen, we need to get a move on. Mom and Dad said to be ready by eight. It's almost nine o'clock," Emily urged.

"Mommy packed my things last night; besides, I'm not going anywhere until I've had my breakfast. So there!" Sara stuck her tongue out at Emily. She lumbered her expanding bulk across the room, stopping in the doorway. "And I don't care what time it is."

"Brat!" Emily shouted to her sister's retreating back. Soon Sara would be the size of a house if something wasn't done about her weight. She'd try and talk to her once they were at Uncle Alex's. Sara didn't seem to act as rotten when they visited their aunt and uncle. Emily was really looking forward to this visit. She'd always felt extremely close to Uncle Alex, plus he had all those wonderful golden retrievers. At this stage in her life, she figured, this was about as close to heaven as she could get.

Emily heard the electric garage door open, reminding her it was time to leave for Asheville. She grabbed her diary, which she'd caught Sara snooping in the other day. She stuffed it in the bottom of her book bag for safekeeping. She glanced around her room one last time, just to make sure she wasn't leaving anything important behind, then closed her door and headed downstairs.

She couldn't wait to leave what she privately referred to as the "ice palace." Her mother was so finicky, always afraid a speck of dust would ruin the ridiculous white furniture throughout their house. Aunt Kate's house was so much more relaxing. They didn't even care if the dogs jumped all over the furniture. Aunt Kate would never have white furniture either. Hers was worn and soft, and so what if there was an occasional mass of dog hair? Emily liked the casual life and loved all the animals roaming in and out of the house. Emily figured her mother would have heart failure if an animal of any kind entered their house.

Emily walked into the kitchen just in time

to see Sara seated at the breakfast bar with egg yolk smeared across her fat face. Emily grabbed a paper towel, dampened it, and gave it to Sara. "Wipe your face. It's time to leave. If we don't get on the road, we'll end up spending the night in one of those twenty-dollar hotels with the scratchy sheets that you hate."

Sara snatched the paper towel from Emily and halfheartedly wiped it across her mouth. "I hope you're satisfied!" Sara tossed the wet paper towel on the kitchen floor.

"C'mon, Sara, don't be such a pig. Let's go. Dad's waiting in the car." Emily picked up the paper towel and tossed it in the garbage can under the sink. "They're waiting, Sara," Emily said, enunciating each word slowly.

"Mommy isn't in the car yet," Sara retorted.

Emily rolled her eyes. "Yes, but she's almost ready. I just heard the door slam." Her mother always hated the fact that they drove to North Carolina instead of flying. If anything cramped her style in the slightest, her mother always let those around her know it. Door slamming had become quite popular the past year.

Reluctantly, Sara shoved away from the

table and followed Emily out the garage door.

Emily tucked her luggage in between Sara's in the back of the Explorer. She climbed into the backseat and took a paperback novel from her book bag. She hoped reading would prevent Sara from aggravating her with all kinds of questions and stupid comments. She loved her little sister, but sometimes she wished her parents would exercise a bit more control over her behavior. She was beyond spoiled and had no real friends at school, so most of her free time at home was spent tormenting Emily with dumb questions and dopey comments.

Emily winced as she heard the front door slam. Her mother must be ready to leave. She didn't dare look away from her book. When her mother was in one of her moods, Emily knew from experience that it was best to remain quiet. Sara was sure to provide her mother with plenty of distraction.

Wearing white slacks and a lime green silk blouse, Debbie Winter appeared to be dressed for one of her charity luncheons, certainly not a lengthy automobile trip. Emily observed her mother sliding onto the front seat. Her short brown hair was shellacked to her head and she was wearing too much eyeliner. Her eyelashes were so thickly coated with mascara that she looked like a goblin of sorts. *Why can't she be more like Aunt Kate?* Emily could almost guarantee Aunt Kate wouldn't wear white slacks and a silk blouse to go on a road trip. Most likely, she'd have on jeans and a comfortable T-shirt. She certainly wouldn't have bothered with all the makeup and hair spray. Emily just shook her head and immersed herself in her novel.

"Is everyone all set to go?" Don Winter asked as he shifted into drive.

"I guess we'd better be set, you're certainly not waiting around if we're not." Sarcasm spewed from Debbie's pink-glossed mouth.

At that precise moment Don Winter's jaw clenched and his steel gray eyes blazed with fire. He drew in a deep breath, then released it through his nose. "Then let me repeat myself. Are we all set for the drive to Asheville?" He peered over his shoulder at Emily and Sara in the backseat. When there was no response, he put the Explorer in gear. "I guess this means we're ready." Without another word Don Winter drove slowly through Quail Lake, the exquisite gated community in Naples. They passed the state-of-the-art fitness center, a ballroom that no one seemed to use, or even wanted to, for that matter, the spa and massage center. They even had a room exclusively for birthday parties. A Tuscan-style fountain held center stage next to the exit gates. A guardhouse that looked like a small mansion lodged two elderly men in uniforms; both seemed about as excited to be at their jobs as a ballerina in a football stadium. Don waved to the men when they stopped at the gate. A kaleidoscope of flowers decorated the road into the gated community. Yellow hibiscus and red geraniums dotted the edge of the concrete walkways. Purple, red, and yellow bougainvillea vines were in full bloom. In a few short weeks the gardeners would be removing the dead leaves, and another plant or bush would dominate the landscape. Quail Lake homes were selling for millions of dollars. Don wanted to scale down to something smaller when the girls went to college. If he could make a hefty profit from the sale, then more power to him. Debbie refused to discuss selling their home. She'd said this was her home, and there wouldn't be any more talk of selling. He'd acquiesced for the moment, but knew the decision was only temporary.

Two months ago Don had had a cell phone installed in the Explorer. Not being used to hearing a phone ringing in the car, he almost swerved into oncoming traffic as he pulled onto Highway 41.

"Hello."

"I thought you'd be rolling up the mountain by now. What's up?" Alex Rocket's cheerful voice sounded as though he were in the car with them. Modern technology still amazed him.

"Hey, you big dope. I'm just now getting on the road. We got a late start." Don glanced at Debbie picking at some imaginary speck on her slacks.

"Big dope, huh? I'm not the one who's late." Alex's zany laughter could be heard over the wires.

"Three women. It takes time."

"I bet it does. I called to see if I could give Emily a surprise. Ginger just had another litter, I thought she might want one. What do you say? I wouldn't want to give her a puppy without your permission."

Don quickly scrutinized Debbie's white slacks. She couldn't deal with a human hair in her perfectly decorated home, let alone dog hairs all over the house. "I would love to say yes, but Deb isn't very fond of animals. The hair and all. I'm sorry." Don wouldn't have minded a pet, but Debbie would rather die than entertain the thought of one.

Don heard Alex's sigh over the phone.

"No problem. I just know how much Emily loves dogs."

"Maybe when she's on her own she can take a few dogs off your hands. Right now she's pretty involved with school and sports. She made the girls' basketball team again. You should see her. Reminds me of you, Rocket Man, when we were in high school."

"I haven't been called that in ages," Alex said wistfully. "Tell Em I'll expect a game of one-on-one while she's here."

Don smiled. "You can count on it. If the traffic isn't too bad and the girls are up for the ride, we should be there late tonight, if not, midmorning tomorrow."

"Either way, we'll be here waiting. Kate can't wait to see the girls."

"They're excited, too. See you soon, old man." Don pressed the End button and placed the phone back in its stand.

"Alex and Kate are really anxious to see the girls," Don said.

Debbie looked at her husband of seventeen years. Suddenly, she couldn't remember what had attracted her to him in the first place. "Kate's barren. She warms up to any kid."

"That's a mean thing to say. She loves the girls and you know she does," Don replied, an edge to his voice.

Debbie snickered. "I didn't say that she didn't like the girls. I simply stated a fact. The woman is barren. She uses the girls as substitute children."

"That's not true, Mom," Emily said.

"As if you would know. Wait till you have children of your own before you voice an opinion on something you have no clue about. You're just like your father. You think you know something about everything."

"Debbie, that's uncalled for." She'd been in a bad mood for days. Don was sick of her. "Stop taking whatever's crawled up your ass out on Emily."

Emily wanted to say more in defense of Aunt Kate, but an argument with her mother was the last thing she needed at the moment. She resumed reading her novel.

"I'm not taking anything out on Emily. I'm just going along for the ride, Don. We could've flown to Asheville, but as usual, you have to control whatever we do. I'm surprised you didn't tell me what to wear." Debbie rolled her eyes and picked at her perfectly manicured oval nails.

"Let's not start, okay? We've got a long ride ahead of us, and I'd like to drive in peace."

"If you'd fly, we wouldn't have to suffer

through this long, boring ride," Debbie shot back.

"I like to drive. It relaxes me. You know that."

"Yes, I do. I always do whatever you want, and I'm getting sick and tired of it. Don wants this, Don wants that. What about what Debbie wants? When is that going to matter? Or is it?"

Don floored the gas, passing a semi on I-75 at breakneck speed. He now wished he'd sent Debbie ahead on a plane. She'd spend the next ten hours bitching and complaining. He was tired of it already and they'd been on the road barely an hour.

"Well?" Debbie persisted.

Shoulders tense with both hands in a death grip on the steering wheel, Don had a vision of wrapping his hands around his wife's neck, squeezing until she drew her last breath. God, this was a marriage? Lately the word *divorce* kept creeping into his mind, but each time he thought about it, he'd remember all of his hard work and just how much he had to lose. No, he'd put up with her crap a while longer.

With both girls in the backseat, Don mentally calmed himself. He didn't want them to be as miserable as he was right now.

"For once let's just enjoy being together.

Before long the girls will be away at college. There won't be any more family vacations. Plus, just think of all the free time you're going to have while the girls stay with Alex and Kate. Two weeks in the Caribbean seems like a fair trade to me." Don knew he was using their cruise as a means to bribe Debbie, but if that's what it took to keep her trap shut for the remainder of the trip, then fine. Once they were aboard the cruise ship that sailed out of Cape Canaveral, she could kiss his merry old ass. He'd gamble and drink. If he were lucky, hell, he might even pick up a woman who was willing to enjoy him as a man and keep her thoughts and opinions to herself. If only.

Don cast a glance at Debbie. A flicker of a smile touched her lips. No doubt she was thinking of all the free time she would have without the girls underfoot.

With just a hint of churlishness, Debbie said, "I suppose I can call a truce. For now."

Don shook his head in bewilderment. Later there would be hell to pay. At present it just didn't matter. Whatever it took to shut her mouth, he was willing to do. He wanted to arrive in Asheville without a murder rap against him. He'd never resorted to physical violence, but he could almost imagine the pleasure he would feel smacking Debbie right in her mouth. He smiled. She'd been nothing but a social-climbing bitch since they'd moved to their new home in Quail Lake. He heard rumors about her from the husbands of the wives she socialized with. Apparently they were laughing behind her back. No matter what, she would always be the girl from the Brooklyn deli with the New York accent. No matter how many elocution classes she took, she'd always sound rough and unsophisticated. Don suddenly realized he was disillusioned with life, especially his marriage. Where was all the fun and companionship he longed for? His marriage to Debbie was a mistake, nothing more than a sham. Once aboard the cruise ship, he was going to take a good, honest look at his situation. Nothing like sailing the Caribbean to contemplate one's life.

Don decided that changing the subject was in order. His thoughts were turning too bleak.

"Thanks, Deb. Now, who wants to go to Krystal for lunch?" Don loved the minihamburgers even though they gave him horrible indigestion.

"I do! I do! Can I have a dozen? Please, please!" Sara shouted from the backseat.

"Gross! You're getting bigger by the

minute, and you want a dozen hamburgers," Emily said in disgust.

"Emily, that's not a very nice thing to say to your sister. Sara is still a growing girl. She needs three meals a day, though I have to agree with Emily. A dozen hamburgers is too much. You can have six with some french fries and a vanilla shake if you want," Debbie explained to Sara.

Sara looked at Emily and mouthed *bitch.*

"Mom, I don't think that's the healthiest lunch for Sara. She needs some lettuce without salad dressing and a glass of water." Emily laughed at the look of horror on Sara's pudgy face.

"That's enough. Both of you. Sara, you might want to listen to your sister's advice. She's been there, she knows what it's like." Don peeked in the rearview mirror and winked at Emily. Emily had never been overweight, but if a little white lie stopped an argument, what could it hurt, Don asked himself.

"Dad! That's just so not true!" Emily rebutted.

"You're just too young to remember. Now, let's look for a Krystal billboard. All this talk of food is really making me hungry."

"Me too," shouted Sara. She began to hop up and down in the backseat.

"Sit down, you brat! You act like a starved Ethiopian. Can't you be still for just one minute?" Emily wished they were at Uncle Alex's already. It was getting extremely hard to remain in such close quarters with Sara acting like a rabbit.

Sara gave Emily the finger.

Emily yanked her sister's middle finger, then pulled. "Ouch!" Sara screamed.

"Enough of you two!" Don yelled.

"She flipped me off!" Emily declared indignantly.

"Liar!" Sara screamed, then she began to howl at the top of her lungs. "She's a liar, she's a liar! Mommy, why does she always make up lies to tell on me?"

Emily jabbed her index finger in Sara's face hoping to make her point. "You are totally losing it, Sara. You're sick."

"And now we have a shrink in the family. Emily, you need to keep your opinions to yourself. Sara doesn't have a clue what getting 'flipped off' means." Then Debbie added hatefully, "I can't wait to dump you off at your uncle's."

Don shook his head in dismay. "Deb, I think that's enough. The Krystal's just ahead. Let's stop and grab a hamburger. I want you two girls to stop arguing with one another."

"But, Daddy," Sara interrupted, "I didn't do that." Sara looked Emily straight in the eye. "She's just a big fat liar. I hate you!" Sara stuck her tongue out at Emily.

Emily replied dryly, "Yeah? Well, the feeling is mutual."

"What's that supposed to mean?" Sara wailed.

"If you'd pay attention in school, you'd know, dummy," Emily added.

Debbie leaned over the front seat to peer at her oldest daughter. "I forbid you to speak another word to your baby sister. You'll have her corrupted. Now, not another word out of you."

Emily turned white and chewed her bottom lip, something she only did when she was upset. Her mother had such a distorted view of Sara. It was obvious the kid needed help. She prayed Sara didn't act like a jerk once they arrived in Asheville. She would hate for Aunt Kate and Uncle Alex to see Sara at her worst. They'd never want her to visit again. They passed billboards advertising Café Risqué, a men's club whose girls didn't look much older than Emily. Signs for South of the Border must've cost the owner millions because they appeared before every exit. They'd stopped there on many occasions when the girls were small, but the place no longer amused them as it once had.

"There it is," Sara shouted, pointing her pudgy finger at the sign.

Don took the next exit and pulled into the Krystal parking lot. "Let's go inside and see if we can act like a civilized family." Don caught Debbie's gaze. If looks could kill, he'd be in a coffin. He couldn't stand the way she spoke to Emily. As soon as the girls were out of hearing distance, he was going to tell her a thing or two.

"Welcome to the land of fine dining," Debbie said as she opened the car door.

Don ignored her comment. This wasn't fine dining, just something different. Did everything always have to be about making an impression with his wife? He wondered.

Sara flew out of the car and raced inside. Emily hung back until both of her parents were inside. Once inside, she slid into a booth and prayed Sara would behave. Sara was out of control, not just in her eating habits. She had a problem telling the truth. Emily couldn't understand why her parents babied Sara all the time. It wasn't healthy. No wonder the poor kid didn't have any friends her own age. She acted like a six-year-old, and her parents continued to encourage her.

The smell of fried onions and grease made her nauseous. She didn't see how Sara or her mom and dad could eat this crap. She'd have some fries and a Coke. That was all her stomach would allow. Emily couldn't wait to eat Aunt Kate's home-cooked meals. She was a professional chef. Sometimes her meals were gourmet, other times she would make something as simple as meat loaf with garlic mashed potatoes and gravy. It didn't matter what she made, it was always delicious.

Don carried a tray laden with the mini-hamburgers he loved. Fries and Cokes were passed around. Sara grabbed at her food like a starving animal.

"Where's my milk shake? Mommy said I could have one!" Sara's shrill cries drew curious glances from the other diners.

Emily prayed she'd be sucked up in a big black hole. Embarrassed, she took a drink of Coke, her eyes downcast. *Three more years,* she told herself. She would go to college. No more of these humiliating family outings. No more Sara. Part of her felt bad for her little sister and the bad thoughts she always seemed to have where Sara was concerned, then another part of her wanted to smack her square in the face every time she opened her mouth.

"Shhh, Sara." Debbie turned to her husband. "I told you to get her a milk shake. Is that so hard to do? Get her one," Debbie demanded to Don.

Without saying another word, Don walked up to the counter, returning minutes later with Sara's large vanilla shake. She hurriedly crammed her straw in the shake, then started slurping like a cow.

Debbie placed a hand on Sara's belly. "Not so fast, honey. You'll get a stomachache."

"Okay, Mommy. I was just so thirsty. Can I have dessert if I eat everything on my plate?" Sara glanced at Emily, then back at her mother. "Please?"

Briefly Emily wondered what the odds were against her sister *not* eating everything on her plate. Into the billions, no doubt.

"Let's not go overboard," Debbie said to Sara.

Emily couldn't believe her mother. One minute she was as wicked as the Witch of the West, and the next, she'd make Glinda the Good Witch seem like a bitch. She would talk hateful to her or her dad, and in the next breath she was as sweet as the dessert Sara was assured of.

As though on pins and needles, Sara anxiously asked, "Does that mean yes?"

"Of course, but we'll have to hurry. Your father wants to drive straight through to Asheville. We won't have time to stop for dinner."

Don kicked Debbie in the shin under the table. "And Mommy wants to get there as soon as possible, too. She can't wait to rid herself of you two." This was said with a smile, but Don was serious. He knew his wife, he'd had her number for a long time. He knew he was playing her games, but sometimes he couldn't help himself.

"C'mon, you said it yourself, let's not argue. Get Sara an apple pie and let's go," Emily said as she eased out of the tiny booth and headed to the car. The bickering over Sara and her eating habits was unbearable. The kid would be lucky if she didn't have heart disease and high blood pressure before she was old enough to drive.

Don gathered the empty boxes and plates and tossed them in the large garbage can by the exit door.

"Emily's right. Get your dessert to go." He looked at Debbie and Sara. "And both of you go to the restroom before we get back on the road. I don't want to stop at every other exit because one of you has to pee all the time." After years of road trips Don had learned Debbie's tricks. For spite she'd tell

CHAPTER 2

Asheville, North Carolina

Kate was careful not to make too much noise as she removed bowls and utensils from the cupboard. Don and Debbie had arrived after midnight and would most likely want to sleep in. She wanted to make a hearty breakfast for everyone. She'd start them off with her homemade blueberry pancakes. She had thick-sliced hickory-smoked bacon and a special bottle of homemade syrup straight from Vermont. Fresh oranges for juice for the girls and grapefruit juice for Debbie. She was sure she still drank grapefruit juice. She'd been on a diet ever since Kate had met her and, other than alcohol, Kate had never seen Debbie drink anything else.

Kate loved the early mornings. Always an early riser, she'd cherished this time for as long as she could remember. She would start her day with a good strong cup of tea.

him she had an upset stomach just so they would make numerous stops. She only did this to make them late, because she knew he was extremely punctual. Again, he questioned why he'd remained married to her for seventeen years.

Hesitantly, Sara got up from her seat, stopping briefly to snatch a french fry she'd missed. "I'll take a hot fudge sundae with double fudge and extra whipped cream."

"Sweetie, Krystal doesn't have sundaes. Either an apple pie or a chocolate chip cookie. Which do you want?"

Sara took forever to decide.

Don persisted. "C'mon, Sara. We need to get back on the road before midnight."

She placed a fat index finger against an equally fat cheek. "Would it be okay if I had one of each since it'll be a while before I get to eat again?"

Debbie turned to Don. "Sure, honey. Don, get the dessert while we use the restroom."

"Let's make it quick," Don said to their retreating backs.

Desserts in hand, Don made his way to the Explorer. Emily leaned over the front seat to open the driver's door for him.

"Is she still eating?" Emily asked.

"No, now it's the bathroom, but I bet you

can't guess who this dessert is for." He held up the box containing the apple pie and chocolate chip cookie. "One for the road."

Emily smiled at her dad. "You mean two."

"Yeah, I guess I do. Let's just try and keep the peace with your mom and sister. Once we arrive in Asheville, your mother will be nice to everyone. You know how she likes to make a good impression on Alex and Kate."

Emily nodded. She knew, but she also knew her mother didn't impress them at all. Not that they'd ever said anything to her. It was just something she could sense. She felt ashamed of her mother sometimes and hated herself for feeling that way. Maybe she'd understand her mother when she was older. She hoped so.

Fifteen minutes passed, and her mother and Sara had yet to emerge from the restroom. Just as Emily got out of the car to go check on them, they materialized.

"What in the world were you two doing in there for so long?" Don asked as he pulled out of the parking lot.

"Sara is constipated," Debbie reported.

Emily had to bite the inside of her mouth just to keep from laughing out loud. If she couldn't go to the bathroom now, just wait a while. Once those miniburgers navigated their way through her sister's gut, she'd have

the Hershey squirts for days. Just imaginin this brought an even bigger smile to he face. Maybe she'd crap herself. It would serve the little brat right if she did. Maybe then she wouldn't be such a pig in the future.

"Mommy!" Sara shrieked

"It's all right, honey. You can't help it if you're sick. It's her nerves." Debbie turned around to look at Emily, who was trying very hard not to laugh at the topic of conversation.

"Emily, badgering your sister has got to cease. She has a nervous stomach as it is. All the bickering has wreaked havoc on her bowels."

"We get the picture, Debbie. Now, can we talk about something else?" Don flashed a grin in his rearview mirror at Emily.

She smiled back.

For once they were on the same page.

Alex wasn't a tea drinker, so she bought the best roasted coffee beans she could get at the Daily Grind, a local grocery specializing in gourmet coffees and hard-to-find food items. She readied a pot of coffee, then took the blueberries she'd recently picked, put them in a colander, and rinsed them in the kitchen sink. Kate loved her kitchen almost as much as she loved the art studio that Alex had built for her right after they'd married. It was a loft just above the kennels where all the dogs were kept. When she needed inspiration, she'd simply walk downstairs and play with all the wonderful retrievers Alex bred and raised. Almost always, she'd go back to the studio exhilarated and would work at her pottery wheel for hours. Kate planned on showing the girls how to use it during their visit this year. Though she had wanted to let Emily try her hand at the wheel a couple of years ago, for fear of hurting Sara's feelings, she'd waited until both girls were old enough. That way she could teach them together. At fifteen and twelve, Kate figured they were both ready.

Kate finished her prep work for breakfast and sat at the old oak table in the corner of the kitchen. She sipped her tea, enjoying the quiet. Though it wasn't cold, she lit a fire in the fireplace. Early mornings in the mountains of North Carolina were always a bit on the chilly side, even in the summer. It was these mornings Kate liked best. She loved the pungent woodsmoke billowing from the chimney, the damp, earthy smell from the moist soil, the buds that dotted the hundreds of trees in early spring. She opened the window over the kitchen sink to admire the view. As the sun ascended above the mountaintops, clearing away the purple-gray fog suspended over the Blue Ridge Parkway, Kate observed the first rays of daylight. *This is God's country,* she thought. Never had she seen a sunrise like that on the parkway. In the fall, it was breathtaking. Golds, reds, and oranges, ranging in hundreds, the colors decorated the mountains like thousands of brightly colored gems.

The hint of Old Spice sent her spinning around. "Morning, sweetie." Alex wrapped his arms around her waist. Kate took in a deep breath, loving the smell of Alex's freshly showered still-moist body against her own.

"Coffee's almost ready," Kate said.

Alex dotted kisses along her jawline. "That's not all that's ready," he teased.

Kate stepped out of Alex's embrace, playfully swatting him on the chest. "Hey, we have company, or did you forget?"

Alex smiled. "That's never stopped me before."

After thirteen years of marriage, Kate was as much in love with Alex as she'd been the day they'd married. Their love life hadn't slowed down a bit either. She was lucky. She'd heard other women talk and knew that her and Alex's relationship was unique, one of a kind. She was so happy, she felt a little bit guilty that her friends didn't share with their husbands what she and Alex had together.

"Well, for now you'll have to wait." Kate poured coffee into Alex's favorite golden retriever mug. "Here you go."

Alex took a slow sip of his coffee. "You don't have to wait on me, Kate."

Kate pulled out her chair and sat across from her husband. "I know that. I do things for you because I want to, not because I have to. You know that, too." She reached across the table and rubbed his forearm. Being married to Alex was easy.

Alex held a palm up. "Okay, okay. You can pour my coffee anytime."

"And mine, too," Don said.

Kate stood and gave Don a hug. Alex grabbed him in a bear hug and ruffled his perfectly combed hair. For a split second, Don looked miffed, then he raked his fingers through his messed-up hair. "Damn, buddy, I just spent ten minutes combing this do."

"And you can still see your bald spot," Alex teased.

"Hey, Alex, that's not a nice thing to say to company, especially before he's had his coffee," Kate added. She poured Don a cup and placed it before him on the table.

"So, how long is the cruise gonna last this time?" Alex asked.

Debbie and Don were avid cruisers and had been on more than fifty cruises since they'd married. The four of them often joked that Don and Debbie had spent more time on water than land.

"Two weeks. I hope that's okay with you both," Don replied.

"Of course it is. We're thrilled the girls still want to come for visits. I know they're getting older, and that's when you usually lose them to boys and makeup. I plan to teach them how to use the pottery wheel this visit," Kate said.

"Emily will love that. She's always had a keen interest in your work," Don said. "Sara, on the other hand, I'd be careful. She's going through somewhat of a clumsy stage right now. Make sure nothing valuable is in her path."

"Are you talking about me, Daddy?" Sara whined from the doorway. "You know I hate it when you do that." Sara trudged across the kitchen and plopped down on her father's lap. Kate thought she was too big for that but kept the thought to herself.

"Are we having breakfast?" Sara asked of no one.

"I'm making blueberry pancakes and bacon. How's that?" Kate announced.

"Goody! I love pancakes. Can I have six extra-big ones and six pieces of bacon? And make the bacon very crisp the way Mommy does," Sara said matter-of-factly.

Don added with a smile, "Debbie burns the bacon."

Sara crossed her arms over her hefty middle. "She does not! I like it that way. She cooks anything I want just the way I want it, too!" Sara glared at Kate as if daring her to contradict her.

"Well, then if you want your bacon well-done, that's exactly how I'll make it." Kate winked at Don and Alex. "Sara, why don't you run upstairs and see if Emily wants to have breakfast with the rest of us."

"Do I have to? I hate her. She's such a bit— , I mean brat. She won't let me look at her diary anymore. Mommy says it's 'cause she's hiding something."

"Sara, don't call your sister names, and you should be ashamed for snooping. You're old enough to value Emily's privacy, and so is your mother. Now run upstairs and tell Emily it's time for breakfast," Don ordered. "And leave your mother alone. She'll want to sleep in, I'm sure."

Reluctantly, Sara slid off her father's lap and headed for the stairs. Once she was out of earshot, Don spoke in low tones. "We've been having some problems with Sara. I think she's jealous of Emily, being older and all. Emily does get to do a lot more than Sara. If she gives you any problems, don't let her have dessert. That's the worst punishment she gets."

Alex and Kate looked at each other. Kate spoke first. "I doubt we'll have trouble with her. She's always been so sweet. Twelve is a tough age. Not a little girl, but not a young woman either."

"Well, let's just hope she doesn't act up. I've had enough of her tantrums," Don said.

Kate placed a hand on Don's shoulder. "She'll be fine. You and Debbie enjoy the cruise and let us enjoy the girls. This might be the last time they'll want to spend their spring break with us. They're growing up so fast."

Half an hour later, full of pancakes and

bacon, Alex excused himself to tend the kennels.

"I thought you hired someone to help out," Don stated.

"Gertie. She's the best thing that ever happened to me. Well, except for Kate." Alex winked at Kate as she filled the dishwasher. "Her brother, Reece Wilkes, has been my attorney for the past eight years. He's very well-known around Asheville. He recommended her one day when he came for a visit. Little did I know she'd worked for Kate's parents years ago. Gertie never had any kids of her own, so she's devoted her life to the care of animals. I don't know how I ever ran the kennel without her."

"Apparently you've managed to make a living playing with dogs," Don said flatly.

Kate closed the door to the dishwasher a bit too hard. She turned around to face Don. "And has done a damned good job." Don was always quick to make snide comments about Alex's chosen profession. Her mother and father had once owned the kennel. The kennel and the animals were very dear to her.

"Hey, you two, let's not start this again. We've been over this so many times, I've lost count. I didn't want to study veterinary medicine. I wouldn't have had the guts or the heart. I like raising the pups, seeing that they go to good homes. That gives me more satisfaction than all the money in the world could," Alex said. "And who cares about money anyway?"

"Some of us weren't born with a silver spoon crammed down our throats," Don responded. "Some of us have to work our asses off just to make a decent living."

Alex's parents were extremely wealthy, and Don had always resented him for it even though he rarely mentioned it.

Kate stared at Don. He was well over six feet tall, his black hair always perfectly combed, nothing ever out of place. He was too perfect. And he was also jealous of her husband. Kate had figured him out the first time they'd been introduced. Even though they'd been friends since elementary school, Kate often wondered if Don had stayed close to Alex because of his family's money. When one didn't have it, one always wanted it. Her parents taught her that. They'd been quite well-off themselves, yet lived a simple life raising dogs. Her childhood had been almost perfect. She wished her parents were still alive. She thought about them every day and missed them terribly even though they'd been dead since her freshman year of college. Being an only child of older parents had its downside.

Kate wondered if Debbie and Don knew how fortunate they were to have two beautiful daughters. She'd give anything to have Alex's child.

Apparently Sara was going through a difficult period, but Kate had faith. She knew Sara would get through this awkward phase and laugh at herself in the years to come. Being twelve was tough.

Emily ate in silence as Kate finished the breakfast dishes. She'd had half a pancake and some orange juice. Unlike Sara, Emily was a bit on the thin side. Kate briefly wondered if Emily had an eating disorder, then pushed the thought aside. Emily was too sensible, and she'd always been taller than average and a tad on the lanky side. Emily reminded her of herself at fifteen. Mature beyond her years. Kate was sure Emily was eating enough to satisfy her hunger, and she wasn't going to make an issue over something that wasn't a problem.

Emily got out of her chair and walked over to the sink. She rinsed her plate off and placed it on the bottom rack of the dishwasher. "Something wrong, Aunt Kate?"

Kate smiled at Emily. "Just woolgathering, that's all. You do this when you're old."

"You're not old, Aunt Kate. You're

younger than Mom and Dad."

"So? What's that supposed to mean?" Kate asked.

"I just never see either of them woolgathering."

Kate laughed loudly. "Oh, Emily, I'm sure they have their moments, too. You're just not around to catch them in the act, that's all."

"I suppose they do," Emily said.

Kate could hear the slight hesitation. "Is there something more?"

Emily shook her head, "I'm going to the kennels. I can't wait to see the new pups."

"Why don't you see if Sara wants to go. I'm sure she'd love to see the new puppies, too."

"I don't know if that's a good idea or not," Emily said, her voice low and eyes downcast.

"Why would you think that?" Kate questioned.

Emily looked around the kitchen, then took a step forward where she could stand next to Kate. She looked behind her one last time before speaking. "Promise not to say anything?"

Kate knew trust was an important issue among teens and would do everything in her power to keep Emily's trust, but if what she was about to say was something Kate thought Don and Debbie should know, she wasn't sure if she could keep her promise, but she wasn't about to tell this to Emily. She took a deep breath, "I promise." For a second she felt like hiding her hands behind her back and crossing her fingers, but she was too old for that, and it didn't mean anything anyway.

"We have these neighbors, the Conzelmans. They live two houses down from us. They've been retired for I don't know how long, but they're the sweetest old people." Emily smiled. "You know what I mean. Anyway, they have three cats, Snuggles, Eddie, and Clovis. They're inside cats, but Snuggles — he's the oldest — escaped the other day. Sara found him in our backyard."

"I hope she took him home." Kate remarked.

"I did. But before I took him home, I saw her dragging him around our backyard by the tail. Poor Snuggles was screeching. You know how cats sound when they cry? It was almost like a real baby. I peeked out the window thinking a little kid was lost or something. That's when I saw her pulling the cat around. I ran outside and grabbed the cat and took him home. I didn't tell Mom or Dad, but I did pinch the crap out of Sara."

Kate couldn't imagine anything worse. "Why didn't you tell your parents?"

Emily shook her head. "It doesn't do any good. Sara simply lies her way out of whatever she's accused of and blames me or whomever she can get away with blaming. I'm not sure she can be trusted around the puppies."

Alarm bells rang in Kate's head. She'd recently read that kids who were cruel to animals were at high risk for severe emotional problems. Emily was too young to deal with this. Don said they'd been having trouble with Sara. Maybe she should insist they get her into counseling. Who knew what would happen if her behavior problem wasn't diagnosed and treated?

"I'm glad you told me. I'll tell you what we can do." Kate's mind whizzed with ideas. "We'll make sure Sara isn't alone with the animals." She wouldn't have to break her promise to Emily, but she would mention to Alex that they needed to supervise Sara carefully when she was with the dogs. "For now, I'll just keep this between the two of us, but if I think your parents need to know, I'll have to tell them."

"That's cool. I trust you."

"Thanks, Emily. That means a lot." Kate gently patted Emily's back. "Now, why don't you go out to the kennel; I'm sure Alex is waiting for you. I'll keep Sara occupied until your mother gets up."

Emily hesitated. "There's more." She scoped out the kitchen as though she might find another set of ears eavesdropping on her conversation. When she was satisfied all was clear, she continued her story. "Sara has a mean streak. More serious than you know. I know Mom and Dad are aware of it, but they don't do anything, except bribe her with dessert."

Kate could see by the look of anguish on Emily's face that her younger sister's behavior was very worrisome to her.

"It's just these tantrums she's having. Her eyes glaze over, it's almost like she's another person. Last week I caught her snooping through my drawers. I chased her out of the room into the kitchen." Emily paused. "There was a knife on the kitchen counter. Sara grabbed it and said if I told on her for snooping, she'd slit my throat."

"Emily, you've got to tell your parents. This is very abnormal behavior, not some childish prank."

"I know, but it's like I said. They'll baby her, and she'll promise never to do whatever she's in trouble for again, then it'll be back to her same old crap."

Kate would talk with Alex later. Then they could decide what to do.

"I can't imagine Sara doing something so mean, but she's still a young girl. I doubt that she was serious." Kate wasn't one hundred percent sure of this, but for now, she'd keep the thought to herself.

"You wouldn't say that if you'd seen the look on her face. Aunt Kate, she truly scares me. I just want you and Uncle Alex to watch out. There's no telling what the little monster will do at this point," Emily said.

Kate nodded, forced a smile. "I'll keep that in mind. Now why don't you run along to the kennels. Alex is waiting for you."

"Okay, I'd like that. Thanks, Aunt Kate. I feel better with you knowing what's really been going on with Sara."

"Don't worry about her just now. Let's just enjoy this visit." Kate ruffled Emily's smooth blond ponytail. "Now get out of here and have some fun."

"I knew I could count on you," Emily shouted as she headed for the kennels.

Kate was extremely worried about Sara. If she would threaten her sister with a knife, who knew what else she would try. She was going to speak to Alex as soon as they had a minute alone. Together they could decide if this was something they needed to share with Don and Debbie before they left on their cruise, or if it was something that could wait. Kate didn't like to put things off. She'd find a few minutes to corner Alex during the day. Something told her they shouldn't put off having this discussion.

CHAPTER 3

"Do you believe Emily?" Alex asked Kate. She'd repeated Emily's concerns to Alex while he took a shower. She didn't want to take a chance of being overheard. The bathroom was the safest place in the house at the moment.

"Of course I do. Emily doesn't go around making up this kind of stuff. And besides, what would be the point? She's very concerned about Sara, and, frankly, I'm a little nervous having her in the house for two weeks."

There was something unsettling about the twelve-year-old. It wasn't just the things Emily had revealed to her. There was more. The word *evil* kept coming to mind. Kate couldn't mention that to Alex. At least not yet. She'd do her best to get through the next couple of weeks. She'd just have to be extra vigilant. In two weeks, the girls would return to Naples with their parents. She and

Alex would go about their daily lives as before.

Alex turned off the shower. Kate handed him a large bath towel as he stepped onto the pink, fluffy rug.

"I think your worry is unnecessary. This is probably just some preteen phase she's going through. Maybe she's trying to get attention. We'll keep our eyes and ears open. I'll put her to work in the kennel with Gertie." Alex laughed. His eyes crinkled at the corners when he smiled. Kate loved to see him smile. It could brighten the worst of her days.

Kate tossed the towel over the hamper and handed Alex a dark green bathrobe.

"We might need to warn Gertie. Let her know what Emily's observed. If anyone can help straighten out a rotten kid, it's Gertie," Kate said. She knew this from personal experience. She wondered if Gertie had the skills to handle a child like Sara. Maybe she should tell Debbie what Emily had witnessed. No, she would wait. She'd made a promise, and she would do her best to keep it.

Besides, Gertie had worked for her parents for twenty years. Kate remembered getting scolded by Gertie on more than one occasion. She had to admit, Gertie had always been fair and wise with her discipline. She'd covered her rear more than once with her parents. Right when Kate thought she was about to get away with her so-called crime, Gertie always seemed to have an appropriate punishment. Like the time she'd caught her and Jocelyn Myers drinking Boone's Farm strawberry wine. It'd been on a Friday night. Jocelyn was sleeping over. Both of them figured they'd try drinking, then spend all day Saturday rehashing their experience. Gertie'd had other plans. At five in the morning Gertie slipped inside her room, woke them up, and demanded they go downstairs and wait in the back of her truck. Thinking this was some kind of terrible joke, Kate refused. Gertie left the room, only to return a few minutes later with three empty bottles of Boone's Farm. Kate knew then that she and Jocelyn were caught. With Gertie at the wheel and both her and Jocelyn in the cab of the truck, Gertie drove down the bumpy driveway, careful to hit each pothole in the road. She'd driven them to the local soup kitchen. They'd spent the day with massive hangovers serving breakfast and lunch to a few down-on-their-luck drunks. She'd never looked at wine the same since.

Yes, Kate thought, *Gertie might be just*

what Sara needs. Some good old-fashioned discipline, and Sara will be right back on track. Kate couldn't wait to see the change in Sara when Don and Debbie returned from their cruise. They would thank her and Alex, praising the miracle.

"If she's anything with kids like she is with the animals, then Sara will straighten out in no time," Alex observed.

"Then let's just hope Emily's concerns don't manifest."

Kate took a pair of soft, worn Levi's and gave them to Alex. He'd had them since his college days. Alex was still as trim and handsome as the photos in his high school yearbook. Actually, Kate thought him even more handsome. He'd certainly been something to look at in high school. Both he and Don had their pick of the girls, according to Don, but it was Alex they'd always gravitated toward. Kate could see why, but she knew it was more than his good looks. Alex was the kindest, most gentle man she'd ever known. There was an air of goodness about him. Kate knew she was biased, but anyone who'd ever met Alex would agree. He was top-of-the-line.

"So what's got into your head all of a sudden? You look way too serious," Alex said as he pulled on his jeans.

Kate laughed. "Actually, I was thinking how lucky I am."

"And what brought this on?"

"I don't know. Just thinking about my life. Being married to you. It's the best." Again, Kate flashed a big grin. Alex took her in his arms.

"I'm the lucky one. You're a dream come true, Kate. The day I purchased the kennel changed my life. I have you, a terrific career, animals I love. What more could I ask for?"

Kate knew, but didn't want to voice her thoughts. Alex stepped out of their embrace and gazed into her green eyes. "I know what you're thinking, and it doesn't matter. I've told you that a hundred times. What will it take to convince you?"

"I know, I just can't help thinking a child would be the icing on the cake. Our lives would be, oh, I don't know, more fulfilled," Kate explained.

Kate had spent the first six years of their marriage trying to become pregnant. When that failed, she tried in vitro fertilization for another three years, and still no child. She'd finally made peace with the fact that she would never have children with Alex, or anyone else for that matter. Alex had gone through a series of tests himself, but he was fine. It was her. For some reason, she wasn't meant to have children. She'd accepted it, but she didn't like it.

Alex took another step back. "Do you really think a child would make us . . . complete? You know better. As long as we have each other, that's all we'll ever need. We both agreed this was acceptable."

"I know, it's just when the girls visit, I realize what I'm missing. I've accepted the fact, Alex, but I'll never like it, no matter what we discussed." Kate reached for Alex's hand. "I didn't mean to imply anything more, Alex. It's just something I'll always wonder about. Now, what are your plans for the day?"

Alex shook his head, sending droplets of water flying across the bedroom. He reminded Kate of one of the dogs after bath-time.

"I'm going to have Emily and Sara help me bathe the pups. You know what a job that can be. Gertie's expecting two families this afternoon. They've met all the adoption requirements as new pet parents." Alex laughed. "All except for Gertie's seal of approval."

Kate knew that if Gertie had any doubt about their puppies' prospective family, they would not get the puppy, come hell or high water. Alex took his business very seriously.

Gertie hadn't made a bad call yet, and Kate didn't think she ever would. Gertie took painstaking care in her decisions.

"Just don't leave Sara alone with the dogs," Kate said.

"I won't. I'll tell Gertie to keep an eye on her. She won't do anything, Kate. She's just a kid, who's hormonal and confused. Remember being twelve?"

She did. It was tough, but she'd never felt the urge to hurt an animal, or a human for that matter. Her pillow took a lot of hits, but that was acceptable.

She nodded in the affirmative. "I do. You're right. It's a difficult age, but let's not forget what Emily said. No matter how sweet and loving Sara can be, we don't want the pups to suffer in any way."

"I'm not about to let anything happen to the dogs, don't worry," Alex assured her as he tucked his shirt into the waistband of his Levi's. He wrapped a leather belt through the loops, hooked the buckle, then sat on the bed to lace up his work boots.

Kate sat down beside him. "I'm not worried, really. I guess I'm just overly paranoid. You're right. She's probably hormonal, and who knows what else is going on in her head. Maybe you can get her to open up to you while she's helping with the dogs."

Alex stood up, ran both hands along his thighs as if to remove something from the palm of his hands. "I'll see what I can do. Meanwhile, entertain Deb and Don for me, at least till I have the dogs bathed."

"I will, but remember, we're going to dinner with them tonight. I'm going to ask Gertie to keep an eye on the girls while we're out. I don't feel comfortable leaving them alone just yet."

Alex laughed. "Whatever you say. I'll tell her myself. Now, go do something fun. Don't you have a cooking class next week?"

"Yes, I do. I thought I'd try a couple of my new concoctions out on you and the girls. Emily loves to try new food."

"Sounds like a plan. Just remember, Sara will want dessert."

"I'll make something light," Kate added.

Alex gave her a quick kiss and headed for the kennel.

Kate prayed Sara wouldn't cause any problems during her visit. She was very concerned about her but didn't want to overreact. She'd talk to Debbie at dinner. For the moment, she had plenty to keep her occupied.

She had several recipes she wanted to work on for Chloe's, the restaurant where she worked part-time and taught cooking classes two evenings a week. She was in total bliss during her eight-hour shift. Cooking was her passion. Seeing the delight on the customers' faces was beyond awesome. She'd thought about opening her own restaurant; but with her pottery and the kennel, she knew it was more than she wanted to take on at this point in her life. Maybe when they retired, she and Alex would open a restaurant where the customers could bring their animals along. It was becoming all the rage in New York City. She didn't see this happening in the South for quite some time. Still, it was a possibility for the future.

Kate returned to the kitchen, hand-washed the skillet she'd used for the bacon, wiped the counters down, and took a package of frozen shrimp out to thaw.

"My, my, aren't we the busy little housewife," Debbie remarked as she stood in the doorway.

Kate jerked around. "You scared me!" She put her hand against her chest. Her heart stuttered. It was just like Debbie to sneak up on her.

"Sorry. I was in search of someone who could tell me where in the hell my girls are. Emily knows I like my juice before I get out of bed. Where is that little tramp?"

Kate had to grab her left wrist with her right hand to keep from slapping Debbie. Why in the hell did women like her have children? Why were they *allowed* to have children? No wonder Sara was having problems. Kate would bet her last nickel Debbie was at the root of Sara's behavior.

She drew in a deep breath, then counted to ten before answering. "The girls are helping Alex with the dogs. Don said you'd want to sleep in."

Debbie pulled the belt of her gold silk robe tighter, then yanked the refrigerator door open. "You have anything to drink?" She peered at the contents on the shelves, saw a pitcher, took it out, and looked at Kate. "A glass would be nice."

Kate realized that she didn't really like Debbie all that much. She'd ignored Debbie's rude, catty behavior for years. It was time to put a stop to it. "How many times have you and Don brought the girls here to visit?" Kate questioned.

"Why are you asking me that now? I want a glass," Debbie stated. Her New York accent had become more prominent. Kate thought she sounded as though she'd swallowed a bucket of gravel after an all-night smoking session.

Kate spoke slowly. "I would've thought

you would remember where the glasses are. You've been here enough times to know. If you want to be waited on hand and foot, I suggest you wait till the cruise gets under way. Unlike your girls, *I'm* not your maid."

Debbie's mouth hung open, and Kate was reminded of a slobbering baby that had yet learned to control herself. "What the hell is this all about? You got a rag up your ass or what? I simply want a glass to drink from. What is it, Kate? You have PMS? Or is it baby-envy?"

Kate felt heat rise from the pit of her stomach to the top of her head. Her hearing seemed distant, as though she were listening through a tunnel. "The glasses are in the cabinet next to the sink."

Kate walked out of the kitchen in a daze. In a matter of minutes, she'd ruined her day. She'd always walked on eggshells with Debbie, careful not to offend her. Alex and Don were the best of friends, she really wanted to be friends with Debbie, but she knew now it wasn't going to happen. She'd tried for years. Debbie had just pissed her off one time too many. Why would you call your fifteen-year-old daughter a tramp for not bringing you a glass of juice? She'd cancel their dinner plans. Tell Alex she had a headache. Don and Debbie could think what they wanted.

"Hey, wait a minute . . . I need something to eat," Debbie shouted.

For once, Kate wanted to be anywhere but the kitchen.

CHAPTER 4

"Was Don upset that I didn't show for dinner?" Kate asked. It was after midnight. She was tired and wanted nothing more than to go to sleep. Alex had gone to dinner with Don and Debbie. She wanted to hear how the evening turned out.

"No, he wasn't upset. He was curious, though. I told him you weren't feeling well and decided to stay home. Debbie must not've said anything to him about your argument."

"It wasn't even an argument, really. I don't know what came over me. One minute I was ready to make her breakfast and in the next it hit me just how much I couldn't stand her. I still can't believe she'd call Emily a tramp. That was the last straw. I couldn't care less if I never lay eyes on the woman again."

"Well, you might have to put on a show for the girls. Don and Debbie are leaving in the morning."

"Of course, I wouldn't think of acting so juvenile in front of the girls," Kate stated adamantly.

Alex pulled her next to him, until her head was resting on his chest. "You never act juvenile, Kate. I'm sure Deb had it coming. She's always been a bit of a bitch." There was a time when Alex didn't think so, but that was better left unsaid. The past was prologue.

"Yeah, and I just lowered myself to her level by reacting."

"I wouldn't get too upset about it. She wants to get the hell out of here, according to Don. She can't wait to get on that cruise ship so she doesn't have to, quote, 'look at me or those brats' for two weeks."

"Women like her shouldn't have children," Kate announced.

"You're probably right, but there isn't a damned thing we can do about it. On the upside, they'll be gone tomorrow, and we'll have nothing more to do than enjoy their girls."

Kate smiled. "Yes, I guess I can make nice to Debbie one more time, just for the privilege of having the girls." Kate thought about the future. "What'll we do when they're grown and don't want to spend their spring breaks or summers with us any-more?"

"We'll worry about that tomorrow. For now, what do you say we finish what I wanted to start this morning in the kitchen?" Alex pulled her on top of him. He traced his lips over the soft bend where shoulders met neck. Soft and smooth.

Kate sighed with pleasure. "I believe I'll take you up on that offer, Mr. Rocket."

Later, relaxed and content, Kate drifted into a satisfied sleep.

She'd smiled so much the past three hours, Kate thought her face would crack. She was glad finally to have a moment to be by herself. Don and Debbie left without incident. Both girls seemed glad to see them leave — *she* certainly was. Debbie had hugged and air kissed her good-bye as always. She and Alex promised to take extra good care of the girls, as usual, then their guests were off. She'd just finished cleaning up the kitchen. She'd made a huge breakfast for everyone. Had it not been for Sara, the food and effort would've been a total waste.

Alex and the girls were at the kennel waiting to send off one of the pups. Gertie had approved an adoption late yesterday afternoon, so he wanted to be there for the final send-off. The family was due to arrive sometime before noon, leaving Kate free to work for a couple of hours.

She decided to go to her studio to finish a piece that she'd been preparing for an upcoming exhibition in Asheville next month. The theme was cooking, and she was extremely excited. She'd been working for three months, hoping to have her first samples of earthenware ready in time for the show. If all went according to plan, she'd have her own line of baking dishes available to the public in another year. It was something she'd always wanted to do, and after a great deal of procrastination, she'd finally made the commitment.

Kate went upstairs to change into her work clothes. Old jeans covered with paint and hardened with clay and a UNC sweatshirt constituted her usual working attire.

She left through the back door in the kitchen following a well-worn footpath. This allowed her to come and go to her studio without being seen by Alex's clients. Though once she was inside the studio, she could hear the dogs barking and playing.

She removed the key from her jeans, taking a moment to listen for Alex and the arrival of the new family. She didn't hear anything, so she assumed the buyers had yet to arrive. Maybe Alex and the girls were at Gertie's. She lived in the small guest-house her parents had built on their property years ago. When Kate was in high school, she would occasionally spend the weekends ensconced in the private quarters with a good book and plenty of popcorn. There was nothing she liked more than to lose herself in a novel. She'd been a bookworm most of her life and still enjoyed reading when time permitted. She slipped the key into the lock, sure that Alex had taken the girls to Gertie's.

Kate twisted the doorknob and tried to push the door open. Something heavy leaned against the door, causing it to drag. She didn't remember leaving anything that could've fallen so close to the door. She gave an extra shove, and the door swung open. She stopped. Clearly this wasn't her studio. Like a sleepwalker, she stepped outside of her studio and entered again, thinking this time she'd awaken and the view would be different. Yes, it was real. Very real. Her entire collection for the upcoming exhibition was scattered in a million little pieces all across the wood floor. She pushed the door aside and stood in the middle of the room. She whirled around, trying to absorb the significance of what she saw. Her entire collection of earthenware destroyed. She walked through puddles of glass, thankful she was wearing sneakers instead of flip-flops. Stooping, she picked up several shards of red clay. There were no words. Numb, she walked across the room, hoping against hope that the three pieces she hadn't quite completed were still on the shelf where she'd left them. No, they were gone as well. Every single piece destroyed. She took in the shattered red earthenware. Months of work, ruined. She needed to call Alex, possibly the police. She walked across the room, her sneakers crunching on the debris as she made her way to the phone.

She dialed Gertie's number.

"Damn." Kate thought for sure that Alex and the girls were at Gertie's. Gertie wasn't answering the phone. She always picked up when she was at home. Kate wound her way through the glass. She gave a last look before heading to the kennel. She was at a loss. Who would do something like this? And more so, why? It wasn't as though she had competitors at the exhibition. All the artisans were excited about their work, but there wasn't one of them who would go to such lengths to sabotage her work. Again, there was no reason.

Kate entered the kennel, straining to hear

Alex or the girls. Nothing, except the sweet sound of puppies at play. They must be at the house. Kate looked at her watch. She'd only left the house ten minutes ago. Surely she would've passed them had they been leaving Gertie's or the kennel. The path from the kitchen led to both the kennel and the cottage.

Kate raced back to the house. "Alex, Gertie. Anybody here?" She waited. Nothing.

She went upstairs just to make sure. "Alex?" No answer.

Her hands shaking, she went to the kitchen to use the phone. She called the police to report the break-in at her studio.

"Is this an emergency?" the female operator asked.

Kate shook her head, "Uh, no, I don't think it is. But yes, wait. I can't find Alex or the girls." She ran her fingers through her hair, suddenly alarmed even more. "No, I can't find my husband, or the kids. They . . . He must've taken them. Oh God!"

"Calm down, ma'am," the voice encouraged.

Kate shouted into the receiver, "Just send the police, hurry!" She slammed the phone down. Did whoever broke into her studio have Alex and the girls? And Gertie, too? Were they still at the kennel, waiting for her?

Maybe they were still inside her studio. She had a small bathroom near the back. She hadn't thought of going inside. There was no reason. Until now. She looked around the kitchen. She needed a weapon. She snatched a Henckels butcher knife lying on the countertop. Funny, when she'd used it that morning, she never thought she would have to treat it as a weapon. She gripped the knife in her right hand, careful to keep the blade downward. She raced out the back door, then slowed as she approached her studio. She was about to push the door open when she heard sirens in the distance. Thank God. Now, if she could find Alex and the girls. Deciding to wait for the police, she jogged down the footpath to the winding road that led up to the house. Three police cars raced up the drive.

"Here!" She waved at them, then remembered the knife in her hand. She hung on to it, just in case.

A tall, broad-shouldered officer got out of the car. He had close-cropped hair and dark, piercing eyes and wore his uniform as though it were made by a top-notch designer, exclusively for him. "I'm Officer Furdell, ma'am," he said by way of greeting. "I was the first to get the call."

"Someone broke into my studio. My

husband is missing, and so are the kids. I was about to go back inside my studio, there's a bathroom, thought they were hiding . . ." Kate saw the police officer's eyes lower to the knife at her side. "I thought I might need a weapon. I went back to the house searching for Alex, and, well, I called . . ."

"Slow down, ma'am. Let us have a look around first."

Kate nodded, "Of course."

"Stay here by the vehicle."

"Okay."

Two more officers, both as large as Officer Furdell, sprang from their cruisers and followed his lead.

Kate couldn't believe this was happening around her. Police, her studio, and worst of all, Alex and the girls, nowhere to be found. She said a silent prayer that it was all some kind of sordid joke and she'd laugh about it later. Dear God! What would she do if something were to happen to Alex? And the girls as well. She'd promised Don and Debbie she'd take good care of them. What would they think if they knew Sara and Emily were missing? She would have to contact them soon. She had Don's cell number and would make the call. Later, when she had some news of Alex and the girls.

The sound of laughter caused her to look over her shoulder. Coming up the drive was Alex's old Ford pickup, Alex at the wheel, Gertie riding shotgun, and Emily, with three other children, in the back! Laughing. A white Lincoln Town Car followed them up the drive.

She dropped the knife and ran toward the moving truck. "Alex! Oh my God, you're alive! Where were you? What happened to the girls? The studio is destroyed!" She said this so fast, she knew it would take a few seconds for Alex to absorb.

He shifted his battered vehicle into park and jumped out. "My God, Kate, why are the police here?" He nodded toward the three patrol cars.

"There was a break-in. My studio, someone destroyed all of the earthenware I'd made for the showing in Asheville. I called Gertie, she wasn't there. Then I realized you and the girls were missing. I . . ." Her words faltered as she realized what a fool she'd made of herself. Standing in the bed of the truck were Emily and three small children. The car behind them had shut off its engine. A couple in their early thirties emerged from the car with looks of bewilderment on their faces. "Ivee, Ashleigh, Edyn, come over here, please." Three girls, all with bright red hair and freckles, slipped over the bed of the truck, dropping to the ground.

Kate looked at them, then back at Alex. "The Taylor family?"

Alex nodded. "They were lost. They called, and I told them I would meet them at the base of the mountain. I guess I should've told you I was leaving. Gertie and Emily went along for the ride."

Kate glance at the couple. "What about Sara? Where is she?"

Alex looked at Emily, who looked at Gertie. Gertie was the first to speak. "Sara said she wasn't feeling well and went back to the house."

"We thought you knew," Emily added.

"I went to the house. She wasn't there, or if she was, she must not have heard me calling." *Or,* Kate thought, *she just didn't answer.*

Alex motioned to the couple still standing alongside their car. They walked over to where Kate stood. "We're the Taylors. I'm Kathy, and this is my husband, Fred." Kate shook Kathy's hand and nodded to Fred.

"You all must think I'm crazy." Kate laughed.

"Not to worry. We all have 'those' days now and then. We got lost. I kept asking Fred to stop for directions." Kathy offered Kate a conspiring smile. "You know men and directions. Before we wound up in Outer Mongolia, I called and asked Alex to meet us."

Kate smiled at the younger woman. "That seems reasonable to me. I bet you all would love to see the new addition to the family."

"Yeah! C'mon, Mom, we want to meet Rosie." All three girls bounced up and down, barely able to contain their excitement.

"Rosie?" their parents asked in unison.

"That's what they've decided to call the new puppy," Kathy informed them.

"I like that name," Emily said.

Kate motioned for Alex to step aside. "Where do you think Sara is? I'm sure she's not at the house. I just hope to heavens she's . . . Ohmygod! Alex!"

"Kate, what is it?"

"What if whoever broke into the studio took Sara?" Kate's heart was beating so fast, she was sure it would explode from her chest any minute.

"Calm down. I'm sure there's an explanation for all of this. Let's wait and see what the police suggest. I'm going to take the Taylors to meet Rosie. Emily, wait here with Kate."

Emily nodded. The Taylor family got back into their car and followed Alex's truck to the kennel.

"Aunt Kate, do you think Sara's okay? I mean, I'm sure she is, but when she said she wasn't feeling well, I thought she'd gone to the house to tell you."

Kate didn't want to scare Emily any more than she was already. "As Alex said, there's an explanation for her . . . disappearance." Kate couldn't stand to think further about Sara. *One minute at a time,* she told herself.

The three police officers sauntered across the drive, all appearing as if they were on a casual call. A cat stuck in a tree, Kate thought.

"Ma'am," Officer Furdell said, "there doesn't seem to be any sign of forced entry. The bathroom is empty. We searched your house and the small cottage as well. The only thing we saw was a young girl sound asleep in one of the upstairs bedrooms."

"Oh, thank God Sara's safe! I don't see how I could've missed her. But if she was sleeping, she must not've heard me call."

The two officers smiled and returned to their cruisers. Officer Furdell reached in his breast pocket and pulled out one of his cards. "If you have any more problems, just call. I'm at a loss as to what happened in your studio, ma'am. I'm going to write up a vandalism report. If I were you, I'd change all the locks just to be on the safe side. This could be the work of some bored teenagers. You know how they are." He gestured toward Emily. Kate wanted to say unfortunately she hadn't experienced the pleasure of raising a child, but decided it didn't matter. She gave Emily a wan smile.

"Thanks. I'll have Alex change the locks today." She shook his offered hand, and, with a quick nod, he returned to his patrol car and headed down the drive.

"I need to check on Sara."

"I'll go with you. I can't believe she didn't hear you. She's a light sleeper. Or nosy, I'm not sure which. She never seems to miss anything at home. She'll be surprised when she realizes she missed the cops. I can't imagine her sleeping through those loud sirens."

Kate couldn't either but didn't say so out loud. She berated herself for the negative thoughts she had concerning Sara. Something was going on with her, and Kate was going to get to the bottom of it. Suddenly, she knew she didn't need to change the locks on the doors. She knew exactly what had happened to her studio. Until she could prove it, however, she would remain silent.

Chapter 5

"Sara, you should've told me you were here. You scared us half to death," Kate explained.

"I'm sorry, Aunt Kate. I was just so full from breakfast. That raw bacon you served made me so sick, all I wanted to do was lie down and rest. I might be poisoned."

"I'd give her an enema. That'll clean her out. Just in case she's poisoned," Emily said.

Kate laughed. "I think she'll be okay. I'll make sure you eat lightly for the next twenty-fours hours. If you're no better, then I'll take you to the emergency room myself," Kate informed Sara.

"I'm okay. Now. This happens only when I eat raw pork. Mommy cooks it well-done, like I told you before," she snapped.

"I promise this won't happen again. Emily, Alex is still at the kennel with the Taylor family. Why don't you run down there and see if he needs any help. I'm going to stay with Sara a while before I tackle the mess in the studio."

Kate hadn't mentioned one word about the police or the so-called break-in to Sara. She wanted to watch her, see if she hinted at anything about it, which would cast suspicion on her.

"You're sure you don't need me here? I can start cleaning the studio when the Taylors leave."

"No, I don't want you to risk hurting yourself, just go see if Alex needs your help. Tell the Taylors I've got a sick child and can't say good-bye. I'm sure they'll understand."

"Okay." Emily paused, glaring at her sister. "Don't give Aunt Kate any trouble."

"See, this is what she does all the time! She blames me for stuff I don't even do. I can't wait till Mommy gets back. I'm going to tell her —"

"Enough, Sara," Kate admonished.

"Well, I am going to tell her about almost dying from food poisoning. I bet she'll never let me out of her sight again. She won't want to go on one of those stupid cruise ships ever again!" Sara whirled out of the room like a fast-moving tide.

"Of course I'll tell your mother you were sick. Which reminds me, I need to call them before they arrive in Cape Canaveral," she said to Sara's back as the obnoxious child raced out of the room.

Kate shook her head and left the room, with Emily at her heels.

"She's so mean, Aunt Kate. I don't believe she was sick, do you?"

"I don't know. I do know that I didn't serve raw bacon for breakfast. It was probably too much grease. She's at a difficult age, Em, remember that." That was lame, but it was all Kate could come up with.

"Yeah. Okay," Emily agreed. She left through the kitchen, heading for the kennel.

Finally, with a few minutes to herself, Kate sat at the kitchen table in order to contemplate her next move. Of course she'd have to clean up the studio. She would call Nancy and tell her she wouldn't be able to make the exhibition after all. There were plenty of other artisans who could take her space. Then she would talk to Alex. She'd tell him her misgivings. From there, they would decide what to do.

She'd wait until the girls left before she would allow herself a pity-party over the destruction of her earthenware and the lost opportunity. Months of work, gone, in the blink of an eye. She had an idea of what might've ignited Sara's desire to destroy but wouldn't mention it just yet. She hated to accuse anyone without hard evidence, especially a child; but in this case, she felt she had good reason to be suspicious of Sara.

Suddenly, Kate wished the two weeks were over, then felt a flash of guilt. She'd enjoyed so many summers and spring breaks with both of the girls, especially now that they were older. She loved teaching them new things, loved to see the smiles of satisfaction when they discovered something that excited them. This particular visit had just gotten off to a bad start.

Trying to talk herself out of her negative thoughts, Kate opened the freezer in search of something to prepare for dinner. She took out a whole chicken and placed it in the sink to thaw. She'd make her favorite chicken with yellow rice. That shouldn't hurt Sara's stomach. For dessert she'd serve lime sorbet with sugar cookies. She took frozen cookie dough she'd made earlier in the week from the freezer and placed it on the countertop. When she was stressed, cooking acted like a sedative to her. She started to relax as she set about her simple tasks.

Kate cooked the rice and put it inside the fridge for later. She sliced the partially frozen dough, placed the round circles on a cookie sheet, and put them on a shelf in the refrigerator. With nothing more to do in the kitchen, she knew it was time to confront the disaster that awaited her in the studio. She grabbed a broom and dust pan from the utility room, along with a couple of brown paper bags. Taking the same path she had earlier, Kate wondered how it was possible that she'd missed Sara in the act of destroying her earthenware collection. Why hadn't she heard the pottery as it shattered? She'd been occupied with thoughts of Debbie and Don, but had she been that distracted? Admittedly, yes. She'd been so intent on her thoughts, she hadn't paid much attention to anything around her. She prayed she was wrong about Sara, but she knew there was no other explanation.

Once inside the studio, Kate dispassionately swept the remains of months of hard work into the paper bags, telling herself there would be another time for her dreams. She'd start a new project when things slowed down at the restaurant. She still had her cooking classes to keep her busy, not to mention all of the baking she did for the restaurant and its many customers during the Christmas season. Once the holidays were over, she and Alex would go back to sharing the events of their day together over a nice glass of wine and a meal prepared by her. Sometimes they would go out, but mostly, they liked being alone at home together. It wasn't unusual for Alex to make several nighttime trips to the kennel when he had a new litter of pups. Evenings out weren't that frequent either, and that was fine by her. She liked their life as it was, and hated the thought of it changing. She told herself this visit with the girls would get better, it *had* to. She still wasn't sure what, if anything, to say to Sara. For the moment, she would wait and discuss it with Alex.

Half an hour later, Kate disposed of the last bag of broken clay in the garbage can. It was hot, and she wanted to get a shower before Sara woke up. If she was even asleep at all. Kate glanced around the studio one last time just to make sure there were no broken slivers of pottery. Her gaze swept the long, narrow room. Sun from the skylight twinkled leaf-shaped patterns over the oak floors. She didn't see a sparkle or anything she thought could be a sliver of glazed clay. She'd just be careful not to wear flip-flops in the studio for the next few weeks. Not that she had any reason to work in her studio for a while. Since her collection of earthenware was long gone, she closed the door without another glance. Later, she would return and decide on a new pattern. She'd never be able to re-create what had been destroyed.

Back inside the house, Kate was quiet as she took the steps to the upstairs bedroom where Sara was napping. She wasn't trying to be sneaky. She just wanted to make sure that if Sara was sleeping, she didn't wake her. A crack in the bedroom door revealed Sara curled into the fetal position. Her eyes were closed. Kate gave the child the benefit of the doubt. She would assume she was truly sleeping. With her hand on the knob, she was about to close the door when she spied Sara's sneakers on the floor. One shoe lay on its side, revealing the bottom of the shoe. Embedded in the beige-colored rubber sole were several shards of red earthenware. Her hand shook as she quietly opened the door. Careful not to disturb Sara, she scooped the shoe off the floor and hurried out of the room. Kate entered the master bedroom, then closed and locked the door behind her. She placed the sneaker on her bed. Before she had second thoughts, she went to the bathroom to get a plastic bag from beneath the sink. She put the shoe with the slivers embedded in the sole in the bag. She took the bag to her closet. Once inside, she stood there in a daze. Both sides were filled with her clothes. Alex's were kept in a smaller closet in the second spare bedroom. Someday she'd downsize and wouldn't need the entire closet. Riffling through the clothes at the back of the closet, Kate found an old leather jacket she hadn't worn since high school. She tucked the shoe in the inside pocket. She wasn't sure why she did this, but it seemed like the right thing to do. Kate didn't know how to approach Sara with the incriminating shoe, but at least she had tangible evidence that there had not been a break-in. That part was a relief, but knowing that Sara was responsible for the damage alarmed her even more, especially after the conversation she'd had with Emily. Sara needed help, and she needed it soon, before her shenanigans escalated into something much worse. Kate remembered what Emily had told her about Sara and her mistreatment of their neighbor's cat.

Sara needed help.

And she needed it right away.

Chapter 6

Because of bad weather in the Caribbean, Don and Debbie arrived to pick up the girls a day early. Kate had managed to keep Sara out of trouble for the remainder of her stay. After much thought, she'd allowed Alex and Gertie to believe they'd had a burglar. She knew she should've told Alex that Sara was responsible, but something held her back. She hated being deceitful, but Alex enjoyed the girls' visits so much, she just didn't have the heart to tarnish his image of Sara. She, too, had enjoyed Emily and Sara, even if Sara had complained constantly. She reasoned that it had taken twelve years to turn her into a spoiled young girl. Kate knew she couldn't expect a miracle in the short time she'd spent with them. She decided to speak privately with Don before they left.

As usual, Kate made a hearty breakfast for everyone. Pecan waffles, sausage patties, and pan-fried new potatoes with onions and green peppers. She sliced cantaloupe and honeydew melons for herself and Debbie. After they'd finished their meal, Debbie went upstairs with the girls to help them pack. Alex and Don drank their coffee while Kate put the dishes in the dishwasher.

With all the pups adopted out from the last litter, Kate knew Alex wouldn't be in a major rush to head out to the kennels. She needed to get him out of the room for a few minutes. "Alex, why don't you run upstairs and help Deb take the girls' luggage to the car."

Alex stood up and stretched. "I think she wants me to get to work."

Don laughed. "Then you'd better get your ass out of here."

Alex gave Kate a hurried kiss on the cheek.

Kate didn't have much time. She dried her hands on a kitchen towel and grabbed the pot of coffee. She refilled Don's cup and her own with the last two cups. Don made things easy for her when he said, "Is there something you want to talk about?"

She nodded. "It's Sara."

"I figured as much. What mischief did the little monster get into this time?"

Kate wished it were something as simple as childhood mischief. "I'm afraid it's more than that, Don. She seems to have trouble telling the truth. I don't know if she mentioned this to you or Deb. The day you left —"

"Don, get the hell out here!" Debbie shouted from the living room.

He stood. "Duty calls. And Kate, thanks for taking care of the girls. As for Sara, I know she's a handful. I think being the youngest is hard on her. I'll keep an eye out, though."

Before Kate could even begin her account of what had happened, Don left the kitchen. She followed him, but much to her dismay, Debbie and both girls were ready to leave. Their luggage was already in the car. Now all she needed to do was say her good-byes. She really needed to talk to Don about Sara. She would call him as soon as they returned to Florida. It might even be easier that way. Kate wouldn't have to see the look on his face when she told him about the incident in her studio. Yes, it was better that way. After all, what could Sara do in the next twenty-four hours while they were all in the car together?

"We had a great time, Aunt Kate. I can't wait till Christmas break. You're letting us come up then, right, Dad?" Emily asked.

"If Kate and Alex still want to have you, it's fine with me. Debbie?" he questioned.

"Whatever, Don. You'd think you girls would want to be with your family at Christmas, but as usual, you both do whatever you want." Debbie glanced at the gold Rolex watch on her wrist. "We need to go. I don't want to get a late start."

Kate hugged both girls. "We'll see you at Christmas this year. Make sure and send us a list so I'll have plenty of time to send it to Santa." She'd been saying that to the girls for as long as she could remember. And even though, obviously, neither of them still believed in Santa Claus, they still continued to send her long lists every year.

"I don't want to come here for Christmas. It's too cold," Sara said to her mother.

"That's months away, Sara. We'll discuss it later." Debbie nudged Sara toward the front door. "Let's get in the car."

Kate and Alex hugged the girls one last time. Don gave Alex a quick hug, while Debbie gave her usual air kisses.

"Call us when you get home so we know you made it," Alex said to Don.

"Remember, I've got that cell phone in the car if you need to get in touch before we get home."

"I'll do that. You be safe, old man." Alex placed a hand on Don's shoulder, gave a quick pat, then a nudge, pushing him toward the Explorer. "Now get out of here. Take care of those girls."

"Will do," Don said.

As they traveled down the winding drive, Kate watched them leave. She experienced an eerie feeling, so strange in fact that she was uncomfortable. She stood on the front porch until their vehicle was no longer in sight. A sinking feeling in the pit of her stomach caused her to run to the edge of the drive. She needed one last look at their car. She didn't know why, but something about their departure nagged at her in a bad way. She shook her head, telling herself it was because she'd let Don leave without speaking about Sara. Never mind that she'd almost convinced herself it was better to do over the phone. No, this was more. Something she couldn't quite put a finger on.

Kate went back to the house, feeling bereft. She should've been happy to have her home all to herself again. She and Alex could go back to their normal routine. Gertie would take care of most of the work at the kennel, allowing them the evenings together. But something continued to raise the hair on the back of her neck. Ominous and menacing feelings destroyed her composure.

She shook her head to clear her negative

thoughts. *This is stupid,* she told herself. She wandered back to the kitchen, where she felt most comfortable. Wanting to take her mind off the girls, Kate decided to work on one of the dishes she'd been thinking about for the restaurant. The Ladies Club was having their monthly luncheon next week. She wanted to try something different, and they would be the perfect group. Kate always gave them her recipes to try out at home. Not once had Kate heard a complaint. A few of them had even called her at home for ideas on what to make for their husbands' dinner parties, kids' birthdays, and even a bar mitzvah. She loved sharing her knowledge of food with others.

Kate took all the ingredients she needed from the fridge. She sliced a lime and squeezed the juice into a bowl. A dollop of horseradish, fresh garlic, and olive oil followed. She whipped the mixture with a fork, then dabbed her finger in the bowl and licked it. "Not bad." A little ground black pepper and another touch of olive oil should do the trick. She knew most members of the Ladies Club were always watching their figures, so instead of the traditional fat-laden mayonnaise dressing used in Crab Louis, she wanted something light, with just a hint of citrus flavor. As she tasted, she made notes in a spiral notebook. Later, she would write out the exact measurements, but for now she simply listed the ingredients.

Half an hour later, Kate finished in the kitchen. Feeling depressed, she went in search of Alex and Gertie. They'd all go out for dinner and celebrate. What, she didn't know. What she did know was that she needed to be around friends and family to distract her from her dark thoughts.

Deciding they truly wanted to celebrate, Kate, Alex, and Gertie took the extra time to drive to the Grove Park Inn in Asheville. With three different restaurants to choose from, they selected the Sunset Terrace, noted for the best views in town of the Blue Ridge mountains.

They ordered twelve-ounce filets, topped with a Cognac-mushroom sauce. Roasted fingerling potatoes with rosemary butter and a sun-dried tomato Caesar salad completed their meals. After finishing their dinner, Kate felt more relaxed than she had in two weeks.

"I'm glad I don't eat like this often. I wouldn't be able to move," Alex observed.

"Are you saying I don't feed you enough?" Kate asked teasingly.

"More than enough. These portions are

enough to feed a family of four," Alex replied.

"I don't think so. Look at Sara. Why, I never saw a girl eat so much," Gertie added.

Kate's stomach flip-flopped. She didn't even want to think about Sara, let alone discuss her eating habits. She couldn't say this to Gertie or Alex without revealing why, so she said nothing, waiting for Alex to comment. When he didn't, Gertie continued, "There's something about that child that isn't right. I don't know what it is, but I bet she's gonna be trouble when she's older."

If she only knew, Kate thought.

"She's young. Don told me she was jealous of Emily. I think she'll grow out of whatever's bothering her soon enough. She's at a tough stage. I think she just wants Debbie's attention," Alex said to Gertie.

"You could be right, but I think it's more than that."

Kate perked up. "What do you mean?" Did Gertie know something more about Sara's behavior that she hadn't told her?

"Something I can't put a finger on. She's a schemer, that much I do know. I'd watch that one if I were her parents. She's going to break their hearts." Gertie shook her head, her soft gray curls bouncing as she did so.

"Let's change the subject." Kate's thoughts formed into words before she could stop them.

"Yes, let's talk about that vacation we've been putting off for the past three years," Alex said.

Alex had been so busy with the kennels and Kate with her cooking classes and work at the restaurant, they hadn't even considered taking a vacation. Oh, they talked about it, but that was it. Now was a good time.

"Oh, a vacation sounds wonderful, Alex. But where would we go? I can't think of a place that's more beautiful than our front yard," Kate said, and she meant it. Her and Alex's home had a prime view of the Blue Ridge Mountains. In the fall, Kate could hardly stand to work inside. The springtime was just as remarkable. The winters in Asheville weren't bad either. At that moment, Kate felt as though her life couldn't have been more perfect.

"We've never been on a cruise. Don left some pamphlets for us to look at. Maybe it's time we sailed the high seas."

Kate laughed. "I don't think sailing to the Caribbean would be considered the 'high seas,' but I'd certainly be willing to see what a cruise has to offer."

"I'll look after the dogs. Bella isn't due for another month, so that should give you plenty of time to take a cruise," Gertie commented.

Bella was Alex's favorite, and Kate knew he'd want to be the one to help bring her pups into the world. Even though she wasn't due for another month, Kate didn't want to take a chance. Bella could have the pups early. It would break Alex's heart if he was gone when she delivered.

"Maybe after Bella has the pups we'll go," Kate suggested.

Alex reached for her hand, giving it a squeeze. He didn't want to leave so soon either, Kate thought. She placed her hand on his forearm, gently caressing the firm muscles.

"What, you don't think I can take care of Bella?" Gertie asked.

Alex laughed out loud. "I think you're more than capable, old girl. I trust you more than anyone. You should know that by now. We're just in the planning stages anyway. Kate might hate the thought of going on a cruise. No land in sight for days. Nothing to do but lounge by the pool, drink those funny little fruity drinks with umbrellas.

Have some young stud waiting on her hand and foot. Plus, she wouldn't be able to prepare our meals. I don't know if she'd like that or not."

Kate gave a playful punch to his shoulder. "And you are so full of it, Alex Rocket, your eyes are swimming in it."

"I know you. After two or three days with nothing to do, you'd go stir-crazy."

Kate knew he was right. "Maybe. We'll think about a cruise. Later. For now, I think we need to pay the check and go home. Our waiter is giving us the evil eye."

It was after eleven and the restaurant had closed at ten. "Leave a super-big tip, too," Kate added.

As they were getting ready for bed, Alex seemed on edge. Kate asked if something was bothering him.

"Nah, just tired. It was a long two weeks. I'm ready to settle down into our routine again. How 'bout you?"

"The visit did seem a bit longer than normal. I guess it's because we're getting older and don't have the energy we used to," Kate hedged.

"I suppose you're right. It stinks," Alex said.

"What?"

"You know. Getting old."

Kate smiled in the mirror. Alex was lying on the bed with a Stephen King book opened, lying on his flat stomach. She tissued off the remainder of her eye makeup. "I think getting old is a wonderful thing. It sure beats the alternative." She thought of her parents. She only wished they were here with her. She wished she could tell them she had married Alex. They would've approved.

"I suppose you're right about that, too, Mrs. Rocket. Now, get that butt of yours over here so I can give you a kiss." Alex smoothed the rumpled sheets, then motioned for Kate to lie down beside him.

After a passionate, fun-filled tumble, Kate fell asleep with absolutely nothing on her mind.

And tomorrow was a brand-new day.

CHAPTER 7

Alex and Kate hadn't heard a word from the Winter family since they'd gone home two weeks ago. Don had called Alex telling him they'd arrived safely, and that was it. Not another word. Kate thought this odd, but didn't mention it to Alex. He'd had enough on his mind the past few days. Bella was delivering early, just as she'd anticipated. Alex spent most days and nights at the kennel with Gertie. Jay, their vet, had spent the last twelve hours with Bella. She was having a rough delivery. Kate prayed she and her pups survived. Alex was worried, and it showed. He'd barely slept the past week. Kate had supplied hot coffee and plenty of sandwiches for him and Gertie while they remained at Bella's side. Dinnertime rolled around. Kate still hadn't heard a word on Bella's condition from Alex or Gertie. She decided to visit the kennel to see for herself. She grabbed a sweater from the hall closet, slipped on her sneakers, and stepped outside.

Kate shivered at the shock of cool air that greeted her when she opened the back door. A cold front had moved in from the north. She hoped it wasn't a sign of a bitter winter ahead. While she loved fall-like weather, cold weather sometimes depressed her. Both her parents had died in a terrible car crash on a bleak winter day in January. Even after all these years, driving in snow and ice still made her nervous. Though it was chilly, winter was still months away. She was glad.

She entered the kennel. Voices raised in excitement greeted her.

"That a girl! I knew you could do it."

"Would you look at . . . him! He's one big boy!"

"Wait . . . wait, I'll be damned! Here comes another!" Jay shouted.

Kate stood in silence as Alex, Gertie, and Jay surrounded the laboring Bella. Alex held one puppy; it looked as though Gertie had two. Jay was about to deliver another.

"And would you look at this! I think she's the runt of the litter." Jay held the pup up for inspection.

Whimpering puppies and a happy Bella. Tears moistened her eyes. A beautiful sight for sure.

"I see I arrived just in time," Kate announced. "Looks like a happy crew to me."

"Bella had four pups! I can't believe it. She's such a good girl, aren't you?" Alex rubbed between Bella's ears. She growled. "I know, I know. It's hands off for now."

Jay checked to make sure all of the puppies were healthy. Bella was worn-out from labor and delivery; but other than that, she appeared to be in good health. Kate saw the happiness in Alex's eyes as he stared at the puppies. She could only imagine how happy he would've been to be a father.

"I think this calls for a toast," Kate said. "I've got a bottle of champagne I've been saving just for such an occasion. I'll run up to the house. Be right back."

She returned within a matter of minutes and poured champagne into red plastic cups. "I'd like to propose a toast." Kate viewed the smiling faces surrounding her. "Here's to Bella and her crew for making it the perfect day. And to Alex. For making all my days perfect."

Cheers were given by all. After they finished the rest of the champagne, Kate and Alex left the puppies with Gertie and Jay. Both were tipsy. Their mood exuberant.

Kate was reminded once again how good her life with Alex really was. It was almost too good, she thought. No, it was just perfect. Nothing would ever change her feelings for Alex. And Kate knew Alex. He would always love her, stick by her, no matter what. They would make it to the "till death do us part" for sure.

Arms wrapped around one another's waists, they made their way to the kitchen. Kate brewed a pot of coffee. It was too early to call it a night. Besides, they knew Gertie and Jay would come up to the house when they felt Bella was ready to be alone with the pups. Maybe she'd be a little more sober by then.

She drank two cups of coffee to Alex's four. She wasn't much of a coffee drinker, but it was the only beverage she knew to lighten the load when she had one too many.

"I'll have one more cup, and that's it. This crap tastes like . . . crap," Kate said to Alex.

"Then why drink it?"

" 'Cuz I had too many glasses of champagne." Kate's words were slurred.

Alex laughed. "I think you'll be okay, hon. It's not like you drink all the time."

Alex was right, hence her inability to handle a couple of glasses of champagne.

"I'm gonna go upstairs and shower 'fore Gert 'n Jay get here." Kate stood on wobbly legs.

"Need some help?" Alex asked.

"I'll be jus' fine. Back in a flash." Kate whirled out of the room, waving her arms like a bird.

Alex just laughed at her. She rarely drank. He was happy today. Bella and the pups had survived. Gertie was the best damned employee there was. Jay took excellent care of the animals. Marriage to Kate was beyond his wildest dreams in every way. Nothing in his life was bad. He thought that was good. *Heck, I'm a tad on the sloppy side of drunk myself.*

He was about to go upstairs to join Kate in the shower when the phone rang. He hoped it wasn't Jay or Gertie calling from the kennel to say something had happened to Bella or her pups.

"Hello," Alex said into the receiver. Again, he said hello. Nothing. The phone went dead. "Well, make up your mind." He placed the phone back in its cradle. It rang again.

"Yes, hello." Alex raised his voice. If it was a phone solicitor, he hoped they would hang up on him when they heard his unfriendly tone.

"It's me, Alex."

"Why the heck didn't you speak up? I've been wondering why you haven't called, old buddy. Think you're too good to call your best friend? You down there in Florida with all those swanky houses you're working on, huh? All those rich folks," Alex teased. "I'm glad you called. I have some good news. I was going to call you tomorrow anyway."

"Alex, wait. I have something I need to talk to you about. It's very serious. Do you have a few minutes?" Don asked.

"I always have time for my best bud," Alex replied, wondering what Don could mean.

"Have you been drinking, Alex? You don't sound so good."

"We had a bottle of champagne. I might've had one too many slurps." Alex burped into the phone. "I did have one too many. But hey, I'm a big boy. I can handle it. Why so serious, my friend?"

"I've . . . I'm not sure how to say this," Don stated seriously.

"Like I always say, 'say it the way you're supposed to.' Hit me, old man. What's up?"

"It's Sara."

"Is she okay? She didn't get hurt or anything, did she?" Alex asked, all traces of his liquor wit gone.

"Physically, she's fine. Or at least she says she is. I would think you'd know more about this than I, Alex."

Alarm bells rang loudly in Alex's ears.

"Why would I know this, Don? I haven't seen or spoken to Sara since you all left."

"I know that," Don said, his voice even more somber.

"Then get to the point. Is Sara all right or what?"

"No, she's not, Alex. She's in a very bad way. Deb has had to take her to the hospital twice in the past two weeks. She's been having anxiety attacks since she left your house. The doctor gave her sedatives to calm her."

Alex shook his head, hoping to clear the alcohol fog in his brain. He still couldn't understand why Don was telling him all of this. Maybe he needed money? That had to be it. Maybe Sara needed to be hospitalized, and he couldn't come up with the cash.

"Listen, Don, you know if you need money for hospital bills, just say the word, and it's yours. I'll have my bank wire it first thing in the morning."

"I don't need your damn money, Alex. I need you to shut up and listen to what I have to say. Just one time, I wish you wouldn't mention money."

Alex was puzzled. Don had never had trouble accepting loans from him in the past. Had his pride kicked in all of a sudden? Alex didn't care if Don paid him back or not. They'd been best friends since elementary school, they were as close as brothers. Maybe even more. Money was beside the point as far as Alex was concerned. He had plenty of it to share with his friend. He'd always made sure Don knew that, too.

"Hey, I'm sorry. What's wrong, Don?"

Alex could hear Don's intake of breath. "This isn't easy for me, Alex."

"Okay. Just spit it out. We can deal with it, no matter what it is."

"Sara . . . she says the last time you guys came to Florida to visit us . . . she says you, uh . . . you touched her, Alex. Sara says you touched her in an inappropriate way."

Silence. And more silence.

Alex's hand shook, and he felt the blood flow from his face to his feet. Surely he hadn't heard what he thought he'd just heard. "Say it again, Don. I'm not quite sure I heard you. Apparently, I did have too much to drink."

"I think you heard me right the first time. Sara says you've been touching her for years. She says it only happens when you all come to our house to visit, except for one time during Easter break. Goddamn you, Alex! How could you? She's just a little girl! I swear, if I was in the same room with you right now, I would kill you with my bare hands! You son of a bitch! Do you realize what you've done to her? You've ruined her for the rest of her damned life," Don sobbed into the receiver. "You bastard, I loved you. And now look at us."

More silence.

Alex cleared his throat. He downed the cup of cold coffee in front of him. His hands trembled like dry leaves. "I don't know what to say, Don. This is . . . I don't know why . . . I would never . . . Let me talk to Sara. She's just, hell I don't know what I'm saying."

"There isn't anything left to say. You've molested my daughter. My best friend, more dear than a brother to me. I don't think there are any appropriate words for a conversation of this nature. You've ruined my little girl, Alex. I'll see you in hell before I allow you to get away with this. I will see you in hell, old man!" Don shouted, then slammed the phone in Alex's ear.

He continued to hold on to the phone as though it were a lifeline of sorts. If he hung it up and acknowledged his conversation with Don, that would make it real. There had to be an explanation. Surely, Don was playing a cruel joke. But to do so at Sara's expense wasn't like Don. He could be a prankster, but this went too far, even for

Don. No, there had to be another explanation. Maybe he had a bet with a friend down there in Florida, maybe Don just wanted to see how many hoops he'd jump through before he got in his truck and hightailed it to Florida to kick his ass. But that was too lame even for Don. The only possible explanation — and this was too far-fetched to imagine — was that maybe Sara had really convinced her father that he'd touched her.

God, it was sick to even think about, let alone actually doing something as repugnant. *Him* a child molester. He couldn't imagine something happening to him like this in his wildest dreams. Maybe tomorrow he would wake up and he'd find out this was nothing but a dream.

"Alex. Alex, are you okay?" Kate's voice sounded tinny, like it was coming through a deep, dark tunnel. Kate shook him. "Alex, you're scaring me!"

Alex gazed around the kitchen looking at all the familiar things that he and Kate had collected throughout their marriage. Now it was all a joke. A dirty, filthy joke.

Ruined.

Tainted.

"If you don't speak up, Alex, I'm going to have Jay give you a shot of whatever he gives to crazy horses. I thought I heard you talking when I got out of the shower." Kate was basically sober. She still had a slight buzz, though nothing she couldn't handle.

"That was Don on the phone," Alex said, his words coming out like an automaton's.

"It's about time he called. Are the girls okay?" Kate waited for Alex to answer.

"No."

"God, Alex, what's happened! Was it Emily? Sara?" Kate was almost screaming at him, yet he remained seated at the table. He was like a zombie in another time zone.

He stood up and went to the kitchen sink. He splashed cold water on his face, hoping its briskness would wash away all that he was feeling. He cupped his hands together and drank greedily from the faucet.

Kate had never seen Alex like this. It frightened her. "I'm going to call Don myself if you don't tell me what happened. I'm scared, Alex."

Kate's words brought him out of his daze. She would be changed forever when he told her what Don accused him of. His sweet, perfect Kate. Any shred of innocence she'd ever had, gone. He had to get himself together. For Kate. They would get through this together. He prayed she would believe him. Hell, this was Kate. Alex *knew* she would believe him.

"Don says they've had to take Sara to the hospital twice. She's been having anxiety attacks since she came home."

Kate knew why. The little monster was having a guilt attack. "I'm glad. It serves her right for what she did. She's old enough to know better, Alex. I know I should've told you, but you and the girls were having so much fun, I hated to put a damper on things."

"Kate, what are you talking about?"

"The studio. There was no burglar, Alex. It was Sara. I've known about it all along. I waited to see if she'd come clean while she was here, but she didn't. I was going to tell Don, but they left, and I never got a chance to. I've been meaning to call them since the girls left and tell Don what she did, but then I decided against it. It was over. I figured Sara would apologize when she was older. I think she knew I suspected her."

Alex couldn't believe what he'd just heard. "You're telling me that Sara destroyed all of your earthenware, and you did nothing about it! Kate, why in the hell didn't you tell me? I would've told Don. And then he would've . . ."

"Would've what? Said she's 'at that age' and gone about his business. That's what

Don would've done. He sure as hell wouldn't get her the help she needs."

"I hate to say this, Kate, but it might've made a big difference if you'd at least told Don. You didn't have to tell me. Now, though, this is only going to make things look worse."

"Alex, speak in English or say something that I can understand. You're not making sense."

"Don called and told me Sara told him that I had . . . touched her."

If Alex were to have slapped her in the face, it wouldn't have been as shocking. "What?"

"You heard me. Sara told Don and Debbie that I touched her inappropriately."

"This has got to be some horrible joke. Why would Don do this to you? To us?"

"I've asked myself that same question more times than I can count. He was serious, Kate. He said Sara told him I'd touched her when we visited them in Florida. Said it'd been happening for a long time."

Kate turned ten shades of white, then red. "That little monster! Why would she do this to you? There has to be a mistake, Alex. I'm going to call Debbie myself. I'll clear this thing right up." Kate hoisted herself up from the chair she never quite remembered seat-ing herself in. She grabbed the phone from Alex.

"Don't, Kate. Don was serious. He wouldn't joke about something like this."

"Then what? You're supposed to sit back and do nothing! I don't think so! This could ruin our lives, Alex. Have you thought about that?"

"This is as much a shock to me as it is to you. I don't know what to think at this point. I suppose I should wait to hear from Don again."

"Did he actually say he would call you back?"

Alex thought for a minute. "No, he didn't."

A sharp knock at the back door caused Alex to drop the phone. Kate about jumped out of her skin. "Who's there?" Suddenly paranoid, she peered through the curtain, hoping that whoever was there would just go away.

"Kate. Alex, it's Gertie. Open up."

Gertie. Jay. Bella and her puppies. Had it only been an hour ago that they'd celebrated the birth of the tiny creatures? It seemed like days.

"Gertie, sure, come in." Kate unlocked the door, which she didn't remember locking. Was this what fear did to a person? Did you do crazy things that were out of character and not remember?

"You two look worse than Bella. Gosh, was the champagne that bad?" Gertie asked.

"Sit down, Gertie," Kate said.

"You two want to tell me what's wrong? Neither damn one of you look worth a plugged nickel."

Kate glanced at Alex, silently asking his permission to tell Gertie what they'd just learned.

"Alex just got off the phone with Don. It seems Sara's been having anxiety attacks since she got home. They . . . She said that Alex had touched her." Kate let out a deep breath and inhaled.

For once, Gertie was at a loss for words. She stared at Alex, then back at Kate, her warm brown eyes filling with fire.

"Well, I hope to hell you're not gonna take this sitting down! Have you talked to the girl? What in the world would she do something like this for, what would she hope to gain? I knew that kid wasn't right the first time I laid eyes on her. She's always been on the sneaky side, even as a toddler. What can I do?"

Gertie was being Gertie. Thank God. Kate and Alex needed her unabashed common sense now more than ever.

"I don't know what to do, Gertie. I've never even imagined being accused of something so horrendous in my life."

"You're gonna need a lawyer, I can tell you that. My brother ought to be able to recommend a good defense attorney. I'll call him right now."

Gertie's brother was a first-rate attorney, known far and wide in North Carolina. Sadly, he didn't do criminal law.

She took the phone into the living room. She spoke to her brother for five minutes, then returned to the kitchen. "This is gonna get a lot worse before it gets better."

"I knew today was too good to be true. It's time for old Alex to fall."

"And I'll be there to catch you, Alex. You can count on it," Kate said.

CHAPTER 8

"Since the child maintains the alleged molestation took place in Florida, if this goes to trial, we'll have to go to Florida." James Conroy, Alex's criminal defense attorney, made it a practice to tell his clients the whole truth and nothing but. There was no point in mollycoddling them.

"Do you think this will actually *go* to trial?" Kate asked.

"Right now I can't say for sure, but most likely not. I do know that if Alex turns himself in, it will look better in the eyes of the court."

Kate and Alex had lived in a whirlwind for the past three days. They'd heard nothing more from Don. Gertie's brother had recommended James. As soon as they told their story, James contacted the authorities in Collier County. As expected, there was a warrant for Alex's arrest.

"So we drive to Florida, Alex turns himself

in, gets bailed out, then what?" Kate asked.

James Conroy was tall and pencil-thin with thick blond hair. A goatee softened a pointed chin and a mustache covered a thin upper lip. He resembled a young professor. If Kate had seen him on the street, she would've thought him the scholarly type, not the high-powered criminal defense attorney he was reputed to be. Clear blue eyes met hers. "I'm afraid it's not that simple."

"What do you mean?" Kate asked.

James's office was located in downtown Asheville. It was on the tenth floor of the Bank of America Building. This afforded him a much better view than any of his peers had. The Blue Ridge Mountains dominated the skyline. Gray fog layered the mountains in early morning, reminding him of Los Angeles, his hometown, only there the fog was more smog than anything else. He gazed out at the view, then directed his attention to his client. He spoke in a cultured voice, each word precise and clear. "If the child alleges the molestations took place in Florida, it's in their jurisdiction. The sheriff's department will send a pair of deputies to extradite Alex. Once he's processed, he'll be formally charged at an arraignment hearing. We'll make our plea to the court at that time."

"And what about bail? Just how does that work?" Kate persisted. Alex was still in a state of shock. Kate asked most of the questions while he stood by and listened. This was a nightmare, and both of them wanted nothing more than to wake up with it all behind them. From what James said, it didn't appear that it was going to be as simple as they'd hoped.

James sat down at a large mahogany desk, its surface clean except for a legal pad, a cup of sharpened pencils, their tips facing forward, and a banker's lamp. The wall behind him held certificates showing that he'd graduated from Yale Law summa cum laude. "I know this isn't what you want to hear, but it's the way it is. Bond for an accused child molester in the state of Florida is very difficult to obtain. It can be done, but it is going to take a large amount of cash. Of course, at the conclusion of the legal proceedings the money is returned to whoever put it up."

Alex stood up and walked across the office to gaze out the window. Several seconds passed before he turned to James and Kate. "So in essence what you're telling me is that I'm guilty until proven innocent? And that, if we're lucky, I'll be able to avoid going to jail because I happen to be wealthy?"

Kate was beginning to hate the law with every passing minute. "What do you mean? Alex may have to stay in jail until he proves his innocence? He didn't do anything! Why wouldn't he be able to get bail set? This is the most absurd thing I've ever heard of!" Kate was roaring, pissed as hell, and didn't care who knew it.

"I don't make the laws, Mrs. Rocket, but I do have to follow them. All isn't lost, though. Are you prepared to put up at least five hundred thousand to assure your presence at trial? It might take a million, given the seriousness of the charges of molestation over a long period of time."

"That's not a problem," Alex said. "If you can get the judge to set bail, it will be paid. In cash."

"That's good. Okay. In the meantime, Alex, you're going to have to prepare yourself, just in case, for a few weeks in the Collier County jail. From what I understand, it is the cream of the crop. Air-conditioned, three good meals a day. Books, television. Try to think of this as a restful vacation, should worse come to worst."

Kate flew out of her chair, stood in front of James's desk, and pounded her fist on its surface. "Are you out of your mind? A restful vacation? Do you realize the stigma that

Alex will have to carry around for the rest of his life? This isn't some . . . some traffic ticket! This is my husband's life we're talking about!" Kate reeled backward and collapsed into the chair she'd just vacated. She held her head in her hands. Sobs racked her shoulders. Alex stood behind her, placing his hands on her shoulders.

"She's right, James. I can't stand back and do nothing. Isn't there some way to prove Sara is lying? What about her destroying Kate's studio? Kate still has her sneaker with the glass embedded in the sole. Doesn't that prove she's capable of making this up? Where is the actual proof?"

Behind Kate, Alex remained rigid. The nightmare worsened by the minute. His muscles tensed, he wanted to hit something or someone, anything to relieve the intense anger building in him.

"That's the downside of an accusation of this kind. You have only the victim's word. Unless there is physical evidence, bruising, swelling, bleeding, it's up to the court to decide guilt or innocence. We'll order a psychiatric evaluation. My investigator will check her school records, friends, anything she's been involved in for the past several years. If we need to go back further, we will. Since she's stating this began when she was five or six, there should be some pattern of behavior that proves she's had issues with telling the truth."

"I just remembered something," Kate said. "The first day the girls were here, Emily took me aside. She asked me not to say anything to her parents. I didn't, but now I wish I had. Emily saw Sara terrorizing their neighbor's cat. Said she was dragging it around by its tail. The poor thing was screeching like a baby. Emily thought Sara was out of control. She even mentioned how she told lies. Isn't this something we can use?"

James wanted to reassure the Rockets, but he also wanted to be honest with them. "It could be. We would have to get Emily's testimony on the record. She's underage. That would require her parents' permission. It's something to work with."

"What about having her subpoenaed?" Kate questioned. "Wouldn't she be forced to tell the court what she said to me that day in the kitchen?"

"Courts don't like to subject children to testifying, unless it's a dire emergency."

Alex backed away from the chair. "What the hell would you call this, then? It's a goddamn emergency to me. My life and Kate's are at stake. I don't think there is anything else this could be called but an emergency."

Kate agreed. Had she been too hasty in hiring James Conroy?

"You're right, Alex. I don't mean to imply otherwise. I want you to trust me. If you don't, I can't help you. I want you to tell me everything you remember about those times you and Kate visited the Winter family in Florida. That is, if you want to."

"I don't have much choice, do I?" Alex observed. "God, it's been a long time. Kate, when was the last time we went to Florida?"

"Year before last."

"This might make my job easier. Go home tonight. Both of you sit down with a pencil and paper. Write down the dates of the visits. Be as accurate as possible. Tell how long each stay lasted. Were you ever alone with Sara? Emily? For how long? Anything you think of, I need to know. We've got a long road ahead of us, but I have no doubt we'll get this resolved."

"When will they extradite me to Florida? I have a business to run. There are arrangements to be made. Just in case," Alex said.

"I'd say three or four days at the most. They don't waste time. Get your personal business in order and let me take it from there. Now, I can't do this for free, so there is my fee to discuss."

"Of course, I wouldn't expect you to do this for nothing. Money is not an issue. Whatever you need, I'll write you a check, or cash if you prefer."

"I'll need twenty-five thousand as a retainer. If this doesn't cover my initial expenses, I'll discuss that with you when and if." James stood up, held out his hand. Alex shook his hand, and Kate simply nodded.

"I'll bring a check tomorrow if that's convenient," Alex told James.

He released Alex's hand. "Of course. I'll see you both tomorrow morning, around nine."

"We'll be here," Kate said as she stood from the chair. Her legs felt like Jell-O. A tremor like nothing she'd ever experienced ripped through her like gale-force winds.

The drive back home was torturous. Few words were exchanged. Kate felt the tension but didn't know what to say or do to relieve it. When they reached the house, Alex escaped to the kennel and she to the kitchen.

Three hours later, she'd made a hummingbird cake, two blackberry pies, and three dozen biscuits. She was wrapping the biscuits in plastic when Alex and Gertie joined her. Kate sliced one of the pies, filled the coffeemaker with water, and scooped coffee into the filter. Gertie and Alex sat at the table, both silent as mimes. Kate waited for Alex to speak up, and when he didn't, she did.

"So. What do you think of James so far?" Kate wanted Alex's honest opinion. There was something about him she didn't care for, but if he had the charges against Alex dropped, or at least proved his innocence, that was all that mattered. Kate sliced three pieces of warm pie, placing them on small saucers. The coffeepot gave its final gurgle. She took three mugs from the cupboard, filled them, and set them on the table. Cream and sugar from the fridge, then Kate sat down.

"If he gets this mess cleared up, he'll be my best friend for life," Alex said as he sliced into the pie.

Kate wanted more than that, she needed to know if Alex felt any reservations. This man held a power more awesome than Alex realized. Kate wanted the assurance that Alex was ready to put their future in this stranger's hands.

"Are you sure you're comfortable with him? Can we trust him?" Kate asked.

Gertie spoke up. "If my brother says he's good, then he's good. Reece won't recommend anyone who isn't the best in his or her field. Kate's right, though. You have to trust him. If you feel the slightest doubt, then at least get another attorney's opinion."

"I don't think that'll be necessary, Gert. I trust him. His credentials are impeccable."

Kate had reservations about the young attorney, but maybe it was nothing; maybe she was just being overly paranoid. She would wait and see. If he didn't work out, they could always hire another attorney. If Alex felt comfortable with him, that was all that mattered.

Alex pushed his plate aside, took a sip of coffee, and cleared his throat. "Kate, there's something I want to tell you."

For a split second Kate stopped breathing. "What is it, Alex? Please, don't tell me this is —"

"Dammit, Kate. You don't believe there's any truth to this garbage?"

Her eyes felt like someone had poured buckets of chlorine in them. She'd cried more in the past twenty-four hours than she had in her entire lifetime. She wiped her nose with her knuckles. Her hands shook as she reached for her mug of coffee. "That's preposterous. You just scared me, that's all. What is it you want to tell me?"

"I've been talking to Gertie. She's with

me on this, right, Gert?" Alex asked.

"I am."

This was harder than he expected. The odds were slim that he'd ever need to implement his backup plan, but Alex wasn't a betting man. He preferred a sure thing.

"I've had Gertie's brother Reece draw up the papers to put the house, the land, and the kennel in Gertie's name. I know it's not rational, but if something were to happen to me, you wouldn't have to worry. Financially, at least." There, it was out. Kate observed him as if he'd lost his mind.

"You really think this is necessary? Not that I don't trust you." She reached for Gertie's hand. "It's just . . . it seems so final."

"We don't know what will happen, Kate. If this goes to trial, which I pray it won't, but if it does, I want to know that you're taken care of. Gertie will disburse any money we need for attorney fees, basic living expenses, and, of course, bail if we can get the judge to agree. I can't help but think that Debbie will try to sue the pants off us if she gets the chance. With all of our assets in Gertie's name, no one will be able to touch anything."

"Okay. I can live with these arrangements. Now, about that list James wants, let's get that out of the way." Inside, Kate was slowly falling apart. There she was sitting at the old oak table that had been in her family for years, talking about protecting their home, everything they'd shared, just to ensure that Alex's best friend didn't try to take it all away because of a lie. If she managed to get through this, she really didn't know what they would do. For starters, they'd have to relocate. The damage to Alex's reputation would be irreparable. They'd have to start fresh in another state. Maybe even another country. This was like a soap opera, only the drama was very real.

Kate took a pad from the kitchen drawer and placed it in front of Alex. "Let's get this over with."

"I'll go check on the dogs. Bella is getting pretty jumpy with her babies," Gertie said.

"Thanks, Gertie. I don't know what we'd do without you." Kate gave the older woman a tight hug. Alex nodded at Gertie.

"You're gonna be just fine, Alex. Just fine," Gertie called over her shoulder.

Kate closed the door and leaned against the frame. "She's right, you know. A few weeks, and this will all be behind us. We can move on."

Alex's blue eyes filled with anguish. "I don't know if we'll ever move on and put this behind us, Kate. We're just getting started, and already I feel like I've lost. I know that's being negative, but there doesn't seem to be much we can do. Pray that if this goes to trial, a jury will see Sara for the little manipulator that she is."

"I've said more prayers the past three days than I've said in my life, Alex. We'll get through this." *We have to,* Kate thought, *because life won't be worth anything without Alex.*

"I hope you're right. Let's take this pad and pencil to bed. I'll bring up a bottle of wine. We'll be more relaxed. What do you say?" Alex was trying so hard to lighten the mood. They'd been so down since Sara's accusation.

Wine was the last thing Kate needed, but if it helped Alex take the edge off, then she'd drink an entire vineyard's worth.

"I'll just be a minute." Kate took the cups and saucers off the table. She rinsed them with scalding-hot water until her hands were beet red. Then she put them in the dishwasher and wiped the tabletop and counters. She refilled the creamer and sugar bowls. She swept the floor, then took a damp mop and began scrubbing the already clean tiles. An hour later she was exhausted. All she wanted to do was lie down. She didn't want to remember all their visits with the Winters, didn't want to imagine what Sara had told her parents about Alex. Poor, innocent Alex. He wouldn't hurt a flea. He couldn't even smash a spider. He'd scoop it onto a paper, or whatever happened to be handy, then release it outside. Kate had yet to meet the man who could compare to Alex. Knowing she couldn't stall any longer, she turned off the kitchen lights. Upstairs, Alex was sound asleep, the paper and pencil tossed aside. Knowing this might be the last restful night Alex would have for a while, she curled up next to him.

She was so very tired. Mentally, she'd never been this tired. Kate let her mind wander as she drifted off.

Alex looked like he was a hundred years old. His skin, once a warm brown from the sun, was pale and wrinkled like parchment paper. There was no color to his eyes, the pigment gone. His hair had turned completely white.

"I told you we'd get through this, Alex. Why'd you have to go and get yourself locked up? We were winning, you didn't have to accept the plea!"

Tears filled Kate's eyes as she watched her husband through the thick Plexiglas. He'd taken the deal, telling her it was only ten years. Only ten years . . .

Kate shot up in the bed like a missile. Sweat beaded her forehead and upper lip. She still wore her jeans and T-shirt. Her heartbeat quadrupled. She looked over at Alex. He still slept. She wouldn't wake him up. She couldn't tell him about her dream. As a child, she and her friends had always said, "If you tell a dream before breakfast, it'll come true."

Morning was hours away. Kate would not speak of her dream to anyone.

She prayed this wasn't an omen of things to come.

CHAPTER 9

"I know you're lying. You are one sick little girl. I don't believe you for one minute, you rotten piece of dog poop. Uncle Alex wouldn't ever do something so . . . so nasty. Especially to a fat pig like you!"

Emily knew she was being hateful to Sara, but at that minute, she just didn't care. Somehow, she had to help Uncle Alex out of this mess. At fifteen, she didn't know what she could do, but she was sure to come up with something.

"You don't know what it's like, so just shut up. I've been abused. Don't talk to me that way again, or I'll tell Mommy." Sara was delighted with her new role as victim and was going to milk it for all it was worth. She'd told Emily it was terrible, the icky things Uncle Alex did to her, and why *shouldn't* she get some extra sympathy? Her life was tainted forever. Words she'd overheard their parents use.

"You're such a liar, Sara. Do you think for one minute anyone is going to believe you? Oh, I know Mom and Dad do, but they'll soon realize that you're just doing this to get attention. This isn't the way to get it, surely you ought to know that by now. But then again, you are just a baby. Twelve years old. Puh-leeze! And go ahead and tell on me. I don't think anything I do could be as rotten as what you're doing. I'm ashamed to call you my sister!" Emily slammed out of Sara's room and headed to her own just down the hall.

She was still in shock over Sara's accusations. And her parents had actually believed the little liar! They'd talked to the sheriff, and who knew who else they'd told. And Emily knew as well as she knew her name that Sara was making up every detail she'd shared with their parents.

Sara had an appointment with Dr. Chambers tomorrow morning. Dr. Chambers was Emily's best friend's mom, who just happened to be a child shrink. Maybe she would ask Amy to snoop into her mother's files and see what Sara was really up to. Sara should've been sent to Dr. Chambers a long time ago.

She wanted to call Aunt Kate, but her parents had forbidden that. However, they couldn't watch her all the time. She jumped off the bed and went to the piggy bank she had stashed in her bottom drawer. She dumped its contents on top of the bed. Nine dollars and seventy-three cents. That should be enough to make a long-distance call. Without a second thought, Emily hurried to the kitchen. It'd been a while since she'd ridden her bike. That might make her parents suspicious, but she'd deal with that if they caught her.

She went to the garage through the side door off the kitchen. Her red Schwinn lay against the wall farthest from the door. *Good,* she thought. She pushed the button on the wall to open the electric garage door. It wasn't real noisy. If her parents were still lounging by the pool, they'd never hear a thing.

Hurrying, Emily jumped on her bike. Pedaling as fast as she could, she veered around the huge potted plants at the end of the driveway. Once she was out of sight of her house, she slowed down. There was a Circle K convenience store a mile or two down the road. She would make a quick phone call, then be on her way. More than likely, she'd be back in her room before her parents even realized she was gone.

Twenty minutes later, she cruised through

the store's parking lot over to the pay phone at the side of the building. She read the instructions at the base of the phone just to make sure she didn't screw up and lose her money. An automated voice came on the line instructing her to put $2.25 into the change slots. She did, then a few seconds later, Aunt Kate's phone was ringing.

"Hello."

"Aunt Kate, it's me." Emily's hands were shaking. For a second she felt like she was betraying her family, but the feeling left as fast as it came. She was saving a man's life.

"Emily? Why are you calling here?"

"I'm so sorry, Aunt Kate. I know what Sara did." Embarrassed, Emily's eyes filled with tears. She looked over her shoulder to make sure no one saw her bawling. She'd die if someone she knew saw her.

"It's not your fault. We know that, sweetie."

"I just want to help. They've got an appointment for Sara tomorrow. It's Dr. Chambers. She's a psychiatrist. Mom said she would go to court and testify on Sara's behalf. I don't know what to do, Aunt Kate. This is all so terrible." Emily let her tears flow freely, suddenly not caring who saw her.

"This isn't something for you to worry

about. Uncle Alex and I will be just fine. We'll get through this."

"And I'll never get to see you all again!" Emily's sobs were loud. Her nose was running. She used the hem of her shirt to wipe it with.

"We don't know that, Em. We just have to be patient, see how this works out."

Emily nodded, then remembered she was on the phone. "I know. I just hate the thought of what this is doing to you guys. I think Sara is a mean, lying, conniving little asshole, in case you want to know."

Kate's laughter sounded forced. "Thanks, kiddo. It really means a lot that you believe in Alex. I'll tell him you called."

The automated voice came over the line telling Emily to either deposit another $1.25 for the next minute or the call would end.

"Bye, Aunt Kate. I love you!" The line went dead, but Emily was sure Kate heard her. Feeling a little better, she hopped back on her bike, pedaling toward home.

She was able to slip inside without detection. Back in her room, Emily formulated a plan. She called Amy.

"Do you think your mom'll be suspicious?" Emily asked her best friend.

"No. She's too busy to notice. Besides, she'll think she's being a better parent if I take an interest in her work," Amy explained. Her voice held a tinge of excitement. Emily knew she could count on her.

"Her appointment is tomorrow. How long does it usually take your mom to dictate her notes?"

"She does it at the end of the day. Her secretary usually takes a day or so. Don't worry, Em, I know the routine. I'll do whatever I can. I always knew Sara was a little bitch, but I just never thought she'd do something like this. Of course, it could be true. Did you think of that?"

"Amy! I know my uncle, and I know Sara. There's a reason she's doing this. Who knows what it is, but she's too stupid to realize the ramifications of her actions."

"Hell, Em, you sound just like my mom," Amy said.

"Sorry, Amy. This is just really important to me. Uncle Alex and Aunt Kate are like a second set of parents, only better. If Sara succeeds, I'll never see them again."

"I'll get back to you as soon as I have something to report."

Emily smiled. "I knew you'd come through."

"Hey, what are best friends for?" Amy said good-bye.

Having done all that she could for the moment, Emily removed her diary from beneath the mattress. Each day she wrote about Sara and her false accusations against Uncle Alex. Someday, her words might make a difference.

Don and Debbie spent the better part of the afternoon lounging by their pool. After a second pitcher of margaritas, both dozed in the late-afternoon sun.

"Mommy!" Sara shrieked.

Debbie fumbled with the straps on her bikini top, tying them in a loose knot. "What is it now? Can't you see your father and I are trying to relax? This is a very stressful time for us."

Sara plopped down on the edge of her mother's lounge chair. "Mommy, I was just feeling . . . feeling so unclean. I don't think I'll ever feel clean again. Emily makes me feel so dirty, too. She called me a liar today. She said she was ashamed to be my sister."

Debbie inhaled, her nostrils flaring.

"You look like a cow when your nose does that," Sara said.

Debbie placed a hand on her nose. "What am I doing?"

"Your nostrils are the size of a cow's."

"Sara, you're so rude! You should be ashamed," Debbie retorted. "Now, what would you like for dinner? I was thinking about ordering in. We can have pizza from Domino's, or I can call that little Italian restaurant you like so much and have something cheesy and meaty delivered. It's your choice, sweetie."

Her mom sure knew the way to her heart, but this time food wasn't what she was looking for. Sara really needed to talk about Uncle Alex.

"I don't care. Whatever."

"Sara, are you all right?" Debbie questioned.

"No. I told you Emily called me a liar. I hate her. I wish she would leave here. She thinks I'm making up this story about Uncle Alex." Sara's lower lip puckered. "I am not making it up, Mommy. You and Daddy believe me, don't you?"

By that time Don was awake, listening to their conversation.

He patted a spot next to him. "Come here, sweetie."

Sara sat next to her father. "You believe me, don't you Daddy? I feel so bad, but it just was so terrible. He made me look at his . . . his thing. It was so ugly. It wasn't like yours, Daddy." Sara acted coy, almost as if she were flirting with her father.

"Sara Marie Winter! What are you saying?" Debbie zoomed upright in her chair, her eyes focused on Don and their daughter. "Please tell me that I misunderstood you."

Sara opened her eyes wide as though she had no idea what her mother referred to. "I said that Uncle Alex's thing wasn't —"

"I heard you!" Debbie shouted.

"Don, do you want to explain how our twelve-year-old daughter has knowledge of . . . of, you know what I mean?"

"Calm down, Deb," Don said.

"Sara, you're making things sound very vulgar. Now tell your mother exactly what you're talking about."

Sara opened her eyes even wider. "I saw Daddy in the shower one time. His . . . his thing wasn't like Uncle Alex's, that's all. Is that bad, Mommy?"

Debbie shot Don killer looks.

"No, it's not, Sara, but your father should lock the door when he's in the shower."

"Why, Mommy?" Sara asked.

"Because he's a grown man, that's why. A grown man with two teen daughters living under the same roof."

"I'm just twelve, Mommy. I won't be a teenager for a long time."

"Sara, you'll be thirteen in two months. You're closer to thirteen than twelve," Debbie said to her daughter.

Sara began to howl like a coyote caught in a bear trap.

"Stop this nonsense, Sara! You're driving me insane. I can't take much more of it!" Debbie shouted. She was sure Sara's wails could be heard all over the neighborhood.

Sara gulped and hiccuped a few more times before ending her crying jag. "I just feel so nasty, that's all. And I don't want to go to that stupid Dr. Chambers either. I hate her!" She sniffled a few more times.

Debbie's heart softened. Of course Sara was frightened. "Then you don't have to. Why didn't you tell us you were afraid to go? We'll find another doctor, don't you worry. Now, what would you like for dinner?"

Don shook his head. "I don't think food is the answer to Sara's problem. Sara" — Don forced her to look at him — "why are you afraid of Dr. Chambers? Is there more we need to know?"

Sara nodded. "I think she tells her business to Amy. I know she does 'cause I heard Amy say that to Emily. I just don't want this awful stuff to spread around, that's all."

Looking over the top of Sara's head, Debbie raised her eyebrows. "I'll turn her in to the American Medical Association. I never cared for her anyway. And I don't want Emily hanging around with her daughter either. Don, you make sure and explain this to her. Go do it now, before you forget."

Don gave a limp salute. "Sure, anything you say. You say jump, I ask how high."

"Stop being an idiot and just do what I asked. Our daughter's emotional well-being is at stake here, or have you forgotten?"

"I remember, dear. How could I not?" Don went inside in search of Sara's older sister.

Sara reclined in her father's chair. "Now, I need to know why I feel so unclean. That's all, Mommy. I just don't understand!"

Her daughter's wailing resumed. Debbie wished she were back on the cruise ship. No kids. No problems. Just smooth sailing.

CHAPTER 10

The plain white van parked in the driveway. Two sheriff's deputies wearing dark gray uniforms got out and knocked at the front door. Kate had seen them, knew why they were there, but wanted to delay the inevitable as long as humanly possible. Her time together with her husband was about to end, at least temporarily.

Alex waited at the foot of the stairs. He had no luggage, no carry-on bag, no book tucked beneath his arm for this particular trip. He wouldn't need any clothes where he was going either, Kate thought. An orange jumpsuit would be provided for him. This was the saddest day of her life, maybe even worse than when she learned of her parents' death. Losing one's parents was a natural event, something one expected to occur at some point, however tragic the circumstances. Losing one's husband to a false accusation was something totally different, entirely unexpected.

She wanted to be upbeat for Alex's sake. Gertie had stayed with the dogs after Alex left the kennel that morning. He'd said his good-byes to Bella and the others. Kate's heart broke a bit more each time she looked into his eyes. They were so very sorrowful; the spark that once lit them up like jewels was dimmed by sadness.

The time was up. Alex had taken care of the business end of things. Kate knew it was up to her to take care of matters of the heart.

She forced a smile. "Look at this as a break from me and my forcing you to eat all those test meals. I'll see that everything is taken care of, Alex. I promise." Tears filled her eyes. "This won't be forever." She wrapped her arms around his waist and held on for dear life. She never thought she'd lose Alex this way, not in a million years.

The doorbell rang once, then a second time.

Alex removed Kate's arms from his waist. His eyes were shiny with tears, but he wouldn't release them. He had to be strong for Kate. He touched the tip of her nose. "You look like you've got a cold." He smiled at her. She was his life, his everything. Words could never convey his love for her. He touched her again, this time running his knuckles across her cheek. "This won't be forever, Kate. I promise that no matter what happens, I'll come home. We'll be here together again, maybe not like before, but I will be back. I love you, Kate."

She nodded, then went to the door where the two men on the other side would take Alex away from her for a while. They'd had their private moments and it was time to face the music.

"I love you, too, Alex Rocket. Always and forever." She gave him one last smile, then opened the door.

"Alex John Rocket?" the taller of the two deputies asked. He held a sheaf of papers out to Kate. Alex stood by her side. The other deputy removed handcuffs from his belt.

"That would be me." Alex pushed the screen door aside and held both arms out in front of him as the second deputy placed the handcuffs around both wrists. Kate took the papers and stuffed them into her back pocket.

Tears gushed, and she didn't care who saw them. "Oh, Alex!" She ran out the door and grabbed him. She embraced him one last time before the deputies took him to Florida, where he would have to remain until, if things worked out, bail was arranged. "I'll see you day after tomorrow."

Alex simply nodded and walked toward the van, a deputy on either side of him.

Kate watched the van until its taillights disappeared. Once she was back inside the house alone, she sobbed until her eyes were swollen shut. She took Alex's best bottle of Royal Canadian and poured herself a tall glass. She gulped it down, then followed it with another. Her throat burned from the whiskey, but she continued to drink until the bottle was empty.

In a drunken stupor, Kate went upstairs to the master bedroom and fell onto the bed she had shared with her husband. She hugged Alex's pillow, inhaling traces of Old Spice and a scent that was uniquely Alex's. When she awoke, the sun was setting.

She reached for the clock on her side of the bed. "Damn!" She'd lost an entire day. Pulling herself into a sitting position, Kate tucked both knees close to her chest, wrapped her arms around them, and sobbed more. She'd cried so much after Alex left, she was sure she had no tears left. She was wrong. Kate blew her nose on her T-shirt.

At that precise moment Kate wanted nothing more than to get her hands around Sara Marie Winter's fat neck. She wanted to squeeze until the truth spewed forth from her lying lips. Why had she done this? What in the name of God had Alex ever done to the child? Kate tried to think of all the times they'd been with the Winter family in the past thirteen years. She couldn't recall a single time that Alex had been alone for any length of time with Sara, or with Emily, for that matter. They'd gone over this a million times as they were writing the dates out for James. Both agreed that the child had serious mental issues because there was nothing that either of them could recall that remotely hinted at anything even close to inappropriate touching.

If Alex's situation hadn't been so desperate, Kate would've laughed. Who would have thought Alex capable of such a vile act? Kate wondered if Don truly believed Alex had committed an act so unnatural that it was sickening to contemplate. If so, then he'd never really known Alex, even though they'd been friends for most of their life.

Kate ended her pity-party then and there. It would do Alex no good at all. From that moment forward, everything she did would be for Alex. Somehow, she would help Alex escape from this nightmare. She wasn't sure what she could do, but she was always big on gut instinct. When hers kicked in, and said, "Do this or that for Alex," then she would know.

With their future at stake, Kate knew crying and theorizing wouldn't get her any closer to learning the truth about Sara and why she'd accused Alex of such a sordid act. She would leave first thing in the morning for Naples, Florida. Gertie had arranged for her to stay in the house of a friend who was in Rhode Island for the summer. If Alex remained in jail when it was time for her to give up the house, then Kate would rent an apartment. Gertie would remain in Asheville so that Alex's business continued. He'd been worried about leaving the dogs, but he knew they were in good hands with Gertie. Kate trusted her more than anyone else, excluding Alex. Gertie was as good as family.

After a long, cool shower and a couple of aspirins, Kate felt much better. She'd been foolish to drown her sorrows in a bottle, but somehow it'd seemed the thing to do at the time.

Hoping the weather for tomorrow was decent, she flipped on the television in the bedroom in hopes of catching an up-to-date weather report. She'd chartered a private plane to fly her to Naples and knew if the weather was remotely iffy, her flight would be canceled. She turned the volume up as the anchor's animated face filled the screen to make sure she could hear accurately. As the anchor was about to switch over to the weather report, her smiling face became serious. "This just in. Alex Rocket, longtime resident of Asheville, North Carolina, has been extradited to Naples, Florida, to face alleged child molestation charges . . ."

Kate pushed the Off button on the remote and tossed it across the room. "Damn those bastards! How did they find out?" she shouted, knowing there would be no answer. Those newshounds made her sick! Did they realize what they were doing when they reported stories like this? It ruined lives! If this was known locally, Kate couldn't imagine what the media in Naples would be like. Something told her Debbie had a hand in this. It would be just like her to try and gain publicity for Don's firm from this tragedy. The woman had no scruples whatsoever.

Sleep was the last thing on her mind. Kate checked her to-do list one last time before settling in Alex's recliner with the Stephen King novel he'd been reading only a few nights ago. It brought her a little closer to Alex, knowing his eyes had focused on the same words she was reading. When her eyes grew heavy, she laid the book aside and dozed. She was due at the airport at six in the morning. She hadn't bothered setting the alarm. She knew sleep would be fitful at best.

At four, she made a pot of tea, took another hot shower, and waited for the taxi to arrive. She hadn't wanted Gertie to drive her to the airport. She needed to be with the dogs. At five-thirty a horn blared. Kate's taxi had arrived. She was dressed and ready. With one last look over her shoulder, she left the only home she'd known for most of her life.

She gave the taxi driver her luggage and got in the backseat for the ride to the airport. There was no traffic at that early hour, so she arrived at the airport with time to spare. Because she was flying in a private plane, she went to the general aviation area to wait for her pilot and his crew. She and Alex had hired this crew before, so Kate felt comfortable and safe. The weather report was perfect. If only she were flying somewhere exotic with Alex at her side. Then she might actually enjoy the flight. But there would be no pleasure in this trip.

"Mrs. Rocket?"

The pilot and his copilot.

"Yes? Oh, good morning, Joe." She couldn't recall the copilot's name.

"Trent Walker, ma'am." The young copilot shook her hand.

"Trent, call me Kate."

"We've got to preflight the plane. If you want to go ahead and board, it's fine. Candy Lee is getting coffee and muffins for the trip. She'll be here any minute," Joe explained to her.

"Sure, that's great." Kate wondered if they'd heard last night's news. She hoped they hadn't, but if they had, it was already too late. The damage to Alex's reputation was complete. Anything she said or did at this point wouldn't make a difference. She went out to the tarmac and climbed up the small pull-down steps, entering the plane. She sat in a plush seat with plenty of leg room. A headset lay on the seat next to hers. She knew this was rude, but she didn't want to talk. She grabbed the headset, placed it over her ears, and adjusted the music to something light and soothing. She waited for the preflight inspection to end, at which time she'd have to sit up for takeoff.

Chapter 11

Kate woke up surprised to find she'd actually fallen asleep after takeoff and that the flight had passed so quickly. She removed her headset and prepared for the onslaught ahead. She prayed the local media hadn't gotten wind of her arrival. The last thing she wanted was to face a mob of reporters.

Gertie had called ahead and arranged for a rental car with maps and the keys for the house so Kate could go there first thing. She needed to unwind. James would be arriving that afternoon to go over their strategy. Kate needed to be sharp and alert for the ordeal she and Alex would have to endure for the next few days, maybe even weeks. She prayed it would soon be over. She wanted their life back. Oh, she knew it could never be as it was before, but maybe now it could be even better. A tinge of doubt clouded her thinking. In order to escape her negative visions of the future,

Kate grabbed her carry-on and prepared to vacate the small jet. She'd traveled to Naples many times, but never in a million years did she think she'd be visiting Alex in jail. Sara's accusation still shocked her. This nightmare had to end, and soon. Kate prayed for swift decisions with happy endings.

As she walked down the small set of steps to the tarmac, Kate actually felt faint for a second. The humidity was overwhelming, like a wet wool blanket enshrouding her. She took a deep, if somewhat shaky, breath. She hated Florida summers, but the winter was truly perfect. Knowing this, she and Alex had always timed their visits to coincide with good weather. It'd been a long, long time since she faced this kind of heat. If the weather was an omen of things to come, then Kate figured Alex was in big trouble. Again, she tried to curb her negative thinking. It wouldn't do her or Alex one bit of good. *Positive thinking, Kate.*

Determined to get through this ordeal, Kate forced a smile when Joe brought her luggage to the rental car waiting alongside the jet. "Thanks, Joe. I can't tell you how much I appreciate this. I don't know when I'll be leaving."

Joe nodded. "Just call when you're ready.

We'll be here within a couple of hours." He paused for a minute before finishing, "If there is *anything* I can do for you and Alex, just say the word." He looked her straight in the face, his eyes never wavering. Kate was sure he knew why she'd come to Florida in such a hurry. His diplomacy in the matter was more than appreciated.

"I'll do that, Joe. And thanks. Alex will appreciate this." She shook his hand, then took the keys he held out for her.

"The car is full of gas, and it's ready to go," Joe said.

Kate nodded her thanks while he placed her luggage in the trunk of the sleek gray Mercedes. A compact car would've been fine, but dear Gertie, she always selected the best for Kate, no matter what.

Kate gave Joe a quick hug. "I truly thank you. I'll stay in touch."

With a slight nod, he returned to the aircraft.

Kate wondered who else would need his services today. She hoped to return to Asheville within the week, but James had told her they would take this one day at a time. She promised Alex she wouldn't get too upset, but it was a hard promise to keep. Her negative thoughts kept bombarding her with "what-if" scenarios.

Kate adjusted the car's air-conditioning as high as it would go. The back of her neck was damp with sweat. She couldn't wait to take off the black slacks and cream-colored silk blouse. Dressing so formally for the trip was unlike her. Maybe subconsciously she thought looking her best would have an effect on the outcome of what lay ahead. If only it were that simple.

She took the map from the passenger's seat, spreading it across the steering wheel. She was familiar with Naples, but not the area in which Gertie's friends lived, now her new home, however temporary. Naples Municipal Airport was located on Aviation Drive, according to Kate's map. Tracing the directions with her finger, she viewed the route to Highway 41. From there she would travel farther south to Hibiscus Lane, where the Thermans' house was located. She glanced at her watch before putting the car in drive. Not yet noon. She had plenty of time before James's arrival.

As she turned south onto Highway 41, or Tamiami Trail, as it was called by the locals, Kate's heart did a flip-flop. There on the northeast corner of 41 and Airport Pulling Road sat the Collier County Courthouse. That was where Alex's future would be decided. Slowing down to get a good look,

Kate determined there was nothing even slightly threatening in the building's appearance. Several stories high, white concrete stucco, dozens of palm trees, hibiscus plants decorating the lawn. Men wearing dark suits and ties walked in and out of the revolving doors. She couldn't imagine dressing like that in the heat. She shook her head and accelerated.

The usual McDonald's, Wendy's, and Burger King flanked Highway 41. Nothing new. Nothing they didn't have in Asheville. She saw a Wal-Mart sign and decided she'd best stop for a few groceries. She still had to eat, even though she'd lost her appetite days ago. She had to keep in shape for Alex. Kate's decisions on the outside could very well affect Alex on the inside. It wouldn't do for her to get sick.

She pulled into the large parking lot. It appeared as though half of Collier County had decided to make a stop at Wal-Mart. Kate found a parking place without too much aggravation. She made a mental list of what she would need.

Inside the large chain store, Kate grabbed a bag of apples, Earl Grey tea bags, Sweet'N Low, a loaf of whole wheat bread, strawberry jam, and peanut butter. That was enough. If she needed anything else, she'd go to the supermarket. She waited in line longer than she should have and paid for her purchases. Again, the heat battered her as she walked to the Mercedes. Warm and moist, Kate wondered how in the world people stood this year-round. She supposed it was like anything else; you simply got used to it or learned to live with it. If only that were her main concern.

Kate's silk blouse clung to her clammy skin. She cranked the AC up again, shifted into reverse, and maneuvered through the lot until she was at the traffic light leading her back to Highway 41. She ran a hand through her damp hair. The humidity had really done a number on it. Not that she cared. Her curls sprang up like fast-growing weeds. She smiled. Alex liked her curls and could never understand why she hated them.

Kate took the map, which was now lying on the seat. Another block and she'd be at the intersection where she would make her final turn onto Hibiscus Lane. The street sign came into view. Kate slowed down, looked in her rearview mirror. Nothing behind her. She turned onto the street. Any other time this would've been a pleasure. The homes on the street were blocked by high stucco walls and too much shrubbery.

Gertie told her this was a very private area, but until now, she hadn't really understood. This was more than suitable considering the circumstances. The last thing she wanted to deal with was nosy neighbors. She wanted to do what needed to be done to take Alex home. Nothing more. She didn't need to make friends, and she sure as hell didn't need anyone to befriend her.

Kate saw the house number on the dolphin-shaped mailbox. She smirked and pulled into the circular drive. With two blue Wal-Mart bags and her carry-on in one hand, she wrestled with the set of keys. She crossed the beautifully manicured lawn to the enclosed front porch. Opening the door, she saw several editions of the *Naples Daily News* in a pile at her feet. She nudged them aside and slipped the key into the lock of the front door to the house. A gush of cool air greeted her. She sighed. The feeling was wonderful.

Kate deposited her bags on a small table in the foyer. She inspected the great room as she entered. Cathedral ceilings, hardwood floors, and snazzy red sofas bordered the large room. A double-sided fireplace positioned in the center of the room caused Kate to do a double take. Why in the world would one need a fireplace in Florida? She walked farther into the room. Three sets of French doors led to a large swimming pool and Jacuzzi. Several Adirondack loungers were scattered haphazardly around the pool's edge. Potted plants peppered the deck. A table that could seat at least ten faced the canal. A Jenn-Air grill, larger than her stove at home, was situated between a small built-in counter and an oven ensconced in a brick wall. Baking. Outside. In the Florida heat. *Who'd've thunk it?* A sink, fridge, and teak cabinets completed the outside kitchen. Two silver Jet Skis hung in midair above the dock. Under different circumstances, she would've been thrilled with her accommodations. Now it only reminded her that she wasn't living her life as she wanted. She and Alex both were at the mercy of the court and its future rulings.

Ignoring her lavish surroundings, Kate took her bags from the table. A nice double side-by-side fridge, a gas oven, not unlike the ones at Chloe's, and cabinets galore encircled the great room. A small island with a red ceramic sink was centered in the kitchen area. Again, Kate was sorry she was in such a crappy position. She would've loved to cut loose in this kitchen. And she might, she told herself as she put the groceries away. Maybe she would prepare a celebratory dinner for her and Alex when he was released. Yes, that's exactly what she would do.

With thoughts of planning a gourmet meal upon Alex's arrival, Kate found the guest bedroom. It was decorated in a palm tree motif. Not her cup of tea, but it worked there. Celery green walls, a beige comforter with palm fronds looked too inviting. She removed her sticky clothes. Just a few minutes. That was all she needed. She closed the plantation shutters and pulled the switch to turn on the paddle fan. She lay on the bed, her thoughts a whirlwind. Before she realized it, she fell asleep. A loud knock at the front door awakened her.

She jumped up from the bed, off guard in her new environment. She still wore her bra and panties.

Damn. She only meant to rest her eyes for a few minutes. She looked at her watch. She'd slept for over two hours.

The knocking continued.

"Coming," she shouted. It had to be James. She grabbed the much-hated black slacks and blouse, slipped the latter over her head, and raced to the foyer as she stumbled into her pants. A glance in the mirror above the small table said she looked like hell, but she didn't care. At that point all she wanted to do was put this nightmare behind her and get on with her life.

Chapter 12

The court bailiff, a male deputy sheriff wearing the standard gray-and-black uniform issued to the Collier County Sheriff's Department, called, "All rise," in the oak-paneled courtroom. His words echoed in the small space. He was not much taller than she, Kate observed, as he turned to the door that opened behind the judge's bench. Kate, along with the rest of the people in the courtroom, rose.

Tall and thin, with brown beady eyes behind what Kate always referred to as granny glasses, the female judge presiding over the morning's arraignment hearing fanned her black robe around her shoulders like a proud peacock. Her short gray hair had been cut into a distinct blunt bob. *Severe* came to mind. Judge Jean Stowers. Upon hearing the name, Kate thought the judge was male, not that it mattered. James assured her that Judge Stowers was as good as any other judge in the Twentieth Judicial Circuit in Collier County. The second she laid eyes on her, there was something about the judge. Kate couldn't put her finger on it, she'd never met the woman, only knew as much about her as she'd learned from James in their meeting the previous afternoon. Still, she was on edge. Though she'd always relied on gut instinct in the past, Kate hoped for once that her instinct was wrong.

Not more than twenty people were seated in Judge Stowers's courtroom. *Crime must be taking a vacation,* Kate thought as she scrutinized the group. Or was it possible there wasn't a lot of crime in the moneyed town? Probably the latter. James had told her what to expect, but nothing prepared her for the actual vision as Alex, along with three other scruffy-looking men, entered the courtroom through a side door.

Shaking hands covered her mouth to keep her gasp from being heard. James touched her arm and nodded. Only forty-eight hours since she'd last seen Alex, and he'd aged ten years. Kate's eyes filled with tears. Alex, her wonderful, decent, honest Alex. Jailed with a bunch of God knows what kind of criminals, all because of a lie. Her heartbeat increased, sweat beaded her upper lip. This wasn't good.

Dressed in a bright orange jumpsuit with black flip-flops on his feet, his appearance was a shock to Kate. Alex's hands were in handcuffs, and the handcuffs were attached to a heavy chain. The chain was attached to shackles on both feet. Each man was attached to the other. If one decided to run, then they'd all go for the fall. Kate had no idea Alex would be treated in such a . . . criminal manner. He'd come willingly. James said that would be favored by the courts. It sure as hell wasn't doing him any good just then.

Alex, along with the three other inmates, stood in an area reserved exclusively for prisoners. They were seated in what Kate thought of as a pen. Like penned-up animals. She took a deep breath and exhaled. This was worse than she'd imagined. She watched as Alex turned to look over his shoulder. First, to the left, then to the right. Then he saw her and James seated at the defense table.

He smiled.

Kate's heart did a thousand somersaults. She smiled back. Tears streamed down her face. She mouthed, "I love you."

Alex nodded.

Since Alex's name began with an "R," his

case was the last to be heard. James had explained all this to her, but seeing how the system worked was a lot different than someone talking about it. It seemed low-down, almost cheap to Kate, like the men in orange were nobody. Most likely they had families, people who loved and needed them. At least Alex did. Kate listened to the judge as she made her decisions. Though this was only an arraignment hearing, it was significant in the sense that those charged were allowed to stand before the court and state their pleas.

James stood when Alex's name was called.

"Alex John Rocket, you have been charged with six counts of felony sexual assault against a minor child. How do you plead?" Judge Stowers asked. Alex, still grouped with the other inmates, remained silent as James had instructed.

"Your Honor, my client pleads not guilty."

The judge made a notation on a paper handed to her by the bailiff. She passed the paper to her secretary, who was seated next to and below the bench on her right. The secretary, a young girl of no more than twenty, smiled at the judge.

"Is this your plea, Mr. Rocket?" Judge Stowers questioned.

Unprepared for questions coming from

the judge, Alex looked to James for guidance.

"Yes, it is, Your Honor. I plead not guilty."

"All right."

James continued to stand before the bench. "In order to save time in Your Honor's courtroom, I would like to acknowledge that there has not been a bail hearing scheduled. If it please the court, I would like to do so at this time."

Alex looked over his shoulder. Kate's eyes continued to fill with tears; still, she managed a smile.

Judge Stowers spoke to the assistant district attorney. "Mr. Wykowski, is the state prepared to hear bail statements?"

The assistant district attorney, Lyle Wykowski, shuffled through several file folders inside a plastic bin. "We are, Your Honor." He continued to look through the bin while raking a hand through his thick, oily black hair. Coke bottle–thick glasses made his gray eyes appear three times as large. His suit, a black Sears off-the-rack, had been sent to the cleaners so many times it resembled imitation silk. His white dress shirt had yellowed with age. A rust-colored clip-on tie completed his outfit. He kept scratching his nose as he read through the papers he found. It appeared as though he wasn't prepared at all.

Kate watched all this. She thought him sloppy and unorganized. This could be advantageous to Alex's case. She breathed an audible sigh of relief.

"You may proceed, Mr. Conroy."

James walked back to the defense table. He took a manila file folder and removed several sheets of paper. He thumbed through them until he found what he was searching for. "Thank you, Your Honor," James said.

"If it please the court, I would ask that Mr. Rocket be released on his own recognizance."

"You do realize the seriousness of the charges against your client, Mr. Conroy?" Judge Stowers asked from her perch at the bench.

"Yes, Your Honor, I am quite aware of the charges against my client, and I assure you, he is as well. However, I would ask the court to consider Mr. Rocket's past history."

"Does the state have any objection?" Judge Stowers asked Wykowski.

The ADA fumbled with the pencil stuck between his head and ear. "Uh, oh . . . yes, I mean, no. The defense can say whatever they want."

The judge rolled her eyes, then turned to

the defense attorney. "You may proceed."

"Mr. Rocket has no criminal history, not even so much as a traffic violation. He is in no way a danger to the community, Your Honor. He understands that he must follow the guidelines Your Honor may set, if you choose to honor our request at this time. He and his wife have arranged to remain in Collier County until these proceedings are resolved."

Kate held her breath for what seemed like minutes before releasing it. She wanted Alex home, no matter where home was at the moment.

"Mr. Wykowski, I do not care to do the state's job. Do you have anything to add to Mr. Conroy's request?" Judge Stowers shot the ADA the evil eye.

"The state sees no reason to hold Mr. Rocket at this time. However, I would ask that the court issue certain conditions upon Mr. Rocket's release." Lyle Wykowski managed to speak his first complete sentence without blundering his words.

"You have specific conditions, Mr. Wykowski?"

Kate watched the debate between the judge and the ADA. He proved himself more inept with every word that spewed from his mouth. Kate was confident the charges against Alex would be seen for exactly what they were; nothing more than a child trying to gain attention. She caught Alex's eye and granted him another smile, only this time it was for real.

"Given the nature of the charges, the state requests Mr. Rocket wear a monitor."

"Your Honor, this is extremely unreasonable!" James shot up from the defense table. "The embarrassment it will cause to Mr. Rocket is unnecessary."

Judge Stowers pinned James Conroy to the floor with her glare. "Mr. Conroy, it is not the court's wish to cause or bring any form of embarrassment to your client. Your client should have thought . . ." The judge hastily grabbed the papers from her secretary before she finished. "I am going to grant the state's request. In light of the charges, the state is being extremely generous to your client."

"Thank you, Your Honor." James knew when to keep his mouth shut. He hated that Alex would have to endure the indignity of wearing an ankle bracelet, but the judge was right. She could have denied him bail entirely or asked for a very large cash bond.

"Your Honor, I would also like to request Mr. Rocket be placed under house arrest," Wykowski added, as though this additional punishment had just occurred to him.

"I've made my ruling, Mr. Wykowski. The court will let it stand."

"Yes, okay. Your Honor." The ADA shuffled through more unorganized papers in his plastic bin.

Kate was truly amazed the state hired such low-caliber attorneys. In this case, she was more than happy. Most likely their slackness in screening ADAs would benefit Alex.

"Since the Rockets are here in Collier County until this matter is resolved, I'm going to set the date for the grand jury hearing one week from today. Does the state or the defense have any objection?" Judge Stowers asked.

James was surprised at the swiftness of Judge Stowers's decision. He'd been prepared to ask the court to speed things up. Now that would no longer be necessary.

"I have no objection, Your Honor," James stated for the court reporter, who stared at him, waiting for his reply.

"The state doesn't object, either," Wykowski said.

Again, the judge rolled her eyes at the ADA. "Mr. Conroy, once your client has been released into your custody, you will need to take him to the Department of Corrections so that he may be fitted with an ankle bracelet."

"Thank you, Your Honor." James smiled at Kate.

In a matter of seconds, two sheriff's deputies entered the courtroom from the side door the prisoners had used. The accused were whisked away before Kate even had a chance to mouth good-bye to Alex. She told herself it didn't matter because soon enough Alex would be released.

Outside the courtroom, James took Kate's hand and led her into a private conference room. "It will take a couple of hours for Alex's release. From there, I'll drive him over to the DOC building. If you want to meet us there, I'm sure Alex will be happy to see his wife." James said all of this with a big smile plastered across his thin face.

"I can't see him before then?"

"I'm afraid not. The judge released him into my custody. Why don't you go have lunch. There are some great restaurants on the waterfront. You might like Tin City."

Kate didn't even want to think about food, let alone worry about a fashionable area in which to dine.

"Thanks, but I'm going to wait for Alex. I'm sure I can find something to occupy the time." Kate paused. "James, I can't tell you how much this means to Alex and me. I don't know how we'll ever thank you."

James shook his head in the negative. "We're just over the first hurdle. Wait and thank me when Alex goes home for good."

"I'm confident that you'll see that he does go home for good, James. Now, if you tell me how to get to the DOC, I'll let you do your job."

James pulled a yellow legal pad from his briefcase, wrote down the directions. "If you have any trouble, just call this number." He scribbled the DOC's number on the bottom of the page. "They'll help if you get lost."

"I'll see you there." Kate took the sheet of paper, folded it into a small square, and tucked it inside her purse.

Chapter 13

When Kate saw her husband three hours later, she cried in his arms. "Oh, Alex, I'm sorry. I'm so glad you're out of that . . . hole."

"Not half as glad as I am." He wrapped his arms around Kate even tighter, holding her close. "Now, let's get the hell out of here. I want to take a shower and eat some real food."

James left them on their own for the rest of the day. The following morning Alex would undergo a psychiatric evaluation. Then the three of them would spend the next week going over Alex's case.

"Let's go back to the house. I'll make lunch, and you can clean up." Kate didn't want Alex out of her sight. She drank him in as they walked to the rental car.

Alex laughed when he saw the silver Mercedes. "Gertie?"

"How'd you guess?" Kate grinned. "Nothing but the best."

"That's my Gertie. Nothing but the best for my girl." Alex took the keys from Kate. "I might be a criminal, but I still have my driver's license. You relax. You've had enough stress the past few days."

"And you haven't?" Kate dropped the keys into Alex's open palm.

"Yes, I have. I can take it. I hate what this is doing to you. You look worn-out."

They got in the car and headed for the house.

"I am tired, but I don't care. I don't ever want to see you locked up again, Alex, and I mean it. I'll do whatever is necessary to keep you here with me." Kate meant it, too. Even if she had to ask James to do something legally unethical, she would. No way was Alex going to jail for Sara's lies.

"James is confident the grand jury won't formally charge me. That's next week. If all goes as he says, we can go home after the hearing."

"I hope so," Kate said. "But what about . . . you know. This was on the news in Asheville."

"I'm not concerned with what other people may believe. If they chose to think I'm some sort of . . . molester — God, it sickens me to even say that word — then they weren't that crazy about me in the first place." Alex reached for her hand. "If this makes you uncomfortable in any way, we'll move. I don't care where we go. I can take the dogs and go just about anywhere in the world."

"Let's not borrow trouble. We'll get through this somehow," Kate added.

"Thanks for your faith. I don't know what I would do if you didn't believe in me."

"And you'll never have to find out, Alex. I love you, and I trust you immensely." Kate never doubted for even a minute that Alex was innocent of the charges against him. She knew him, knew he wasn't some evil pervert lurking behind a facade.

"James said Sara would have to testify, but there are special circumstances for children. She may give her testimony through closed-circuit."

"Then how will James question her?"

"He'll be able to question her, the same as the prosecution. The jury, if it comes to that, and we don't believe it will, they'll view her testimony by video. And speaking of prosecution, what did you think of Wykowski?"

Alex stopped at the traffic light at the intersection of Highway 41 and Immokalee Road. "From what I hear, he's their best.

Does nothing but sex crimes."

Kate laughed. "Surely you heard him mumbling in court this morning. If he's the best the state has to offer, then we're home free."

"I'm just repeating what I heard from a few of the inmates." Alex made the turn onto Hibiscus Lane.

He whistled. "This is nice." They parked the Mercedes in the garage.

"It was so thoughtful of Gertie's friends to let us stay here. They have Jet Skis, and if you want to try them out later, we can."

Kate unlocked the side door. A blast of cool air hit them as they entered through the garage door leading to the kitchen.

"Maybe later. This air-conditioning feels great. I don't see how anyone could live here year-round."

"Debbie always complained about the heat. Claimed it frizzed her hair," Kate said.

"She's always got something to complain about. I don't see how Don puts up with it."

"Can you imagine her now? I wonder if she's encouraging the media. James said there was an article in the *Naples Daily News* yesterday. Didn't say what the charges were, only that you'd been extradited from North Carolina. I'm sure Debbie will want her face splashed all over the paper. She's always craved attention, good or bad."

"I wonder about Don. We've been best friends since we were, hell, I think I was seven, maybe eight. You'd think he would know me better, wouldn't you?"

It just occurred to Kate that not only was Alex losing his reputation, he was also losing his best friend and his two daughters, who were like his own children.

"Yes, I would. I think Debbie's behind this. I don't know why or anything, but I'd bet my last nickel she's encouraged this accusation of Sara's." Kate took a pitcher of iced tea out of the refrigerator. She poured them each a glass.

"There was a time when Debbie was decent. She was crazy about Don, followed him around like a lost puppy. When Don got his engineering degree, she changed. Got all snooty, started acting like a social climber. It wasn't too long after Emily was born that I really noticed how drastic the changes were. She went back to school, got her Realtor's license, then she started making big bucks. Money changes people, Kate."

"I think it's more than that. She's always seemed so, I don't know, petty, I guess is the word. Makes a big deal out of nothing.

I think she treats Emily terribly. When she called her a tramp, that was it for me. No decent mother would think of calling her daughter such a thing, even if it happened to be true. I know I would never, ever call Emily such a name. Though I have to admit, I have thought of a few choice names I would love to call Sara, but then I realize she's only a child. One with problems, too."

Alex took their glasses and walked to the patio door. "Let's sit by the pool for a bit, then I'll go shower, and you can make us a bite to eat."

"Sounds good, but there is something I have to confess."

Alex shot her a worried look. "And just what would that be?"

"Lunch will have to be peanut butter and jelly sandwiches. I didn't bother with a lot of groceries yesterday."

"I love peanut butter and jelly sandwiches. Especially yours." Alex grinned. "You had me worried for a minute."

"Let me make the sandwiches. Relax for a while, I'll be back in a jiffy." Kate left before Alex could tease her about her play on words.

Kate took her time making the sandwiches. She sliced two apples, arranging a few pieces on each of their plates. She took the pitcher of tea and placed it on a serving tray with the rest of their lunch. If only they were back in Asheville. Alex would be with the dogs, and more than likely she'd be in the kitchen whipping up some new recipe for Chloe's. *Patience,* she told herself. In a matter of days they would return to North Carolina, back to their established routines. If they managed to get through this without too much damage, Kate vowed somehow she would see to it that Sara was punished for her lies. It might take a while, but she and the rest of the Winter family would be sorry they had ever laid eyes on her. Not that she had anything in mind at the moment, but maybe Emily could get Sara to confess. Emily knew the truth, she'd said as much to her on the phone. Then Don would punish her and apologize to Alex. They'd never be best friends again, Kate was sure of that. Maybe if Don found out about Sara and her lies, he could get her the help she needed. And possibly spare another innocent man the humiliation that Alex was struggling with.

Kate took the serving tray out to the patio. Alex was sound asleep in a deck chair. She hated to wake him, but he needed something to eat.

Kate placed the plates and pitcher of tea

on the patio table.

"Hey, sleepyhead." She squeezed onto the vacant spot next to him. "I think it's time to wake up."

He opened one eye, then closed it quickly. "I'm still sleeping. Those cots in the jail did nothing to encourage a good night's rest." Alex hoisted himself up and over to the table.

"If you'd rather nap, why don't you go inside where it's cooler. We can eat later."

"No, I'm hungry. Tired, but it'll keep. I've waited for two long days to feast my eyes on you. I'm not going to waste time sleeping."

"This almost seems like a dream. I keep thinking it's some sort of sick joke Don's playing, then I realize it's not." Kate paused for a minute. "I'm scared, Alex."

Alex took her hand. "I know you are. Hell, I'd be a fool to say I wasn't a little bit scared myself. I've always believed the truth will stand, no matter what. I still believe that, Kate. If not, I wouldn't be able to handle this either. James is a good attorney; he's already had me released on my own recognizance. That's not an easy feat, according to him. Especially with the type of charges I'm facing. I don't want you to worry. In a few days we'll be home, and we can put this horrible incident behind us. Now, let's eat.

I'm starved."

The peanut butter stuck to the roof of her mouth. She took a sip of her tea, then another bite. She wanted to say so many things to Alex, things that she feared if she said them, they'd only cause him more anxiety, so she kept them to herself. She would get through this. For Alex. "I'm going grocery shopping while you take a nap. I can't feed you peanut butter every day."

"Kate, tell me what's really bothering you? I don't care if we eat peanut butter sandwiches or prime rib. Kate?" Alex knew her well.

"It's everything, Alex. I said I was afraid, and I am, that's all. I'm having terrible thoughts about Sara. I guess I feel a bit guilty for having them since she's just a kid. I just want to know why in the hell she'd do this to us. We've always been good to her. I've never showed favoritism to either of the girls, at least I don't believe I have. I want to know why, that's all. Why did the little monster do this? Why now?" Kate shook her head. Each time she voiced what had happened to Alex, it only made her more determined to get to the bottom of Sara's lies.

"Only Sara can answer that. I've gone over our visits so many times, I just can't imagine where this idea came from. Never did I touch her in any way that could be called inappropriate. I'm sure Debbie's behind this. I'd like to think not, but at this point, I'm willing to believe anything, except Sara. You said Emily knew Sara was lying. Think she'd testify in court if it comes to that?" Alex asked.

"She would, but I don't know how Debbie or Don would react. I would think since she's underage, she'd have to follow the same rules as Sara. We'll discuss this with James. Now, why don't we forget about the Winter family and try out those Jet Skis?"

Alex's eyes brightened. "Sounds like a plan to me."

CHAPTER 14

"Unless Sara undergoes a psychiatric evaluation, there is no case," Aaron Hanover explained to the Winters.

"She's been through enough already. I've already taken her to the hospital for the anxiety attacks. That was more than the poor child could handle. I don't want some . . . some stranger asking her questions about this. It'll only upset her more," Debbie explained to the attorney.

She and Don had discussed it and decided a civil suit was warranted as well as the criminal charges against Alex.

"As I said, Mrs. Winter, there isn't a case without expert testimony to back up Sara's accusation. She'll also need a complete physical. If you're unwilling to subject Sara to this, then I'm afraid I can't be of any help to you." Aaron Hanover had been practicing law for more than twenty years. Never in all those years had he met a client he disliked on first sight as much as Mrs. Winter. She was too eager, wanted to know exactly how much money she could get if they won. Aaron was sure she didn't really care about the trauma her child had experienced any more than the father did. He wasn't even sure if the allegations were true.

Debbie shot daggers at the attorney. "Are you sure? This is such a painful time for Sara. She feels terrible about telling on her uncle Alex. I would think someone would have a bit of sympathy for my daughter." She stood and turned to Don. "Let's go. I don't think Mr. Hanover can help us."

"I'm sorry you feel that way, Mrs. Winter. I believe another attorney will advise you to do the same as I've suggested."

Without another word, Debbie yanked Don's hand and tugged him out of the office. Once they were in the car, Debbie continued to rant and rave. "Doesn't anyone care about Sara? My God, look at what she's going through. I hope Alex Rocket rots in prison for what he's done to her. She'll never be the same again." Debbie took a tissue from her purse and blotted her eyes.

Don thought about what the attorney had just explained. He feared that Hanover was right. Sara would need to be examined by a professional, whether or not they filed a civil suit. Debbie wasn't fully aware of the law.

"I think we need to listen to what Hanover has to say. He's supposed to be the best plaintiff's attorney in south Florida. If he wants Sara to undergo a psychiatric evaluation, Deb, we're gonna have to find someone we can trust. Someone who's experienced with sexual abuse."

"How did I know you'd agree with that know-it-all? You men are all alike." Debbie tapped a cigarette out of a crumpled package. "Can't you put yourself in Sara's place, just for a minute? We'll be lucky if the child has a normal life from this point on."

Don sighed. Sometimes he wished he'd never laid eyes on this woman. "Sara needs professional help, Debbie. If there is any hope of her leading a normal life, that's the only way it's going to happen. She needs someone to listen to her, someone objective. We need to consult a psychiatrist."

Debbie blew a puff of smoke from her glossed lips. "Then you take care of this garbage. I'm tired of it already. She's your daughter, too."

"Which is it, Deb? Either you care or you don't. I'm very concerned about our daughter. I'm also burning with rage at the man who I thought was my best friend. If you won't find a professional to help Sara, I will do it myself. She needs help."

"Go ahead, then. I say Sara will be even more traumatized, but you know everything, so we'll do it your way. Let's go have lunch, we have reservations at Tin City."

"You always have to make everything so difficult. I'm taking you home. Screw lunch at Tin City, I can't stand to be around you a minute longer than absolutely necessary." Don punched the gas, pressing Debbie backward in her seat. At that minute, he hated her with every ounce of his being.

Debbie dug her fingers into the dash. "Are you trying to get us killed or what? Slow down right this minute or let me out, you bastard!"

Don eased off the gas, but not because Debbie asked him to. He'd spotted a highway patrol vehicle at the next intersection. Let her think she was controlling the situation. It was the only way to shut her mouth. The last thing he needed was a speeding ticket.

"Let's just go home. I'll take care of Sara, and you can do whatever it is you do."

"So now I don't do anything, is that what you're trying to say? Forget that I go out and bust my ass every day trying to sell these overpriced houses. I guess the next fifty-thousand-dollar commission check I collect, I'll donate it to a homeless shelter. Since I don't do anything."

Another deep breath. "I didn't mean it that way, and you damn well know it. This situation with Sara is getting to both of us. I do appreciate your contribution, no matter what you may think." He knew Debbie worked hard, but she loved it. She liked the social climbing that went along with her job more than the money. It was all she could talk about at times.

Twenty minutes later, Don was on the phone searching for a reputable psychiatrist.

He called Sara into the den.

"What do you want, Daddy? I was watching MTV."

"Sorry to interrupt, kiddo, but this is important." Don motioned for her to sit next to him on the white leather sofa.

"What?" Sara dragged out the word longer than Don thought possible.

"I know you're going to be upset, but I want you to listen. I've made an appointment for you to go to a doctor. She's going to help you talk about what happened with . . . Alex."

Sara screamed, "I told Mommy I was not going! And I'm not!" She stormed out of the room.

Don screamed right back, "Get your ass

back in here, young lady!"

Sara came back to the den, her face mottled with tears streaming down her fat cheeks. "What?"

"You have an appointment tomorrow afternoon with Dr. Kenton. I don't want to hear your whining. Now get out of my sight!"

"I hate you!" Sara screamed as she exited the room.

"Yeah, well, so do a lot of others," Don said, knowing it was childish but unable to help himself.

If there was the slightest hope of Sara leading a normal life, Don knew he would see to it that she kept the appointment, even if he had to drag her by the hair.

It was time she learned to play by the rules.

His rules.

James Conroy placed the call he'd been dreading all morning. There was no way around it, no matter how he tried to talk himself out of it.

He drew in a shaky breath. "Kate, it's James."

"What's wrong? You sound terrible."

He was hoping by the tone of his voice, or at least by his lack of enthusiasm, that she would pick up on why he was calling, anything to save him from saying what he knew the Rockets didn't want to hear. He had really come to like the couple over the last week. Hell, he'd practically promised them this would all be over with before they knew it. He was wrong.

"I was hoping to have better news. Apparently the grand jury has made its decision. They're binding Alex over for trial. I'm so sorry, Kate. I was almost positive that this would go in Alex's favor."

Kate's hands trembled. Her eyes pooled with hot angry tears. *Damn that little bitch! She's about to ruin Alex's life. If I could get my hands around Sara Winter's fat neck right now, I just might choke the life out of her. I can't stand the kid.* Kate knew she'd regret her thoughts later. But not just then. She needed her anger to get her through this. Without it, she didn't know if she could.

"I'll tell Alex," Kate responded.

"I know this isn't what you wanted to hear. I want to go over a few details with you and Alex today. I'll stop by the house this afternoon. Will that work for you both?"

Their life was falling apart minute by minute. If their attorney wanted to make a house call, it mattered little to her. "That's good. We'll be here." Still in a daze, Kate hung up the phone. The Winter family had won the first round. They were out to ruin Alex, or so they thought. While this was the worst news possible, Kate was ready for battle no matter how daunting the challenge. She had to be strong for Alex. Let him know they would get through this, no matter what. They would. She knew they would. They had to.

Alex entered the kitchen. "Who was on the phone? You don't look too happy."

Kate shook her head. "You're not going to believe this."

"Try me. At this stage of the game, I'm willing to believe anything."

"That was James. The grand jury came back, Alex. They've issued an indictment."

Kate watched the play of emotions dance across her husband's face. Surprise, resignation, anger, then acceptance.

"I thought as much. James talks a good talk. This is Florida. They don't take these kinds of accusations lightly, we knew that going in. Let's just hope we can prove otherwise." Alex took a seat at the small kitchen table. "We'll get through this, Kate. I promised you I'd come home. You know I don't make promises I can't keep. Now come here." He motioned for her to take a seat in his lap.

"James wants to stop by today, go over his strategy. I don't know what else there is to say. I've racked my brain for answers, and all I come up with are more questions, and that leads to the inevitable. Why did Sara accuse you of this?" Kate didn't want to talk about Alex's coming home. She was sure that he would. Anything more she couldn't conceive. Kate sat on Alex's lap, her arms around his neck. She breathed in his scent. If she lived to be a hundred, she'd always remember the smell of Alex. Old Spice and Dial soap.

"James mentioned a private investigator he uses. I think it's time we seriously listen to what he has to say," Kate suggested.

"I never thought it would get this far, but you're right. James will start digging up anything he can find on the Winters and Sara. Let's just pray he comes up with something we can use."

"I wish I had told Don about Sara destroying my earthenware in the studio. Maybe he would have thought twice before believing her."

"Sara is his daughter. He has to believe her. If he thought she was lying, what kind of parent would that make him? A rotten one, I can tell you that for sure. It's easier for him to think I'm some sick molester;

that way he doesn't have to question his skill as a father, or ask himself where he and Debbie went wrong. I know Don."

"He certainly doesn't know his best friend. Former best friend, I might add." Kate hated the Winter family. The extent of her rage frightened her. She'd heard all people had it in them to commit murder. She'd always laughed at the idea of such savagery. Now she completely understood. A person could only be pushed so far.

"It's sad, Kate, but life goes on. When this is all said and done, it wouldn't surprise me if Don called to apologize. Like he'd forgotten a birthday or something. That's how he is."

"Then he's even more shallow than I thought. A sociopath is more like it. Adapting as the situation calls for. It'd be a cold day in hell before I'd say a kind word to any member of that family. I'm sorry, but you don't ruin your best friend's life, then say you're sorry."

Her heart broke for Alex and his lost friendship. She knew he acted as though the loss meant nothing, but Alex wasn't that kind of man. The loss probably hurt him almost as much as Sara's accusation. For that, she was truly sorry.

"You're right, but this isn't the time or

the place to contemplate Don and his idea of friendship. Right now, I want nothing more than you." Alex eased her from his lap and led her to the bedroom. Words were unnecessary.

Kate, Alex, and James all sat at the kitchen table sipping iced tea. The weather was still killer-hot, with no break in the humidity. "There is always the possibility the DA will offer a plea. That's standard in this type of case," James explained.

"What type of plea?" Kate asked, then looked to Alex to see if he knew what James was referring to.

"In a case of this magnitude, with six counts the DA usually gets a conviction."

"A conviction! Alex is innocent! I thought you believed us!" Kate yelled. Her nerves were beyond on edge, smashed to smithereens.

"I said 'usually,' Kate. It's my duty as Alex's attorney to tell him when a plea is being offered. I won't tell you what to do, though I almost always insist my clients accept a plea in a case of this kind. But I think Alex's chances of being found innocent are extremely high. That's why I am not going to suggest you even consider the plea," James said.

"Okay, so what's the next step after we tell them we won't accept their plea?" Alex asked.

James took a deep breath. "Then we go to trial and hope for the best."

"You just said you felt Alex's chances of being found innocent were good. So what do you mean, 'Hope for the best'?" Kate questioned.

"Just what I said. There are no absolute guarantees that a jury will find Alex innocent, just the same as there are no guarantees they'll convict him. We have to be realistic."

Kate realized James wasn't as confident as he'd been when he first took their case. She didn't like this and told him so.

"I'm doing the best I can for both of you. Alex, if you want another attorney, now would be the time to speak up."

Alex shook his head. "No, of course not. I'll just go to trial. I'm innocent, and the truth will come out. I have always lived by that motto, and I'm not going to stop now!"

Kate wasn't so sure. Oh, she believed in the criminal justice system, but she was afraid of a jury. She knew just how convincing Sara could be. She'd conned her and Alex all these years, and they'd been as close to her as her parents. She could only imagine what act she'd play for a jury. Still, Alex needed to know she was with him. She'd show her support by believing that the truth would emerge triumphant.

"Alex is right. He's innocent. Anyone with the slightest bit of intelligence will see this. Besides, when it's Alex's time to take the stand, the jury won't have any trouble believing him."

James fumbled with his goatee. "We haven't discussed this yet, but might as well. I don't want Alex taking the stand. It's too risky, and Lyle is much tougher than he looks. Trust me."

"And?" Kate asked.

"Let's just say I don't feel comfortable putting Alex on the stand and leave it at that, okay?"

Kate got up from her chair and dumped her tea in the sink. "What about it, Alex? Don't you want a chance to tell your side of the story?"

He raked a hand through his hair. "I don't have anything to tell, Kate. You know that. I'm going to do as James suggests."

Kate felt like she'd been rammed by a Mack truck. Alex wasn't willing to take the stand, put up a defense? She would. "Then put me on the stand. I'll tell them about Sara, what a conniving little brat she is. I'll tell them what she did in my studio."

"And we might do that. For now, I need both of you to understand that no matter what, I'm on your side."

Alex came and stood next to Kate. "So, how soon can we get this over with?"

"You're in luck. The docket for two weeks from today is clear. The DA has cleared his schedule, so we can get started on your defense right away."

This surprised Kate. "I thought a trial date would take forever. Why so sudden?"

"For starters, this is Naples. There isn't a lot of serious crime. Mostly civil suits, family matters, that type of thing. The judge is ready, the DA is clear, there isn't a lot of investigating that needs to be done, and what there is, we can certainly have it completed long before our two-week starting date."

"Let's just get this over with as quickly as possible. I need to get back to the kennels. Gertie'll be needing a break soon enough," Alex said.

"I'm ready, too. I want our life back, I want to put this nightmare behind us and never think about it again."

"And so we will," James acquiesced. "Let's get started."

Chapter 15

The courtroom was the same one used for the arraignment hearing, only this time it was packed. Newspaper reporters and television reporters from all across southwest Florida were positioned in a section closed off just for the media. Court TV had been given permission by Judge Stowers to broadcast live coverage of the trial. James explained to them that the Polly Klaas case had been instrumental in bringing these types of cases to national prominence. Kate was mortified, to say the least.

Seated directly behind Alex and James, Kate didn't dare turn around to view the people gathered in the courtroom. Somewhere, Debbie and Don were seated. She hadn't spotted them when she entered the courtroom. She was afraid of what she'd do if she saw them. This had all happened so fast. James was true to his word and had done a thorough investigation of the case.

Alex had been examined by a psychiatrist. James had interviewed Sara and was more convinced than ever of Alex's innocence. "The child has major issues," he'd told them, but refused to say anything more. Jury selection had been a breeze, according to James. There were no pretrial motions to contend with, so here they were, ready to begin to let the truth emerge from the wreckage of Alex's reputation and, perhaps, allow him and Kate to recover their lives.

Whispers, paper crackling, and the humming of the remote camera were the only sounds to be heard as the bailiff entered the courtroom. "All rise."

Judge Stowers entered through a door behind the bench and sat down. She shuffled through a stack of papers, then adjusted her half-moon reading glasses. After pounding her gavel twice, she announced, "You may be seated. This court is now in session."

Kate thought the gavel a bit extreme but figured it was for the benefit of the cameras.

"Is the state ready to proceed?" Stowers asked Wykowski.

"We are, Your Honor."

"Then you may begin your opening statement," Judge Stowers instructed.

Lyle Wykowski wore his best suit. A navy,

single-breasted with a crisp white shirt, and a narrow red, white, and blue striped tie. His Coke bottle glasses were the same, but his oily hair appeared as though he'd recently been to a stylist. Gone was the clumsy fumbler from the arraignment.

"I'll be quick, Your Honor."

Kate breathed a sigh of relief. Though Wykowski had cleaned up appearance-wise, she was relieved to see he was as unprofessional as before.

"Be whatever you want, Counselor, just be thorough," the judge admonished.

With a yellow legal pad in hand, Lyle stood up and turned to the jurors, seated to the right of the prosecution table.

"First of all, let me thank you all for performing your civic duty. This is a hardship for some of you. The state acknowledges this and appreciates your dedication. Now I'm going to tell you all a story. It's almost a fairy tale, but sadly, in this fairy tale it will turn into every parent and child's worst nightmare, because you see, there are no happy endings." Lyle paused. He had the jury's undivided attention.

"Once upon a time there was a little girl. She was around five or six years old at the time when the bad things began. She lived with her mother and father and big sister.

This little girl was a happy-go-lucky child. She loved Barbie dolls, animals, and roller skating. All the normal things little girls her age love to do. She liked helping her mother bake cookies, she loved hearing her father tell her bedtime stories, but most of all, this little innocent girl loved the visits from her aunt and uncle. Sometimes she would visit them, other times they would travel to Florida to visit her and her family. It didn't matter to this little girl where she saw the couple. Next to her parents, they were her favorite people in the, and I quote, 'whole wide world.'

"Year after year this little girl looked forward to visits from her extended family. As she and her big sister grew older, her parents allowed the two to spend Christmas vacations, Easter break, and a few weeks every summer with their favorite aunt and uncle."

Kate wished he would get to the damned point. She was already sick of "little girl this" and "little girl that."

The ADA continued with his opening statement. "It was on these many happy occasions that this little girl experienced the most vile, sickening act a child could ever imagine. Her trusted uncle, a man well thought of in his community, a breeder of dogs, a husband to his wife, and best friend to the little girl's father, molested her!"

"Objection!" James piped up.

"What are you objecting to, Mr. Conroy?" Judge Stowers asked.

"I'm objecting to the fact that Mr. Wykowski says my client molested the child."

"That's what this trial is about. Objection overruled. Please continue, Mr. Wykowski."

"Every time Mr. Rocket came to Florida, he sexually abused this innocent, precious little girl. The state intends to prove beyond a reasonable doubt that Mr. Rocket is guilty of all six counts of sexual battery against a minor. That's all, Your Honor."

The judge looked at both attorneys. "Mr. Wykowski, you may call your first witness."

"The state would like to call Dr. Maureen Sheffield."

After the doctor was sworn in, her credentials qualifying her as an expert in her field verified and satisfied by the court, the ADA began his questioning.

"Dr. Sheffield, when did the child in this case first visit your office?" the ADA asked. Because the child was still a minor and the cameras were in the courtroom, Judge Stowers had asked they refer to her as "the child" in order to protect her identity. When it came time to view the video of her testimony, the media would be asked to leave and the cameras would be turned off.

The doctor looked through a binder she brought to the witness stand. "It was ten days ago."

"And how many times did you see this child in your office?"

"I saw her six times in my office and twice in her home," Dr. Sheffield stated.

"And why did you visit the child in her home?"

"It's not unusual for children who have been sexually abused to —"

"Objection!" James shouted. "The court has not proved there was sexual abuse of any kind!"

"Overruled again, Mr. Conroy. That's what we're here to find out," the judge explained for the second time.

"You may continue, Dr. Sheffield," Judge Stowers advised.

"As I was saying, it's not unusual for children who've suffered sexual abuse to display different behavior patterns in the home."

"And did you find the child to act any differently at home than during the visits to your office?"

The doctor looked out into the courtroom,

searching for a set of eyes. Kate turned to follow the doctor's stare. Debbie Winter sat three rows behind the prosecution table.

"Dr. Sheffield?" Wykowski prompted.

"I found the behavior of the child to be exactly the same as she displayed during our visits."

Muffled whispers could be heard throughout the room.

"Order!" Judge Stowers said, then banged her gavel for dramatic effect.

Once again, silence reigned in the courtroom.

"Was this unusual?" Wykowski questioned.

"Not at all."

"Can you explain to the court the types of behaviors most common and uncommon in child victims of sexual abuse?"

"First and foremost, their sense of security is damaged. They may be clingy, whereas before they may have felt entirely comfortable on their own. They may no longer trust those in authority. Some children act violently. Others, depending on their age, may become sexually promiscuous. It varies from case to case. These are only a few of the changes one might expect to see."

"Of the behavioral changes you mentioned, did you have the opportunity to view any of these behaviors during your examination of the child in question?"

"Yes."

"And which would that be?"

Dr. Sheffield smiled before answering. "The child was quite angry."

"Was she violent in any way?"

"Never, just angry. She doesn't know how to release the anger she feels at her abuser; therefore, she exhibits anger at simple, everyday things."

"Could you explain this to the court?" Wykowski asked.

"When I would ask a simple question, such as, 'What is your favorite television program,' she would shout, telling me she hated everything on television. She said the only thing she liked to do was eat."

"And you found that what, Dr. Sheffield?"

"Typical of her situation. The child is devastated, finding her only comfort in food. Her weight is extremely high for a child her age and height."

"I have no further questions for this witness, Your Honor."

"Mr. Conroy, do you wish to cross-examine the state's witness?"

James stood, then walked to the front of the courtroom. After scanning the audience, he walked very slowly to the jury box.

"Yes, I would very much like to question

the state's witness."

"Proceed," Judge Stowers ordered.

"First I, too, would like to thank the fine people of Collier County for giving us their time and their attention. It's not going to be easy hearing some of the things you're going to hear."

"Mr. Conroy, you waived your right to make an opening statement, I'll ask that you question the witness and save your comments for closing statements. If you choose to make one."

"Yes, Your Honor. Allow me to apologize for wasting the court's time." He walked to the witness stand and leaned against the wooden rail.

"Dr. Sheffield, did the child ever come right out and say exactly what it was that my client did to her? Did she give any details at all?"

The doctor looked toward the prosecution table. "Some, yes, but minute detail, no, she was not able to."

"Was the child able to remember any specific times or dates that my client did these things she was unable to describe to you?"

Dr. Sheffield took the pitcher of water provided by the court, poured a small amount into a paper cup, and took several gulps before answering. “No. The child is too young to be able to recall specific dates, times.” The doctor realized her mistake the second it came out of her mouth.

“Then the child can’t possibly be a reliable witness to any of the acts she’s accused Mr. Rocket of, if she can’t remember dates and times, can she?”

“That’s not what I meant . . . She’s too young to recall anything specific . . . She doesn’t know . . .”

“The defense has no further questions, Your Honor.” James left Dr. Sheffield seated in the witness stand for round two.

“Redirect, Your Honor,” Wykowski said, for the benefit of the court reporter.

“Proceed.”

“Dr. Sheffield, the events the child said took place, when she told them to you in the safe confines of your office, no matter how little the detail, did you question her accuracy? Did you believe her to be telling the truth?”

Dr. Sheffield arched her shoulders back, raised her chin a notch. “I am one hundred percent sure the child is telling the truth. The abuse was too exact for the child not to have experienced.”

“Even though she was unable to give you dates and times?”

"Yes."

"I have no further questions of this witness."

Again, the bang of the gavel. "Court will take a ten-minute recess."

Several members of the media scurried out of the courtroom, probably hoping to be the first to report to their respective networks.

James whispered something to Alex, and he laughed.

"What's so funny?" Kate asked as she leaned over the banister.

"James seems to think Dr. Sheffield is a fruitcake."

"I agree. Her answers were so vague, how could the jury even think anything happened to Sara if a professional was unable to provide details? This looks good, doesn't it, James?"

"It's not bad, but remember, the jurors are the ones who will view the video. I can promise you it does go into some detail."

"What did she say? You can't let us observe it the same time as the jury! Who knows what reaction we'll have?" Kate asked James.

"That's the exact reason I do want you to view the tape when the jury does. I want them to see you both with fresh eyes and ears. I want the jury to see the look of shock on Alex's face, and yours as well."

Kate smiled. "I get it. I guess that makes sense, but I can tell you, I am not looking forward to hearing what this sick little girl has to say about my husband."

"Nor am I," Alex added.

"Trust me, I think this will work to our advantage." With that, James thumbed through several papers his investigator had brought in during the recess. He seemed upset at their contents.

The media returned to the courtroom with barely a minute to spare. Reports were filed, and news was made for the first half of the day.

Chapter 16

The hum in the courtroom was like a low note being held by a choir. After the recess, the judge asked all members of the media to leave her courtroom. She instructed the bailiff to observe as a technician provided by Court TV turned off the camera. She wasn't going to tolerate any mistakes in her courtroom, especially during a trial of this magnitude.

An audiovisual technician set up a screen and the VCR for the jurors to view. The courtroom was empty except for the attorneys, the family members of the victim, and the accused.

The jurors were given pads of paper to write their notes on. They would see the video only once.

Kate held her breath as the judge instructed the bailiff to dim the lights.

"Is the court reporter ready?"

"I am, Your Honor. I have all the extra

equipment you requested."

"Thanks, Janice."

"I'm told the video testimony is approximately four and a half hours long. We will view the first hour, then we will take a lunch break."

Kate leaned over the banister, her hand on Alex's shoulder. She couldn't imagine being in his place. Her heart broke a little more for him with each passing day. Her Alex. Good, salt-of-the-earth Alex.

"Are the prosecution and defense ready?" Judge Stowers asked.

Both replied that they were.

"You may begin the tape."

A few seconds later the projection screen, at least eighty inches high, showed a huge Sara sitting on a dark green leather sofa. She wore a pale peach sundress with white sandals. Her hair was pulled back in a ponytail with a white ribbon. *The picture of innocence,* Kate thought. Sara never wore dresses and rarely combed her hair.

"Sara, this is Mr. Wykowski. He works for the state of Florida. He's going to see that the bad man who hurt you is punished. He is going to ask you some questions, okay?" Dr. Sheffield spoke as though she were talking to a mentally challenged two-year-old.

"I guess so," Sara replied.

"Remember, Sara, Mr. Wykowski is one of the good guys that we talked about. You do remember us talking about good guys and bad guys, don't you?" Sheffield asked.

"Yes, of course I do. I'm not stupid!"

Sara being her usual self.

"Of course you're not stupid. Did anyone call you stupid, Sara? Did the bad man call you stupid?"

Kate grimaced. Now Alex was "the bad man."

"Yes, and he called me bad words, too." Sara smiled.

"Why don't you let Mr. Wykowski ask his questions now."

"What's he waiting for, anyway? I want to hurry. I want to go home. I hate this place. I didn't want to be here in the first place. Mommy said I had to. Hurry up, Mr. Wyk— whatever your name is."

"Sara, I know you don't want to be here any more than I do. It's big, brave girls like you that put bad men in jail. Now, I want you to tell me about the first time the bad man, Mr. Rocket, touched you. Can you do that?"

"Sure, I can. I was in bed in my room, sleeping. He was visiting us like usual. I woke up and saw this scary-looking man sitting on the edge of my bed. He was smoking a cigarette. I hate smoking. Mommy smokes all the time. It stinks. But there was this man. I couldn't really tell what his face looked like until he puffed on the cig. He was all aglow then. It was Uncle Alex."

"Then what did you do?" the voice of the ADA asked.

"Nothing. I just pretended to go back to sleep."

A sigh could be heard, but you couldn't tell who it was. The video camera moved away from Sara, then back again.

Wykowski's voice. "Why did you pretend to go back to sleep?"

"I don't know. I think I was scared. Yes, that's it. I was very afraid of the man, Uncle Alex, on the bed. I wanted to scream for my dad, but I knew Uncle Alex would hurt me if I tried."

"Why did you think this? Had your uncle Alex hurt you before?"

"Lots of times. He hit me, pinched me, one time he burned me with a cigarette. I never told Mommy or Daddy 'cause he was their best friend. He never hurt Emily, though. I think he liked her more than me. Mommy said he had good reason to, but she never said what it was. He's a very mean man."

"Let's get back to the night you saw him sitting on the edge of your bed. Can you think back to that night and try to remember what grade of school you were in?"

The ADA was trying to establish a time period, Kate assumed.

"I told you before that I didn't! Why do you keep asking me the same thing over and over?"

"Your Honor, can we pause the recording for a moment?" James asked.

"Yes."

The judge instructed the bailiff to pause the VCR.

"May I approach?" James asked.

Judge Stowers nodded in the affirmative.

"Judge Stowers, I was told the state would have one opportunity to question the child, same as the defense. It appears from what the child is saying that the state has questioned her on more than one occasion."

"Mr. Wykowski, is this true?"

"Yes, it is, but only to the extent of allowing the child to get an idea of what she could expect. In no way was she ever told what to say by me, Dr. Sheffield, or her parents."

"Mr. Conroy, does the state's answer satisfy you?"

"Yes, it does."

"We'll continue to view the testimony."

The VCR was turned on, and Sara's face lit up the screen.

"I'm sorry, but this is what the court needs to find out in order to put the bad man away."

"I was in third grade. I remember now. That's right."

"So in third grade, was this the first time the bad man, Mr. Rocket, came to your room and frightened you?"

"I don't really remember. He was mean all the time. He always wanted to play with Emily. I bet he touched her, too, and she liked it. I'm going to ask her. You should, too. Emily won't tell even if he did. Mommy says —"

"Let's not worry about what your mother says, Sara. Let's get back to the night you woke up when you were in the third grade. You saw Mr. Rocket sitting on the edge of your bed smoking. What happened next?"

"I hate this, but I have to do what's right. Mommy told me always to tell the truth, right, Mommy?"

"Of course, dear. Now tell Mr. Wykowski what happened."

"Okay. Well, I watched him sit there for a while. I think he thought I was asleep, but I was secretly peeking out through my eyes. You know how you close them, and they're like slits? That's what I was doing. He reached beneath the covers and put his hand on my . . . You know . . . on my privates."

Kate tried to see the expressions on the face of the jurors, but the room was too dim.

"Did you have your pajamas on?"

"No, I just had on a long T-shirt and my panties. He pulled my panties down, too. Right to my knees. By then I didn't know what to do. I was just so scared I thought I should keep pretending I was sleeping. I did, and after that he rubbed me . . . there. Then after a while he stopped. I saw he was rubbing his underwear, too."

Kate's stomach climbed high into her throat. She wanted to vomit at the smug look on Sara's face. Though Kate would never know if Don or Debbie coached Sara, she was sure Sara knew much more in the sex department than she'd let on to her parents. She remembered a conversation she and Emily had when Emily had got her first period. Sara seemed more knowledgeable than Emily. She'd even remarked that she'd better not have sex or she could get knocked up. Kate thought Sara must've been around nine at the time.

"Was there another time Mr. Rocket came to your room?"

"Yep. Lots of them. Every time him and Aunt Kate came to visit he came in my room. He would come into the bathroom, too. I was afraid to tell Mommy; she didn't want me to lock the door just in case I fell or something. I never did. Uncle Alex knew this, and he'd come into the bathroom. Once he got in the shower with me. He got his hands all soapy, then he rubbed his . . . his man part. It got all big and stiff. He made me touch it, too. It was all slimy and had these big old veins popping out. I started crying, then he made these terrible noises and turned away from me. When he looked at me again his part was all flat. He said if I told, he would kill my dad. I stayed in the bathroom so long I was wrinkled. I think Mommy had to come and get me out of the tub. I was just so scared."

Kate couldn't stop herself. She bolted from the courtroom in search of the nearest restroom. At the end of a long hall, she found the ladies' room. She shoved her way into a stall. On her knees, she vomited until there was nothing left. She flushed the toilet, then dragged herself to the sink. Splashing cold water over her face helped a bit, but nothing would ever remove the words she'd just heard from the mouth of the most evil child on earth. After she'd composed herself, she went back to the courtroom.

James and Alex were waiting.

"After you left, the judge thought it was time for a break. Let's go to lunch." James guided Kate through the throngs of reporters lining the halls. They were in attack mode. "There's a back entrance we can use."

The trio raced to the basement, then back up two flights of stairs that led them to an alley.

"My car is just around the corner. Wait here, and I'll be right back."

James raced to his car, leaving Kate alone with Alex for the first time since they'd entered the courthouse.

"Kate, I don't know what to say. I'm beyond shocked. I had no idea Sara had it in her to destroy me in such a deplorable manner. I wonder what Don was thinking as he listened to this bunch of malarkey."

"I don't care what he thinks, or his miserable wife. I care what those twelve men and women in that jury box think. Beyond that, I just can't go there now. Alex, this is worse than I thought."

He agreed. "I'd pay big bucks to find out how Sara learned all that sick stuff. Emily sure as hell wasn't a party to it, I know that. Did she look like she was delighted or something to you? It was almost like this was a big game to her. The more she talked, the bigger the tale."

James pulled next to the curb. "Let's get out of here. We've got a couple of hours before we have to be back in court."

They drove for fifteen minutes, then pulled off Highway 41 into the parking lot of what looked like an abandoned strip mall. "I hope the media hasn't found this place. I discovered it last week. They have the best conch fritters in the state. Or so I'm told."

Inside the mom-and-pop restaurant, James ordered boiled shrimp, the famous conch fritters, and bowls of she-crab soup. The waitress handed him a ticket with a number, telling him they'd call when their food was ready. They sat at a rickety table in the corner. The place wasn't much in the way of decorations. Fish netting, with fake fish, sand dollars, and starfish, was plastered on the knotty pine walls. Pictures of men with humongous blue marlins and fish that were unidentifiable were placed haphazardly throughout the restaurant.

"Thirty-two," the waitress called.

"Be right back." Alex left the table to get their order.

Kate had her chance. "Quickly, James, how does it look for Alex?"

"Hard to say, Kate. We'll know more after the jurors view the video in its entirety."

"Talking about me behind my back, huh?" Alex teased.

"No, Alex. I was just asking . . . Never mind. Let's eat." Food was the last thing on Kate's mind. For Alex's sake, she'd eat and like it. The forced cheerfulness between them was starting to frazzle her nerves. She and Alex had always been comfortable with one another. Now it seemed not only had they lost the life they shared, they'd lost the ability to be at ease with one another. Sara had taken more than she realized.

When James tried to drop Alex and Kate off behind the courthouse, the media spotted them. They ran alongside James's vehicle as he slowly nosed his way through the throng of reporters.

"Mr. Rocket, how many other children have you molested?"

"Do you like boys, too?"

"Are you registered as a sex offender?"

The reporters kept shouting their questions at them. It was all Kate could do to keep from rolling down the window and telling them all to screw themselves. She mentioned this to James as they maneuvered their way through the crowds in search of a parking space.

"You wouldn't want that splashed across the front page of the *Naples Daily News,* that's for sure. Remember, this is a big news story for them, and that's all it is. They don't care about the people they're reporting on, just the story. Don't let their comments offend you."

Like hell, Kate thought.

James found a place between a van and a scooter. Miracles never ceased. They needed one then, Kate theorized, as they crept through the hallway, back to the courtroom.

Ten minutes later, court was back in session. The lights dimmed, and Sara dominated the screen once again.

"Sara, tell me about the cigarette burn,"

Wykowski said.

"What's to tell? He burned me. We were having a cookout. Mommy likes to cook."

And that was the biggest piece of fantasy Kate had heard about Debbie since they'd met. The woman didn't know the difference between motor oil and olive oil.

"Uncle Alex was at the grill cooking hamburgers. He had that cigarette hanging out of his mouth like always. I went over to the grill with my plate. Mommy told me to get a hamburger. I always do what she asks. Then when nobody was looking, Uncle Alex took the cigarette out of his mouth. He smashed it on my neck. See?" Sara turned to the camera so her wound was visible.

Kate strained, but didn't see a thing.

"Then what did you do?" the ADA asked.

"I dropped my plate. I ran inside and got an ice cube. I put some aloe on it. It was okay after that. I went back outside and Mommy gave me her hamburger."

"You didn't tell your parents what had just happened to you?"

"Nope. I didn't want Uncle Alex to kill my dad. He'd said that before. I figured he still meant to kill him if I ever told *anything* he did to me."

"Tell me about the times when Mr. Rocket hit you."

"Which time? There were lots of them."

"Just tell me the ones you remember the most."

"I remember all of them. Want me to tell you all of them?" Sara looked to the side.

"Okay, yes. Mommy says to tell all of them. Well, the first time he really hit me, we were in Asheville. It was Christmas. Mommy and Daddy were on one of their cruises. They always go on a cruise when we stay with Aunt Kate and Uncle Alex. I think me and Emily will have to go with them now. But, anyway, it was Christmas. Emily and Aunt Kate were in the kitchen baking cookies. Uncle Alex was in the den watching the television. I think it was the Playboy Channel. I remember telling Mommy about seeing all the naked ladies. So I was just messin' around. I guess I stood in front of the television too long or something. The next thing I remember is Uncle Alex smacking me in the face. I cried and ran upstairs. I so wanted Mommy, but she was on the cruise."

"Did you tell your sister or Mrs. Rocket what happened?"

"No. They never believe anything I say. Like the Conzelmans' cat. Emily swore to Mommy that I was dragging Snuggles around by its tail. But she just lied 'cause she wanted to get me into trouble. That's how Aunt Kate is, too. She believes anything Emily and Uncle Alex tell her. I was glad when my parents picked me up. I told Mommy I never wanted to go back, but she said that would hurt Aunt Kate's feelings and all. I just kept going on the visits."

Emily must have told Debbie about the cat incident. Good for her. A hand came into the camera's view with a paper cup. Gulping noises were heard across the courtroom.

"And when were you hit again?"

Sara rubbed her eyes, then started picking her nose. She rolled a booger between her thumb and index finger. Watching her, Kate gagged.

"We were at our house in Naples. Not the one we live in now, the other one. The one Mommy called a high-priced outhouse."

"Sara!" Debbie exclaimed.

"Well, that's what you called it," Sara said.

Wykowski spoke up, "Sara, let's just talk about Mr. Rocket and the things he did to you. Remember, we're here to make sure that he never does this to you again. Do you understand what I'm saying?"

"Duh! Of course I understand, I already told you. I am not stupid. I told you that, too. Now what did you ask? Oh, yeah, the next time Uncle Alex hit me was at our old house. They were there for Christmas. I can't remember what I was doing. I think I was using the bathroom. Yeah, that's right. I was in the bathroom . . . taking a shower. Uncle Alex came in and . . . uh, he peeked at me. I told him to get out. He laughed. I think I called him a bad word. Asshole, or maybe it was dickhead. I don't remember, but he took off his belt, yanked me out of the shower, and slapped me real hard on my butt. My skin was still wet, so It really stung."

"And you didn't tell your parents about this either?" Wykowski questioned.

"No! How many times do I have to tell you? Uncle Alex was going to kill my dad, I couldn't tell!"

"I'm sorry, Sara. I know this is extremely hard on you. You're doing a great job. Now if you want, we can take a break."

The tape stopped. The lights in the courtroom brightened. Kate looked at the jurors. Their expressions were blank. Poker-faced, each and every one of them.

Judge Stowers announced, "We're going to recess for the rest of the day. Tomorrow the cameras will be dark and the media will not be allowed back in the courtroom until the jury has viewed all of the child's testimony. I would like to remind the jurors that you are not to speak to the media, read a newspaper, watch television, or talk about this case to anyone. Friends, family, anyone at all. Court is adjourned until nine A.M. tomorrow."

The gavel sounded once again. The jurors were allowed to leave first. A deputy escorted them to a bus, where they were transported to a private parking garage that housed their personal vehicles. Judge Stowers took no chances.

Kate and Alex waited until James said the coast was clear before exiting the courtroom. Apparently Debbie was holding court with the media. She would suck up every minute of publicity; Kate knew her well. This wasn't just about Sara, this was about poor Debbie. Kate couldn't stand the sight of her.

Once inside James's car, Kate breathed a pent-up sigh of relief. It was exhausting sitting in the courtroom listening to her husband's life being torn apart by a twelve-year-old. *Thirteen,* Kate thought. *Sara had a birthday recently.*

"I want you both to go home, get a good night's rest. I'll pick you up around seven. That too early?"

"I doubt either of us will get any sleep. Seven is fine," Alex said.

Kate heard the worry in his voice, the fatigue. She knew he was trying to hold it all together. For her. Hell, she was doing the same. They both needed a good scream, something to punch or kick, anything to relieve the bottled-up emotions gripping them. Kate didn't even want to think of their future, at least not beyond tomorrow.

One day at a time.

Just like an alcoholic.

Chapter 17

"You shouldn't watch this stuff. James asked us not to," Kate called out. She was making tea for herself and coffee for Alex. He was in the great room watching Court TV. She brought their drinks in and placed them on the sofa table.

The reporter, an older woman with frizzy red hair and big, chunky jewelry, was interviewing the parking lot attendant from the private garage where the jurors parked their vehicles. So much for secrecy.

"This is ridiculous. What in the hell does he know about your case?"

"He knows the year, make, and model of the jurors' vehicles. At this point, I'm glad this is all they have to report. Once word of Sara's testimony is out, the Rocket name will make headlines all over the damn country. This just sickens me, Kate. What in the hell is this world coming to when children can tell such monstrous lies and get away with it! God-damn that child!" Alex took one of the throw pillows from the sofa, tossing it across the room. "I would like to get my hands on Don Winter. I'd choke the life out of the son of a bitch. Then they'd have a real reason to send me to prison."

Kate stood by silently, allowing Alex to release his anger. He'd needed to do it for days now. He took the remote control, hit the Off button, then tossed the device across the room so hard that it shattered. Kate would replace it.

"Where's all that wine you've been trying to get me to drink? I think I could use a glass right about now."

"I've got something stronger, if you prefer."

"I'll take whatever you have. God, Kate, I don't know why this is happening to us! What did we do to deserve this? Was I mean to Sara? Didn't we always get her the best of anything she asked for? I never scrimped when she asked for those outlandish Christmas presents. Hell, I liked spoiling her and Em. I wanted to buy them more. I wanted to give them each a pup. I wanted . . . Oh hell, I don't know what I wanted." Alex slumped forward, his head in his hands. His shoulders heaved. Kate watched her husband sob. In thirteen years of marriage she'd never seen him cry. Her heart ached at the sight. Knowing Alex wouldn't want her to see him like this, she busied herself in the kitchen, searching through strangers' cabinets for what, she hadn't a clue. Rocks glasses. She was looking for rocks glasses so she could pour Alex a shot of whiskey. She found the glasses and whiskey. Her hands shook like dry leaves as she poured the amber liquid. She took a big slurp, then another. She coughed till her eyes watered. She took another drink. Maybe she'd just get damn good and drunk. She would. They both would.

"Alex," she called, giving him a minute to pull himself back together.

He shouted back with forced cheerfulness, "Bring that drink, woman! I'm dying of thirst!"

"Well, so am I! I say we both get roaring drunk, have wild sex, and forget the world!" The falseness rang in her ears.

"I'm willing to do whatever it takes to forget the world. Now, where's that booze?"

Kate poured them each a full glass of whiskey.

"Let's make a toast," Alex bellowed.

Kate held her glass high in the air, the liquid sloshing over the rim onto the white carpet. She'd pay to have the house remodeled if that's what it took. Alex was happy right then, and she didn't care how many messes he made.

"To . . . to Gertie! The best damn dog sitter in the word!"

Kate clinked her glass to Alex's. "To Gertie!"

They finished, and Kate poured another round.

"Let's toast . . . hell, let's toast Gertie's friends for letting us trash their beautiful home!" Alex was laughing, but it wasn't his real laugh. It was the laughter of a man who was at the end of his rope. A maniacal laugh.

"To Gertie's friends!" Kate shouted, and finished her drink. Her head was fuzzy, her words beginning to slur. She'd had more to drink than Alex, but by God she was going to match him drink for drink. If this took his mind away from the tragedy that their life had become, then Kate would drink till the sun came up.

Another bottle of whiskey later, Kate was passed out on the sofa, with Alex lying across the sofa table.

Six in the morning came bright and early. Kate woke with a neck so stiff, she could swear she'd spent the night in a vise. Alex wasn't willing to move. He swore his skull had been crushed.

Though they'd both had too much to drink and were suffering hangovers from hell, they'd needed the respite. Now what they needed was coffee. And aspirin. And hot showers.

"I'll make ya a bet," Alex mumbled.

"Yeah? What?" Kate whispered. She was certain her head was surely about to explode.

"If you can make us a pot of coffee, I'll turn the shower on."

Kate smiled. "Ouch! That hurt."

"What?"

"Everything. Okay. You do the shower. I'll do the coffee."

Alex continued to lie across the sofa table.

"Go, before I knock you over."

"You're not big enough!" Alex teased.

"Wanna bet?"

"No, I am not a betting man. Or a drinking man. Oh, hell. Why'd you have to turn the lights on?"

"So I could see to make the coffee, smartass. Now get to the shower. I'll join you in a few minutes."

"Okay, but I don't think I'm up for . . . for getting it up. Too smashed last night."

"That makes two of us. Now get!"

Kate forced her way into the kitchen. Each

step felt like a trombone was playing in her head. She poured water into the coffee-maker, scooped in the coffee, and pushed the Start button. She waited for the coffee to perk, then stuck her cup below the drip so she could have the first cup. She hated coffee. How people drank the stuff, she hadn't a clue. But it was the one thing that could reduce the pounding in her brain to that of a soft flute. And aspirin. She couldn't forget that. She sipped her coffee, then poured Alex a cup. She went to the bathroom, where Alex was lying on the floor in the shower. The water sprayed across his nude body. Thoughts of that wild sex they'd never managed to have last night came to mind. No, she couldn't subject her body to the movement required just yet.

"Coffee's on. Get up and sip this."

Kate placed the cup inside the shower. She giggled. "Drink up, before it's cold and full of soap."

Alex gave a halfhearted salute before standing. He took the cup with him. Kate placed her cup next to the sink, then stood in the huge shower with Alex. "This is kinda nice, all these showerheads spewing from every direction. We should do this to our shower when we go home."

Alex slurped down his coffee, then before

she knew what was happening, he turned the water temperature to cold. Icy cold.

"Alex Rocket, you . . . you asshole." Kate jumped out of the shower and wrapped a towel around her.

Alex doubled over with laughter.

Kate beamed. It was good to hear Alex's laughter, because this time it was genuine.

"You'd better hurry and get dressed before I ravage you."

"I kinda like the idea of being ravaged. I'm in no hurry at all, Mr. Rocket." Kate dropped the towel on the floor and stepped into Alex's open arms.

Later, after a second shower and a fresh pot of coffee, Alex got all serious. Kate liked the playful mood so much better. But she knew reality was looming on the horizon. James was scheduled to pick them up at seven.

"Kate, I want you to listen to what I have to say. This might be the last chance I'll get to tell you."

"Alex! After what we just did, you sound like a preacher man." Kate had hoped to lighten the atmosphere once again, but knew it was silly of her. "What do you want to tell me?"

"If things don't go as planned, I want you to know that you'll always be taken care of.

I told you about my backup plan, to put everything in Gertie's name. Well, I did it before the trial started. If the Winters decide to file a civil suit, which James has assured me they will, I don't want them to get their filthy hands on anything I've worked for. This way no matter what, you'll be taken care of. You won't have to work at Chloe's, you won't have to sell your artwork. You can travel the world. Gertie's promised to stay and work at the kennel for as long as you need her. Hell, you couldn't drag her away from those dogs. Kate, are you listening?"

"I am. But, Alex, you're acting as though you've been given a death sentence. James will see to it that you're found innocent. He knows what he's doing. I just hate to hear this, though I understand why you felt you had to go to such extremes. So, it's all legal?"

"Legal and binding. When this blows over, I think I'll leave things in Gertie's name a while longer. Debbie will do anything to get her grubby hands on the almighty dollar."

"Alex, do you think she put Sara up to this in hopes of . . . getting rich from a lawsuit?"

Alex took another sip of coffee. "Anything is possible, but I doubt even she'd stoop that low. I don't think a civil suit was her intention, but you can bet your sweet ass some ambulance-chasing attorney has put the idea in her head by now."

The doorbell terminated further conversation.

"Finish your coffee, I'll get it." Kate went to the front door. "Morning, James. You're just in time for breakfast. I was about to toast bagels."

"Sounds good, thanks."

Kate engrossed herself in the simple task of toasting bagels and spreading cream cheese on them. She filled three glasses with orange juice. "This is it, guys. If I were in my own kitchen, we'd have something a bit more substantial."

"This is fine. It's more than I'd make for myself at the hotel."

They ate in silence. James towered over the small table when he stood. "Hate to break up the party, but if we want to avoid the press, we'd best get an early start."

Kate turned off the coffeemaker and put the cups and plates in a sink filled with hot, soapy dishwater. Then she smeared some lotion on her hands and grabbed her purse. "I'm ready."

They made the trip to the courthouse in silence. Kate prayed for Alex, for James, and, though she would never admit it to anyone, she said a prayer for Sara. Maybe the child would stop this nonsense and tell the truth.

The media was in full throttle. James had to circle the courthouse three times before he found a parking spot that wasn't homesteaded by some form of the media. They slipped inside the courthouse without being discovered. Kate guessed her prayers were being answered. The small ones first.

Alex and James went inside the courtroom ahead of Kate. She lingered at the entrance. A thought had occurred to her on the ride over. She figured it was worth chancing. Right when she was about to give up and go to her seat inside the courtroom, Kate spotted Debbie. Members of the press escorted her up the hallway toward Judge Stowers's courtroom.

When Debbie saw her waiting at the entrance, she stopped. With the media at her heels, Kate knew this wasn't the time to approach Debbie. She walked to her seat and sat down. The room was filling up quickly. The press area was jammed full. The low murmur of voices radiated throughout. Kate tried to make out some of the words, but couldn't. All was quiet as Judge Stowers entered her domain.

The bailiff called his usual, "All rise."

"You may be seated."

The rustling of clothes, briefcases being closed, and the mechanical hum of cameras being turned off filled the room.

Day two of their nightmare had begun.

Again the media were asked to leave the courtroom, and the lights were lowered. For the second day, Sara told her story to the prosecutor.

"Do you recall when Mr. Rocket touched you again?" Wykowski quizzed.

"Yep, I sure do. It was on Easter break. Me and Emily were in North Carolina again. Mommy was on a cruise. Daddy didn't go that time. I remember because he accused her of slutting around, and she got all mad. She didn't even come with Daddy to pick us up."

"Sara, just answer Mr. Wykowski's questions!"

"Go on, Sara, tell me what happened that Easter."

"Okay. We were having an Easter egg hunt. There were some other kids there. Friends of Aunt Kate's. I was running around looking for eggs. I saw Uncle Alex; he was standing behind a tree. I thought he was playing a game or something, so I went over and asked him what he was doing. He grabbed my arm really hard. Then he unzipped his pants. He pulled it out, then put my hand there. It was so gross!"

The screen became all fuzzy. A few seconds passed, then Sara's image filled the screen.

"Is there another incident you'd like to talk about?"

"Yeah, it's the worst. This happened the last time I was at their house in Asheville. Aunt Kate was in her studio. I don't know where Emily was, probably with the dogs. She cares more about the dogs than me. Mommy said this. I was upstairs sleeping when Uncle Alex came into the room. He made me take off my clothes, then forced me to sit on his lap. Oh and he took his clothes off, too. It was nasty. Then he left. I got dressed and went to sleep. Then Aunt Kate came in my room. Somebody had broken into the house and smashed all of her pots. Mommy said it was Uncle Alex's rage. She said it was sexual frustration."

Sara's testimony lasted for another hour. Kate was in shock at the sheer audacity of the child. She certainly didn't act as though she'd been traumatized. Kate recognized Sara's behavior. It was the same way she always acted when she told on Emily for something. She'd acted very pleased with herself. She hoped the jurors picked up on this, but they really didn't know Sara, only what they saw and heard.

Next up was James and his cross-examination. Kate prayed that he broke through whatever psychotic shield Sara had erected around herself.

"Let's take a ten-minute recess," Judge Stowers ordered.

Kate and Alex stayed inside the courtroom while James went for coffee. The media lurked around every corner. James told them to stay put, and they took his advice.

"In a million years, I couldn't make up the sordid lies that child just told. I always knew Debbie had trouble telling the truth, I guess I never realized that Sara is just like her mother."

"If those perverted acts happened to a child of mine, screw going to court. I'd kill the bastard with my bare hands and delight in doing so. The more Sara runs her mouth, the worse her stories get." Kate leaned over the railing, and continued, "I almost wanted to laugh. Isn't that terrible? Your freedom and reputation are in jeopardy, and all I can think about is laughing. It's all so unbelievable. I bit the sides of my mouth to keep from cackling out loud. I remember the day my studio was broken into. That's the day the Taylors came for their pup. She has to know this, Alex. Surely she knows I will tell what really happened that day."

"She's a sick child. I would guess she's a sociopath. She doesn't seem to show any outward signs of real emotion. This is just another day to Sara. She's getting the attention she craves and doesn't give a damn at whose expense."

"I remember Don talking about her and how she'd been acting. I wonder if he questions her truthfulness?" Kate asked Alex.

"If he did, surely he would've put a stop to this goddamn circus act. No, he believes her, Kate. She's his daughter."

James entered the courtroom, carrying a cardboard tray of coffee. "Drink fast, we've only got a few more minutes."

Kate sipped the nasty liquid, wishing all the while for tea.

"My cross won't be near as long as Wykowski's, so we should have the opportunity to question the state's next witness before the end of the day. Sara's medical doctor. I think we'll learn a lot of nothing." James smiled at Alex and Kate.

Judge Stowers went through her routine. When the lights were lowered, Kate leaned forward in her chair. She didn't want to miss one word of Sara's cross.

"Sara, I am going to ask you a few questions, the same as Mr. Wykowski. I want you to think before you answer. Let's try and leave your mother and her thoughts and actions out of your testimony. Think you can do this?" James coaxed.

"Of course. Do you think I'm stupid, too?"

"Actually, Sara, I think you're a very intelligent young lady, smart beyond your years. Now, let's see if we can get to the bottom of this. Remember, I'm in charge, and I am asking the questions. Is that understood?"

Sara rolled her eyes. "Yeah, whatever."

James wasn't treating her like a two-year-old. *Good for him,* Kate thought. Maybe her true colors would shine brightly for the members of the jury.

"Tell me what you were doing prior to the time Mr. Rocket allegedly came into your room while you were sleeping."

Sara squirmed a bit as though she had to think of an answer. Her responses had been instantaneous when the ADA questioned her.

"I can't remember."

"Okay, do you recall the day of the Easter egg hunt?"

"Yeah."

"Do you remember what you were doing

before you joined the group of children outside to hunt for eggs?"

"Why would I remember something that stupid?"

"You tell me, Sara. You seem to recall with great detail the times your uncle allegedly touched you, or exposed himself to you. I would assume that if you remember so vividly these incidents you say took place, you would remember exactly what you were doing before anything supposedly happened. Do you remember what you were doing before the egg hunt?"

"Nope, I don't!"

"Okay, let me ask you this; when you were eight, you said your uncle sat at the edge of your bed and touched you. You told the court that you were frightened, yet you didn't tell your parents at that time, this being before the alleged threat to your father. Can you think why you didn't tell your parents what you thought was happening to you?"

"I didn't just think it, I knew it. If you'd been through what I've been through, you wouldn't remember every last detail either! I am tired of this. I want to go home. I hate you, and I hate Uncle Alex! He has ruined my life!"

The recording went fuzzy. The judge asked the bailiff to turn the lights back on.

Surely there was more. Kate didn't see or hear anything in James's cross that was at all damaging. Maybe Sara's smart comments, but the jury might attribute that to her current mental state. *Please, God, tell me there is something more, something that will save Alex.*

"Is the state ready to call its next witness?" Judge Stowers asked.

That was it! Kate wanted to reach across the banister, grab James, tell him he couldn't do this to them. He was Alex's only chance. As far as Kate was concerned, he'd blown whatever chance Alex might have had. There wasn't one thing in his cross-examination of Sara that favored Alex. If there was something she'd missed, then she would consider herself dense.

"Bailiff, you may allow the spectators back in the courtroom."

When the press and others not directly involved in the proceedings returned, the ADA announced, "The state calls Dr. Edward Smythe."

Dr. Smythe practically floated to the witness stand. His welcome smile lit up the dull courtroom. Warm brown eyes, he smiled at the members of the jury. Kate saw a few of them smile back. So much for the evil doctor she'd been prepared to dislike.

Lyle Wykowski wore the same suit he'd worn the day before. His hair appeared clean. There seemed to be something edgy about him today. Kate observed him as he scrolled through a sheaf of neatly stacked files. Gone was the clumsy oaf from the arraignment.

"Dr. Smythe, how long have you been treating the child in question?"

"Two years." He looked directly at the jurors. He'd done this before.

"Can you give the court an approximate number of times you've seen the child in question."

The doctor examined his notes. "I believe she's been in the office six times. The last visit was almost two weeks ago."

"Tell us about these visits," Wykowski encouraged.

"They were the usual normal childhood visits. Once I treated her for a sinus infection." He continued to skim his notes. "She received a flu shot. Once her stomach was giving her problems. And the last visit, I examined her vaginally."

"Why would a child who is not sexually active need an examination of that kind?"

The doctor drew in a deep breath, looked almost apologetic. "The mother requested I do this. She was suspicious. She thought the child might have been sexually abused."

A hush cloaked the courtroom. Pens and pencils could be heard scribbling across paper. The media was soaking up Dr. Smythe's testimony like a sponge in a lake.

"What did you find during your exam?"

"I found the hymen no longer intact. Some old scarring, possibly where an object was forced inside the vaginal cavity. The area was slightly swollen. The child was very tender during the exam."

Pencils whizzed across tablets, colored pencils in the hands of professionals hurried to capture the images of the twelve faces in the jury box.

"I have no further questions of this witness, Your Honor."

"Mr. Conroy, you may cross-examine."

James hurried to the witness stand. He paced back and forth before questioning the doctor.

"Dr. Smythe, is it possible that the injuries to the child's vaginal area could have been self-inflicted with any number of objects?"

He thought before he gave his answer. "I suppose anything is possible."

"So you agree when I ask you if the old scarring and the recent trauma to the child might have been self-inflicted?"

"Yes."

"No further questions." James sat down while the witness was excused.

Kate's heart flip-flopped. Maybe there was hope after all. James knew what he was doing; she had to trust in him. She smiled at Alex when he turned to look at her. She could feel the eyes of everyone in the courtroom on them. Let them look. They were looking at an innocent man.

"The state wishes to redirect."

"Dr. Smythe, could the trauma to the child's vaginal area have resulted from forced sexual relations?"

"Yes, it could."

"No further questions."

Kate's heart plummeted. She should have expected this. Lyle Wykowski wasn't the half-assed attorney he'd originally appeared. Not by a long shot.

CHAPTER 18

After four days of testimony, both the defense and the prosecution gave their closing arguments. James hadn't scored any more points with the jury as far as Kate could tell. They spent the morning listening to Judge Stowers instruct the jury. Now the jurors were deliberating.

James continued to assure them that the twelve people in the box were good, honest, intelligent people. He was sure they saw through Sara's lies. They'd been deliberating for two hours when the judge informed those who waited inside the courtroom that the jurors were taking a lunch break. She suggested they should do the same.

Kate's hands shook each time she brushed a strand of hair behind her ear. She wanted to go back to the house and wait for the verdict, but Alex wanted to stay. He said the sooner this was over, the better. They would both pack and drive back to Asheville first thing in the morning.

"Let's grab a sandwich in the cafeteria," Kate suggested to Alex.

"You're ready to face the media?"

"I don't care what they say, report, or write anymore. I want to have lunch with my husband, and, by gosh, that's what we're going to do." Kate picked up her purse and headed toward the exit. She knew Alex would follow her.

Ten minutes later, they both had corned beef on rye, with hot mustard and big, juicy dill pickles. Kate was starving. She hadn't been this hungry in days. She devoured her sandwich and was about to ask Alex for a bite of his when James found them.

"They're back. They've reached a verdict."

Kate looked at Alex. They'd only deliberated a little more than three hours. She wasn't sure if this was good or bad.

Alex stood, rubbed his palms across his thighs to brush the crumbs away. "What are we waiting for?"

"Alex, wait." She needed a minute to . . . to look at him. She wanted to see every hair on his head, the smile lines surrounding his eyes. She'd never forget Alex. Hell, she was being silly and morbid. She took his hand in hers. Closing her eyes, she looked at the marbled gray linoleum. Alex did the same.

After she'd finished her silent prayer, she spoke. "Let's get this over with, Alex, so I can take you home."

The three walked back to the courtroom without saying a word. There'd be time for that later, when this was over with. Kate would take James to dinner. Hell, she and Alex would spend the rest of the night toasting their success. Yes, they would be fine — Kate felt it in her bones.

The courtroom was packed to the limit. Newspaper reporters had handheld recorders. Court TV had three reporters waiting outside and one in the courtroom. The local news network anchors waited patiently with their cameramen ready to roll.

The jury waited for the judge to be seated. After she adjusted her flowing robe, she put on her half-moon reading glasses. After she signed a few papers, she looked out at the throng of people in her courtroom.

"Before we announce the verdict I want to make myself perfectly clear. I will not tolerate comments of any kind. I will not tolerate any hand clapping, floor stomping, or any type of unruly behavior. For those who feel they will not be able to contain themselves once the verdict is read, now is your opportunity to excuse yourselves."

Judge Stowers paused for a full minute

before she went on, "Since all here are in agreement with the rules of my courtroom, then let's proceed. Has the jury reached a verdict?"

The jury foreman stood. "Yes, we have, Your Honor."

"Please hand it to the bailiff."

The foreman gave a small slip of paper to the bailiff. The bailiff read the verdict silently, then gave the paper to the judge. After she read it, she gave it to her clerk, whose job it was to read the verdict for the record and for the accused.

"Will the defendant please rise," Judge Stowers said. "The clerk will now read the verdict."

"The state of Florida versus Alex John Rocket. Case number 112159. You have been charged with six degrees of sexual battery against a minor. Count one, lewd and lascivious behavior. We find the defendant Alex John Rocket guilty as charged. Count two —"

Kate grabbed the rail in front of her for support. They'd found Alex guilty! This was a mistake. She looked at James. He'd lowered his head, afraid to look them in the eye. The clerk continued to read the verdict. Six counts of sexual battery against a minor.

Guilty.

Guilty.

Guilty.

The good, honest intelligent people of Collier County found Alex guilty on all six counts.

The courtroom exploded with noise. Judge Stowers banged her gavel. "Order, please!"

The noise stopped.

"Alex John Rocket, do you have anything you would like to say to the court before I pronounce your sentence?"

Kate saw Alex's hands. They were trembling so, she worried he might faint. She might faint. This was a nightmare. Guilty. On all six counts.

Oh no!

"What?" Kate shouted.

"Order! Ma'am, you'll have to leave my courtroom if I hear another outburst like that! Order!" She banged the gavel hard, three times.

Kate looked to James. He hadn't told them sentencing would be pronounced at the time of the verdict! The son of a bitch! He knew all along and hadn't told them. Kate had never felt such rage in her life. She wanted to kill James, she wanted to kill the goddamn judge, but more than anything, she wanted to suck the life from Sara

Winter. She wanted to watch the little bitch beg and plead for her life!

Alex was guilty! No! Sobs racked her body. James turned around and motioned for her to be quiet.

"Drop dead, you inept SOB! You lied to us! I'll see you disbarred if it's the last thing I do!"

"Bailiff, remove this woman from my courtroom immediately!"

"Your Honor, please. This is my client's wife. She is understandably upset. I beg of the court, please let her remain. There won't be another outburst from her."

"Mrs. Rocket, can you remain silent?"

Kate nodded. She'd agree to whatever they asked as long as she could remain at Alex's side. She wasn't the least bit sorry for her outburst. She could not wait to get James Conroy out of the courthouse. He'd be sorry he ever laid eyes on her. She'd tell Gertie's brother what a loser he was. She'd make it her life's goal to ruin him.

When the courtroom settled down, Judge Stowers spoke. "Mr. Rocket, once again" — she looked directly at Kate — "is there anything you would like to say before your sentence is pronounced?"

Kate's heart broke into a million little pieces as she watched her husband stand before the court to accept a punishment for a crime he wouldn't commit if his life depended on it. Kate had always believed in goodness, righteousness, and honesty. Right then and there, everything she'd spent her entire life believing and supporting was revealed as nothing but a lie. All lies. She would never trust again. Never.

"I am not guilty of the crimes I am charged with." Alex turned away from the judge, searching for the Winter family. He saw Debbie and Don seated in the back of the courtroom with big smiles plastered across their faces. "Don, we were friends most of our lives. You know me, or I thought you did. The things your daughter accused me of are atrocious, perverted, and vile. I can only pray that she is able to live with herself as she ages and realizes how her lies have hurt me and my family." He turned around to face the judge. "That's all, Your Honor."

"Mr. Rocket, the crimes you've been found guilty of are horrendous. The state of Florida allows for a set of guidelines to be followed when sentencing. It's at my discretion to sentence you to the maximum or the minimum required by the state. I know you have no criminal history, you've never even received a traffic violation. You're an upstanding citizen in the community where you live. I've read affidavits of more than one hundred people. None of them were negative in any way. However, I must also take the child into consideration. These crimes you've committed upon her will follow her for the rest of her life. She will never again live as a carefree young girl because of you. When you chose to commit these horrendous acts upon this child, not only did you throw your future away, you threw that child's future away as surely as if you took her last breath from her. I have no sympathy for men like you, Mr. Rocket, therefore I feel I must impose the maximum sentence on you. Six felony counts of sexual battery against a minor, for this offense I sentence you to the maximum time of twenty years for each crime. Each sentence will run consecutively. For the record, Alex John Rocket has received one hundred twenty years, the maximum allowed by the state of Florida. There will be no possibility of parole for twenty years." Judge Stowers banged her gavel one last time before sweeping out of the courtroom.

Two sheriff's deputies surrounded Alex. James stepped aside to allow them access. They pulled Alex's hands behind his back and handcuffed him. This was far worse than the two deputies who had come to Asheville to take him to Florida. Then Kate had had hope; now she had nothing.

"It'll be okay, Kate. James, tell her it's going to be okay. I'll call you." Those were Alex's last words as he was taken away to jail. The reporters' cameras clicked like tap shoes as Alex was carted away. This vision of Alex would burn into her brain forever. Till her death, she would retain this image of her husband's last days as a free man.

Now she didn't know what to do. She had nowhere to go, no one to lean on. Just herself. She fled the courtroom, not wanting to give that sorry excuse for an attorney an opportunity to fill her head with more lies. She'd hire another attorney. She'd get Roy Black. He was in Florida. A few year's back he'd defended William Kennedy Smith on rape charges, and his client was found innocent. Yes, that's what she would do. Tomorrow. She would do whatever she had to in order to get Alex out of jail.

Outside Kate realized she didn't have her rental car, since they'd ridden to court with James.

She scanned the area in search of a pay phone. They always had taxi numbers scratched in the glass. She walked a block before she spied a phone booth. Since cell phones were becoming all the rage, phone booths were few and far between.

She dialed the number etched into the glass. Ten minutes later she was inside a Lincoln Town Car with the air conditioner set to blizzard. "Where to?"

Kate recited the address, then leaned against the cool leather seat. Now that she was out of sight of the media, she let the tears she'd reined in flow freely.

"You okay, lady?" the driver asked.

She wiped her tears with the back of her hand. "Yes, just a bad day, thanks."

"I have 'em all the time. Those snowbirds. When they arrive the traffic goes from bad to worse. I wish they'd stay up north, I tell ya."

Before Kate replied, they were turning onto Hibiscus Lane. *Thank God.*

She took a twenty-dollar bill out of her wallet. "Thank you. Keep the change."

"Anytime."

Kate plopped down on the leather sofa in the great room. She knew she was in a state bordering on shock. One hundred and twenty years. It was barbaric. She would get in touch with Roy Black first thing in the morning. For now, she had to call the jail and find out when she could see Alex. She would be brave for him. Once they had a new attorney, Alex would come home where he belonged.

She found the telephone book in a drawer beside the kitchen sink. She dialed the number. It rang twenty-three times before someone answered. She wondered what the hell she'd do if this were an emergency.

"Collier County Sheriff's Department, how may I direct your call?" the automated-sounding voice asked.

"What are the visiting hours at the jail?"

"Inmate's name?"

God, Alex was an inmate now in every sense of the word.

"Alex Rocket."

"Oh, yeah, the kiddie molester. Hang on."

Kate wanted to strangle the girl with the telephone cord.

"He ain't allowed any visitors."

"What? That can't be right."

"Says he's to be processed."

"What does that mean?"

"Didn't your lawyer explain the routine?"

Here we go again. "No, he did not. Why don't you give it a shot?"

"Sure. But you can't hold it against me if I ain't exactly on the money."

"Of course not," Kate said flatly.

"First they'll send him to a reception center. I would guess he'd go to Central

Florida Reception Center in Orlando. Once they get an opening at his designated place of imprisonment, then he'll be allowed visitors. Usually takes a few months to go through the process."

"Is this customary?" Kate asked, knowing she'd be lucky to get an intelligent answer.

"Depends on the case. Your lawyer shoulda explained this to you, Mrs. Rocket."

"Yes, thank you." Kate hung up the phone. When she'd met James for the first time, something hadn't felt right about him. She'd had doubts. Now she wished she had listened to her gut instinct. It hadn't failed her yet, but she'd failed herself by not listening. More than anything, she had failed Alex.

CHAPTER 19

Roy Black explained over the telephone all the reasons he couldn't take Alex's case. He recommended another attorney in Naples, Coleman Fitzpatrick. Kate clicked with him immediately. He assured her he would arrange for a visit with Alex, then he wanted her to relax. He said she should've known beforehand what would happen if Alex was convicted, telling her it was always a possibility. She felt as though she could trust him.

While waiting for Coleman to arrange a visit, Kate occupied herself with cleaning the house she'd lived in for the past few weeks.

She scrubbed the kitchen counters, cleaning out the refrigerator and freezer. Then she polished all the appliances, including the toaster. From there she stripped the sheets off the bed she'd slept in and tossed them into the washing machine. She swept and mopped the tile floors and vacuumed the rest of the house. When she attacked both bathrooms, she scoured shower tiles that didn't need it and tubs that hadn't even been used. After she finished, she took a long soak in the Jacuzzi tub she'd just cleaned.

She knew she needed to call Gertie before she heard the verdict on television, but she'd put it off. Saying this aloud would only make the situation more real. Thank God Alex had the good sense to arrange their finances in such a way that she needn't worry. Gertie would take care of everything. The dogs were in the best of hands, so Kate could concentrate on helping Alex get a new trial, getting him released. She didn't know what to expect at this point. She sure as hell wouldn't sit idly by and allow Coleman Fitzpatrick to make any decisions without consulting her first. She would send a letter to the American Bar Association. James had duped them into believing Alex wouldn't go to prison. Kate sure as hell wasn't going to let another life-altering mistake slip past her.

The phone rang, and she jumped out of the tub to answer it.

"Can you be at the jail in an hour?" Coleman asked.

"Of course."

"I'll meet you in the main building. I'll be wearing beige slacks and a blue polo shirt."

Kate was glad he'd thought to tell her what he'd be wearing. She wouldn't have been able to pick him out of a crowd of three since they'd only spoken on the phone.

"I'll find you. Thanks, Mr. Fitzpatrick."

"Sure thing, Mrs. Rocket."

"Coleman?"

"Yes?"

"Call me Kate." For the first time in weeks, Kate felt like smiling. She hung up the phone and dressed as quickly as possible in navy pants and a red and white striped blouse. She looked like a sailor. She didn't care. All that mattered was Alex. She was going to see him. He'd meet Coleman, and they'd simply have to start from square one.

When Kate arrived at the jail, reporters were still scattered about the parking lot. Court TV's crew had set up a temporary soundstage on the front lawn. She wished she had remembered to wear sunglasses or a hat. Her auburn hair stood out like a black eye. She swerved into the left lane, driving away from the jailhouse.

She parked the Mercedes three blocks away in a Publix parking lot. She'd walk the rest of the way.

Fifteen minutes later she slipped inside the building without being noticed. She gave herself a mental pat on the back.

True to his word, Coleman Fitzpatrick waited discreetly in the main lobby.

Kate hurried over to him. "I can't thank you enough for what you've done."

Coleman shook her hand. "All in a day's work, Kate. Now let's get out of this lobby before those vultures figure out you're here. I've already made the necessary preparations for your visit with your husband. You'll have to show your identification and go through a screening. This is normal and shouldn't take more than five minutes. Follow me."

Kate was impressed. He'd accomplished more in a few hours than James would have in a week. She followed him through a maze of institutional hallways. They rounded a corner and were stopped by a deputy. He ran a wand over them before allowing them to continue down the next hall. They walked a few feet and were greeted by another deputy seated behind a glass wall. "I'll need to see your IDs, please."

Kate removed her license from her wallet and slid it beneath the glass on a metal tray. A visitor's badge was returned to her along with her license. Coleman did the same. A loud click opened a door to the side of the glassed-in office area. Another deputy led them down more hallways. He took a ring of keys from his belt, inserted one into a lock. He opened a heavy steel door. Seated in what looked like a cage was Alex. Glass and wire separated them. Alex sat on a small stool. A countertop was in front of him and an old-style telephone was placed on the wall to his left. Tears clouded her vision. Alex looked terrible. He wore the orange jumpsuit and black flip-flops.

Kate sat across from him and picked up the telephone to her right. "Oh Alex!" She splayed her left hand on the glass. He followed suit.

"This is bad, huh?" Alex joked.

"Yeah. I am shocked, Alex. I want to shoot James Conroy good and dead."

"Mrs. Rocket, careful what you say. Your every word is being monitored," Coleman said as he stood behind her.

"Sorry. I can't help it. Has he been here since the verdict?"

Alex shook his head, then remembered to speak into the phone. "No, he hasn't. I'm sure he has some paperwork to take care of. Remember, Kate, he doesn't have his staff here to assist him. He's working out of his car and a hotel room. I wouldn't be too hard on the guy."

Leave it to Alex to see the positive side of a tragic situation.

"I don't care if he's working out of the White House with the president to assist him! He didn't provide an adequate defense. He never did anything like an effective cross-examination on Sara. He knew that she trashed the studio, that on that same day she told Emily and you that she didn't want to go when you went to meet the Taylors. You were with Emily or the Taylors the entire time before the police arrived to investigate the destruction of my work in the studio. So there was no way in hell that you could have molested her when she says you did. And that's the most recent incident she described, the one she was most likely to remember the details of, so she couldn't have been molested when she says she was. How could we not have noticed that he wasn't providing you with anything like an adequate defense? Do you think he was in cahoots with the Winters or something? He should be disbarred. If I have anything to say about it, he will. The bastard."

"Getting pissed at this stage isn't going to help, Kate. You know that. I'm as shocked as you are, I was sure I'd be helping you pack up. I never imagined it would come down to this."

Alex had aged ten years since the verdict. Bags sagged beneath his eyes, and Kate swore she saw a dozen new creases around the corners of his eyes.

"I've hired a new attorney, Coleman Fitzpatrick." Kate motioned for Coleman to step up and take the phone she held out. He stooped to Alex's eye level.

"I can't say I'm glad to meet you, but I guess I am. What do you think the chances are of cleaning up this mess?" Alex asked.

"We're going to take one step at a time. First, I want you to understand that I won't make you any promises on the outcome. I might be able to get a new trial, I might not. I might try to reduce the sentence, but whatever I do, I won't lie to you or lead you to believe there is hope when there isn't. Right now, the best I could do was finagle this visit. I'll need a few days to get the transcript of your trial. I doubt it's even been typed up yet. From there, I'll see what choices we have. For now, I'm afraid you're going to have to go through the system as ordered. It's not going to be easy, but anything worthwhile never is. Roy Black called and told me everything he knew. What I'll want to do at some point is go over every statement you made to the authorities, everything the Winter girl said. This might take some time, but that's the downside of worthwhile."

Resigned, Alex said, "I appreciate your honesty. So I'm gonna be here a while."

"I'm afraid so. You're going to Orlando's reception center. I checked. You won't be allowed visits, except from me. I can communicate for Mrs. Rocket if needed. She can write letters to you, and you'll be allowed to answer them. That's where we are now. I'll let you have a few more minutes with your wife. Visit's about timed out." Coleman gave the phone back to Kate.

"We'll get through this, Alex. I want you to focus on you, don't let this temporary setback worry you. I can take care of myself. I have Gertie if I need her. She'll come and stay with me if I ask her to. I'm going to look for an apartment here in Florida. I'll go to Orlando; that way we'll be close to one another."

"Kate, I don't want you moving to Florida, I don't care how temporary the situation. You go back to Asheville where you belong. You can write letters just as easily from there as you could in Florida. I mean this, Kate. I don't want you living here alone. Hell, I don't want you in the same state as the Winters. Who knows what they might do next? I won't take no for an answer on this. I hate to sound like a bastard, but I insist you go home."

"Alex! I don't want to leave you here," Kate cried. "This isn't how it's supposed to be!"

"I don't want to be here either, trust me. But this is what we've been dealt. We have to take the punches as they come. Coleman seems to know the ropes. If I can hang tight for a few months, you can, too. Please, Kate, do this for me?"

She nodded. How could she not? It was her Alex locked behind these walls, not her. If he wanted her to go home, she would go even though it broke her heart. She felt like she was leaving him to rot in jail. Sara and her parents should be there. *They* lied, *they* broke the law. Someday, Kate would exact her revenge. For now, she'd live one day at a time.

"Of course, Alex. I'll do anything you ask. I love you."

Alex splayed his hand on the glass. She matched her palm to his.

"I love you, too. Always, Kate. No matter what happens, remember that."

"I will, Alex. I promise."

Chapter 20

Asheville, North Carolina
Three months later . . .

For the first time since her return home, Kate was excited. She was leaving for Florida later in the day. Alex had been sent to Dade Correctional Center in Florida, close to Miami. She'd reserved a hotel for the upcoming weekend. She would be permitted to see Alex both Saturday and Sunday for a full eight hours each day. Coleman had called her the night before with the good news.

Gertie, ever the trouper, continued to care for the dogs, though she hadn't bred any new pups. She told Kate they'd wait for Alex to come home. Kate agreed, telling her it was something for them to look forward to.

She'd been as outraged as Kate when Kate told her the verdict. They spent a few evenings together drinking away their sorrows, then Gertie went back to her cottage. She didn't leave, except to feed the dogs. Kate spent most of her days writing letters to Alex. She told him everything was fine, when in reality, it wasn't. She'd left Chloe's for good. She hadn't been inside her studio since the day she'd cleaned up after Sara's vandalism. She ate when she could no longer stand the pain in her stomach. She drank at least a bottle of wine daily. She'd let herself go. Her clothes hung on her. Her cheekbones jutted out in sharp angles. She couldn't recall the last time she'd shaved her legs. There was no reason to. Alex was gone, and she was miserable. She never let on in her letters, but now she would see him face-to-face. He'd know she wasn't happy. She'd promise him that she'd be happy when he came home. Until then, she was only existing.

She asked Gertie to come along. A few weeks ago, she'd hired a young girl to help out at the kennels. Kate was sure Lauren would be fine if left alone for a weekend. Gertie wouldn't hear of it. She'd insisted Kate go alone, telling her that she and Alex needed as much time by themselves as possible. Kate silently agreed, but hadn't wanted to hurt Gertie's feelings by not including her in the invitation.

She'd hired a limo to drive her to the airport. She was flying commercial. She didn't think she could bear to see the looks of pity on the faces of Joe and his flight crew. Later, when Alex came home, she'd rent the private plane. Until then, she didn't want to explain anything to anyone.

Kate heard the limo as it pulled into the driveway. She turned off the lights in the house, set the alarm that Alex insisted she have installed since he wasn't there, and took her luggage outside.

The driver put her bag in the trunk, opened the rear passenger door, and waited until she was buckled in before he closed it. Impersonal and efficient. Just what she wanted. No small talk or polite conversation. Get her to the airport in time for her flight to Miami, and she would be a happy camper.

Kate arrived at the airport in time to catch her flight. She slept, knowing she needed to do whatever she could to lessen the dark circles beneath her eyes. Three hours later she was at the Hertz kiosk picking up her car. With instructions to the hotel in her purse, she found the Ford Taurus in the assigned parking slot. She drove to her hotel.

After a shower, Kate took a long nap. She dreamed of Alex. Sara was living with her while Alex served his term. Sara kept telling Kate that she'd lied because her mother asked her to. She said she was sorry. She begged Kate to let her go to the authorities with the truth. Kate kept telling her what was done was done.

What was done was done. What was done was done.

She bolted upright in the bed. It was pitch-black in the room. For a moment Kate forgot where she was. Then she remembered. She was going to see Alex in the morning. She'd had a nightmare, that was all. Tossing the covers aside, she went to the minibar. Two small bottles of Chablis later, she went back to sleep. This time there were no dark dreams. Just pure, deep sleep.

At six in the morning, Kate woke refreshed, without the slightest bit of a headache. Wine usually gave her a nasty hangover, but she hadn't drunk all that much. She showered, then shaved her legs for the second time in twenty-four hours. She blew her hair dry and applied cover stick to hide the dark circles. Mascara, blush, and a swipe of coral lipstick. Coleman told her there was a strict dress code when visiting. If she didn't adhere to it, she would be turned away for the day. Not wanting to take any chances, she'd packed a pair of camel-colored slacks that were too hot for Florida weather and a long-sleeved, plain white blouse. Beneath it she wore a cream-colored T-shirt so you couldn't see any skin or bra lines. She'd sweat, but she'd do whatever she had to in order to see her husband.

She found her way to the Dade Correctional Facility without too much hassle. Once she parked in the designated visitor area, she had to walk about half a block to the entrance. She supposed this was for safety purposes; an inmate would have a distance to travel if he decided to leave through the main entrance. She couldn't imagine someone ever being that brave, but then again, she never imagined she'd be visiting Alex in a prison.

She'd been issued a number once her name was placed on Alex's visitation list. She brought the number with her. She entered what looked like a waiting room. There were dozens of other people. Young, old, male, female. Every race you could imagine. Small children raced around chasing one another. She would hate to think of a child of her own having to visit a place of this kind, but that wasn't going to happen. Some of the younger women wore skirts so short and blouses so tight, Kate thought it a miracle they could move. If the dress code was as strict as Coleman said, then these gals were in for a surprise.

A few minutes later Kate heard her name called. She went to the officer at the visitors' desk. She showed her ID, and they searched her purse. Once she went through this, she was sent to another room, where there weren't that many people waiting. This was the clearance room. Kate supposed they were checking to make sure she was a true, bona-fide registered visitor. Another few minutes passed. She was escorted into an area that looked like a ten-by-twelve steel room. She was told she would have to undergo a body search, but she hadn't realized to what extent. The female guard was brisk and efficient as she felt Kate's legs, up and down. She was frisked, then told to walk through a scanner. When no alarms sounded, Kate was allowed to go to the visitation center. This reminded her of the cafeteria in high school. A large square room with long tables and metal folding chairs. Thank God there would be no glass to separate them. In her instructions she learned she was allowed to hug Alex upon entering. Afterward, however, there would be no touching allowed. If a guard saw any, she would be asked to leave, and her next visitation would be canceled. It was almost like she was a prisoner. Kate figured they housed some hard-core killers. Coleman told her to be careful and obey the rules no matter how she felt about them. After going through the process, she knew she wouldn't have any troubles. She would follow the rules to the letter. She would take no chances if violating the rules meant losing what little time she had with Alex.

She sat at the end of one of the long tables. About when she started to wonder where her husband was, she saw him enter the room. His hands and legs were shackled. A guard removed the metal bondage, and Alex walked over to the table.

Kate felt tears fill her eyes. She didn't care. She was with Alex. He walked to her side of the table and took her in his arms. Kate clung to him. She didn't want to let go, but after what seemed too short a time, Alex backed out of their embrace. He'd lost at least thirty pounds. He was too thin. His skin looked yellow, like he was jaundiced.

"I've missed you so much," Kate whispered through her tears.

"Let's sit down. The guards are watching us." Alex's first words to Kate in three months.

She did as instructed. "God, Alex this place is terrible! I can't imagine how you get through each day." When the words were out, Kate wished she could have taken them back. It was terrible of her to say that to Alex. He needed her support, not her criticism.

"I'm sorry, I shouldn't have said that."

He smiled at her, and all was right with the world. "It was my first reaction, too. Surprisingly, it's not as bad as it looks. It's not home, but the guards are decent. The food leaves a lot to be desired, but I didn't expect I'd be eating Chloe-quality food. I'm handling it, Kate, that's about all I can say."

"I'm glad. Not that I'm glad you're here, just that you're able to handle the place. I guess it could be worse." She didn't see how, but didn't dare say the words aloud.

"Have you spoken with Coleman? Anything new?" Alex asked.

"He called to tell me about the visitation. There was no news about your case, Alex. I am so sorry. He only recently got a copy of the trial transcript. What should've taken a few days stretched into a few months. He told me as soon as he had something worth reporting, he'd come and tell you himself. I trust him Alex. It's the system that I don't trust. You were railroaded, bamboozled, and screwed any way you look at it."

"True. But it isn't the system that screwed

me, Kate. It was Sara and her parents. If they had a shred of decency in them, they would've come to me in private. They could've told me what Sara was saying. I think we could have worked this out. If I'd had a chance to talk to the kid, I think she would've told the truth. I'm beginning to believe it was just like you said. I think Debbie encouraged her. Once Sara saw the attention she was getting, I think she went off the deep end. I've had a lot of time to think about this. I really believe they're in it for the civil suit. Has that been filed, or do you know?"

"Coleman said it hadn't, but that wasn't unusual. It may take a few more months, for whatever reason. They can't touch us; remember, Gertie has control of everything."

"How is that old gal? I thought she might come along. I had her name put on my visitation list."

"I asked her to come. She insisted she had to stay with the dogs. She's hired a helper. Her name is Lauren. She looks like a fashion model. Lean, leggy, and blond. Says she wants to be a veterinarian. She's really good with the dogs, and Gertie can't stop talking about her, so I think she'll be around for a while. Gertie said to tell you she's not breeding any of the pups until you're home."

"You tell Gertie I said to get her ass in gear and start breeding the dogs. I've still got families on a waiting list. We don't know when or if I'm coming home anytime in the near future. Life goes on, Kate. I don't want you or Gertie to wait for me. Tell her to start breeding or I will kick her old ass if I ever do get out of this place. Your parents would flip over in their graves if the kennel were to close down. I made a promise to them, and I'll keep it, Kate."

"She just wanted to wait for you. She knows there's a waiting list. I'll tell her to hop to it. Now, tell me how you pass your days while you're here." Kate wanted to talk about something else. She couldn't bear to think of the kennels without Alex.

"They're not very exciting, but it's not as bad as the holding center in Orlando. At least here, we have a bit more freedom. There's a library. I've read every John Grisham book there is. I'm working on another Stephen King now. I never realized just how brilliant he is. You should read his books, the guy has one hell of an imagination. When I'm not reading, I work out. They have a gym. It's not state-of-the-art, but it's better than nothing. A few of the guys here are actually quite decent. They've been screwed, too. It makes me wonder about the justice system, Kate. I realize that Sara was behind all this, but what does it say when a system allows innocent men to rot in jail because they just happened to be the unlucky bastards who were actually innocent, but in the wrong place at the wrong time? Brad and Ron, two of my cellmates, were charged with possession. Neither of them ever took drugs in his life. Then all of a sudden Brad gets divorced, his wife starts dating a cop. Brad thinks the cop is abusing their seven-year-old daughter. Next thing he knows, he's charged with possession of cocaine, and, boom, he's in prison. Same thing with Ron, but no wife involved. A business associate screwed him out of a large sum of money. When he filed a suit in small claims court, the dude lost the case. Again Ron was pulled over on a bogus traffic stop. The officer found heroin in his trunk. That arresting officer just so happened to be the brother-in-law of the business associate."

Kate had watched too many episodes of *Law & Order.* All convicts claimed they were innocent. All had been framed or screwed in one way or another. She'd let Alex continue to believe in his cellmates' innocence. He didn't have many friends right now. He needed someone to confide in while he was in prison.

"Then I hope the persons responsible for planting the drugs get caught. If they're police officers, this certainly wouldn't be a good place to wind up."

"You can say that again. Ron told me a few months before I got here a former cop was killed. He didn't say what he was in for. Apparently some of the guys didn't like his attitude, and they killed him. So, no, I would say a cop's as good as dead once he's inside."

Kate was horrified at the ease with which Alex had adjusted to prison. He spoke as if he'd been there for a long time.

God, I have to get him out of here. He's changing already, and I don't like the changes I'm seeing. I'll drive to Naples before heading back to Asheville. Coleman Fitzpatrick and I are going to have a serious discussion.

Chapter 21

Kate knew their time was almost up. She'd had two wonderful days with Alex, but given the thought of leaving him behind, knowing what she was leaving him to, almost made her wish that she could stay with him, even if it meant she'd have to spend her days in prison. She told him this.

"Somehow I don't think that would be in your best interest, Mrs. Rocket. Some of these men in here haven't touched a woman in thirty years. It'd be like feeding you to the sharks. Besides, I need you on the outside. I'll take care of the inside," Alex teased. His mood had lightened considerably.

"I'll do whatever I can to speed things up with Coleman. Promise me you'll take care of yourself. You've lost weight. I worry about you day and night."

Alex laughed. "They don't have the kind of food you make in here. I can get all kinds of candy and chips from the canteen, but I don't really care to. I'm fine, Kate. Really, the place isn't all bad. I'm not saying I like it here enough to call it home, but for now, I can tolerate it. Besides, I really don't have much choice in the matter."

"I know, I just hate to think of you in here, while I'm at home with all the things you can't enjoy. Wine, good food, the dogs. Me." She grinned.

"I'm a simple man, Kate. You know that. I don't need anything more than the air I breathe and you. If I have those two things, I'm happy. I know I have you, and there is air here even though it's stale and smells like sweat. But it's air."

A bell rang, letting the visitors know they had five minutes before it was time to leave.

"You're too good, Alex. I don't know what I'd do if I didn't have you. Life would be so . . . empty. I wouldn't want to go — never mind. I want you to write me every day. I'll make sure Gertie gets busy breeding the dogs. I'd bet my last dollar you'll be home before we can deliver a new litter."

"I hope you're right. There isn't anything I'd like more. Now, it's time to go. I don't want to see tears, or I'll have to sic one of these female guards on you. Some of them like women, so you better watch out."

Kate smiled and managed to keep her tears from spilling over. "I'll write you as soon as I get home. When I leave, I'm going to drive to Naples to see Coleman. I'll catch another flight out of Fort Myers if I have to. I'll say prayers for you, Alex. I love you." Kate stood, barely able to keep from throwing herself in Alex's arms. Suddenly, that long parking lot didn't seem so long. If she could've stuffed Alex inside her purse right then and there, she would have, just to have him home again.

"Be careful, Kate. Why don't you wait and drive over tomorrow. It'll be dark soon. Alligator Alley is no place for a woman alone. Promise me you'll wait until morning?"

She really wanted to leave that night. But if it meant so much to Alex, she'd wait. "I can do that. I'll go back to the hotel and force myself to soak in that deep tub, maybe pick up a Stephen King novel on my way home."

"You better wait till you get home before you start reading his books. He'll scare the pants right off you."

She laughed. "Okay, I'll stick with romance. Maybe I'll get something by that woman who writes about those big families in Texas and Vegas. I've always enjoyed her books."

"Just be careful. I'll worry until I hear from you. Next week I get phone privileges. I'll call you the minute I can. Be safe, Kate."

"I will. You too. I'll write you. I love you, Alex." Kate wanted to cry so much she could feel the tears ready to flood her cheeks, but she would wait until she was outside in the parking lot.

Alex sneaked his hand on top of hers and squeezed. "Me too. Always. Now get out of here." Before she could respond, Alex had turned around and was walking toward the guards. He was the first prisoner to leave the visiting room. Kate knew he wanted to follow the rules, but part of her felt angry that he'd left before their time was up. This was stupid. Alex didn't want to make any waves.

I'm acting like a spoiled brat. Alex knows what he's doing. He's the one in prison, not me.

Kate headed toward the car. Dreading another night in the hotel, Kate thought of driving to Naples anyway, but couldn't bring herself to break the promise she'd made. She would relax in the hotel. She had seen a Super Wal-Mart on her way to the prison. She decided to stop and pick up a few books. Maybe even a bathing suit so she could lounge by the pool. The more she thought about it, the more the idea appealed to her. She would swim, read, and enjoy what was left of the day.

Kate took the cart offered by the elderly gentleman at the entrance. Wal-Mart was packed with families shopping for groceries, clothes, and other necessities. Then there were the hundreds of people who simply wanted to window-shop.

She cruised over to the book section. After perusing the shelves, she decided on three novels by her favorite authors. Even though it was September, Wal-Mart still had a huge supply of fashionable bathing suits. She scoped out several different styles, then settled on a plain black one-piece. At thirty-six, she wasn't getting any younger. She sure as hell wasn't going to burden the folks at the hotel with the sight of her wearing a skimpy bikini. She'd leave the bikini-wearing to the younger crowd.

After she paid for her items, she drove back to the hotel. She checked to see if she'd received any telephone calls. She hadn't. A quick change, then with book in hand and a bottle of cold water, Kate went to the pool area. Because it was Florida, the crowd was huge. People vacationed in the Sunshine State year-round. Kate had to wait for a young woman to rearrange her family's towels and beach toys so she would have a place to sit.

"Thanks," Kate told the harried mother.

"Kids. You need so much stuff just to get out the door. I can't wait till these days are over," the young mother complained.

Kate just smiled. She didn't want to make conversation, and certainly didn't want to be reminded of the troubles kids could cause. She'd had enough for a lifetime. She buried her nose in her book, hoping the woman would take the hint.

The sun dipped low in the sky. She spent two hours at the pool and forgot to apply sunscreen. On her way back to her room, she realized that her skin was the color of strawberries.

Dammit. With my fair skin I know better than to do without sunscreen. Oh well, sunburns I can live with.

After taking a cool shower, she covered herself with aloe gel she had picked up at the gift shop and slipped on a loose cotton T-shirt. The sheets felt refreshingly good to her warm skin as she slid beneath them. She flicked the table lamp on, picked up her novel, and continued to read about the Coleman family in Texas.

Which reminded her of Coleman. She'd called him earlier. He agreed to make time for her, telling her they'd meet outside the office. He told her the name of a restaurant, saying it was quiet and they'd have no interruptions. From there, he'd agreed to drive her to Fort Myers to catch an evening flight home.

Kate's eyes were getting heavy. She turned off the light and placed her book on the bedside table. She was so tired. The stress, the excitement of seeing Alex, then two hours in the sun were all she could stand. Within minutes, she was fast asleep.

The restaurant where Kate met Coleman was perfect. It was nice, without being fussy. The staff was very professional and the atmosphere relaxing. They were seated at a table in the rear of the restaurant, overlooking the Gulf of Mexico. White-tipped waves crashed on the beaches. Southwest Florida was in for one of its infamous thunderstorms. Had this been a different occasion, Kate would have been captivated, watching the storm thrash and move its way across the sky.

Coleman was polite and professional, and a true gentleman. He pulled her chair out for her, took her bag, and placed it on a chair next to her.

"I hope this weather doesn't delay my

flight," Kate said as she watched lightning zigzag across the darkening sky.

"It's barely noon. This'll be long gone before it's time for you to catch your flight. You get used to it, living here," Coleman observed.

"I would imagine it's like anything else, though I must admit, I wouldn't want to live here in the summer. The heat is almost unbearable."

"Yes, that's why I try and leave every chance I get. I have a cabin in the mountains. If my workload is light, I hop in my plane every chance I get."

Kate liked the conversation and found herself very comfortable talking with Coleman. He was a nice guy. *Like Alex,* she thought.

"You said your plane. What do you fly?"

"An Archer. Something I always wanted to do. A few lessons, and I was hooked. I've been flying for fifteen years now. Have never tired of it yet."

Kate saw the passion in his eyes when he spoke about flying. "I always wanted to learn to fly, but there were so many other things I wanted more. I guess I'll cross that off my life list."

"Why?" Coleman asked her.

Kate snickered. "For starters, I don't think

the timing would ever be right. Alex and all. Then there is my cooking classes. The pottery. I still want to try my hand at another set of earthenware."

He knew about the incident in her studio since it figured so prominently in the attempt to get a new trial on the basis of ineffective counsel, but she'd never told him her dream of having her own line of baking dishes.

"What sort of earthenware?"

He opened the door. What could it hurt to tell him? It was now just another dream she'd have to tuck away.

"When Sara destroyed my studio, I'd just finished a line of cookware. I'd worked on it for months and months. I was getting ready for a show in Asheville. I'd hoped to market my own line of bakeware someday." Kate felt silly explaining this to Coleman. He was a professional man. An attorney. He would probably think her dream silly.

"You mean like Martha Stewart?"

Kate laughed. "Something along those lines. Though not quite as grand. It was something I really wanted to do." Kate looked away from Coleman. The intensity of his stare made her uncomfortable.

"Why would you toss your dream out the window? I would think you'd be . . . I don't know. I guess I've always believed that if you have dreams, you should pursue them, no matter what."

"I used to believe all that, too. But that was before Sara ruined our lives. I don't think I'll ever dream again. My only focus now is Alex. I want to see that justice is done, or I'd never be able to live with myself. That's what you're here for."

Was Kate mistaken, or had she actually seen a look of hurt on his face? She had to be. Coleman was Alex's attorney.

"Yes, it is." He sighed. "I do have a few things to discuss. First, I finally got through the trial transcript. All I can say is if there was ever a case of an improper defense, this one is for the books. Though I hate to discredit a colleague, James Conroy didn't even bother with a defense. Oh, he made a few inquiries into the Winters' financial situation, which isn't good. He could have used that as motivation for a civil suit. Without the criminal suit, there wouldn't have been the need for the civil filings. He could have claimed false reporting of a crime. That's a third-degree felony in the state of Florida. There were many other avenues for him to pursue, even apart from the absolute alibi Alex had for the last alleged incident, Kate."

She shook her head. "It's obvious that

James Conroy is a shyster. I just don't understand why he didn't give the case his best efforts. We told him about the sequence of events the last time Sara and Emily stayed with us. Still, he made no effort to try to discredit her testimony. What's with that guy?"

Coleman looked away. The waitress brought their iced teas and took their order.

Kate knew something was bothering the attorney. "Is there something you're not telling me? Because if there is, and you don't, well, then you're no better than James Conroy!" Kate stood, ready to make a hasty exit from the restaurant.

Coleman grabbed her hand. "Wait, there is more, but I don't want to hurt you and Alex."

Kate sat back down. "Tell me what it is. You have no right to keep something from us if it will help Alex."

He nodded, "You're right. I just hate to tell you what I learned. It surprised me."

"I'm listening." Kate urged.

"James Conroy is a very, very distant relative of Don's. I'm not even sure Don was aware of this. Apparently Don's great-grandmother on his father's side was married to a cousin of James's great-grandfather. It's complicated, but maybe family loyalty played a part in his lack of a defense. This is just a guess. I only came across this information a couple of days ago. My investigator is beyond thorough, and she just happens to be into genealogy. With the Internet, she said you could find just about anything if you search hard enough. And she did. If James knew this, he should've recused himself from the case."

Kate couldn't have been more surprised. "This is shocking! Does Alex know?"

"No, I wanted to get your take on this before I said anything to him."

Kate was sorry she'd jumped to conclusions about Coleman. He really was bothered by this new information.

"It changes a lot, doesn't it?"

"Yes and no. Will it get Alex released? Possibly, but not right away," Coleman explained.

The waitress brought their salads and a basket of homemade cranberry-nut muffins. They ate, stopping occasionally to speak of things they deemed unimportant. Kate did learn Coleman had lost his wife to breast cancer five years earlier.

"I'm sorry. It must've been hard for you."

"It was. Suzanne was a strong woman. She fought the disease until she drew her last breath. We were in practice together. We both had a profound love of the law. When she died, I thought about closing my practice. She would've been disappointed if I had, so I took a few months off. I went to the cabin. I had never been there without Suzanne. It was strange. All of her things are still there. I can't bring myself to pack them away. I guess that's stupid after all this time." Coleman lowered his eyes. He busied his hands spreading butter on a muffin. Coleman was a compassionate man who obviously had loved his wife deeply.

"She sounds wonderful. I would have liked her."

"Yes, there wasn't anyone who didn't. And if there were those few who had reservations about her, she'd have them on her side in no time. She was the light of my life."

"Then you were a very lucky man to have loved so deeply." After the words were out of her mouth, Kate wished she could take them back. This talk of love and sorrow hit too close to home.

"Yes, I was. I see the same type of love between you and Alex."

Kate was surprised he would even say this. She liked him more and more. Maybe when this was all over, she and Alex would invite him to North Carolina.

"I'd only been out of college a year when

I met Alex. My parents had died in a terrible crash. I thought I'd never find happiness after their deaths. I was very close to both my parents. Alex knew them before they died. He'd purchased the kennels from them. They wanted to retire, and selling the kennel was such a big decision for them. When they met Alex, they felt like they'd been blessed. He loved animals as much, if not more, than they did. I wish they'd lived long enough to see Alex and me married."

"They would have approved of Alex. He's a decent man, Kate. I can tell these things. I'll do whatever I can to see that he's out of that pit. I promise." Coleman looked at her from across the table. She knew he would keep his promise, too. He was that much like Alex.

"Something tells me that you will do just what you say. I thank you for that, Coleman. I just wish we'd hired you before it went to trial. Maybe if I had, Alex wouldn't even have gone to trial."

"One never knows, Kate. Now" — he looked at the chrome watch on his wrist — "if we want to beat the traffic, we'd better head out. I-75 is a killer this time of year, what with all the tourists. You won't have to rush once you're at the airport."

"Thanks."

Coleman took care of the check, even though Kate had tried to insist. It was a business meeting, after all. She excused herself to the ladies' room. She brushed her hair and put on lip gloss. She had good feelings about Coleman Fitzpatrick. Her gut feeling told her he would get Alex out of that hellhole. And this time, she was going to listen.

CHAPTER 22

Don calculated that he had enough money left in his accounts to cover the mortgage for one more month. He wouldn't pay Emily's and Sara's tuition again this month. Debbie could. She was making all kinds of money selling real estate. What the hell she did with it besides buy clothes, he hadn't a clue. Every day she came home from work and informed him she'd been on a wild shopping spree. She'd bought the girls Louis Vuitton purses last week. She'd paid $1,500 apiece for them. That would have covered their tuition for another month. He hadn't told her of the dire straits they were in financially. If things at work didn't change soon, he'd have to ask his wife for money. He'd never asked her for one red cent. It was going to kill him when he did. She'd never let him live it down either.

His only hope was receiving a substantial amount from the civil suit they'd filed.

Though it had been several months, they had yet to receive any word about the status of their case. Debbie was supposed to take care of that, too. Obviously it was too much to ask. He made a mental note to call their attorney Monday.

Thinking of the civil suit, he thought of Alex. Old son of a bitch. How could he have stooped so low? While Don would admit Sara was a handful, now more then ever, she could never have made up the stories of all the abuse she suffered at the hands of his best friend. She was supposed to be in counseling, but when Don questioned Debbie about it the other day, she told him that Sara was fine. He didn't think so, but she was a woman. She knew about things like this. If she said Sara was okay, then he would assume she was. There was a part of him that had wanted to believe in Alex's innocence. But he couldn't. Never in a million years would a child of his construct a tale so filthy. Sara loved going to Alex and Kate's. She would never have jeopardized her relationship with them. The last trip had been the straw that broke the camel's back, according to Debbie. Sara was so frightened of Alex and what he was doing to her, she'd had anxiety attacks. For once Debbie did what he would have done. She'd sat Sara down and practically forced her to tell her what was bothering her. When Sara started talking about sexual abuse, Debbie said, she was flabbergasted. The two of them talked for days before Debbie let Don in on the topic of their conversations. When she did, he'd had no choice but to call Alex. From there, they'd let the authorities take over. Alex would remain in prison for at least the next twenty years. He deserved to die in jail for all that he'd put Sara through. The civil suit had been the icing on the cake as far as he was concerned. Alex had millions. There could not have been a more perfect time to get his hands on some of that cold hard cash.

The engineering firm he'd worked for was about to file Chapter Eleven. Too many good deals gone bad. He would open his own company as soon as he got his money from the civil suit. All he had to do was hang in there a while longer.

With his finances temporarily settled for the moment, Don had promised the guys from the country club he'd meet them for an afternoon round of golf. Debbie would have to see to it that the girls had something for dinner. For weeks now he'd brought home takeout, chicken from Publix or some crap from Taco Bell. He'd take the girls out for pizza once in a while when they got tired of eating the food he brought home.

What I wouldn't give for a home-cooked meal. Kate can cook like no one else. I would give a hundred bucks for a slice of her pot roast. Screw it, I'll eat at the club. Again.

"Where are you going?" Debbie peeked inside the den.

"To the club. I told the guys I'd play some golf with them."

"Don't you ever stay home on weekends?" Debbie nagged.

"No, not when you're here."

"You're a real prick, you know that?"

"I've been called worse."

"Deservedly so. The girls want to go to the movies tonight. I can't take them. I've got a house to show."

"The girls can go to the movies without me tagging along."

"No way, Jose. I need you to drive them. Emily only has her learner's permit."

"Sorry. No can do." Don delighted in pissing her off. Their marriage was a sham. When Sara reached eighteen, he was out. No questions. He wouldn't spend another minute listening to his wife moan and groan. He'd move to another country to get away from her. *Just five more years, and I'll be on my merry way.* He couldn't help but smile at the thought.

"What's so funny? If I remember correctly, you are the girls' father. You're as responsible for their care as I am. I have to show this house. It could mean a huge commission for me."

For me, Don thought.

Maybe he'd give in. This time.

"What time does the movie start?"

"Seven. It's out at ten, so you'll have to stay sober long enough to get them and bring them home."

Don shrugged. "Then maybe you better pick them up. I don't think I can stay sober that long. No, wait. Maybe I'll send a taxi to pick them up. You'll be too stoned to remember where they are."

"What are you talking about?" Debbie asked.

"Do you actually expect me to believe I don't know what a frigging pothead you are? You smell like a weed factory, Deb. I'm surprised you haven't started snorting cocaine. That'll be next."

"Nuts to you, Don. Just pick up the girls. I have to leave."

She stomped out of the den, and he heard the electric garage door open. *Good. Having her out of the house is like manna from heaven. I just might cancel my round of golf and stay home. I might even join the girls for a movie. But that will humiliate them, so I'll pass on that.*

Debbie found the joint she'd rolled in her makeup case. She lit it up and inhaled. She held her breath until her eyes watered. She needed to relax. *A joint now and then doesn't hurt,* she decided. *Hell, half the people I work with toke a doobie once in a while.*

She wondered how Don had found out she was into pot. Not that she gave a rat's ass. He drank too much. She was convinced that if his liver wasn't pickled already, it would be soon enough.

So we both have our vices. Who cares? I need something to get me through the days.

This was especially true since the business with Sara's being molested had started. Debbie knew that the kid was a real mental case. She also knew that she might be to blame for some of it, but so was Don. He never gave Sara enough attention. He was always lavishing his affection on perfect little Emily. Sara was smart enough to see the difference. She was a sad kid, Debbie thought. She took another puff of the joint, held the smoke in her lungs until it felt like they would explode, then exhaled. She opened all the windows so her car wouldn't smell like weed when she drove her clients to the house out at Marco Island.

She needed this sale badly. Her credit cards were maxed out. She owed that stupid little drug dealer in Fort Myers a fortune, in cash, for all the pot she'd been buying. She'd tried to talk him into sleeping with her in exchange for the dope, but he'd told her he was gay.

Just my luck to proposition a drug-dealing fag. Oh well. If he keeps on nagging me for the money, I'll turn him in to the police. Nothing in life is fair.

She arrived at her office. Before she went inside, she took a bottle of Nina Ricci from the glove compartment and sprayed herself with it. It stank, but she didn't care. One of the girls at the office had given it to her last Christmas. It had been in her car ever since.

She checked her makeup in the vanity mirror. Her eyes were glazed over. She spent most of her nights consoling Sara through another one of her nightmares. At least that's what she told the girls in the office when they asked. They accepted her explanation without question. The prosecution of Alex Rocket for molesting Sara had been major news.

Once inside, she took care of some paperwork she'd been putting off. There was so much more to selling houses than running around from showing to showing. She'd love to see Don turn out as much work as she did. He thought she was stupid. She knew they were broke. Had seen it coming for a long time. They'd mortgaged their asses to the hilt. Don kept pretending they were rolling in the dough.

Didn't he stop and think that I have access to all our accounts? He must be dumber than dirt. Unless, of course, he has an account I'm not aware of.

She doubted it. He wasn't smart enough to be that devious. All he cared about was his Conehead-looking hair and making an impression on the guys at the country club. She should've reeled Alex in when she had the chance. He was a much better catch. Even now, she would take him over Don. She knew he wasn't the sick, perverted bastard Sara made him out to be.

How well she knew.

CHAPTER 23

Coleman couldn't wait to give Alex and Kate his news. They would be on cloud nine. He'd worked extra hard on Alex's case. There was something about the couple that reminded him of his marriage. They were as dedicated to one another as he and Suzanne had been.

He hadn't wanted to make this call from work, so he waited until he got home. He took a shower, poured himself a glass of sweet tea. The view from the master suite terrace was remarkable at that time of day. He took his drink upstairs, along with the portable phone.

He dialed Kate's number from memory.

"Hello."

"Kate, it's Coleman. How are you?"

"Coleman, hello. I'm well, how are you?"

"I couldn't be better. I've waited all day to talk with you."

"I've been home all day. I guess I didn't

hear the phone ring. Is everything all right?" He heard the worry in her voice.

"Actually, you didn't hear the phone because I waited till now to call. I wanted to make this call from home."

"Is it that bad?" Kate asked.

"No, it's that good. I didn't want my associates to see the look on my face when I told you the news. They already say my head is big enough for ten men."

"Then spill it, Coleman." He heard the joy in her voice. He was thrilled he had the ability to make her happy. She deserved it.

"I've hemmed and hawed around, not wanting to mention this to you or Alex until it was a sure thing. Today I learned it was a sure thing. I'm going to tell you. You can tell Alex when he calls you tonight."

"Coleman! I'm on pins and needles. Tell me!"

"I got Alex a new trial. The appeals court has thrown out the original conviction on the grounds of ineffective counsel on the part of a lawyer who seemed to have a conflict of interest. His case has been referred to the bar for investigation."

Silence.

"Kate? Are you there?"

More silence.

"Kate, I'd hate to have to jump in my

plane and fly to North Carolina."

"I'm sorry." She sniffed, then blew her nose into the phone. "God! I can't believe this. I'm crying, in case you're wondering what that noise was." She laughed loudly into the phone.

"I've heard a woman cry, Kate. I figured you would. Hell, I would cry after what you and Alex have been through."

"So when is the trial? Can Alex come home while he waits? Give me all the details."

Kate was on cloud nine.

"It won't be on the court docket until spring. The court's backlogged for the next few months. Alex will be out of prison within the next few days. From a legal point of view, he has not been convicted of any crime. He may have to stay in Collier County until his second trial is over, but he should be a free man. I don't see how there will be any problem with his getting bail."

"I don't know what to say or do to thank you. If it wasn't for you these past few months, I would've gone crazy. You're a good friend, you know that?"

"Yes, I do, and I feel the same way, Kate. You're good people. Now as to what you can do to thank me, I think a large check is in order." Coleman smiled. He didn't care if Kate or Alex paid him a penny. He was just glad that he was instrumental in seeking justice for a man who deserved it. He could feel Suzanne smiling down on him.

"You name it, and it's yours. Any amount. Hell, I'll sell my soul to pay you."

"I'll let the billing department send you a statement. And I wouldn't want you to sell your soul. What I want you to do is this; hang up the phone so the line is free when Alex calls. You can call me back with his reaction."

"Thanks. Dang, all I do is say thanks to you. Anyway, thanks, Coleman. I'll call you after I speak with Alcx."

He placed the phone on the table next to him. Hc hadn't been this satisfied with a case since Suzanne was alive. Sometimes life was good.

Instead of calling Gertie, Kate ran to the cottage, the portable phone in her hand. She banged on the back door. "Gertie, it's me. Open up."

She heard the old woman cuss. It was getting harder and harder for her to move around with her arthritis. Kate wished she would retire.

The door opened.

"Well, it must be awfully important for

you to come to the cottage. I can't remember the last time you were here. Come on in, it's chilly outside."

Kate hadn't even thought of grabbing a sweater on her way out. She was too excited.

"So, spit it out," Gertie coaxed.

"Coleman just called. Alex's conviction has been overturned. He's getting a new trial!"

Gertie stopped dead in her tracks. Kate watched the look of surprise travel across the older woman's face. If ever there was joy in a pair of eyes, Gertie's shone forth as bright as the north star. "I knew that man was good, but I didn't think he was that good. Well, it's a damned good thing. I'm getting old. Alex needs to get his ass back home and take care of you and the dogs." Gertie smiled and wrapped her arms around Kate. "I've prayed for this day to come. The good Lord was listening this time."

"Alex is supposed to call tonight." She held up the portable phone. "I didn't want to miss it."

"He's going to be one happy man when he hears the news. I'm afraid he's been depressed the past month. His letters haven't been as upbeat."

"I thought so, too, but when I asked him, he just said he was tired. Told me that sleeping in a prison was one of the worst things about being there. Well, once Coleman gets him out of that place, he can sleep all he wants. I'm giddy, Gertie. I can't believe he's finally coming home."

Kate's phone rang.

"Hello?"

She waited for the automated voice to say she had a collect call from a correctional institution. Push one to accept, two to decline. Yeah, yeah, she'd heard this a thousand times, and it'd never taken this long to get the call through.

"Kate, it's me."

"Oh, Alex, I am so glad to hear your voice. I have the most wonderful news. Coleman called a while ago. Your conviction has been overturned. You'll be getting a new trial, Alex. You're coming home!"

"You're serious?"

"I wouldn't joke about this, you know that. He said the new trial was scheduled for the spring. You'll be out on bail while you await trial. We might have to live in Naples, but who cares? I'd commute from Timbuktu if it meant your freedom."

"Well, all I can say is, *Yeah!*" Alex shouted so loud Kate had to hold the phone away.

"Is that the best news or what?" Kate asked.

"Yes, it is. Damn, I can't thank the man enough. I don't know how I'm going to stand it in here until I can go home."

"Oh, Alex, maybe I shouldn't have told you," she teased.

"Hmm, and I would've had to smack your butt good, Mrs. Rocket. I've been in here a while, I think I can stand it a bit longer."

"I bet you can't wait to tell those two friends of yours, Ron and Brad. Maybe Coleman could take a look at their cases as well. I'll ask him about it."

"Thanks, I'm sure they'll appreciate the effort. It's not like either of them has a lot of money to hire a top-notch lawyer. I think both of them had public defenders."

"I'm going to ask Coleman to look at their cases when I call him back. He wanted to hear your reaction to the news."

"You can tell him that thank you doesn't begin to cover it. Write him a check for double the amount, Kate. If he doesn't accept it, then give it to some organization he's interested in. We owe him my life."

"His wife died of breast cancer a few years ago. I'll make a large donation in her name. Coleman would like that. Is this surreal, Alex? I was starting to think Coleman wasn't on the ball."

"Not Coleman, he'd jump through hoops

for you, Kate."

"For me? You mean for you, Alex. Coleman is dedicated to seeking justice. He told me so himself. More than once, too. His wife was in practice with him. He still loves her, Alex, I can see it in his eyes when he talks about her."

"He likes you Kate, a lot," Alex teased.

"Please, don't tease me that way. It's not funny. I admire and respect Coleman. And you should, too."

"I'm sorry, Kate. When he talks about you, there's this light in his eyes. And I do respect him. He's a good guy."

"Coleman's eyes light up when he talks about all women, Alex. Trust me." Kate laughed. Alex had nothing to worry about.

The beeping noise came over the phone line letting them know they had thirty seconds before the call ended.

"I love you, I'll call tomorrow, Kate. Thank Coleman." Then the phone was disconnected.

Kate didn't see why they couldn't make another call as soon as the last one ended. Fifteen minutes wasn't enough time. But Alex would be out of prison very soon.

"Gertie, I'm going back to the house to call Coleman. If it gets too cold, you come up to the house. It's too big with just me. It needs some life inside."

"You're gonna get life when I send half of those dogs up to the house. Alex wouldn't want them out in the kennel, even though there's heat."

"You can bring all the dogs to the house anytime you need to. If I'm not there, you know where the keys are."

Kate hurried out into the cool autumn air. Fall had arrived in all its glory, and she barely noticed it. She'd been so busy writing letters to Alex and wallowing in pity that she hadn't really taken the time to stop and look around her. Things would be different from that moment on. No looking back. She and Alex did have a future together. She would never take anything for granted again.

She put the kettle on for tea and lit a fire in the kitchen fireplace. She always preferred to sit in the kitchen. It was cozy and warm. She'd make a cup of tea and call Coleman. The teakettle blew its whistle. Kate took Alex's golden retriever mug out of the cabinet. She'd been too sad to look at his favorite cup since he'd been in jail. Now she was going to drink out of it, sort of like a private toast to Alex. She poured hot water over the tea bag. While it was steeping, she dialed Coleman's number.

"It's me." She didn't even wait for hello.

"And?"

"He was so excited he shouted over the phone. I had to hold the phone away from my ear, he was so loud. And he says thank you isn't enough. He told me to double your fee and donate a big chunk to a charity of your choice. I told him about Suzanne, I hope you don't mind. I thought we could donate something to the American Cancer Society in her name."

"She would've loved that, Kate. Thank you. I'll thank Alex when I see him. I just got off the phone with a friend of mine who happens to be a friend of the warden. Alex should be released as early as next week. No promises, since things like this usually take some time in Florida, but I think I can make it happen."

"That soon? That's fantastic. Should I make plans to head your way then?"

"Give me a day or two. I wouldn't say anything to Alex just yet in case it takes a bit longer."

"I won't. But he will be so thrilled. He told me knowing he has the possibility of coming home makes it just a little tougher to stay there, but he said he would hang in."

"Okay, as soon as I have word, I'll call

you. I can come pick you up myself if you'd like."

"You know what, I just might take you up on that offer, Coleman Fitzpatrick, I just might."

"All right, Mrs. Rocket. Good night."

And it truly was a good night.

It'd been three days since Kate had talked to Coleman. She'd tried his office, but was told he would be in court most of the day. She had tried his house for the past two evenings, and there was still no answer. She was sure he'd have some news of Alex by now. One way or another. She hated being left in limbo. She even thought about working in her studio but couldn't bring herself to just yet. A few clients from Chloe's called wanting to know if she'd cater their Christmas parties. She'd declined, but was now having second thoughts. With nothing on her hands but time, she might change her mind. She could do all the cooking right there in her kitchen. As far as delivery, she wasn't ready to take that step just yet. There were too many people who knew about Alex. While she wasn't ashamed, she just wasn't ready to face her former clients and colleagues.

An idea sprang into her mind. She'd get

out the Christmas decorations. She'd always loved the holidays. If Coleman called, she'd box up a few and take them to Florida. Christmas wasn't the same in Florida, but this year it wouldn't matter where she was during the holidays because she wouldn't have to spend them alone. Actually, she'd been dreading the approaching season, but now she looked at Alex's imminent release as a true gift from God. Yes, she'd get the decorations down and start going through them. She had all of her parents' decorations. Her mother had saved every single ornament Kate had ever made.

She hoofed it to the attic and brought down the boxes that held her childhood treasures. It would be a pleasant way to pass the evening. She even made a pot of hot chocolate and lit the fire in the den. It was as cozy as ever. The only thing missing was her husband. And the girls. They were always here when she decorated the tree. Though she felt sad at the loss of Emily, she would never be able to look at Sara again without thinking about choking her. But she would deal with that another time. She hadn't really given much thought to the future as far as a relationship with Emily went. She would be eighteen in a couple of years. Kate would never turn the child away. She loved her like a daughter. She'd been so consumed with the trial that she hadn't really given any thought to Emily. She would like to send her something for Christmas, but it wasn't time this year. Maybe next year.

Kate opened the first box. Extra careful of the fragile ornaments, she unwrapped the tissue paper around each and every one. She'd glued macaroni to a paper plate to make a wreath. Must have been first grade; the green paint she'd used was all but gone. Glitter still sparkled in a few places. She removed a hot pink star made out of dough. She remembered making this particular decoration. She'd been in fifth grade. Not wanting to make a Santa or tree or an angel like the rest of her classmates, she'd opted for the star. No gold paint either. She'd gone with hot pink. Her mother had laughed at her choice of colors. Fluorescent colors were all the rage. Next, she held a small bell. She hadn't made this. It'd been given to her by a girl in her third-grade class. Natalie. She remembered. Natalie's parents were Jehovah's Witnesses. Natalie told Kate she really hated that they didn't exchange gifts. She'd told her mother, and they'd gone together to pick out a special gift for Natalie. The bell had been Natalie's gift to her.

Kate had given her a charm bracelet in the shape of a heart. Natalie had hidden it from her parents, but Kate knew she'd cherished the gift. Kate's childhood held so many happy memories. Her parents were older when she was born, but they never acted any different from the younger parents of her friends. In fact, Kate remembered them being more active than her friends' parents had been. She still missed them to this day. Good people gone way too soon.

She tackled a second box. It was filled with decorations she and Alex had purchased after they were married. She remembered going to the Hallmark store at the mall. They'd bought all kinds of fun, silly ornaments. Then Alex had disappeared only to return with a gift-wrapped box. He told her it would always be their special ornament, the one they would pass on to their children and grandchildren. Of course, at the time they hadn't known Kate couldn't conceive. Inside the box was a crystal star with their wedding picture etched in the glass. Inscribed in the crystal: *Our first Christmas as a family.*

Kate had cried, and Alex laughed at her for being so sentimental. It was always the first ornament placed on the tree. Yes, she would take this to Florida. Together, they'd hang it on whatever kind of tree they wound up with. She'd get something new this year to celebrate Alex's release.

Kate relaxed in Alex's chair with her cup of cocoa. She was about to pick up her book when the doorbell rang.

Gertie. She probably had the dogs. Kate hurried to the door. It was downright cold. Gertie should have called her to come get the dogs. Kate certainly wasn't doing anything important.

The chimes again.

"Come on in, Gertie," Kate called out. Why was she at the front door anyway? She never used the front door.

Kate pulled the heavy oak door aside. No Gertie. She stepped out onto the porch to see if she'd gone around back. There was no trace of her. She was about to go back inside and get a sweater when she heard something that sounded like a car door closing. She walked around to the driveway. A silver car — she hadn't been expecting company. The person driving flicked on the headlights. Apparently whoever it was saw her and shut the engine.

Kate waited while the visitor walked up the drive to the porch.

"Kate, is that you?"

"Coleman? Coleman Fitzpatrick, what in

the name of Pete are you doing in Asheville? I've tried to call you for two days."

"Kate, can I come inside? I'm not used to this weather. Florida living spoils you."

"Of course. Come on. I have a fire in the den and a pot of hot chocolate."

Coleman followed Kate inside. He dreaded telling her the news. A phone call would've been sufficient, but he couldn't do that to Kate.

He entered a brightly lit room. Big sofas and large chairs were scattered haphazardly about the room. The stone fireplace took up one wall. Coleman liked what he saw. Homey, nothing pretentious, just like Kate. If he remembered right, this was Kate's childhood home.

She continued on to a bright red kitchen. Copper pots and a red stove. So like Kate. She took a cup from the cabinet. "I might have to heat this a bit. I was going through some old Christmas decorations." Kate stopped. Coleman wasn't there to chitchat. "Why are you here?"

He pulled out two chairs from the old oak table.

"Are you going to tell me, or do I have to guess? It's about Alex, right? Coleman, if you're hiding him out in the car, I'll never forgive you! Did you bring him home?"

She wasn't making this easy. "Kate, I want you to sit down. No, I don't have Alex in the car. I promise you. I wish I did, but I don't. Please" — he motioned toward the chair — "sit down."

She did as he asked. "What?"

He was about to tear her world apart. There wasn't a nice way to do this. "Kate, yesterday there was a fight at the prison. Alex was involved. Some guys in the showers. I'm sorry, Kate. Alex was killed."

Time stopped.

"Say that again?" Kate asked.

"Alex was defending one of his friends. Someone got hold of a shiv. They used it on Alex. He didn't make it, Kate. God, I am so sorry."

Her body went limp, and her world turned black.

Chapter 24

Orlando, Florida
Seven years later

The Internal Revenue Service office was like any other government office. Dull and boring. The employees were hardworking and dedicated. Auditing was a serious business, so they took their jobs seriously. At lunchtime, they discussed dividends, tax shelters, and capital gains. They all knew the numbers for each and every tax form ever published. For the numerically challenged, it was the job from hell. For those with a mission, to work at the IRS was the chance of a lifetime.

Kate Rocket had worked her way up to supervisor of the Orlando office. She'd never missed a day of work. Never called in sick in the five years she had worked there. Never took a vacation and always ate her lunch at her desk. She did not socialize with any of the employees. She was punctual to a fault. All who worked with her, especially the new agents, called her "Killer Kate" behind her back because working with her would kill you. She knew what they said about her. She had a job to do. She didn't care to learn about her workers' personal lives. She didn't want to give them an opportunity to ask about hers. There was nothing to tell. She lived in a one-bedroom condo. She had a bed, a couch, and a small table in the kitchen. She had five different suits she wore to work: gray, black, brown, dark green, and burgundy. She wore plain white blouses with all of them. Black or brown shoes with beige nylons. She wore her hair in a topknot. She usually had a pencil or two tucked within the nest of her hair. She had nothing fancy, nothing to distract her from her job. At 8:00 A.M., she went to work and left at exactly 5:00 P.M. She went home to her empty condo. She did not cook. Her small freezer was packed with Stouffer's and Healthy Choice frozen dinners. She had toast and coffee for breakfast every day. A tuna sandwich for lunch. In five years, she'd never strayed from this routine.

That was about to change. Tonight was the seventh anniversary of Alex's death. The first year after Alex was murdered was a blur. The second year she spent planning. All of her and Alex's holdings remained in Gertie's name to this day. Since moving to Orlando, Kate hadn't touched a penny of their money. She lived on what she earned as an employee of the government. She had excellent health coverage and a small life insurance policy.

Alex's killer had eventually died of his wounds, inflicted by Alex. She supposed there was some sort of justice in that, but it hadn't eased her grief. Coleman had made all the arrangements for Alex. He'd been cremated. His ashes were the only possession of her former life that she'd allowed herself to bring with her when she decided to relocate to Orlando.

It hadn't been an easy decision given what she'd set out to do. She'd had to find the perfect job to fulfill her plan. That it was in Orlando was even better. She'd gone to a training center in DC for a few months after she was hired. She was a quick learner. Computers were her only friend now. Kate took to computers like a duck to water. She could find almost anything she needed to know. The one extravagance she allowed herself was a top-of-the-line computer system with 512 megabytes of RAM and an 80-gigabyte hard drive. She could view CDs and some DVDs. She had six USB ports, a camera, and a two-channel audio speaker. She had a scanner, a printer, and a fax machine. She'd recently purchased a digital camera. That was enough for her needs. Y2K had been a threat to those with a computer system of any kind. Banks, department stores, gas stations, anyplace that depended on Internet services, their computers would supposedly crash. Just as Kate had predicted, it never happened.

Kate didn't feel the least bit of guilt for what she was preparing to do. It was all she had lived for the past five years. She had to do this. For Alex. For herself. And for all the innocent men who died in prison.

Tomorrow her coworkers would be shocked when she didn't show up for work. After a while they would call only to find her telephone disconnected. Since her address was in her personnel file, they would come to check on her. She had arranged for her utilities to be disconnected at eight tomorrow morning. Garbage pickup had been discontinued. She didn't need to worry about closing her bank accounts. She wouldn't be making any deposits. She did all of her banking online. She received no mail, other than advertisements, so she didn't need to cancel any magazine subscriptions. She wouldn't be forwarding her mail to her new address. That was the point. She wanted to disappear. When she felt it was safe, she would call Gertie and tell her she'd moved. Only the name of the town, never the address. She hadn't seen Gertie in five years. She called her once a week from a different pay phone each time. She wanted nothing that could be traced back to her. Investigators were sharp, with all the technology a mere click away. From that day forward, she hoped that finding her would be very difficult, if not impossible. And if she was found out, she'd simply face the music. She didn't have much of a life anyway. It mattered little to her whether she spent the remainder of her life in some crummy rental apartment or a jail cell.

Kate Rocket had a mission to fulfill.

She removed all her clothes from the closet. She placed them inside a dark green lawn and leaf bag. Her shoes went, too. From the top shelf in the closet she removed a small black duffel bag she'd ordered from L.L.Bean. She had two pairs of jeans, a pair of khakis, a pair of black capris, and five white shirts she'd purchased online from The Gap stuffed inside the bag. Ten pairs of Victoria's Secret plain white briefs and three bras. One long nightshirt. She had a pair of black slides and a pair of white Nikes. Kate was amazed. A person never had to leave her home. One could even shop for groceries online. She might utilize that particular extravagance after she settled in her new apartment.

Next, she went to the small bathroom. She had two bottles of Suave shampoo and conditioner. Two tubes of Crest toothpaste, two unopened toothbrushes, and three bars of Dove bath soap. Ten Daisy razors, three packs of dental floss, and a large bottle of Scope mouthwash. She grabbed the light blue can of Secret deodorant. Anyone would use the products she did. There was nothing special about them at all. She peered beneath the single cabinet and removed a generic box of tampons. At forty-three, she needed them less and less with each passing month.

She looked around the place she should have called home for the past five years. There were no pictures to remove from the walls, nothing personal. No magnets collecting on the refrigerator. Once she removed her clothes and toiletry items, the apartment could've housed anyone at all. She thought about tossing all the frozen dinners, but at the last minute changed her mind. The next tenant might enjoy them.

Her computer system would go with her. She still had the original cartons they came in, so they were easy to pack. With all the electronics gone, the room was as empty as Kate's life. She didn't know what the future held. Only one thing mattered to her at this stage. She must avenge Alex's death, or else he'd died for nothing.

The last thing on her list was a disguise of sorts. Her hair made her visible. As much as she hated to, she knew it had to go. She went to the bathroom with a pair of hair scissors she'd ordered. She removed the elastic that held her hair in a loose knot. She shook her hair out, like a dog shook after a bath. She remembered Alex when he would bathe the dogs. He'd get as wet as they did.

She grabbed a handful of hair and started cutting. Twenty minutes later she had a cute bob. A box of Nice'n Easy waited. Cool brown, the color said, but Kate knew it would be closer to black, the color she wanted. She'd seen women who had what she called "witch black–bottled" hair. It was extremely unnatural. That wasn't the look she was aiming for. Forty-five minutes later she viewed her handiwork. Not bad. She had contacts to turn her green eyes brown. She had a cosmetic case full of eye shadow, mascara, and every shade of lipstick in the rainbow. She had never worn much makeup. She spent a few nights trying some tricks she had read about. They were quite drastic. She would now be one of those women who couldn't leave the house without "putting her face on."

She went through the apartment one last time. It was after ten, dark enough that she could begin loading her car. She had a Ford Explorer, so there would be room to spare once she filled it with her meager possessions.

When she finished, she took the large garbage bag and placed it next to the Dumpster. She didn't want to throw the clothes in with all the smelly garbage. Maybe someone who needed them would find them.

As she pulled out of the parking space, Kate felt an odd sense of freedom. All that she'd studied, planned, and plotted was about to come to fruition.

Kate settled into her new apartment with ease. The complex was adults only, and was occupied mostly by retirees. That was good. They'd be too busy playing golf and cards to bother with the new tenant.

Her last trip to Naples had been lunch

with Coleman Fitzpatrick. She often thought about him. He'd been devastated upon hearing the news of Alex's death. So much so that he immediately flew to North Carolina in his private plane. He'd had some weather delays. Kate remembered trying to call his office and home repeatedly. They were going to bring Alex home after his new trial exonerated him, but it had never happened. She'd paid Coleman an exorbitant sum of money and donated an equal amount to the American Cancer Society in his wife's name.

He would call daily, and twice he came knocking on her door. She begged to be left alone. She couldn't face him. There was too much of a connection between him and all that had gone wrong in her life. Not that she ever blamed him. He'd finally given up on trying to reach her. She'd liked Coleman and hated to lose his friendship. He was still in practice, according to his firm's Web site. She would've liked to call him but couldn't.

This apartment had two bedrooms. She used the second as an office. If anyone were to ask, she planned to tell them she did medical billing from home. Lots of people did that. She knew because she had actually taken an online course. You never knew.

She knew that Emily was in vet school,

though she was unable to find any current employment records. Debbie had her own real estate firm. That surprised her. She knew a few years back Don had filed for bankruptcy, but Debbie's name wasn't on the file she'd looked at. There were no current employment records for Don either. The past three years he had received no income whatsoever. Working with the Internal Revenue Service had opened all kinds of doors for Kate. She could take away a person's livelihood with the stroke of a few keys.

While sabotaging the Winters financially was on her list, it wasn't at the top. Sara would be twenty years old now. She was a big girl. Kate figured it was time for her to face the music. If Sara was attending college, Kate had been unable to find out where. That was a big reason for her move to Naples. If Sara was still living there, Kate could watch her.

Sick as it sounded, Kate actually liked spying on people, getting information that no one else seemed to be able to find. Maybe she'd been a private investigator in another life. Whatever, she seemed to have a knack for it.

She had a schedule and would stick to it if she hoped to accomplish anything. That day she would drive to Debbie's office. She might go inside and ask about a rental. She needed to be able to come and go freely. If she could get by Debbie, she'd get past anyone.

She blew her hair into a curl-free bob. She still had trouble recognizing herself when she looked in the mirror but figured that was a good thing. Contacts in place. Heavy eye shadow and loads of thick gloss on her lips. She wore the black capris, slides, and a white T-shirt. She looked like anyone else, well, maybe minus the makeup. Hell, she looked like Debbie. The woman wore so much makeup, Kate used to wonder how often she had to buy it to balance supply and demand. Weekly, from the looks of her. But that was years ago. Maybe she'd changed with age.

Kate had practiced speaking with a strong Southern accent. She had a slow drawl as it was, but when she enhanced it as she'd done, she sounded nothing like the Kate Rocket Debbie knew.

She waited until midmorning to go to the real estate office. If Debbie was true to form, she wasn't an early riser. Kate believed her chances of "bumping into" her at this time would be greater.

Driving down Highway 41 brought back

memories of the short time she'd spent in the city. If she could turn back the clock, Alex would be alive. In a way, she blamed herself for Alex's death, believing that if she'd insisted on speaking to Don long ago about Sara's mental status, he might've taken her to get the help she'd needed. She should have confronted Sara about the destruction in her studio. Most of all, she wished she'd paid closer attention to the premonitions she'd had when they'd agreed that James was the best possible attorney for Alex.

The directions she printed out from MapQuest were right on the money. She made two right turns, then a left. The Century 21 office was located in a newly built strip mall. Pastel colors, pink and lavender. Kate thought it looked like something at Disney World, but this was Florida. Everything was flashy, designed to entice.

She checked herself in the mirror one last time. Taking a calming breath, Kate got out of the car and walked directly to the office. A set of chimes resting against the door emitted a soft tinkling sound when she entered. She found herself in a reception area decorated in pale white furniture with lots of plants and dozens of the latest fashion magazines, which were stacked on small white tables throughout the area. A small television set held center place, with a group of comfortable chairs placed in a semicircle off to the side.

A young girl hurried to the reception desk, a half-moon area that led to what appeared to be several small offices behind her. She was tall and thin, with perfect features. Nothing too big or too little. Long brown hair and dark eyes. Very pretty. Kate had secretly hoped she would find Sara in her mother's office, whining, "My mommy said this, or my mommy said that," but she wasn't that lucky.

"May I help you?" the young woman inquired.

Here goes. "Yes, thanks. I am new to the area. I have a couple of months left on my rental lease. I thought it was time to look for a house."

"Well, that's what we do. We find homes for people." She took a clipboard with several sheets of paper attached and gave it to her. "This is a questionnaire we ask all of our prospective clients to fill out. Helps us to find just the right home for you and your family. It narrows down the list of possible properties."

"Of course." Kate took the clipboard and sat down in the television area. Her back was to the wall to the left as you entered. That allowed her to view the front door and still be able to glance at the reception area.

Kate decided it was best to stick as close to the truth as possible. She was single. Divorced. Worked in medical billing. Price range. She didn't want to go too high, but then the lower-priced properties were probably listed with the junior sales staff. She'd go for the moderate-priced. The high two hundreds. She thought her chances of Debbie taking her as a client were slim. She didn't want that anyway. She wanted to see her and get past her. Then, if she made enough visits to the office, possibly she would learn more about the owner and her family. She returned the clipboard to the receptionist.

"If you'll have a seat, I'll look this over, and we'll be right with you. Would you like coffee or a Danish while you wait? We have a kitchen for our clients to use." She smiled at Kate.

"That would be great. I didn't bother with breakfast. Thanks."

The girl walked around to the side of the reception desk and opened the door. Kate couldn't believe her luck. There fifteen minutes and already she was inside the inner sanctum.

The receptionist led her to a small kitchen at the end of a long hallway. She could see inside each office as she passed, provided the doors were open. "You can help yourself. There's juice in the fridge." The girl left the room.

Kate grabbed a muffin and poured herself a cup of coffee. She took a few bites, deciding she was hungry after all. She peered down the hallway, left then right. Nothing. Before the girl came back, Kate hurried out of the kitchen and down the hall. If she was caught, she'd say she was searching for the ladies' room. Slowly, she stopped to peer inside the open doors of the offices. Nothing looked lavish enough for Debbie. She'd have the best digs in the place, that much Kate knew. Still favored white furniture, from the looks of the waiting area. Kate would hate to pay her maintenance on such frivolous furniture. It must cost a small fortune to keep it clean, and Kate figured Debbie would have to replace it every few months at that.

At the opposite end of the hallway Kate hit pay dirt. An office the size of her apartment's living room. White furniture, glass-top desk. No plants, not a thing to create a comfortable atmosphere. Cold and sterile came to mind. Knowing this might be her only chance, Kate slipped inside the office and closed the door. She didn't know what she would say if she were caught; she sure as heck couldn't say she was looking for the ladies' room. She'd worry about it when and if. A tall glass shelf held plaques of different sizes and shapes. Apparently Debbie'd won quite a few honors in her career. One hundred million dollars in sales. Not bad, Kate thought. Voted best real estate office by the Better Business Bureau. She scanned the rest of the shelves, looking for a family picture, but found nothing. Behind the desk there was a door that Kate figured led to a private bathroom. She hurried inside. There on the side of the vanity. A small frame. Both girls. Kate picked it up. Before she chickened out, she stuck the frame in her pocket. She hurried back to the kitchen. Later she would peruse the photo. She sat down and took a sip of the disgusting coffee.

"Ma'am?"

"Yes?" Kate asked.

"I think we've got something for you to look at later this afternoon. Would that be possible?"

"I would love to. Yes, thank you. This is great."

"We aim to please."

"I guess you do. How many agents do you have?" Kate asked as she followed the girl back to the front.

"I think we have around thirty, but that figure can change daily."

"Why is that?"

She looked behind her. "I shouldn't say this, you being a new client and all."

"I'm good at keeping secrets," Kate encouraged.

"The owner. We call her Ms. Winter White. She does love the color. Anyway, she's not always the easiest person to work for. Very moody."

Office gossip. Kate couldn't be more pleased.

"I know what you mean. I used to work for a woman who was the same way. Every day when I came to work I thought it was going to be my last. She was a real tiger."

"Yeah? Well, Mrs. Winter can be a real B-I-T-C-H." She spelled out the word to Kate.

"How so, if you don't mind my asking?"

"Like I said, she's very moody. If her daughter is here, you might as well kiss a pleasant day goodbye. They fight like cats and dogs. None of us can stand the little witch. She's just like her mother."

"So she has a daughter?" Kate hoped the girl's loose lips would reveal which daughter she was referring to.

"Actually, she has two. I think the older one moved away years ago. Some of the girls that worked with Mrs. Winter said the older girl didn't get along with her parents. I think someone said they haven't spoken since the girl graduated from high school. But you know how office talk is. Who knows? But you're not here to listen to this silliness. I'm sorry, I guess I shouldn't have told you all that."

Kate held up her hand. "Hey, not to worry. Sometimes you need a good gab about the boss. I've had my share."

"Well, I hope you'll still consider us as your Realtor."

"Of course I will. Now, what about those houses you want me to look at?"

"I'll get the agent. Hang on a minute."

Kate sat down in the waiting area. She couldn't believe her good fortune. An office gossip. Maybe she'd make friends with her, invite her to lunch. A few minutes later, Kate was escorted to a junior agent's office just as she figured. They made arrangements to view a three-bedroom condo later that afternoon. Kate thanked the agent, Randi, and left the office.

Inside her car, she took the small framed picture out. It was Sara and Emily, but it'd been taken a long time ago. If what the receptionist told her was correct, then this picture had to have been taken before Emily graduated. She looked at Sara. She was at least fifty pounds heavier than she'd been as a preteen. She wore as much makeup as her mother. Her brown hair was frizzy just like Debbie's. *Debbie Junior,* Kate thought. Emily, on the other hand, looked nothing like her mother or father. She was still tall and thin. Her long blond hair reached her waist. She was a beautiful young woman. Kate's heart lurched at the sight of her. She put the photo inside her purse. She had no intention of returning it.

Kate had some time to kill before seeing the condo. She drove around the town familiarizing herself with the area. It had grown by leaps and bounds since she was there last. Shopping centers at every intersection. Gated communities. Movie theaters. The roads had been four-lane. Progress. The medians were lined with palm trees and multicolored annuals. Very pretty.

Before she realized where she was headed, Kate found herself on one of the lesser-traveled roads. She knew what she was doing. She was looking for Coleman Fitzpatrick's office. He was still located in the same building. Low-key, nothing extravagant, but she remembered the elegant decor inside. He'd told her Suzanne had decorated it personally. Lots of antiques and comfortable sofas and chairs.

Tempted to stop and say hello, Kate floored the accelerator. She couldn't see Coleman. He would want to know what she was doing in Naples. And there was no way on earth she was going to tell an attorney her plans.

Unless she wanted to go to jail. And she didn't. At least not yet.

CHAPTER 25

Sunlight streamed between the wooden slats on the plantation shutters. Don moaned and rolled over. He'd closed them last night. The bitch must've opened them that morning before leaving for the office. He didn't remember how much he'd drunk the previous night at the club. One of the waiters brought him home. He didn't know which one, hell, he didn't care. He'd lost his license three years ago. It'd be another two before he could have it reissued. Four DUIs. Driving under the influence.

He forced himself into an upright position, dragging the bedsheets with him. He had on the same clothes he'd worn yesterday. He smelled like alcohol and sweat.

He needed a shower, but wasn't sure if he could make it. His head thrummed with pain; his throat was dry and soured. He managed to stand up. One foot in front of the other. Left. Right. Left. Right. Ten more.

One. Two. Three. Four. He knew exactly how many steps to the shower. He'd counted them once. At least he could still count, he thought. He turned the shower on. Ten showerheads. He stepped inside, letting the hot water pummel against him. He leaned against the cool marble for ten minutes before he felt stable enough to grab the bar of soap. He lathered up and shampooed what was left of his hair. He found a razor and a can of shaving cream placed on one of the built-in shelves in the shower. Nothing too good for the Winter family, was there? He made a half-ass attempt to shave without slitting his throat. That was something because the way his hands shook, he was surprised he hadn't sliced his jugular years ago.

He'd taken a dump on life six years ago. First, he'd lost his job at the engineering firm after they filed bankruptcy. He tried to start a firm of his own. With his ass mortgaged from here to hell and back, he hadn't been able to get the business loans he'd needed. He'd gone to every bank in town. Then to Miami. Fort Lauderdale. No one wanted to lend him a nickel, much less the two million he was asking for. He'd hoped for something from the civil suit they'd filed against the Rockets. That had remained tied up in the court for four years before he'd finally accepted the fact that even in death Alex had bested him. The son of a bitch. Before he was even arrested, he'd made sure his fortune was untouchable. Don had hired numerous attorneys in hope of finding something that would allow Alex's fortune to spill into his open hands. There was no way. He'd finally given up. Debbie had even hired and paid for a few attorneys herself. Even she, the invincible Mrs. Winter, hadn't been able to break through the chains Alex had placed on his fortune.

He stepped out of the shower, pulled a thick white bath sheet from a white wicker basket, and wrapped it around his middle. He'd gone to pot, he thought as he viewed himself in the mirror. He couldn't remember the last time he'd seen the inside of a gym. His skin looked flabby, like the old men at the club. Too much sun, too much drink. *Screw it,* he thought as he turned away from his reflection.

In the kitchen, Don poured the leftover coffee into a mug and drank it even though it was only at room temperature.

Now, what should he do today? Like he had a choice. He'd call a taxi to drive him to the club. He'd hang out at the bar for most of the afternoon. From there he'd make an attempt to act like he had something to come home to, then he'd drink until he passed out. Sometimes he didn't even bother coming home. They knew he was a drunk at the club. If he got rowdy, they'd have one of the waiters drive him home. He rarely got rowdy anymore. It wasn't worth the effort.

He remembered the day his life had taken a turn for the worse.

Debbie and the girls had gone shopping as usual. He had been searching for a pack of matches, of all things. He'd taken to enjoying a pipe now and then, but only when the girls were out of the house. Even though Debbie smoked Kool cigarettes like they were going out of style, he couldn't find a damned match to save his life. He'd searched the drawers in the kitchen. Nothing. Then he remembered Debbie sometimes lit up in bed, of all places. He went to their bedroom in search of a light. What he discovered changed his life forever. How he wished he'd never started smoking a pipe.

He knew Debbie wrote in a diary, a journal, whatever the hell they called them nowadays. He wasn't the least bit interested in learning her innermost thoughts or deep dark secrets. Whatever she wrote about, he was sure it would be of no interest to him whatsoever. The search for matches had certainly changed that.

As he'd rummaged through the bedside table drawer, he found her journal lying open, her schoolgirl curlicues glaring up at him. It wasn't the handwriting that got his attention. It was the words.

I told Sara she had to do this. I promised I would make it worth her while for the rest of her life. She didn't seem to give a damn one way or another. She told me she knew about Emily, and that was all it took. Sara didn't like her sister anyway. Though I don't like the fact that my two girls hate each other, I have found a way to make it work for me. Don would kill me if he ever found this out. He won't. He's too busy trying to make a good impression on those worthless bastards he works for. Did I pick a loser or what? I should've gone after Alex when I had the chance. He'd offered to take care of me and the child, but he never mentioned marriage. I wanted all or nothing. I sure as hell wasn't going to be Alex Rocket's handy piece of ass. I thought there was hope for Don. See what I get for thinking?

The next entry overwhelmed him.

Yes! That son of a bitch was convicted! I told Sara she should consider acting. She would get an Oscar for her performance.

He'd never read any farther. In turmoil over what to do, he decided he'd speak with an attorney. They were bound by attorney-client privilege, so no matter what happened, he would have that security. A week before his scheduled appointment, Alex was killed in a prison brawl. Don had started drinking that very day and hadn't stopped.

That bitch and his evil spawn had lied about his best friend. They'd killed Alex as surely as the man who'd shoved the knife into his gut.

Daily he lived with the torment. Each day he contemplated taking his life, but then he thought how much satisfaction that would bring Debbie and decided against it.

He went back to bed with a half-full bottle of cheap vodka. Maybe he'd die in his sleep. Sometimes he prayed that he would just so he didn't have to face another day. He was finding it harder and harder to live with what Debbie had forced Sara to do. Sara didn't seem to care one way or another. All she thought about was men and food. Don knew she was a slut, and he didn't care. He kind of hoped she'd get some sort of sexually transmitted disease. Maybe that would slow her down. Debbie had allowed her to go on birth control when she was fifteen. God, he hadn't said a word. No, all he'd cared about was making money and a name for himself. At least Debbie was right about that.

The icing on the cake, the straw that broke the camel's back, whatever you wanted to call it — he had always suspected Emily wasn't his child. But never in a million years had he thought his best friend had slept with his wife. Not good old Alex. He was too good to do something so . . . male.

Emily sure was a chip off Alex's old block. She loved animals. Hell, she was studying to be a veterinarian. Alex would be proud of her had he lived.

Don wondered if Alex had ever suspected that he knew of the affair between him and Debbie. If Alex had, he'd certainly never given it away. *Just goes to show you how much you think you know someone and, boom, they go and pull something you would never have dreamed of.*

Even though his best friend had screwed around with his wife, got her pregnant, then went on with his life, Alex hadn't deserved to die. Don had spent many hours wondering why Debbie put Sara up to such a charade. He had yet to figure it out. He'd tried looking through more of her journals and found nothing. He concluded that Debbie was jealous of Kate and her life with

Alex. She did what she did out of pure spite, and nothing more.

He took a swig of vodka straight from the bottle. It had little effect on him. He finished it off, then went in search of another. One thing he could thank Debbie for: she kept him supplied with plenty of booze, took care of the household bills, and basically left him alone. He wasn't even sure why they were still married. The girls were grown, and he was sure that Sara couldn't have cared less if her parents were married, divorced, or dead. Emily had split after graduation and rarely called. Debbie probably liked having him around just so she would have someone to lord it over. She was that way.

The shrill ringing of the phone made him jump, spilling liquor all over the white sheets. Who cared? The phone continued to ring.

He leaned across the bed and grabbed the portable phone from the nightstand.

"Yeah?" he called into the phone. He'd lost whatever class he had long ago and knew it.

"I'm looking for Don Winter," a male voice said.

"You are, huh? Well, who's looking, and I might see if I can find him." Don laughed at his own sick humor.

"My name is Coleman Fitzpatrick."

Isn't he the attorney who got Alex's conviction overturned right before Alex was killed?

"So what do you want with me?"

"Then I'm speaking to Mr. Winter?" the voice on the other end questioned.

"No, this is a recording. Of course it's Mr. Winter."

"I see. I have caught you at a bad time, I take it," Coleman said.

"Why do you think that?" Don asked. He was having fun screwing with the man.

"You sound . . . tired."

"You mean drunk? Yeah, well, I am. I'm drunk all the time. I like it, too. So what do you think of that, Mr. Coleman?"

"I think that's a sad place to be, Mr. Winter. Now, if you would like to know why I'm calling."

"Hey, that was my next question. So, what do you want?"

"I know you were a good friend of Alex Rocket's."

Don felt like he'd been kicked in the gut. "So? The man's dead."

"I'm aware of that. I'm trying to find his widow, Kate Rocket. I thought you or your wife might have . . . I thought you might know how I could locate her."

"Well, if that doesn't beat a rug to shreds.

hy in the hell would you think me or my vife would know where Kate is? Her perverted husband molested my daughter. Do you think we cared what happened to her? Hell, no, we don't."

"Then I'm sorry to have bothered you. Thanks for your time," Coleman said.

"Hey, wait a minute. Don't hang up. Haven't you called that dog house in North Carolina? Kate's probably there with a new man to look after her parents' puppies. Yeah, I bet that's exactly where she's at." Don laughed into the phone.

"Thank you for your time, Mr. Winter."

Click.

Damn, he hung up. Wouldn't you know it, just when I had Alex on the brain, I hear from his old attorney. Will miracles never cease.

Still, he was curious, even though he was half-lit. He'd call Debbie at her office. She was nosy as hell. She might know what Coleman Fitzpatrick wanted.

He dialed her private number. If she was there, she would answer.

"Debbie Winter," she said when she picked up the phone.

"It's me."

"What, you're out of booze already?" she said.

"No, I'm not. I was going to tell you that

a certain lawyer called, but if you're goin
to be a bitch, forget it."

"What lawyer?" she urged.

He could hear the sudden tension in her voice. Maybe she was in some kind of trouble. He could only hope.

"Coleman Fitzpatrick."

He heard her intake of breath.

"What did he want?"

"I don't know. He was looking for Kate."

"After all these years, why would he be looking for Kate? Unless there's money he's been hiding. I bet that's it. Did he leave a number? I'll call him myself."

Leave it to Debbie to figure money into whatever the man wanted. She could be right. Why else would he be looking for Kate if not to tell her Alex's fortune was hers? "I'll check Caller ID for his number. Hold on." He looked at the clear plate on the handheld phone. "It's 550-9188."

"I'll call you back," Debbie said, then hung up on him.

Figures. The greedy bitch is at work already. But if she comes up with some extra cash, more power to her.

Don Winter was past wanting to open his own office. His brain was fried from drinking too much. Besides, he was beyond caring at this stage of the game.

Suddenly a thought occurred to him. An epiphany, you could say. He had a treasure chest of secrets he could use to blackmail his wife.

Why hadn't he thought of that before? Too much alcohol, he supposed. He'd back off for a while. See what she came up with on Fitzpatrick. If there was nothing to gain from him financially, maybe it was time he started making his wife pay for her sins.

Yes, it was time Debbie was punished for all her lies.

And he knew just where to hit her.

Right in the good old pocketbook.

No one valued money more than his wife.

No one.

Debbie wondered what Alex's attorney could want. It had to be more than searching for Kate. He had an investigator. If he wanted to find her that badly, he would have. No, she knew it had to be something else. She knew Fitzpatrick was the last man, outside of the inmates, to see Alex alive. Could he have known something he shouldn't have? Had Alex revealed the secret that he swore he would take to his grave? She doubted it, but she wasn't going to take a chance. Because of her secret, she'd never had to worry about finances. If

Don had known, he would have sweated bullets. After all these years, he was still mooching off the money good old Alex had put in trust for Emily, with Debbie as the trustee. She laughed at the thought, but Alex's money had also enabled her to open her own real estate office, which in turn supported Don's drinking habits and Sara's eating habits. Emily, though unbeknownst to her, would never have to worry where her next meal was coming from. Let her think good old Mom was working her ass off to send her to that stupid animal school. She was so much like Alex it was pathetic. Animal lover. Friend of the friendless. An aid to the elderly. It almost made her gag, Emily was such a do-gooder. At least she didn't have to look at her. She called now and then, but had never returned home since her high school graduation.

No one else knew her secret. Except Sara, the nosy little bitch. All those years ago, she'd overheard her and Alex talking about Emily. They had planned Alex's downfall, and it had worked. She'd done what she had to do for her family. Anyone else in her shoes would have done the same thing. She never thought Alex would be convicted, but she hadn't realized what an accomplished actress Sara was. When he was sent to rison, she'd felt a little bit of guilt, but not for long. Alex Rocket thought he was better than most. Well, she would have the last word. Lo and behold, she did, and it was even better than she could have imagined. She wondered what Kate would think if she knew how Alex had betrayed her? Debbie laughed. Maybe she would try to find her, too. Later. For now, she had a phone call to make.

Punching in the numbers, she looked at her nails. She needed a manicure. She would ask her manicurist to start coming to her office. Debbie didn't have time for such menial tasks.

"Hello," the male voice said.

"Is this Coleman Fitzpatrick?" Debbie asked in her sweetest voice.

"Yes, it is."

"This is Debbie Winter. I'm sorry if I'm disturbing you. My husband, he's not well, called me. He said you called. I'm afraid he can't be of much help these days. He's been quite sick for the past few months."

"Ah, Mrs. Winter. Yes, I spoke to your husband. I explained that I've been searching for Mrs. Rocket. I thought there might be an off chance you all might know how to get in contact with her."

"Absolutely not! After what Alex did to

my daughter, why, they're the last people on earth I'd want to stay in contact with. Pardon me for asking, Mr. Fitzpatrick, but aren't you an attorney? Don't you have an investigator to do your dirty work?"

"Yes, I am an attorney, and yes, I do have an investigator to do, as you put it, my 'dirty work.' We were unable to locate Mrs. Rocket. That was my reason for the call. As I said, I had hoped there was a chance you or Mr. Winter would know how to reach her."

Debbie's brain was spinning in circles. Something was up.

"I have no reason to stay in touch with Kate. We never liked one another in the first place. Mind if I ask why you want to get in touch with Kate after all these years?"

"It's personal, Mrs. Winter, I'm sure you understand. Thank you for taking the time to return my call."

Dial tone.

He'd hung up on her. Well, she still had a few contacts and more than a few tricks up her sleeve. She would find out exactly why Coleman Fitzpatrick wanted to contact Kate. She'd bet anything it had something to do with Alex's estate. This Fitzpatrick might hold the key to Alex's protected fortune.

She'd been around Naples long enough to earn a few favors. Debbie would spend the rest of the day on the phone calling them in.

"Melanie, can you come back to my office?" Debbie called over her intercom. Melanie, she thought, that was the girl's name.

"Yes, Mrs. Winter?" Melanie said. "What can I do for you?"

Debbie liked this girl. "I'm going to be in the office the rest of the afternoon. I'll be on the phone. Hold all of my calls, reschedule any appointments for the day. And more than anything, I do not want to be disturbed unless the place is on fire. Do you think you can do this for me?"

"Of course, Mrs. Winter. Is there anything else?"

"No, now go on. Get back to the reception desk. And remember, don't bother me unless it's life or death."

"Of course, Mrs. Winter."

Debbie thought her new receptionist might be a bit of an airhead. But if she followed the rules, she'd see to it that she kept her job for a while. She had no tolerance for laziness and stupidity. Some of the girls she hired to man the phones didn't have a clue how to put a call on hold. God, what was this world coming to?

She remembered her days at the deli in New York. She'd been in high school. She practically ran the business, from placing all the food orders to planning the menus. She'd never really learned to cook, but she could make a mean hoagie when she wanted to. She'd had to work in order to eat. Her mother was drunk most of the time. Her father had left when she was young. She didn't remember that much about him. Her goal in life had been to leave New York and marry a rich man. She'd met half her goal. And while she wasn't rich, she didn't have to roll change to eat.

She got up from her desk and closed the door. Melanie had forgotten to close the damn thing when she left. Maybe she was stupid after all. Oh, well, Debbie had more important things to occupy her time.

Coleman was tired. He wasn't getting any younger either. He'd spent the first half of his day on the telephone, something he wasn't very fond of, but he knew it was necessary. He was going to retire. He'd sold his house three months ago. He had six months before the new owners moved in. *Halfway there,* he thought. *Time flies.*

He had made a promise that he'd yet to

fulfill. If he didn't do this before he formally took off for the mountains, his retirement would consist of nothing but looking for Kate Rocket so that he could make good on his promise to Alex. He'd tried numerous times to get Kate on the phone after Alex's death. Twice he'd flown his plane to North Carolina, thinking that if he were at her doorstep, she wouldn't be able to turn him away. She surprised him when she refused to see him. He'd thought they were friends.

He'd never opened the large manila envelope Alex had entrusted to him. It was for Kate's eyes only. He respected that. As far as he was concerned, he had three months to find Kate.

His investigator had located her three years ago in Orlando. He'd even come up with an address. Coleman had made a few trips to Orlando, but he'd never found her. He had a feeling Kate didn't want to be found. He understood her grief. He'd lost his wife to cancer. All those years ago he'd wanted to offer comfort to Kate. He could have told her that time does ease the pain. He had good memories of his wife. Kate had had good times with Alex. It was just the last half-year of his life that they'd agonized over the arrest and the trial. It had been a sad time for the couple.

e more attemp

he'd cross that

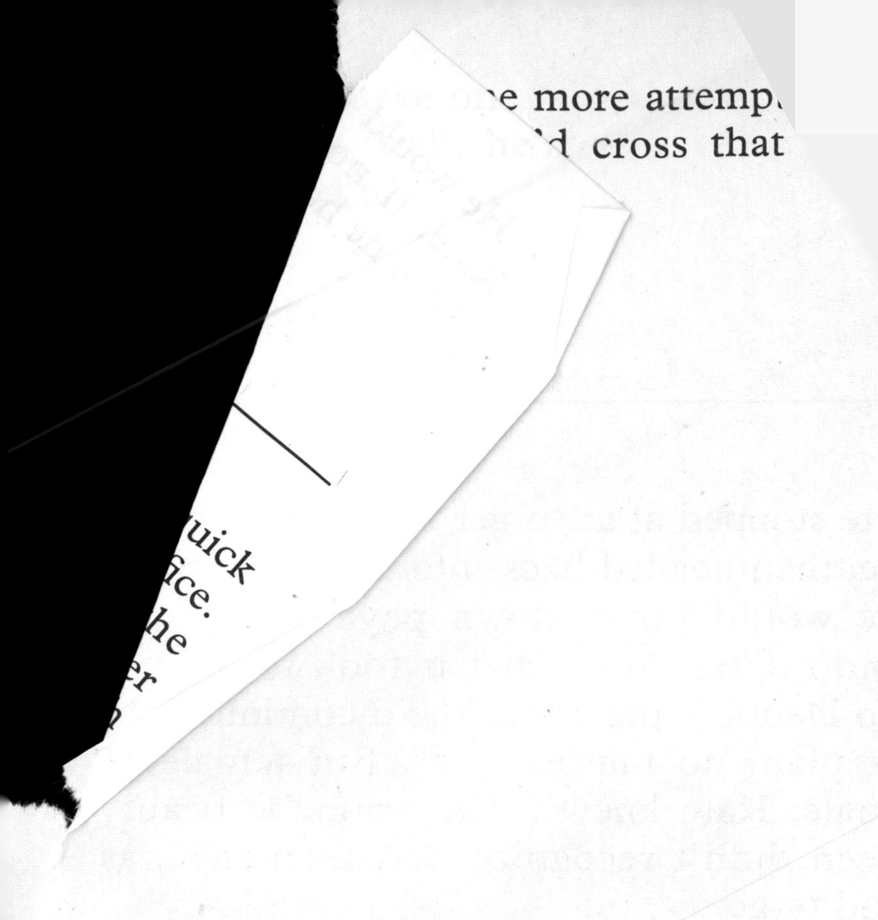

uick
ice.
he
er

CHAPTER 26

Kate stopped at a Burger King, had a q
bite, then headed back into Debbie's of
She would put a down payment on t
condo if that was what it took to get h
into Debbie's presence. She'd continue wit
her plan, no matter what. But female to female, Kate knew if the wannabe beauty queen didn't recognize her, then she was good to go.

Kate waited in the parking lot for another half hour to kill some time; she didn't want to seem too eager. She brushed her hair and reapplied her lip gloss. She added a touch more blush to her cheeks. Five minutes later she was in the reception area for the second time.

"Mrs. Ramsey, you're a little early. I'm not sure if Randi's back from her last showing. I'll check."

Rocket wasn't the most common name. Ramsey was her maiden name, so she felt comfortable using it. If she tried to pass herself off as Cindy Lou Who or Suzy Q, she wouldn't be able to keep up with her own lies. It was best to keep it simple.

Kate remained at the reception desk. She peered down the long hallway, hoping to catch a glimpse of the owner, but the door to her office was closed. Did this mean she was in and working, or did the other associates keep the door to the boss's office closed when she was out of the office? Kate would see if she could pick up anything from — she leaned back to look at the nameplate by the girl's computer — Melanie. Yes, Melanie liked to gossip. She was back. "Randi isn't here. Why don't you relax with a magazine while you wait. We've got all the current issues."

"Uh, you know, Melanie, I could use a Coke or something cool to drink. Would it be okay if I waited in the kitchen area?"

"Oh, I'm so sorry! Of course. How rude of me. Mrs. Winter would kill —"

"What am I going to kill you for this time, young lady?" Debbie Winter asked as she rounded the corner.

"Oh, uh nothing. Mrs. Winter, I was just telling Mrs. Ramsey that she could wait in the kitchen. She's got an appointment with

Randi, but she isn't back from the last showing."

Kate stood three feet away from Debbie. She hadn't even glanced her way. She was still Debbie. Too much makeup, though Kate thought her clothes were fine. She wore a pair of white linen slacks with a pale pink blouse. Pink sandals matched her blouse. She'd learned a bit of style since she'd seen her last.

Debbie glanced at her watch. "What time is the showing? I may be able to take, what did you say your name was?" Debbie asked Kate.

"Mrs. Ramsey. Kate Ramsey." She waited for some sign of recognition. So far so good.

"Tell Randi to report to my office when she returns. It shouldn't take this long. Mrs. Ramsey, I would be happy to show you the property. I'm Debbie Winter, the owner." She held out a professionally manicured hand.

Kate was nervous, but didn't want it to show, "If you're sure. I wouldn't want to cause you to neglect any of your clients." The Southern accent was strong. Kate hoped Debbie didn't pick up on its falseness, even though she thought she sounded okay.

"No, I've cleared my calendar for the day.

I was about to go home. Melanie, get the paperwork on Mrs. Ramsey."

"I had a condo I wanted to see."

"Yes, but if you're not happy with it, we can see if we have something else listed as well. Mrs. Ramsey, let me let you in on a secret. Property in Naples is hard to come by. If you see something you like, you'd best snatch it up. It goes like that." She snapped her manicured fingers.

"Of course. Then let's get going. I do have a schedule to stick to as well." Kate knew she sounded snotty, but she was not going to let Debbie dictate to her. She didn't care if she was the owner of the damned real estate office.

Debbie paused before heading out the door. "Melanie, if a Mr. Fitzpatrick calls back, give him my cell number."

Kate was surprised, but Fitzpatrick wasn't that uncommon a name. It couldn't be Coleman. Could it?

"I'm sorry. This man called me this morning. He's an attorney looking for an old friend. I thought I might have something to tell him. So are you new to the area?" Debbie asked.

It took Kate a minute to find her voice. "Yes, I've been here a few months. I was divorced, needed a change."

attorney looking for an old friend. What the odds?

"You'll find plenty of eligible bachelors here, but most of them are too old to enjoy, if you know what I mean. I have a friend who might be interested in meeting you." She felt like she was on an auction block as Debbie scrutinized her.

Kate felt sure she was hearing things. They were walking to what Kate assumed was Debbie's car. She was trying to fix her up on a date? She couldn't imagine what she'd do if they spent a couple of days together. She'd have her married off. Damn, was this how Debbie sold a hundred million dollars' worth of real estate?

"Thanks, but I'm not dating yet. I have . . . I want to enjoy being alone for a while."

Debbie unlocked the door to a sleek white Jaguar.

"Suit yourself, but the nights can get lonely."

She'd opened the door. This was too easy. "You're not married?" Kate asked.

Debbie drew in a deep breath. "Yes. My husband is very ill. I don't expect him to live much longer."

Don is dying?

"I'm sorry. You look too young to have a husband old enough to die."

Debbie snorted. "How old do you have be? Oh, forget I said that. My hubby isn dying of some terminal illness. He's jus pickling his liver."

Kate smiled. "Oh, well, that's too bad."

They drove along Highway 41, the road to everywhere in Naples. They made a few stops and turns. "Vanderbilt Beach is a great place. This price is too good to be true. You won't find another condo like this. Come on."

Debbie showed the parking lot attendant her ID, and he gave her a pass. They parked in what little shade there was.

Kate followed Debbie. For a minute she felt like an idiot, pretending to be someone she was not. Then she thought of Alex. This was for him, no matter how stupid it suddenly seemed.

The air-conditioning inside the lobby felt wonderful to Kate. There was no way in hell she would buy a condo there, beachfront or not.

"This is on the tenth floor. Faces the Gulf of Mexico."

Off the elevator, they found the unit for sale.

Debbie fumbled with a ring of keys, then swung the door open. She stood aside as Kate entered.

Debbie closed the door behind her. "Don't want all this cool air escaping. We're footing the electric bills for the owner until we sell."

Kate walked around the condo while Debbie pointed out the obvious. "The kitchen has new Jenn-Air appliances. The carpeting in all the bedrooms is new."

Kate listened as Debbie gave the stats on the condo.

"Of course, the main attraction is the view." Debbie pulled the floor-to-ceiling blinds open. It was a beautiful view, Kate had to admit. White beaches and aqua green water.

"What do you think?" Debbie asked. She reminded Kate of Carol Merrill from *Let's Make a Deal* as she held her palm out toward the Gulf.

"Impressive." *And I'll pick door number three,* Kate thought. She smiled.

"So? You want it or not?" Debbie persisted.

She wondered if this was the technique she used with all of her clients. If so, Kate found it hard to believe she'd sold a hundred million dollars' worth of real estate.

"I'd really like to look at more property. This is the first place I've seen."

She whipped the blinds shut. "Well, don't say I didn't tell you. This will be gone in a week, if not less."

"I'll keep that in mind." Kate couldn't wait to get back to her car. Debbie was still the same self-centered bitch she'd always been.

"I'll see what Randi has listed. You know, I walked out of the office without the damned paperwork. That's not like me," Debbie said.

Kate was surprised she'd actually admitted she had faults. Debbie had always been quick to blame others for her shortcomings.

"That's fine. I have things to do this afternoon anyway."

When they climbed in the Jag, Debbie turned the air-conditioning to high. "This heat frizzes my hair. I'll never get used to it. Thank God for central air and swimming pools."

Kate smiled. Debbie had always worried about her hair. Nothing new there. She'd hoped Debbie would mention her children, but since they were headed back to the office, Kate decide now was the only chance she would get.

"Debbie, do you have children? I can't remember if you said you did or not."

Debbie shot her a glance that said she knew she was full of it but answered her anyway. "I have two daughters. They're vn. The oldest is training to be a damned , do you believe that? My youngest, well, e hasn't found her place just yet. She ielps out at the office occasionally. What about you, do you have kids?"

Kate didn't know whether to tell the truth or lie. She decided to go in between. "I had a stepdaughter."

"Had? Did she die or something?"

Kate was still shocked at her crassness. "No, her father and I divorced."

"So she didn't like having a stepmother, huh?"

Kate rolled her eyes. "Actually, we got along quite well. There was a situation that she couldn't control. I haven't seen her in a while."

"Take my advice. Forget about her. Kids aren't all they're cracked up to be. I spent the best years of my life raising two selfish little girls. How do they thank me? One goes away to college, and the other, well, she's a real prize. Something's wrong with her. She's not right in the head, hasn't been since she was a kid, but that's an entirely different story. Oh don't get me wrong, I love my girls. I just wish they were more like me."

And God help us all, Kate silently prayed.

They pulled into the parking area before

Kate had a chance to reply.

She didn't want to go back inside the office. "I'm running late, Debbie. I'll c
Randi tomorrow and see what other listing
she has for me." She took her keys out o
her purse.

"Well, whatever. The client is always right. If you change your mind about that date, call me. This guy would be perfect for you."

"Thanks, but like I said, I'm not ready to date."

"Whatever, later." Debbie entered the office with a wave of her hand.

Kate jumped in her car, cranked the engine, and put the AC on. It was hotter than hell inside the vehicle.

She'd learned so much today. She'd already surmised that Emily was studying to be a veterinarian. Now she knew it for sure. How wonderful!

Kate was so happy for her. Emily had always loved animals as much as Alex did. He would've been so proud to know that all that time she'd spent with him at the kennel had made such an impression.

And then there was that message Debbie had left for Coleman. Kate couldn't imagine what the chances were that Coleman would contact Debbie in hopes of finding her. Maybe someday, when she accomplished oal, she would call him. She'd prepared this for the five years she had spent rking at the IRS. She wasn't going to al-w a friendship to stand in her way, no matter how nice Coleman had been to her in the past.

Then there was Sara. It was evident she was giving her mother a hard time. This didn't surprise Kate. Years ago she remembered Gertie telling her she thought Sara had mental problems. She'd been right.

Don was an alcoholic. That really didn't surprise her at all. He always overindulged. Year after year, what could you expect? That must be why there were no employment records for him. It looked like Debbie was the breadwinner these days.

It was time to put her plan into action. She now knew where her first magical strokes would take her.

"What the hell do you mean my account is overdrawn? I've never bounced a check at this frigging bank. You go back and check your records. I have thousands of dollars just sitting in your bank!" Debbie was so pissed she broke one of her cardinal rules about smoking in the office. *The hell with it, I own the damn place.*

"What? When?" Debbie shouted to the

bank manager. "I'm coming down there right now."

If she found out Don had managed to get access to her bank accounts, she'd throw his worthless ass out in the street. *I don't know why I keep him around anyway. He's as useless as tits on a boar.*

She raced down Highway 41 to the Sun Bank. Telling her she was overdrawn by $43,000! She knew to the penny how much money she had in her accounts. There was plenty to cover her expenses each month. She was not overdrawn. One of those teeny-boppers that worked at the bank had screwed up her accounts. If she had to rip each and every hair out of that stupid bank manager's head, she would. He'd assured her this wasn't a mistake. He said that she herself had made the withdrawals.

She practically skidded into the bank parking lot. She raced inside the bank. They wouldn't screw with her money. They were about to find out how pissed she was.

She entered the bank, bypassing several customers waiting in line. "Where is the manager? He just called me. You tell him Debbie Winter is here, and I want to see his ass now!" She slammed her fist down to emphasize just how mad she was. An older woman in line jumped. "Sorry," Debbie muttered as she waited for the manager.

A small man, typical of what you'd imagine a bank manager would look like, came running out of the back office. For a minute, Debbie thought he was a dwarf. *Damn, men keep getting smaller and smaller. What the hell happened to tall, dark, and handsome?*

"Mrs. Winter? I'm Sheridan Finkel. Please, let's go to my office."

Sheridan Finkel? If she hadn't been so upset, she would've laughed at the name.

"Mr. Tinkle, Finkel, whatever, I want to see these so-called major withdrawals I'm supposed to have made."

They entered the typical square box — plain desk, two chairs, and a plant in the corner office — de rigueur for most banks. *They must mass-produce this crap,* Debbie thought as she sat down.

Finkel hit a few keys on his computer screen, then hit the Print button. "This is the most current printout of your account, Mrs. Winter. As you can see, most of the withdrawals were made using Internet access. I took the liberty of checking your banking history. You do use the online service quite often." He gave her the papers.

She scanned them. "I did not take this much money out of my account! Where the hell is it? It didn't just magically form legs and walk out of this bank. I want you to find out who took my money! If I find one of your tellers has dipped into my accounts, this bank will have my name on the sign. Do you understand, Mr. Finkel?" Debbie stood to leave. It didn't matter what the papers read; she hadn't made any withdrawals from either of her accounts.

"Mrs. Winter, the only other option you have is to make a deposit to cover the insufficient funds; otherwise, I'll have to close your account permanently. Do you understand?"

"No! I don't! I don't care what you have to do to get my money back, I want it back in my account before the end of the day, or else I'm calling the Troubleshooters! They'll have this on every news station in the state. You'll have customers emptying out their accounts faster than I can say fraud. Do you understand?" Debbie peered into the little man's face.

"Ma'am, I'm going to have to ask you to leave. If not, I'll be forced to call security. Please."

"I'll leave, little man, but I'm coming back with my attorney. You've not seen the last of me!" Debbie stormed out of the bank.

Kate observed this while she waited to open her new account. She now had over ifty thousand dollars to deposit, but she would wait until she had the account set up for Internet access. Then she would transfer Debbie's money back into her bank, just a different account. She finished the paperwork required for opening new accounts. She would be able to view her transactions by two o'clock the next day. *Payback's a bitch,* she thought as she drove off.

This was just the beginning. All the years working with the IRS, studying the use of computers, not to mention the dozens of courses she'd taken over the years. She had enough power to hurt a lot of people with her skills. She was a regular hacker. She would have fun tonight.

She arrived at her apartment with a big smile plastered across her face. She took out a frozen dinner, looked at the ingredients, and tossed it in the garbage. She hadn't prepared a decent meal in ages. It was time she started living. She would celebrate the occasion by cooking a nice meal for herself. Before she could change her mind, she grabbed her purse and car keys.

She hadn't really grocery-shopped for years. She'd bought crap. It was a miracle she didn't have high cholesterol and heart disease with the bad food she'd been putting in her body. She would make a ni[illegible] pasta dinner with a salad. That would b[illegible] enough for starters. Maybe when all of this was behind her, she could enjoy cooking again. That is, if she didn't get caught. But prisons needed cooks, too.

She paid for her groceries with cash. She wondered how Debbie was going to pay for her next purchase, whatever it might be. She had a few more moves to make, then the Winter family would be cash-locked, credit-locked, whatever you wanted to call it. Debbie would be begging to sell doghouses when she was through with her. Another thought occurred to her. *There's a licensing board for Realtors. Surely it has some kind of code of ethics. I'll find out.*

Back at her apartment, she spent an hour making dinner. She recalled the meals she used to make for Alex. He liked everything, had never complained about serving as her official guinea pig when it came to trying new recipes. Even after all these years, she still missed him.

While waiting for the water to boil for the pasta, she minced garlic, onions, and mushrooms. She sautéed them with butter and a touch of olive oil. A few dribbles of real cream and a splash of wine. She made a salad with endive, radicchio, and romaine.

crumble of blue cheese, a handful of walnuts. She added a touch of balsamic vinegar to the salad, a dollop of olive oil. She inhaled. Her apartment smelled like home. Suddenly she felt the need to talk to Gertie. Her old friend was getting up in years. Kate couldn't forget about her. Gertie had devoted her life to her parents and then to her and Alex. She wished she would retire soon. Lauren was still in college. Gertie wanted her to take over when she graduated. Kate had an inkling of an idea, but she'd wait before she mentioned anything about it to Gertie.

The pasta was boiling, and the salad was ready. She'd break her rules just this once. She would call Gertie from home. Since she'd been gone, Gertie had moved into the main house. She hadn't wanted to, but Kate had insisted. It was closer to the kennel, plus she hated to leave the big old house empty. Gertie brought some of the dogs back with her each afternoon, and that was fine with Kate. Before she changed her mind, she dialed her old number.

Kate kept an eye on the boiling pasta.

"Hello."

"Hi, it's me." She never said her name when she called. She knew it was silly, but it was one of those precautions that she'd insisted on.

"Well, hello, me. It's about time yo called," Gertie replied.

Kate heard the smile in her voice. "I had to move. That took a few weeks to orchestrate. How are you? And tell me the truth."

"I never lie to you K— , kiddo. I'm okay. Arthritis is still giving me fits, but other than that, nothing new except more pups."

"Wonderful. I'm sure you'll find good homes for them."

"Don't I always?"

"Yes, of course you do. Now listen to me. I am getting things done here. All the years of planning are about to come to fruition. I observed a reaction to some of my work just today. It was quite satisfying."

"I bet it was. I hope to high heaven you know what you're doing. I think you should just forget this crazy plan and come home."

When their conversations got to this point, Kate knew it was time to hang up. "I'll call you soon, Gertie. Love you." She hung up the phone just in time to keep the pasta water from boiling all over the stove.

She drained the pasta and poured her homemade sauce over the top. She sat at the small table in the dining room and ate every last bite on her plate. It'd been so long since she'd had a good meal. She told rself she didn't have time to focus on erself while she was planning and plotting. t was too distracting. She'd lived like a nun for years; now that she was putting the plan into action, she would reward herself by living the way she wanted.

When she was done eating, Kate carried her dishes to the small kitchen, rinsed them, and put them in the dishwasher.

An hour later, she'd found just what she needed — access to Debbie's credit cards. There were several. Visa. MasterCard. Discover. American Express. All had balances, but none were extremely high. A few clicks of the keyboard, and all read differently. Now all of her cards were maxed out and a hold placed on all the accounts until all balances were paid in full.

Next, she'd check the Board of Realtors' code of ethics. After finding what she needed, she decided it would require some digging. Had Debbie ever misled a prospective client into believing the property they were selling or buying was worth more than its actual price? Possibly Melanie could fill her in. This meant another trip to her office. Kate would make up an excuse for stopping by unannounced.

Next Kate discovered that there were three mortgages against the Winter home.

An hour later, they were all in the final stages of foreclosure. It might take a few days for the bank to generate the required paperwork, but it would happen. Maybe Debbie could move into the condo she'd tried to sell Kate.

Finally she accessed the three credit reporting agencies: Experian, Equifax, and TransUnion.

Don's credit rating was low, the bankruptcy still showing. Debbie's wasn't all that terrible. Not yet. It would take a few weeks for the credit card companies and her mortgage company to send the required reports to the three reporting agencies, but it would happen.

Kate made copies of the night's work and locked them inside the small fireproof safe she'd bought just for this purpose. Rain, fire, she wasn't taking any chances. A hurricane, she'd grab the safe and go. Then Kate did a sweep of her computer's hard drive, erasing the evidence of where she had "been," so to speak.

A pinch of guilt rushed over her. She was ruining a family's livelihood without their having any knowledge of what was about to befall them. Then she remembered Sara's sick video testimony. She remembered how that testimony had in essence killed Alex and destroyed her world. What she was doing was mild by comparison.

After taking a long, leisurely shower, Kate went to bed with a book. She hadn't read for pleasure in years. She had the latest Stephen King novel beside the bed. One of Alex's favorite authors.

A perfect ending to a perfect day.

CHAPTER 27

Coleman had hit another dead end that evening. It appeared Kate Rocket had fallen off the face of the earth. His investigator had uncovered an interesting clue earlier in the day, however. Kate had recently walked away from her job as a supervisor for the Internal Revenue Service in Orlando. Apparently she was their most dedicated employee. When she didn't come to the office for three days, they filed a missing persons report. Her apartment had been swept clean by the Orlando Police Department. Nothing showed foul play of any kind, and there was nothing indicating where she might have gone. She'd had her phone and utilities disconnected but left no forwarding address. Nothing with the postal service either. For some reason, Kate Rocket did not want anyone to know where she lived.

Coleman couldn't come up with a good reason for Kate's subterfuge. He simply wanted to give her the envelope that he'd sworn to deliver. Then he could retire to his cabin.

Coleman had always wanted to open a small business of some sort. Maybe a mom-and-pop store out in the country, though he wasn't really sure. But he was sure he wasn't ready to quit working. It was just that he was tired of practicing law. He was young enough to have a second career, and he was going to find something that suited him. But first, he had to find Kate Rocket. Damn that woman. He'd never forgotten her. If things had been different he would have pursued a relationship with Kate, certainly something more than friendship. He'd been attracted to her the first time he saw her. Since Suzanne's death, there hadn't been any woman he'd really wanted to spend time getting to know.

It wasn't like that with Kate. From the very beginning, he had wanted to know everything there was to know about her. But circumstances said it wasn't the time or place, much less the right woman. Hell, for all he had known, Kate could have remarried.

He'd have his buddy at the phone company check her North Carolina number one last time. If he didn't find anything, he wasn't sure what his next move would be. Change his will and leave the letter for Kate? He laughed. He would find some way to get Alex's letter to her. He wasn't giving up just yet.

He would never forget the day at the prison when Alex had asked him to give the letter to Kate should something happen and he didn't make it home. Coleman had laughed at the time, telling him he had a second chance now that his conviction had been overturned. But Alex had insisted.

Coleman gave his word, but apparently there was more than the letter. Alex seemed upset. The lawyer had asked him about it and Alex had told him that sometimes you make a mistake, one small mistake. It's that mistake that changed everything for him. Coleman hadn't known what he was referring to, but thought it might have something to do with the envelope he'd been asked to pass on to Kate. Now that Alex was dead, Coleman wondered exactly what mistakes and secrets the envelope held. It went against his ethical code to look inside the envelope, no matter how curious. No, he would find Kate. The contents of the envelope were for her eyes only.

Kate was amazed at what a good night's

sleep did for her mental status. She woke up earlier than usual. She spent three hours on the computer double-checking her work. She saved the information again and did another sweep on her system. It was time to make that unexpected visit to the real estate office.

Melanie was at the reception desk. Good.

"Hi, Melanie."

"Oh, hi, Mrs. Ramsey. Did you have an appointment?" Alarm chiseled the girl's pretty face into stone.

"No, I was wondering if you or anyone here in the office might have found a bracelet. I was sure I had it on when I came to the office yesterday."

Melanie relaxed, her features back to pretty. "I don't think so, but if you'd like I can buzz the agents who are in the office to check."

"Would you? I hate to ask, but this was a special bracelet," Kate said, crossing her fingers behind her back the way she had done as a child. What lengths she was stooping to these past few days. *All in the name of justice,* she told herself.

"Of course. I have jewelry, too. I know what it's like. Why don't you have a seat, and I'll call the agents right now."

"Thanks, Melanie. I really appreciate this.

I know you're busy," Kate cooed to the young girl.

"Sure, just give me a few minutes."

Kate sat in the same chair as before. She had a bird's-eye view of the front door and the hall behind the reception desk. She took a magazine and thumbed through it. *Lord, I am so out of date with my clothes. I'll revamp my wardrobe once I complete my mission. If I don't get caught.*

The chime bell tinkled on the front door. Kate looked at the man walking up to the reception desk. This couldn't be happening. This kind of stuff only happened in soap operas.

Coleman Fitzpatrick in the flesh.

Her hands shook. She brought the magazine as close to her face as she could without its being too close. She peered around the edge of the magazine just to make sure she wasn't hallucinating. No, she was sure this was Coleman. He'd hardly aged a day in the last seven years.

Melanie put the phone in its cradle. "Is there something I can help you with?" she asked Coleman.

"Yes, is Mrs. Winter in? I need to talk with her. It's personal."

"No, she's gone for the day. Again. I can tell her you stopped in if she checks in later," Melanie suggested.

Coleman seemed to be considering her suggestion. "No, that's fine. Thank you. I'll see if I can catch her another time."

"Mrs. Ramsey?" Melanie called to her.

Coleman turned away from the desk heading for the door. Kate shoved the magazine so close to her face, she felt like her eyes were crossed.

"Kate? None of the agents found your bracelet," Melanie said.

Kate wished she would shut up until Coleman left the office.

Melanie walked to the other side of the reception desk and over to where she was sitting. "Mrs. Ramsey, are you all right?"

Kate nodded.

"Then take that silly magazine away from your face!" Melanie teased. She took hold of the glossy pages and yanked the magazine away from her face. This was something out of a nightmare.

"Melanie, please!" Kate shouted at her.

Coleman Fitzpatrick stopped just as he was about to leave.

Shit! Kate hadn't disguised her accent at all.

He turned around. Slowly, he walked to where she was seated. He looked at her as though he was seeing a ghost. Melanie took a step back to observe them. This was getting worse by the minute. All the years of work were about to go down the drain.

She stood to leave. "I'll call you, Melanie," Kate said.

With Coleman at her heels she exited the office. She would take her business with Coleman outside. She didn't want to provide Melanie with anything to report to her boss when Debbie checked in.

"Kate Rocket, is it really you?" Coleman asked once they were outside.

"In the flesh." Her heart sank as she said the words.

"Well, I must say you look a bit different than the last time I saw you. How are you, Kate? What are you doing in Debbie Winter's office? Why didn't you answer my calls? I've been searching for you for years!" Coleman gushed.

She took a deep breath. *Perhaps,* she thought, *I can make this work to my advantage. How? I haven't gotten to that part just yet. But I will.*

"You ask a lot of questions, Coleman. Why don't we go someplace where we can talk. In private."

"Of course. Would you like to have lunch?"

"No, I . . ." *There really isn't any reason not to have lunch with Coleman. He's an old friend. And I certainly don't owe him an explanation about why I'm here.* "Actually, lunch would be nice."

"Let's go somewhere private where we won't be disturbed. I can't believe I found you after all this time, Kate." He smiled and shook his head. "You can't imagine how many man-hours I've spent searching for you. Then bang, I walk into a local real estate office looking for you, and there you are."

Kate stopped dead in her tracks. Why was Coleman going to Debbie's office looking for her?

"Did I say something to frighten you, Kate?"

Maybe lunch wasn't such a good idea after all. "You know, I've changed my mind. I just remembered an appointment. It was good seeing you again, Coleman. We'll have that lunch another time. See you." She bolted to her car before she changed her mind. She crammed the key into the ignition. Shifting into drive, she peeled out of the lot. Two minutes later she saw Coleman's face in her rearview mirror. He'd followed her!

After he searched for me all these years, what else did I expect him to do. I cannot believe my own stupidity. Now I'll have to explain to him why I ran away.

She saw a Taco Bell up ahead and pulled into the parking lot. Coleman followed her, just as she knew he would.

They got out of their vehicles at the same time.

Coleman spoke first, "Kate, when I asked you to join me for lunch, well, I had something more . . . Well, let's just say Taco Bell wasn't first on my list."

Dear Coleman. He had the grace not to humiliate her. She didn't deserve him as a friend.

"They have really good burritos."

"Then let's go have lunch." Coleman took her hand, leading her inside the fast-food joint.

She wanted to jerk her hand out of his. She felt sparks when he touched her. Damn, she had been away from human contact far too long. She would make friends when all of this was over. She didn't know where she would end up, but she knew she had to finish what she had started, what she had planned for so long, and put it behind her. She was allowing herself to become . . . *Hell, I don't know. I just know that Coleman's touch bothers me.*

"Kate?"

"Yes, I think I'd like a burrito. Cheese,

extra lettuce, no beans."

"I'll have the same," Coleman told the pimply-faced teenager wearing the standard purple uniform. "And two soft drinks."

He led her to a small table by the window. "Wait here," Coleman said, with a wink.

She nodded. Five minutes later he was back with their order. He spread out napkins for plates, peeled the paper from the straws, then gave her a packet of seasoning sauce.

"So, it's been a long, long time, Kate. Tell me about your life now."

Something told her she should trust Coleman with her secrets. Later. Maybe.

"After Alex's death, I wasn't up for much of anything. Poor Gertie. Had it not been for her, I would have gone stark raving mad. She was a godsend."

Coleman listened. "You said 'was.' Does that mean she's gone, too?"

Kate laughed. "Hardly. Gertie'll outlive us all. She's a good old gal."

"Yes, I remember her well." Coleman paused, unsure if he should bring up the subject. "All the times I called you, why wouldn't you speak to me? I have wondered throughout the years what I might've said to offend you. I even made a couple of trips to North Carolina hoping to see you. And I had an envelope from Alex."

"What envelope?" Kate asked.

"The one that Alex left for me to give to you should he not come home."

That's why Coleman pursued me all those times?

"This certainly is a surprise. I thought all of Alex's things were returned when you brought his ashes."

"They were, but Alex made me promise that I would personally see that the envelope was placed in your hands. Evidently, he didn't trust the mail or anyone else to give it to you."

"Then where is it?" Kate asked.

Coleman laughed. "Well, I don't carry it around with me, if that's what you mean. It's in a safe place."

"Is that why you were looking for Debbie? Did you think I would have stayed in touch with them after all the sorrow and pain they caused?"

Coleman took a healthy bite from his burrito, then wiped the dripping sauce from his chin. "This is good. Messy but good. I was at the end of my rope. I'm getting ready to retire, Kate. Before I could do so, I had to see that the envelope and whatever it contained was placed in your hands. I was getting desperate when I called the Winters. I thought they might have contacted you."

"No, not once that I was aware of," Kate replied.

Coleman wiped his face again. "Then I can finally retire in good conscience. I've kept my word to Alex."

Kate's eyes filled with tears at the thought of Alex. Though she thought about him constantly, considering what she'd involved herself in, the pain of losing him had lessened with time. To hear about Coleman's dedication to him simply brought back all the memories of the time Alex spent in prison.

He reached for her hand across the small orange tabletop. "Kate, I'm sorry. I know all of this comes as a big shock to you. It's been over seven years now. You've gone on with your life?"

If he only knew.

She shook her head. "I suppose you could say I'm stuck in a time warp. I haven't accomplished much of anything since Alex's murder. I moved around, took a government job, then I decided a change was in order. I came to Naples."

"I would've thought this place would hold too many bad memories for you."

"I guess it does. Maybe that's why I'm here. To put an end to the bad memories, the bad times. Maybe I can start a new life."

"You say this as though you haven't exactly made the decision to move on, Kate. Tell me the real reason you moved here."

Kate looked at Coleman, really looked at him. He was a very attractive man. Why hadn't she noticed that before? Dark hair, graying at the temples. A deep tan. Eyes as green as grass. Coleman Fitzpatrick was truly a handsome man. She wondered if he'd ever remarried. She looked at his hand for a ring. Nothing.

He saw her.

"I've never remarried. What about you?"

"You read my mind. I was wondering the same about you. No, I haven't even dated since Alex's death. I . . . I was very focused on my work. There was so much learning required, I didn't really have time to think about dating." It was true, but she couldn't tell Coleman what she'd spent all that time learning.

"Let's do this. I'll make something for dinner at my place tonight. You can come, enjoy a quiet evening with an old friend, and I can give you Alex's envelope."

"Yes, I should do that, I suppose."

Coleman raised his brow. "If it's going to cause you any hardship, I can bring it to wherever you're living."

"No, I'll have dinner with you." She took

a deep breath. She didn't want Coleman in her apartment. If he saw the command center she'd set up in the spare room, he would know she was up to something, and she felt like he already suspected she was doing more than coming to Naples to banish old memories. "Just give me your address, and I'll find you."

Coleman gave her the address and told her what time to arrive. Kate felt a tad excited as she drove back to her apartment. She had a date. Sort of. Well, not really. An evening with an old friend. She would enjoy her time with Coleman. He hadn't said where he was retiring to, but Kate knew it wouldn't be in the state of Florida.

Before leaving for dinner, Kate booted up her computers. She checked all of her work to see if anything had changed. Nothing. She checked the credit reporting agencies, even though she knew it would take a few weeks for them to list all the discrepancies in Debbie's credit history. She hit a few keys and discovered the mortgage company had already issued a certified letter of foreclosure. That was quick, but Kate figured with all the technology available in today's world, there really wasn't any reason to delay the process.

She took her time getting ready. Now she wished she had something other than the jeans, khakis, and black capris to wear. Deciding on the khakis for coolness and comfort, she wore her usual white T-shirt. She spent little time with her hair and makeup since she wasn't trying to hide from Coleman. She didn't even bother blow-drying the curls from her hair. She looked in the mirror. Her face was recognizable without the contacts and all the war paint.

Following the directions Coleman had given her, she was surprised to discover he only lived fifteen minutes away. A gated community, but older. There were no guards waiting at the entrance, just an electronic gate with a button to allow the gates to open and close. Not very secure, but as Kate traveled through the winding roads, she saw that most of the homes were very grand. They probably had killer security systems.

At the end of Willow Lake Drive, Kate saw Coleman's SUV parked in the drive. She'd wanted to bring something to contribute to the meal, but he had insisted on cooking for her himself. Said he enjoyed puttering in the kitchen now and then. She'd stopped at Publix and purchased a bouquet of flowers. She couldn't arrive empty-handed. The envelope was uppermost on her mind as she rang the doorbell. Should she insist Coleman allow her a few minutes alone with the contents before dinner, or should she wait until she could be alone? She didn't know and would play it by ear.

The door opened. Coleman wore khaki shorts with a yellow polo shirt. Wisps of dark, wet hair curled around his face. "I just got out of the shower. I hope you haven't been here long."

That explained his hair. "No, I just got here." Kate walked into the foyer. Marble floors, Tiffany chandeliers. Nice, but not too stuffy. "This is a beautiful home. I had no idea you lived in such splendor."

"Yes, it is nice. Too big for me, though."

Coleman was looking at the flowers she had hanging at her side.

"Oh, these are for you. Us. Dinner."

"Thanks, I think there's a vase in the kitchen. Now, if you will follow me." Coleman turned on his heel, and she followed him to a huge kitchen.

Viking range, Sub-Zero refrigerator. "Nice," Kate said. "Did your wife spend much time in the kitchen?"

"Actually, she didn't cook at all. Said it was a waste of time."

Kate laughed. She looked all around the

kitchen. "This is a chef's delight, Coleman. Too bad it isn't used as it was intended."

Coleman rifled through several cupboards before he found a vase. He filled it with water and placed the flowers inside. "What gave you the idea it's not being used?"

"I don't know." Kate laughed again.

"Actually, I'm somewhat of a chef. I lied. I do a little more than putter in the kitchen. I create!"

"Well, I am truly surprised."

"I don't tell everyone I meet that I'm as at home in the kitchen as I am in front of a judge. Wouldn't want to ruin my image."

"And just what kind of image would you be ruining if your secret were discovered?" Kate inquired.

"Oh, you know, the macho man thing. Me Tarzan, you Jane."

She laughed. "Somehow I find that hard to believe. Suzanne was a lucky woman."

A look of sadness swept across his face. "And I was a lucky man. She was a great wife even though she hated to cook."

"Then we have something in common other than tragedy."

"Yes, we do. I knew you were very involved with a restaurant at one time. Alex told me you taught cooking classes. I hope you won't be grading tonight's meal." He winked at her while he rinsed his hands.

Kate was enjoying the light conversation. It had been way too long since she'd shared such an exchange with anyone. She really missed life.

Coleman watched her. "Why the look of gloom and doom? Surely you don't think my cooking is that bad without having tried it yet."

She shook her head. "I was thinking that it's been a long time since I spent an evening with a friend, that's all." She offered him a watery smile.

"You didn't go out much in Orlando?"

"There wasn't time. All the classes I had to take." Kate felt a half-truth was better than nothing. She really didn't want to explain the past five years of her life. "Why don't you give me the envelope. I'll look through it while you 'create' unless you need my assistance."

Coleman dried his hands on a tea towel. "Of course. I should have given it to you when you arrived. I'll go get it from the den."

He returned to the kitchen with a standard manila envelope. Kate sat at the island in the center of the kitchen. "I'm almost afraid to open it."

"Well, I wouldn't be, it's from Alex. He

was very serious the day he gave it to me." Coleman returned to his work at the sink.

"Could you tell me about that day before I open this? I know it sounds silly, but if you could."

"It's not silly at all, Kate. Of course I can tell you. But first, let me check my creation in the oven, then we can talk over a glass of wine." Coleman peered inside the oven and smiled. "Delightful. Now the wine."

He had a built-in minicooler beneath the counters. He removed a bottle, took a corkscrew from a drawer and glasses from an overhead rack.

Kate followed Coleman outside to the pool area. A huge rectangular pool dominated the entire space. There was a rock waterfall at the end of the pool and lots of flowery plants. The patio furniture was dark green and gold, blending into the wild growth of greenery that wound its way on both sides of the pool screen.

"This is nice, Coleman, I bet you stay out here most of the time."

He opened the wine, poured them each a glass. "I do, but I prefer the real outside. This is a great place to relax, though. You want to go for a swim after dinner?"

"No, I'm afraid I don't have anything to wear. Does that sound like a typical silly girl or what? No, really, I didn't bring a suit."

"I guess we're too old to even consider skinny-dipping," he teased.

Kate blushed, something she hadn't done since college. She was glad for the twilight. "I have never skinny-dipped in my life, Coleman!"

"Then you don't know what you're missing. So, we'll see how the evening goes."

Kate looked at him with eyes as round as saucers. "I don't think so."

He burst out laughing. "I'm kidding. Loosen up, Kate, I'm just having fun."

Then he doesn't want to go skinny-dipping?

"Oh, I know. I was just . . . Never mind. Why don't I look at that envelope and put the mystery to rest."

"I thought you wanted to hear about the day he gave it to me."

"Yes, of course, please tell me." She took a sip of her wine. Nice.

"It was the day after I had told him about the conviction being overturned and the new trial he would get. He stressed to me over and over that I was not to reveal the contents of the envelope to you unless he died. Said he'd made a promise about something many years ago, and he wanted to keep it. Alex was a man of his word, I know that. We spoke about the case, the reasons he thought Sara might have made the accusation. He asked me several more times if I would swear to do as he instructed. I assured him I was a man of honor. Sounds silly, I know. I remember using that phrase, too. Alex liked that I did. I could tell.

"He told me a bit about his first marriage and when his wife died. He'd done his grieving, but there seemed to be something he kept holding back. Maybe that will be explained when you read what's inside." He drank the rest of his wine, pouring another glass for both of them.

Kate thought about Coleman's last conversation with Alex. A few things puzzled her. She had no idea why he would have brought up Anna, Alex's first wife, who had died from leukemia. Alex never talked about that period in his life. He was young when he married. By the time he'd realized it was a mistake, Anna was diagnosed with the fatal disease. He'd told Kate he wasn't the kind of man who could walk away and leave her, knowing she didn't have long to live. She'd respected him for his decision, but now wondered if there was something more to that period of Alex's life than she'd been told.

"This is personal, Kate. I'm going to leave you alone for a bit. I've got a salad to prepare and a tasty dressing to go along with it. While I'm working in the kitchen, why don't you look over the contents?"

"If you're sure you can't use me in the kitchen, I'd appreciate the time alone."

"I'll be just fine. Now go on and open that damned thing," he joked as he went inside.

Left alone with Alex's letter — and Kate was sure that was what the envelope held — she was almost afraid to open it. She was nearing the end of her involvement with the life she and Alex had led. After his death she'd made a promise to herself — Alex's death would not be in vain. She would do whatever it took to clear his name and make the Winter family pay for his death and the anguish they'd caused.

Utilizing the legal system hadn't really been an option. She knew there was no chance to win in a courtroom. What charges could she bring against the Winters since Alex was dead? Defamation of character, at best, but that wasn't what she wanted. She needed to dispense justice herself, directly, to those who had caused Alex to die.

Sara Marie Winter and her mother.

Kate opened the gold-colored clasp on the envelope. Inside were several sheets of a yellow legal tablet folded in half. She remembered that this was the kind of paper the inmates wrote their letters on. She had dozens of Alex's. Removing the papers, Kate saw that her hands were trembling. She suddenly wasn't sure that she wanted to read the contents of Alex's letter. After all the nights she had cried and prayed for just one more word from her beloved Alex, she finally had her wish. That old phrase, "Be careful what you wish for," came to mind. Alex was getting the last word. The question was: Did she really want to hear it?

Of course, she had to. She opened the first sheet of paper. There were all kinds of numbers. She ran her gaze up and down the columns. The numbers to all their accounts. Gertie had them. Kate had never really thought about this since she knew Alex took care of it. But what if something were to happen to Gertie? Alex had known Kate would need these numbers. Still thoughtful, even in death. She brushed a tear from her cheek.

The next paper was addressed to Emily. She thought it odd. She would find a way to get it to her. She didn't feel comfortable reading something Alex had written to her. They had a very special relationship. Kate placed the folded sheet of paper aside.

The next paper she opened was a letter to

her. She wiped more tears with her knuckles.

Chapter 28

My Dearest Kate,

If you're reading this, I am no longer here on earth with you. I hope I'm somewhere above smiling down on you and the dogs. Crazy, that I would mention the dogs, but I think of how happy I was when I found the kennel and bought it from your parents. To get you as an added bonus, Kate, that was more than any man deserved. I have truly had a blessed life. Except for the past few months, there is nothing I would change. But being human, I have made mistakes, as you well know! As a young man, I made my share of mistakes, and you know what most of them are. However, one mistake I made so shamed me that I could not bring myself to taint the purity of our marriage by revealing it to you . . .

Kate read the rest of the letter, then ran

inside the house. She grabbed her purse from the small table where she'd left it in the foyer. She had to leave.

Coleman couldn't imagine what the letter could have said to send Kate flying out the door last night. He had no clue where she lived or a telephone number where he could reach her. Now he almost wished he'd looked at the contents of that damned envelope. Would this never end? He couldn't begin to imagine how Kate felt. She'd lived this life for the past seven years, ever since Alex's death. He needed to find her. He called his investigator.

"Then that's good news. I can try the number. If it works, I'll get back to you. Thanks." Coleman hung up the phone. Who said there wasn't a Santa Claus?

He dialed the number given to him by his investigator. Figuring he would give it one more try, they'd made contact with the powers that be at BellSouth in Asheville. Sure enough, the Asheville number where Kate lived with Alex had just received a long-distance call from the 239 area code. This was good. Coleman held the phone with his shoulder.

"Hello."

"Kate, is this you?" He heard paper rustling on the other end of the phone.

"How did you get this number? It's supposed to be unlisted."

"I have my ways, but that doesn't matter right now. I've been up all night worrying about you. Why did you race out of here last night? You know I ruined dinner."

Kate gave a halfhearted laugh. "I'm sorry about the dinner. I just needed to be by myself."

"I'm teasing about the dinner. I was worried about you. After all these years, don't you know you can trust me? Whatever is going on in your life, you can talk to me. We're friends, remember?"

Kate thought about her so-called life. She had stopped living in every sense of the word. All those years in Orlando. She had deprived herself of everything. She'd even given up her love of cooking, telling herself that since Alex wasn't there to eat with her, there was no reason she should care what kind of food she ate. She'd consumed so many frozen dinners, she'd lost count. Her need for revenge was all she'd lived for. And now, she wasn't so sure about that revenge. The contents of Alex's letter had changed all of that. She really needed someone to talk to.

"Kate?"

"Can you reheat last night's dinner for lunch?"

"I can do even better," Coleman replied.

"On such short notice?"

"Absolutely. We chefs keep the pantry stocked. Just in case."

"Can you make tea?" Kate asked. "I haven't had a decent cup of tea in days."

This sounded nothing like the woman who'd raced out of his house last night. Hell, she sounded like a changed woman, even in the short time he'd had her on the phone.

"I can make a better pot of tea than Earl Grey."

"Then expect me in twenty minutes." Kate placed the phone on the desk next to her. She looked at all the expensive electronic equipment she'd spent so much of her life learning to use. Now she wasn't sure if she could continue her quest for justice or revenge, whatever she wanted to call it. She thought it was more the latter. Alex was gone and he wasn't coming back. He'd made his share of mistakes, but his mistakes had provided another reason for her to question her motives.

Maybe she would tell Coleman after all. He was her friend, and that was what a friend was for. A shoulder to lean on.

Exactly twenty minutes later she parked in Coleman's drive. She was barely out of the car before he came running outside. He still wore the same clothes from last night.

"Coleman, you look like hell!"

"Well, I'd like to say the same, but it would be a lie. Come in. I've got some hot tea that's going to blow your mind."

"That strong, huh?"

"Nope, it's that good." He took her hand in his as they entered the house.

"I'm sorry the way I bolted out of here. I . . . there's something I'd like to talk about. I want to wait until I have a cup of that tea, though. And something to eat. You know, I don't think I had anything to eat yesterday. No wonder my stomach feels as hollow as a cheap chocolate bunny."

"A cheap chocolate bunny?"

"When I was a little girl my mother always gave me a chocolate bunny for Easter. It was solid, she would say, not one of those 'hollow cheap chocolate bunnies.' "

"I see."

He led her back to the kitchen. She would have loved to cut loose cooking there, and told him so.

"Then you'll have to come over sometime and make dinner. I would love to watch a pro at work."

Kate laughed. "Yeah, me too. I'm not a pro, I just enjoy cooking. I do love to bake."

"I'll make dinner sometime, and you can whip up some scrumptious dessert. How does that sound?"

"I would like that very much."

"Here, taste this." He poured her a cup of tea.

Kate blew into the cup, then took a sip. And another. "This is very good. Now, you'll have to tell me the secret."

"I will. Someday. Right now I want you to talk to me. I want to know where you've been all these years." He paused, then took her hand again. "I've missed you, Kate."

She had missed him, too. She just hadn't realized it. "I missed you, too. It's funny. We've been apart all these years, and I feel like you've been around forever. Kinda like an old shoe."

He laughed. "Kate, you amaze me. An old shoe, huh?"

"Oh, Coleman, you know I didn't mean it that way. Just comfortable, I guess. Even though most of our time together has been stressful, Alex's case and all, I always felt better about things after we would talk. Is that silly?"

"Not at all. I used to think . . . never mind. It doesn't matter. Let's focus on the future.

Now, there was something you wanted to tell me."

"You have to feed me first. Remember the bunny."

"I just happened to have a decent chilled crab salad waiting in the fridge. With homemade croissants just waiting to be slathered with butter."

"And I thought you didn't bake," Kate quipped.

"I don't, but the Publix bakery makes a decent croissant. Of course, anytime you want to make your own and use me as a taste tester, I'm all yours."

Kate smiled, recalling all the times she'd used Alex for the same thing. "I'll consider that."

They both ate seated at the center island in the kitchen. The crab salad was excellent. "Maybe sometime we could share recipes," Kate teased.

Coleman jumped out of his chair, opened a kitchen drawer, and pulled out a stack of spiral notebooks. "I've been writing them down for years. Take them if you like. When I retire, I'm going to put all of my recipes on my computer. Then I can e-mail them across the world."

Kate thumbed through the notebooks. "Wow, I am impressed. You're actually organized, too."

"It's the only way I could ever find anything, though I have to admit, Suzanne suggested the system."

"Smart woman," Kate said. She took another croissant and bit into it. "Decent." She finished her salad, another croissant, and tea. Coleman waited patiently.

"So, what is it you want to tell me?"

Kate pulled away from the island. She stood up and stretched. "Let's go sit beside the pool, do you mind?"

"Best place in the house. Come on, I'll bring the teapot."

After they settled in, Kate wasn't sure where to begin. "I haven't been honest with you. And a lot of other people as well."

Kate watched him for any sign of judgment. Nothing. Yet.

"When Sara accused Alex of doing all those horrid things, I wanted to choke the life right out of her. I couldn't, I knew that. Or I couldn't and get away with it, that's what I thought. Alex was already in a hell of a mess, and I certainly did not need to add to his troubles. When you came to the house and told me Alex had been killed, I spent week after week plotting Sara's death." She took a sip of tea.

"Kate, let me say this. If you're waiting

for me to judge you for whatever it is you may or may not have done, I'm not here to judge you. We all screw up. I've spent my life defending people. Most of them just made a simple mistake. But in the eyes of the law, some mistakes are a crime. Now, before you go any further I want to assure you that whatever you tell me stays in this room. As your friend, Kate, not as an attorney. Nonetheless, would you please hand me a dollar as a retainer so that just in case, I can claim attorney-client privilege to protect you from having to reveal in a court of law anything you might tell me."

After handing Coleman the asked-for money, Kate said, "Thanks, Coleman. I was sure I could trust you, but I've always known that." She realized what a waste the past five years had been. But she wasn't going to abandon her plans, just rework them a bit.

"I felt horrible having those kinds of thoughts about a child. The second year, I decided it wasn't just Sara that I wanted to get even with. Debbie was also a thorn in my side. I never really liked her. Now I like her even less. Hell, I don't like her at all. When she and Don brought the girls for all those visits, I thought it best to pretend I enjoyed her company. We had nothing in common, except the girls. You know that Alex and I weren't able to have children." Kate paused. This was the hard part. She hadn't come to terms with it yet, but she would. She wanted to.

"I often wondered why you two never had kids. Suzanne and I chose not to, now I wish we had. But go on."

"Alex was married right out of college. Her name was Anna. She died of leukemia not long after they'd married. It was a sad time for Alex. Inside that envelope that you've waited so long to give me . . . Alex and Debbie had a one-night stand. Emily is Alex's daughter." Tears were streaming down Kate's face. She rubbed her eyes with the hem of her shirt. She'd said it. *Emily is Alex's daughter.* There'd been no anger or jealousy when she read this, only relief that a part of Alex lived on.

"So. What happens now?" Coleman asked.

"All those years when Debbie and Don brought the girls to visit, it was so Alex could be with his daughter. She looks so much like him, I don't see how I missed it. He and Debbie swore they'd never tell Don or me because they knew how much it would hurt Emily and us. Debbie can be a real bitch, but she agreed. Alex set up a trust fund for Emily. She'll never have to work a day if she chooses not to. But I've learned she's studying to be a vet; it's so like her. She adored the time she spent with Alex at the kennels. While I loved the dogs — heck, I miss having them around more than you know — it's Emily that the kennels should belong to. Not me." Kate felt light, almost as though she were floating. She hadn't felt this way since before Alex died.

"And just what are you going to do about that?"

Kate looked at Coleman as though he'd lost his mind. "There isn't really anything I can do, is there?"

"Don't you think Emily would want to know Alex was her father?"

"Maybe. But it's not my place. The decision not to tell her was made by her parents. I don't see that I have any right to shock her with something like this just now."

"Have you thought of discussing it with Debbie and Don?"

"No! I'm sorry, I don't think I can. At least not yet. There's more than I'm telling. For now, I need to keep it this way. I need some time to think through what this means. For me and Emily. And Don. Alex said he didn't know. What if Don really knew, but Alex wasn't aware of it?"

Coleman poured the last of the tea into

her cup. "You've got a lot of thinking to do, Kate. Lots of decisions to make before you can move forward. I don't envy you."

"Thanks for being my friend, Coleman. You've helped me more than you know. I have some things I need to do now." Kate took the empty cups and pot to the sink and hand-washed them.

"Suzanne always washed that particular pot."

"It's a very rare piece of china, Coleman. Never serve me tea in it again."

"Oh, well, so much for getting out the good china to impress. Next time you'll get a mug from the law office." He raised his hand, then lowered it. He took her hand in his, and very slowly brought it to his lips. He placed a kiss on her hand. So light, Kate could barely feel his lips against her skin. His light touch sent flames soaring through her.

Before she let this go further, and she now knew that was inevitable, she removed her hand from his.

"I'll be back for that mug of tea, Coleman. I promise."

Chapter 29

"I will sue the pants off you, do you hear me?" Debbie slammed the phone down. Her life was falling apart.

"What are you complaining about now?" Don asked, his voiced slurred already. It was noon.

"What do you care? As long as you have that bottle to wrap your lips around, you're as happy as a traveling salesman with the farmer's daughter, aren't you?"

Debbie was in their bedroom, digging through some boxes at the back of the closet.

"What are you looking for?"

"If you must know, I have a banker's box full of bank statements in here. I need to look at them. If you'd stay sober long enough to have a decent conversation, you would know we're in deep shit, Don. The rug is about to be pulled out from under me. You too." She found the box in question and hefted it onto their bed, white sheets and all.

"What are you talking about, Debbie? Does everything always have to be such a frigging drama with you?"

"Well, well, I am impressed. You can speak more than three words at a time."

"I'm not drunk. I know you find that hard to believe, but I haven't had anything to drink today."

"You sure as hell sounded drunk about two seconds ago. Are you pissing it out that fast?" Debbie shot a look over her shoulder. Don was pacing the room.

"I'm serious. Look at my hands." He held his hands out in front of him. He could barely control the trembling.

"Then go have another drink. Listen, my life is falling apart. You couldn't have picked a worse time to go on the wagon. Again." She thumbed through the file folders in the box. "How many times has it been now? I've lost count."

"Stop for just one minute. I think I have something you might want to hear. Our lovely daughter called looking for you. She was screaming and crying."

"Which one?" Debbie asked, not really interested in either of her girls at the moment. She had more important things to worry about.

"You have to ask?" Don plopped down on the bed, causing the box of papers to topple over.

"Dammit, you can put this back. I'm off to the bank." Debbie stuffed the bank statements in her purse.

"Sara is pregnant."

"Says who?" She didn't have time for Sara's dramatics.

"She called from the doctor's office. She wanted to talk to her mommy." Don said the last word in a babylike voice.

"You don't like Sara, do you? You never have. It's always been Emily, Emily, Emily." Debbie laughed. "If you only knew. Tell Sara to call my cell if she calls back. I've got to get to the bank. Someone is out to destroy me, and I'm going to find out who."

Don watched her. "Debbie, what did you mean by that remark you just made?"

She rolled her eyes. "Kiss off, Don. I'm outta here." She swung her purse across her shoulder like it weighed a ton.

"I know Emily isn't my daughter."

For once Debbie didn't have a smart comeback. She stopped and turned to look at her husband. "What?"

"Do you really believe I'm that dumb? I might be a drunk, but I am not a stupid one. Come on, Deb. Look at Emily, then look at Sara. While Sara is the spitting image of you, Emily is Alex Rocket made over. The female version."

The room was silent. "What would you like for me to say?" Debbie asked.

"Nothing, because there is nothing to say. You seduced my best friend."

"Just remember, your best friend molested our daughter, or have you forgotten in all that alcohol fog you've lived in for the past three years?"

"Despite what you think, I'm not drunk every hour of the day. I am drunk most of the time, I'll admit. Did you ever wonder why I started drinking so heavily? Did you ever care to find out if I had a problem?" He held his hand out. "Don't answer. I already know what you'll say."

"Because we've had this same conversation a thousand times, Don. You drink because you're a failure. You lost your job, you fell into a sinkhole. End of story. Not my fault."

"Think, goddamn it!"

"I don't know what you're trying to tell me, so it'd be best if you just spit it out. I have got to go to the bank."

"Yes, I know. You've told me enough. You're going to stay here and listen to what

I have to say. The bank can wait."

Debbie sat down on the edge of the bed. She took her purse off her shoulder and set it by her feet. She held out her arms as if she were embracing the world. "Okay. I'm all yours. Say whatever it is you need to say, so I can get the hell out of here."

"I know what you and Sara did. I have proof."

Debbie fumbled with her watch. She laughed, but it wasn't her usual smart-ass laugh. "Whatever. I have no idea what you're talking about, Don."

"Yes, you know exactly what I'm talking about. Don't deny it. Stop this damned lie that you're living. I can't take this crap anymore. Do you ever stop and think that you killed a man?" Don stumbled over to the bed, grabbing Debbie's arm. "I'd love to smack your goddamn face. I've wanted to for years, but I won't give you the satisfaction. Get the hell out of here. Now!"

Debbie raced out of the room so fast, Don expected to see smoke in her wake. She was a real prize. He'd just confronted her with the worst news possible. She didn't give a damn. Someone had to. He was so very tired of his life. If he could have only started over, he would never, ever, not in a million years, have married the woman he'd tied himself to. He'd rather be a monk.

Debbie tried to light a cigarette as she drove to her office. Her hands shook worse than Don's had. She pushed the lighter in again. She removed it, this time able to light the wobbling cigarette.

The shit had hit the proverbial fan, and she was directly in the line of fire. She could deal with Don; he was a drunk, everyone knew it. If he ran his mouth to his cronies at the club, they'd chalk it up to too much to drink.

Sara was pregnant. Debbie would insist she get an abortion. No way was she taking care of another brat. She would talk to her tonight. She was supposed to be on birth control. At twenty, she should know better.

Damn, just one more complication I'll have to take care of. Why does life have to be so hard? No, why did I marry such a wimp? Why is my daughter such a tramp? Ironic, that Emily is the only decent one in the bunch, besides me.

She parked in her reserved parking place. They weren't expecting her. More than likely she'd catch them lazing about when they could be making her money. The mood she was in, she'd fire them all.

She bolted through the front door. Looking around the front office, all appeared normal. For once. She went to her office to get the rest of the bank statements.

"Melanie." Debbie pushed the intercom button from her office.

"Yes, Mrs. Winter."

"Has Sara called?"

"Six times. I told her to try your cell phone. She said you had it turned off."

Debbie grabbed her phone from her pocketbook. She flipped it open. Damn, she'd forgotten to turn it on. "Yes, it seems I forgot. Tell her if she calls again —"

"Sorry to interrupt, but Sara is here, Mrs. Winter. She's in the kitchen."

"Oh, well, thanks."

Debbie walked down the hall to the kitchen. Figures — where there was food there was Sara. She should insist on her having that new gastric bypass surgery all the fat movie stars were having. After the abortion.

"Mommy," Sara cried, as Debbie entered the room. "Oh, it's so terrible, and so not my fault. I don't know what I'm going to do. I'm still a girl. I told Joshua, but he . . . He raped me. Oh, Mommy, what am I going to do?"

"Oh shut up. For Pete's sake. I know

you're knocked up. You can have an abortion."

Sara stopped crying. *She would make one heck of an actress,* Debbie thought. *Of course, as fat as she is, she won't get the chance someone like Emily could.*

"Who told you?" Sara asked, all traces of whining gone.

"Your father. Exactly how many people have you told, Sara? You don't want this getting out. It could work against you, if you know what I mean."

"I don't know what you're talking about, Mommy." Sara stuffed a blueberry muffin into her mouth.

"You need to get your act together. Don't tell everyone you meet about this. Now, how far along are you?" This could be taken care of. It would take a bit of orchestrating, but Debbie was good at this.

"The doctor said I was about twenty-two weeks." Sara unwrapped another muffin.

"Oh, my God!"

"What's wrong with that? You asked me, and I told you." She crammed half the muffin in her mouth.

"What in the hell do you do with the allowance I give you every month, besides eat? Did you forget to buy your birth control pills, or did you eat those, too? What the hell am I going to do now? You've really made a mess of things, Sara. You should be more like your sister. At least she has the good sense not to go and get herself pregnant by some loser piece-of-crap boyfriend!"

Sara looked at her mother. "Josh isn't a loser!"

Debbie closed the door. No doubt the office staff was getting another earful of Sara's moaning and groaning.

Debbie yanked what was left of the muffin out of Sara's hand. "Sit down and shut up."

Sara did as she was told. Debbie sat across from her in a metal chair. Sara was so huge, she had to sit on the small love seat. "It's illegal to abort a fetus at twenty-two weeks. And don't give me any of your 'Mommy' crap, okay? You're twenty years old! It's time you acted like an adult. It is too late for you to abort this child! Does that mean anything at all to you?"

Sara seemed puzzled. Debbie knew Sara was a bit slow, but most of it was an act. *Hell, she's as devious and cunning as I am.*

"I guess I'll have to have a baby. Me and Josh can get married. You and Daddy will have a grandkid."

"It's not quite that simple. God." Debbie stood and started pacing. She was as bad as her drunken husband. Her world was crashing around her. "Sara, Josh is a loser. He quit school in the eighth grade. I doubt if he even knows what a sperm is. His parents live in a bus, Sara. Do you want a child of yours to be raised like a homeless person? Do you?"

"It's not so bad. I stay there sometimes. We build fires and roast hot dogs. I love them when they're burned just a tinge."

Sara was truly a genetic screwup.

"Well, no daughter of mine is going to raise her child in a goddamn bus. Do you understand me? You will not under any condition marry that hot dog–roasting uneducated moron you call your boyfriend. Can't you just imagine what kind of father he would make?"

Sara smiled. "Couldn't be any worse than Daddy. All he does is drink and go to that stupid club."

Debbie thought Sara had a point, but she wasn't going to give her credit for it.

"Your father is a very well-educated man. He's had some issues with alcohol in the past, but he's getting things under control. Now I want you to go home. I'm going to make sure you get the proper medical care while you're pregnant. Then, the very second you deliver that moron you're bound to give birth to, you will put it up for adoption. Is that understood?"

"But, Mommy, what if Josh wants this baby?"

"Sara, do you or Josh have any clue how much it costs to raise a child? No, don't answer that. You don't, and I'm sure he and his parents are clueless. And I am not so young that I'm ready to raise another child."

"You'd be a grandmother. You wouldn't have to."

Sara was truly simple.

"And I am too young to be a grandmother! You will do as I tell you or else!"

"Or else what, Mommy? You'll tell on me for making up all those lies about Uncle Alex? Lies that you made me tell. No, don't answer that, Mommy."

"Go home, Sara. I want you to spend some time with your father today."

"But what about me? What am I supposed to tell Josh?"

"Tell him to keep his pecker in his pants for a while, that's what you can tell him. Now get out of my sight. I've got to clean up another mess."

Sara inhaled, then exhaled. Her breath slapped Debbie in the face like old tuna.

"Go home and shower, Sara. Brush your teeth. I'll be there in a while."

"Okay, Mommy."

After Sara left, Debbie felt like she'd been caught in a whirlwind. She should have had her tested years ago. She had to be borderline retarded to act the way she did.

Debbie had received a letter from the bank. Her home was going into foreclosure. Someone was screwing with her. She was going to find out who, and when she did, she would make that person wish they'd never laid eyes on her.

Kate knew that, in good conscience, the only thing for her to do was confess what she'd done. She called Coleman and asked him to come to her apartment. It would be easiest to explain things if he was there.

Coleman arrived ten minutes early.

"So this is where you've been hiding."

"I guess you could say that. I think it will be easier for you to understand what I'm about to say if I can show you a few things. Follow me."

Kate took him to the small room she'd converted into an office. "Sit down." She directed him to a kitchen chair she'd brought in earlier. She sat next to him in her desk chair.

"I told you I wanted to ruin the Winter family."

"That's only natural after what they put you through. I've heard my share of stories from people, Kate."

She typed her password in and logged on to the Internet. She took the disc from her minisafe and inserted it into the computer. A few strokes later, she brought up the information she wanted Coleman to view.

"Knowing I couldn't do physical harm to either of the two, I thought about Debbie. Money has always been her top priority. Even over the girls. She came from a poor family. She spent most of her high school years working in a deli her mother owned. I guess because she was subjected to — I wouldn't call it poverty by any means, but the blue-collar life of her mother, I think she longed for wealth and the status she assumed it would bring. I'm speculating here, so bear with me. After I came to my senses, I decided the best way to hurt the Winters was financially."

She whirled around in her chair, allowing room for Coleman to get a bit closer to her monitor. "This is what I've been learning the past five years."

Kate allowed him to read the financial reports on the screen. "After working with the IRS for all that time and taking all the courses I could, I can get into just about any system. Banks, schools, credit card companies. Pretty much anything."

She waited for Coleman to comment. Nothing. She went on with her story.

"I hacked into Debbie's bank and emptied both of her accounts. She's now forty-three thousand dollars overdrawn. The bank obviously believes she took the money herself. It was an Internet transaction. I'm sure the bank manager thinks Debbie was lying when she told him she hadn't a clue what was happening to her money. Said she was going to sue the bank."

"How did you know this?"

"I knew about when Debbie would learn of her accounts being overdrawn. The Sun Bank calls their clients first thing if the account is in the red. Debbie's been a good customer, so they called her, I'm sure. Knowing how they work, I was at the bank opening a new account when she came storming in. She was furious. I guess you could say I laughed all the way *from* the bank."

Kate watched Coleman, gauging his reaction.

"I'm listening, Kate. Go on."

"I hacked into the credit card companies' databases. Deb had several cards, all with balances, but nothing terribly high. I maxed out all the cards and put a hold on all the accounts. I learned she had three mortgages on her house. I tampered with the mortgage companies' figures, and now the Winter home is in foreclosure."

Coleman grinned. "I hope to hell I never piss you off."

"So, tell me what a horrible monster I am."

He ran a hand through his hair. "I'm not going to say what you're doing is right, but I will say I can understand why you're doing it. Revenge is sweet, especially when you can choose the method by which it's delivered. I wouldn't want you to get caught, Kate. Some of these acts are federal. Bank tampering, for instance. I suppose you were aware of this from the beginning?"

"I was. And I didn't care if I got caught. That was what enabled me to continue with my plan. I didn't have a life without Alex. It didn't matter if I spent the remainder of my life a free woman on the outside or inside a jail cell."

"And what's changed about that now?" Coleman asked.

"I want to live again. I don't want to spend the rest of my life behind bars. Alex wouldn't have wanted to see me end up this way."

"No, he wouldn't. I assume you're going to tell me that you have something else in mind?"

"Sort of. I haven't worked out all the details. It's my hope that when all is said and done, Alex's death will be avenged and the Winter family will suffer, but in another way. That's the part I haven't quite worked out yet. So that's why you couldn't find me the past five years. I didn't need any distractions in my life. If I was to ruin the Winters, I had to concentrate on that and nothing else. There wasn't room in my life for anyone else."

"Are you telling me you have room in your life for someone now?" Coleman asked.

"I would like to try and make room for someone, Coleman. That's all I can promise at this point." Kate couldn't commit to anything more.

"Seems fair to me. Now that you've cleared up the past five years, tell me what can I do now to help you . . . move things forward?"

Kate was dumbfounded. Coleman wanted to help her?

"You'd be willing to . . . This is illegal. You just told me so. I can't ask you to break the law. Hell, you're an attorney."

"I know. I won't break the law, Kate. But

there are ways between the cracks."

"I never had any intention of keeping all that money. After I read Alex's letter, I think I've been given a bargaining tool."

"Want to explain?" Coleman quizzed.

Kate had spent most of the night reworking her plot. It wasn't foolproof, but it wasn't illegal either. She explained her plan to Coleman.

"You've an excellent mind. You would've made a powerful opponent in a courtroom. So, when do we get started?"

"I say there is no time like the present."

Kate and Coleman spent the afternoon making plans. If all turned out well, she would walk away from this a free woman. First, she had a lot of hacking to do.

Debbie couldn't concentrate on the contract she'd been reading for the past hour. Her world was unraveling minute by minute. She hadn't convinced that idiot at the bank that she wasn't responsible for overdrawing her accounts. She contacted her attorney as promised, but he hadn't come up with anything yet. Said it would take a few days. Well, dammit, she didn't have a few days! Lawyers. Always thought the world was on their time clock. Their slow-ticking time clock. Billable hours, they called it. Debbie knew exactly how long it would take for Simon Lewis to get his ass to the bank. Unless he crab-walked, there was no way in hell it should take a "few days."

Of all times for Sara to get herself knocked up, she has to do it now? That girl amazes me. One minute she acts like a three-year-old and the next she acts like a woman of the world. Sara knows how to play people around her.

Of course, she'd learned from a master. Debbie was an expert manipulator. Only she chose what and whom she wanted to manipulate much more carefully than her daughter.

What a loser Josh was. She could just visualize Sara and him raising a child together. She certainly had her work cut out for her with that girl. But she couldn't think about Sara or Don now. If something didn't happen soon, they'd all be penniless and out on the street.

Debbie knew someone was after her. She didn't know who it was or why they had chosen this time to screw with her, but she would find out. When she did, there would be hell to pay.

Meanwhile, she had an office to run. For a while, she hoped. Until this crazed stalker or whatever the hell she wanted to call the person was found out. Indeed, for all she knew, she could lose her office that very day. Simon had told her to go to the police. She'd been very adamant when she said no. They were the last people on earth she wanted poking into her business. She obviously could not explain why that was so when Simon had asked. She had simply said no and left it at that. He couldn't bring them into this without her permission. Let him do the job himself. That's what she paid him for.

Debbie thought about her life growing up. She'd had to work her ass off at the deli. When her mother hadn't been drunk, she'd been on her ass like white on rice for something all the time. Had she taken care of next week's order? Where were the menus for the next week? Why did she order that brand of cheese? Had she done her homework? It was constant. The only time she got any relief were the times her mother was passed out drunk. Which was often, but not often enough, as far as Debbie was concerned. She wanted a different life. She didn't want to sell ham and cheese and smelly sauerkraut. She wanted luxuries. Nice homes and cars. Clothes that were the envy of all. But most of all, she wanted a man in her life to take care of her. When she met Don, she thought she'd found the perfect man. He was as ambitious as she was. He hadn't had an easy life either.

Together they would change their lives. She'd had such good intentions. Then she met Alex Rocket. After meeting him, she decided she'd made the wrong choice. Alex had so much money, he didn't know what to do with it. It was family money, but Alex was an only child. He'd get his hands on it eventually. He already had quite a stash if you saw the car he drove, the clothes he wore. Don told her Alex was down-to-earth. Money meant nothing to him. His parents bought the clothes and the cars. Alex was content to drive an old beat-up pickup that had belonged to his father when his father was a young man.

Debbie didn't believe Don for a minute when he'd told her about Alex. She tried to make a play for him on more than one occasion, but nothing ever came of it. He would tease her, telling her he had a girl. Anna. She was so delicate and sickly the first time Debbie met her. Alex had married her. Hadn't even invited her and Don to the wedding. Though, to be sure, he hadn't been invited to theirs. Who would have wanted to attend anyway? She and Don had married in the courthouse one rainy afternoon. Still, she was shocked to learn Alex was married. All chances of snatching him, gone.

Then Anna got even sicker. She didn't know how long they were married, but Alex was shocked when she died. Don and Debbie went to offer their condolences. They'd stayed for a few days. Then Don had to go back to work. They had just moved to Florida. Don was working his way up the ladder. Debbie insisted he go home without her, telling him she'd stay with Alex a few more days.

One thing led to another. During Alex's mourning, she'd seduced him. Emily was the result.

A couple of months later, she'd gone to Alex telling him she was pregnant with his child. There were some doubts on his part at first. But then Emily was born. As she grew older, she became the exact image of Alex. They'd decided not to tell anyone what had happened between them. Debbie agreed, but inside she was seething. He could sleep with her, but he wouldn't marry her. She told him she would divorce Don. Alex insisted he couldn't hurt his best friend any more than he had already. He had promised to take care of Emily for the rest of her life.

And Debbie had promised herself she would get even with the son of bitch one day. And she had.

Chapter 30

Kate spent the rest of the afternoon working at the computer. She had a lot of work before her, but knowing what her ultimate goal was, she didn't mind. The only regret she had was that she'd lost five good years of her life. She would soon be forty-four years old. While she wasn't an old maid by today's standards, she wasn't some young hot chick either.

She was excited that Coleman was helping her. She would call Gertie. There was nothing more to hide.

She punched in the number.

"Hello," Gertie said. In the background, the dogs were barking up a storm.

"It's Kate, Gertie. I take it I caught you at the kennel?"

"Yes, these little critters. They want their food. Why are you calling back so soon? You're not in jail, are you? If you are, I would hire that same attorney Alex had. The one in Florida. He'll be able to help you."

"Gertie! First, I'm not in jail, so you can stop worrying. Secondly, I'm calling to give you the good news."

"Okay, lay it on me."

"I'm calling off the plot. Things have changed. Oh, Gertie, I feel like such an idiot! All these years. I could've been helping you. I could have done a number of things. All I wanted was revenge. Why didn't you try and stop me? Never mind. Don't answer that. You did. I know that." Kate paused to take a breath.

"Well, I don't know what changed your mind, but whatever it is, I'm glad. Now when are you coming home?"

Kate hadn't thought that far ahead. She didn't really know where home was at the moment.

"I don't know. I'm still working on some things here. Gertie, Coleman Fitzpatrick is here. He's helping me." Kate waited.

"Gertie, did you hear me?" Kate asked.

"Yes, yes, I heard you. I thought you said you were finished with your schemes and plots. What in the world did you go and involve a legal man in all this mess for?"

Kate laughed. So like Gertie.

"He's not involved in any scheming. As you said, he's a man of the law. He's going to help me make things right. Sort of undoing what I've done, but in a different way. A legal way this time."

"So, has this Fitzpatrick kissed you yet?"

"Not hardly! Why would you ask such a silly question?"

"You sound happy, Kate. For the first time since Alex's death, you sound like the old Kate. The happy Kate. When you said 'Fitzpatrick,' something in your voice changed. I know these things, dear."

"Well, I like the man. I'll admit that. He's a wonderful friend. And to answer your question, no, he has not kissed me!" The kiss on her hand didn't count. Or did it? She'd had such a reaction. She felt silly. Like a schoolgirl.

"As soon as he does, I'll know. I'll be able to tell. And, Kate, don't drive this man off with your need for revenge. Second chances only come around once. Now, I have a crew of animals to care for. Call me soon."

Kate smiled as she replaced the phone in the cradle. Gertie knew her better than anyone. She hadn't had a chance to examine her feelings for Coleman. Whatever they were, they were still at the brewing stage. If asked, she had to admit she was attracted to him. He was the first man since Alex that she'd allowed herself to get close to. And it had only been a few days, but there was something simmering between them. When this was all over, she would take a closer look at her feelings. But first she needed to right the wrongs she'd been focused on for so many years.

She spent the next few minutes defragging her computer. That might take a while, so she was ready to implement round two of her plan.

This was going to be the hardest part. She and Coleman had gone over it until she was blue in the face. There was no other way.

She'd made a late-night trip to Wal-Mart. What would people do without the Wal-Marts around the world? Open all night for people like her. She'd purchased color stripper and a hair color as close to her own as she could find.

Now, as she stood in front of the bathroom mirror waiting for the solution to work its magic, she wondered what Debbie's reaction would be when she walked into her office. Would she put two and two together? Would she recognize her as Kate Ramsey, the woman who'd looked at her condo?

It didn't matter. Either way, she was going to go through with her plan. She was secure in the knowledge that once Debbie knew it was her who'd basically put the screws to her the past few days, she couldn't go to the police. Kate held too many aces. Debbie was going to go along with her plan. She had to. If not, Kate would go for round three.

Thirty minutes later, her reddish brown hair was almost back to its natural color. Another half hour to let the new color set, and she would be Kate again, just minus the long hair.

When she'd rinsed her hair in the shower, she got out and toweled off. Her reflection surprised her. She was pleased with what she saw. She hadn't done that bad a job on her hair. Cutting or coloring. *Who knows? Maybe I have a knack for doing hair.* She laughed. She added a bit of blush and mascara before getting dressed. Jeans and another white shirt. This would get old after a while, she thought. She wore her Nikes. In case she had to run.

Get real, you're being ridiculous! She was not afraid of Debbie. She was afraid of her own reaction to the vile Mrs. Winter. As Kate Rocket. Kate Ramsey was already history.

She drove directly to the real estate office. When she pulled into the parking lot, she waited for a few minutes before going inside. She hadn't rehearsed what she would say. She knew the words would come to her as soon as she saw Debbie.

She entered the reception area just as she had the day before.

"Melanie," she called.

"Be right there!"

Apparently the girl was in the kitchen. Kate could smell popcorn.

She didn't bother sitting down; she wanted to go right to the main office.

Melanie came down the hall with a paper bag of popcorn and a soda in her hands.

"Mrs. Ramsey?"

So much for her not recognizing her.

"Yes, Melanie, but it's really Mrs. Rocket. I don't have time to explain. Somehow I'm sure your boss will at a later date. Right now I need to speak to Mrs. Winter."

"You should have called first. You just missed her. She said she had an emergency at the bank. She didn't know when or if she'd be back for the rest of the day. I'm sorry. Is there something Randi can help you with?"

"No. Does Mrs. Winter have a cell phone?" Kate asked.

"Of course. All the agents have a cell phone. Mrs. Winter supplies them with one; if not, well, who's to say when a client would call and they —"

"Sorry, Melanie, I don't have time to listen to your story. I want you to listen to me. What I am about to tell you and how you react could mean your job. Do you understand?" Kate hated to do this to the girl who'd been so sweet to her, but she didn't have time to worry about it at present.

"What is it?" Melanie asked. She didn't sound so sweet after all.

"I want you to call Mrs. Winter. Tell her there is an emergency at the office. She needs to return right away."

"I don't think so, Mrs. Ramsey. Not now. She just learned her youngest daughter is pregnant. She's screamed at me so much the past two days, I am not willing to suffer her wrath."

"Even if it means your job?" Kate persisted.

"I don't mean to be rude, but I don't think you have the power to control what Mrs. Winter does with her employees."

So Melanie wanted to get smart. Okay, Kate would play her game.

"That's fine. I know where she banks. And I know why she's there. So, when she does come back, tell her she had an opportunity to get all of her money returned. She'll know what I'm talking about. And you can tell her that you decided that wasn't important enough to call her. You have a great day, Melanie."

Kate was almost to the door before Melanie shouted, "Wait!"

She knew Melanie would see things her way. She stopped and turned to face the girl.

"Yes?"

"Wait. I'll call her. But if I get fired for this, you better believe I'm going to tell her how you came in here and bullied me into doing this."

"I don't think you'll get fired. Now make the call before I change my mind."

Melanie dialed Debbie's cell with shaking hands. Kate hated what she was doing, bullying a complete innocent, but it had to be done.

"Yes, I'm sorry. I know you said not to call. Well, there is a woman here that says she will get your money back. Yes. In the office. Right here. She wants to speak to you."

Melanie gave Kate the phone.

"Hi, Debbie, how are you?"

Nothing.

"Who is this?"

"Oh, I think you know exactly who I am. Does the name Alex Rocket ring any bells? I tell you what, I've got fifteen minutes to kill. I can either spend them waiting for you to return from the bank, or I can drive to the police station. I'm going to be nice and let you decide for me. You like to make life-altering decisions, don't you, Deb? No, don't answer that. Be here. Fifteen minutes."

Kate pushed the red End button on the phone.

"I'm going to wait in Mrs. Winter's office. You did good, Melanie. Thanks."

Kate was shaking like Jell-O as she sauntered down the long hall. A few of the associates watched her from their desks.

She entered the chrome-and-white office. She sat in the white leather chair behind her desk. She could just imagine the look on Debbie's face when she saw her sitting there.

Just to be spiteful, Kate poked a few keys on Debbie's keyboard. She'd locked her system down. No one in the office would be using the Internet or the computers. For a while. Kate laughed.

Less than fifteen minutes later, Debbie swooped down the hall and into her office. She stopped dead in her tracks when she saw Kate.

"Long time no see. Well, not really. By the way, I did enjoy viewing the condo. You might want to tone down on —"

"What in God's name are you doing in my office?" Debbie kicked the door shut as she leaned across her desk.

"Sit. Debbie. Sit." Kate pointed to the chair across from her.

Debbie sat down in the chair usually reserved for her clients.

"You're just like the dogs Alex breeds. I guess I should say 'good girl.' "

"I'm giving you thirty seconds to tell me what you're doing here, or I am going to call my attorney."

"Call your attorney?" Kate gave a harsh laugh. "What do you think your *attorney* will do to me? Say, 'Shame, shame, go away. Come again another day'?" Kate stood up and peered out the window behind her. "I have a proposition for you."

"You don't have anything I'm interested in, so why don't you leave. Your perverted husband ruined my life and my daughter's life. Personally, I think you have a lot of nerve shoving your way in here like you own the place."

Debbie grabbed a cigarette out of her purse. Her hands trembled as she tried to light a match. Debbie stood up.

"Sit down, goddamn you. You are going to listen to me. Put that cigarette out!" Kate raised her voice so loud she knew the office staff heard her. She didn't really care.

Debbie sat back down, stubbing the cigarette out in an ashtray. "This better be good, Kate Rocket. Now, say what you have to say, then get the hell out of my office!"

Debbie sounded like a deflating balloon. Nothing but hot air coming out of her mouth.

"Does Emily know Alex is her father?"

"So, you found out. Mr. Perfect wasn't so perfect, was he? Yeah, we had a fling. Big deal."

"It was a big deal to Alex. He took care of Emily. I know that, and I am proud he did. I always knew she was different from you and Sara. Speaking of, I just learned that your little monster is pregnant. Does she know who the father is? Forget I said that. Now, I'm going to tell you what I'm here for. Aren't you just dying to know?"

"Actually, I'm not. I don't really care to listen to anything coming from your mouth. Do you think you can walk in here and ruin our lives just because you . . . you get the urge?"

"No, actually I spent quite a few years planning what I would say to you when I saw you. Now, where is Emily?"

"She's at vet school, not that it's any of

your business. Alex might have been Emily's father, but I am still her mother. There is nothing you can say or do to change that. I know, I know, you were always so jealous because I could have children and you were as dried up as an old tumbleweed. So Emily isn't really of any concern to you."

"You're wrong. I think she is. Now, before we spend the rest of the day acting like fishwives, I have a proposition for you."

Debbie shot a half-smile at her. "You don't have anything I want, Kate Rocket. God, I can't believe you!"

"How are things at the bank? Were they able to find all the money missing from your accounts? And your mortgage company? Have they told you your home is in foreclosure?"

All the years Kate spent sacrificing herself were worth it just for the look of shock on Debbie's face. "How do you know about that?"

"Oh come on, Debbie. You aren't that stupid! Then again, maybe you are. You never were the brightest star in the sky, if I remember correctly. I guess that hasn't changed much either."

Debbie remained silent. Kate saw fear in her eyes. She wondered if Debbie knew the fear Alex felt as he was being stabbed to death. The fear he'd felt when he'd been convicted for a crime that never happened.

"Tell me what it is you want."

"We're going to play give-and-take. I have something you want. You have something I want. Is that simple enough for you?"

"Just spit it out, Kate."

"We're playing this game on my terms, Mrs. Winter, not yours, so shut up!" Kate shoved the monitor off the desk, sending it crashing to the floor. Next, she hurled the ashtray into the air like a Frisbee. Ashes went everywhere.

"What —"

Kate held up her hand. "My terms. Remember that."

Debbie leaned back in her chair as Kate came to her side of the desk.

"These are my terms. Listen, because I'm only going to say them once. Tomorrow at noon, that's twelve o'clock, big hand on the twelve, little hand on the twelve. Are you getting this? I can speak slower if you'd like."

Kate loved the looks racing across Debbie's face. She'd give a million dollars if Alex could be there to witness them.

"Are you?" Kate shouted.

"I'm getting it, okay?" Debbie shouted back.

"You don't have to raise your voice, I can

hear you just fine. Now, I was saying. At noon tomorrow I want to see you, Don, Sara, and Emily at this location." Kate tossed a slip of paper to her.

"Are you out of your mind? Emily hasn't been home since she left for college. What makes you think you can convince her to come home?"

"Tell her Aunt Kate is waiting to see her. I promise she'll come. I know her better than you might think."

"And what do I get in return?" Debbie shot back.

"Oh, you'll have to wait. I'm not telling you now. That wouldn't be fun at all. Be at that address tomorrow. Twelve o'clock sharp, or all that cash that's just hanging in cyberspace will mysteriously work its way into . . . the account of some more deserving person. Perhaps someone like Donald Trump or Warren Buffett.

"Now, I want you to have a nice day, Mrs. Winter. And by the way, if I find out that you've reprimanded Melanie in any way for her very, very small part in this, well, I think you know what I can do. You'd best get busy. Bye now." Kate practically floated out of the office.

Kate watched Coleman watch her. They'd

been up all night planning their strategy. It was eleven forty-five. Fifteen minutes to see if Kate's plan would work.

"What will we do if Emily doesn't show?" Coleman asked Kate.

"Oh, I think she will. Debbie can be very persuasive when she needs to be, especially if the almighty dollar is at stake. I've thought a lot about getting even with Debbie and Sara these past years. I wanted it more than anything. And now I just want it to be over. I want to move on."

"I understand. I can't wait to get to my cabin in the mountains." Coleman was smiling.

"You really enjoy your place, don't you?"

"More than anywhere I go."

"You know, you've never told me where your cabin was. Is there a reason?" Kate hoped she wasn't putting him on the spot. Maybe he liked having his privacy. Maybe he didn't want her or anyone else to know the location of his cabin.

"No, there is no reason. I thought Alex might have told you. We'd talked about spending a few quiet days there when he came home. Black Mountain, North Carolina. I love it there, too. You'll have to come and stay at the cabin, Kate. I have a state-of-the-art kitchen. Anything I want, I just hop into my plane and fly to Asheville, Charlotte. It's the best of both worlds. Here in the winter, there in the summer."

Kate looked at him like he'd lost his mind. "And here I thought your cabin was in . . . heck, I don't know where, but not in North Carolina. So, when you came to tell me about Alex, did you go to your cabin then?"

"I did."

"Well, I don't know what to say. We were practically neighbors."

"Will you go back to Asheville, Kate?"

"I haven't given it much thought, really. I don't want to stay here. I suppose I should at least go hang with Gertie for a while. Give her a break. She hasn't had a vacation in five years."

Coleman walked over to where she was sitting. He took her hand and pulled her into a standing position. Kate knew what was about to happen. There was no way she was going to stop him either.

With the gentleness of a whisper, Coleman touched her lips with his. Gently, then firmly. He pulled her close to him, closer than she'd ever been. She felt all of him next to her, wanted all of him. In every way there was to want, she wanted. All or nothing. Slowly, Coleman broke the kiss. "Would it be presumptuous of me to invite myself for dinner now and then?"

Kate smiled and gazed up into the verdant eyes of the man she'd fallen in love with. "Coleman Fitzpatrick, you'll have dinner with me if I have to come and get you myself."

"Just dinner?" he teased.

"Coleman, we're just at the appetizer phase, but dessert is looking pretty good."

He burst out laughing. "Oh, Kate, I'm so glad . . . I'm so glad we found one another after all these years. I feel like a kid right now!" Coleman picked her up and whirled her around.

There was a knock at the door. Both of them looked at their watches.

Twelve o'clock. On the dot.

Coleman answered the knock.

"Mr. Coleman, they're here. I was told to set up first."

"Yes, anywhere you'll feel comfortable."

Coleman had insisted on using his office, then he'd gone on to suggest a court reporter and a videographer. Kate told him she didn't know if the Winter family would allow the relevant portions of their conversation to be taped. Coleman had explained that was part of the package. Said to insist or there was no deal. Now she was glad she had gone along with the plan.

The court reporter and videographer were ready when they were needed.

Coleman asked his secretary to show the Winter family to his office and to show the stenographer and the cameraman in when he called for them.

Kate stood beside Coleman. She needed his support to get through this. She'd been hard and toughened by her experience, but now, she wanted Coleman to stand with her as she implemented the final phase of her revised plan.

Debbie, Don, and Sara came inside the office. Sara weighed at least three hundred pounds. Kate drew in a breath as she looked at her. She was obviously very pregnant. She wore as much makeup as her mother. A black T-shirt with the name of some rock band stretched across her huge belly. Debbie wore white as usual. Don lingered in the background.

"Kate," he said when he saw her. She nodded, but didn't say a word.

"Emily had to use the ladies' room. She came right from the airport. I told her we couldn't stop until we arrived," Don said to her and Coleman.

Kate was shocked at the sight of Don. He'd lost weight. His skin was flabby, sallow. Gone was the handsome man of the past. He appeared shrunken into himself. Kate felt a wave of pity. He hadn't done anything to make Alex's situation any better, but Kate knew he'd truly believed Alex guilty. She wondered how he felt now.

A few minutes later, Emily was escorted into the room. Kate took a deep breath, then walked across the room to take the girl in her arms. She didn't care what Emily's mother or father thought. This was Emily. Alex's daughter. Overcome with a powerful feeling of love for the young woman, Kate thought she would back out, but then she knew she had to continue. Emily had to know Alex for what and who he was.

Almost bashful, Emily spoke to her. "You're beautiful, Aunt Kate! I love the short hair."

Kate touched her hair. "You haven't changed, Emily. You are still as pretty as a picture."

"Can we get this show on the road instead of you two cooing over one another like two lost loves," Debbie said to them.

"Mother, do you always have to be so crude? I haven't seen Aunt Kate in almost eight years, or did you forget that, too?"

Kate felt the hostility between the two women.

Coleman stood up. "I think we're ready to

get started. This is a bit unorthodox, to say the least. Emily, I'm Coleman Fitzpatrick. I was Alex Rocket's attorney."

She held her hand out to him.

"What's wrong, Mr. Attorney? You too good to shake my hand?" Sara Winter blurted.

"No, Ms. Winter, I'm not too good to shake your hand. I just find that the idea of doing so sickens me," Coleman responded.

Sara looked at her mother and was about to start one of her tantrums, when Debbie told her to shut up.

"If we could get started. Kate."

"Thanks, Coleman. Thank you, Emily, for coming here. I know you haven't been home since your high school graduation, so I want you to know that I really appreciate the sacrifice."

Debbie rolled her eyes.

"Sara, I swore I would never speak to you again after what you did. The current set of circumstances dictates that I have to speak to you."

"I don't care if you talk to me one way or the other. Do I have to hear this crap, Mommy?"

"Sara, sit your fat ass down and shut up!" Debbie shouted.

Kate stood behind Coleman's large desk.

"Before we bring in the court reporter and the videographer, I have some things to say. For the past five years I have done nothing but plot and plan the ruin of the Winter family." Kate paused, wanting to see the expressions on their faces. Debbie continued to roll her eyes, while Sara chomped on a piece of gum. Don hung his head. Emily listened to every word Kate was saying.

"And I had almost reached that goal when, a few days ago, Coleman found me. He gave me a letter from Alex, a letter I was never to see unless Alex was dead. We all know what happened to Alex. First, he was accused of a crime so filthy and vile that I can't bear to think about it. Then he was convicted. Finally, he was murdered a few months later — after he'd learned that his conviction had been overturned and he was getting a new trial. Is that justice?

"Alex was innocent of all the charges against him. I know it. There are at least two people in this room that know it as well."

No one spoke. "In my quest for revenge, I learned a skill that I thought would help me. It did, but as things turned out, not quite the way I had planned. When I first learned of Alex's murder, I wanted to kill you, Sara. I could think of nothing that would please me more than choking the life out of you! Then I remembered that you were a child, by and large a product of your environment. It was your mother at whom I needed to direct my anger. And that is what I did. Debbie, would you mind telling Sara why she is here today?"

"I know why I'm here, I'm not stupid!"

"You said those same words when you gave your testimony. I don't think you're stupid at all, Sara. I think you're a pitiful, miserable excuse for a human being. Go on, Debbie, explain why you and your family are here today."

Debbie looked at Kate. If ever there was murder in a woman's eyes, it was in Debbie's.

"A few days ago I got a call from my bank. They said I was overdrawn by forty-three thousand dollars. Then I received a certified letter from our mortgage holder. They were about to foreclose on our house. All my credit cards are on hold."

"Why didn't you tell me this?" Don asked.

"Oh, you're too damned drunk to understand anything. When did you start caring anyway?" Debbie tossed at her husband.

"Please, all of you, let's stop arguing. Aunt Kate, can you tell me why I'm here?" Emily asked.

"Just a moment, Emily. Coleman, would you please have your secretary show the videographer and the court reporter in."

After the two newcomers entered and got themselves set up, Kate looked at Debbie. "You want to do the honors?"

"Emily, all those years ago" — Debbie looked at both of her daughters, but her eyes rested on Sara — "Alex did not molest Sara." Silence, except for the sounds of the video camera shooting and the court reporter taking down what was being said.

"But you said" — Sara cried out before she was cut off by her mother.

"Forget what I said and keep quiet. For once, Sara, keep your flapping jaws shut!"

Emily looked at her mother, then at Sara. "Then . . . Uncle Alex died . . . ohmygod!" She started to cry. Kate walked over and gave her a tissue.

"Debbie?" Coleman urged.

"Emily, I need you to listen. I want you to hear what I have to say. You're a grown woman now, you have a life of your own, but dear old Aunt Kate here, in all those years while she dropped off the face of the earth, Kate Rocket had a plan.

"Debbie, either you come out and say it or I will. I've waited too long to hear this, there's no need to make it any worse for

Emily than it's going to be," Kate admonished.

"Okay, here it is. Pure and simple. Twenty-four years ago I had a one-night stand with good old Alex Rocket. You, my dearest daughter, are the result!"

Emily observed her mother and father. "But, Dad, did you know?"

Kate thought Emily was taking the news remarkably well.

"Yes, Em, I knew. But only after Alex was in jail, though I had suspected for a long time I was not the man who had fathered you. But I still loved you no matter who your biological father was. That never changed, even after I found out who that man was. You were a great daughter." Don wrapped his arms around her. "You still are. It's me that's been such a waste. I've let your mother dictate to me for too many years. I was always too busy trying to climb to the top. I wanted to be somebody. Somebody like Alex. I've failed miserably, Emily. All I can ask is that you forgive me." Don's shoulders shook with sobs.

No one in the room said anything. There were no words left to say.

"Then why are we here? Why do we have to have these" — Emily pointed to the court reporter and the videographer — "people here, recording our every word?"

"You can thank Aunt Kate for arranging this."

"Is this true?" Emily questioned.

"Yes, I'm afraid it is. I've waited so long to clear Alex's name. He was so ashamed when the charges were brought against him. He worried more about me than himself. What would this do to Kate? He always wrote that he was sorry. He had nothing to be sorry for! He died because of a lie!

"In exchange for Sara's coming clean, I've agreed to help your mother clear up her banking problems, clear up her mortgage problems, and clear up the problems with her credit cards. And in turn, I get to remove the stain from Alex's name. I hope to air this on the six o'clock news tonight!"

"That wasn't part of our deal!"

"No, you're right, it wasn't. Did you really believe having Sara confess was enough? All of the people who loved and cared for Alex have the right to know he didn't die in prison as some dirty child molester!"

"So now you want to drag my family through the mud? Is that what you want, Kate, an eye for an eye?" Debbie screamed at her. The veins were bulging in her face. "Because if this tape is made public, you will have ruined me and my family!"

"I know. Now, perhaps, you'll know what it feels like. Don, is there something you want to say? I know Coleman spoke with you this morning. He didn't tell me what you wanted to say, only that you'd like a chance to get a few things off your chest. Do you still want to go through with it?" Kate asked.

"Yes. Sara, I'm sorry if this hurts you. We've shoved your problems under the rug far too long. I told your mother you needed help all those years ago. She supposedly took care of it, and I led myself to believe that she had. I know better. It wasn't just you that needed the help. Debbie, you were instrumental in bringing the charges against Alex. When I thought you were having heart-to-heart talks with Sara, you were telling her things to say! How could you? Alex was my best friend! Not only did you sleep with him, but as far as I'm concerned, you killed him, too!"

More silence. Even Sara was at a loss for words.

"Sara, you were a child when this happened. I don't hold you fully responsible, but you knew better. You knew early on that Emily was Uncle Alex's child. And you wanted to see him suffer just as much as your mother did, didn't you!"

"I did what Mommy told me to do, that's all. I —"

"Other than jealousy," Don interrupted, "I'll never know or understand what motivated you, Debbie, but one thing I do understand for the first time in my life. I will never allow you to control me again. You've ruined Sara, and for that we are both going to have to get her help. The second I leave this room, I'm going home. I am leaving, and I never want to see your lying, conniving face again! Do you understand?"

"Whatever, Don. You're such a drunk. Now, Kate, you've got what you wanted? How about doing what you promised?"

After the court reporter and the cameraman left, Kate went over to Coleman's computer. She had already replaced the money, cleaned up everything in Debbie's accounts. For show, she had told Coleman she needed these few minutes of glory. Since she had admitted nothing to anyone but the Winters, and she knew full well that neither Emily nor Don would ever testify against her, no matter what Debbie did, she wasn't concerned about being brought to justice for her criminal activity.

Emily said nothing to Kate, but Kate knew she would come around. Don apologized again. Debbie and Sara were bickering before they were out of the room.

With the transcript of relevant portions of the meeting in the court reporter's capable hands and the video available for airing by the anchors of the six o'clock news in Naples, as well as Asheville and surrounding areas, Kate felt she had accomplished what she'd set out to do all those years ago — ruin the Winters family, or at least half of that family.

As a bonus, Alex's reputation would be restored, and she could get on with her life. The rest would take care of itself.

Kate looked at Coleman. "What do you think about making dinner for a hardworking girl?"

"Only if she'll kiss the cook!"

Kate welcomed Coleman into her arms.

Epilogue

One year later . . .
Christmas Eve

Snowflakes as big as dinner plates rained down in the darkened sky. Opalescent starlight hid behind clouds. The moon peered out from the top of the Black Mountains in the distance. The cabin sat on the side of the mountain, smoke billowing from its chimney.

Inside, the cabin was full of laughter and cheer. Heavenly scents of baking cookies wafted through the cool night air. Emily Winter thought it resembled a scene from a Norman Rockwell painting.

She hoped she was still welcome. It had been a long time, but she was ready to forgive Aunt Kate. She hesitated before knocking. This wasn't her home, this was Coleman's. He might not want her here after all. Aunt Kate had sent her dozens of letters inviting her to the mountains. In each letter she'd asked her to spend the holidays with them, and Emily decided that she wanted to share this special holiday with someone she truly loved and who loved her in return.

Well, here she was. Do or die. She tapped on the door. She heard laughter and a baby crying. *A baby? Odd, Aunt Kate never mentioned anything in any of her letters about one of her friends having a baby.* She knocked harder a second time.

The door swung open as she was about to knock again. "Emily!"

"In the flesh."

Coleman opened the door, "Come in, you'll freeze your butt off out there. Let me take your coat."

Emily knew Aunt Kate and Coleman had married in June. She was happy for them.

Emily stepped inside. The cabin looked like something from a fairy tale. A Christmas tree, at least fifteen feet tall, stood in the corner. Red, green, blue, and every color under the rainbow sparkled from the glow of the lights. A gold star shone as bright as the fire in the stone fireplace at the opposite end of the room. This is how Christmas at Aunt Kate's had always appeared in her dreams.

Red sofas and dark green chairs were scattered all about the giant room. People were grouped in small circles. Young and old. Bing Crosby singing "White Christmas" played softly in the background. Tears filled her eyes at the scene. Uncle Alex — her dad — would've liked this.

Coleman took her coat as she observed the festivities. "It's kind of a Christmas party, wedding reception, and baby shower all rolled into one."

Emily smiled. "That sounds wonderful. Now, where can I find Aunt Kate? Oh, wait, let me guess. She's in the kitchen?"

"Where else? Go on in and surprise her. This will be her best present yet," Coleman encouraged.

Emily followed the scent of baking cookies to the kitchen. She watched the merriment. This was what she wanted, only with three kids and ten dogs. She saw a golden red–colored retriever curled up in a corner, its tail wagging ninety miles a minute.

She took a step, then another before she stopped. Aunt Kate was pulling trays from a huge oven. Three other women were filling baskets with the cookies as fast as they could take them off the cookie sheets.

Unaware of who she was, one of the women invited her to grab a basket. Emily did as instructed. Aunt Kate replaced one cookie sheet with another before she saw Emily standing next to her in the cookie assembly line. "Emily? It's really you!"

She grabbed her and hugged her, then pushed her away in order to look at her. "You are so pretty, Emily. You look like an angel."

"It's okay to say I look like Uncle Alex. I know I do."

"Oh, Emily, this is the best holiday of my life! When did you get here?"

"Just a few minutes ago. Coleman let me in."

"Sit, sit. You don't have to work. We're baking cookies for the dogs at the local shelters. Just don't take a bite. I don't think this recipe is meant for human consumption."

"Is Gertie here?"

"She's around here somewhere. I practically had to drag her here. She refused to leave the kennel, unless Lauren — she's worked for Gertie since high school — agreed to come and stay at the house."

"Sounds like Gertie, stubborn as ever."

"Who said I was stubborn?" Gertie entered the kitchen. "Emily? Why, I'll be a monkey's uncle. Kate didn't tell me you were coming. My Lord, you've gotten so . . . grown-up and so pretty. Looks just like

Alex. Come here and let me hug you." The two embraced. Gertie's eyes filled with tears.

"This is the best gift an old coot like me could have. Kate, why didn't you tell me the girl would be here?"

Emily looked at Kate.

"It was a surprise, Gertie. For everyone."

Emily mouthed *thank you* to Kate.

"So, does she know about the little princess?" Gertie asked Kate.

Kate gave Gertie a shut-your-trap look. Emily had seen them at it before.

"What little princess are you talking about?"

"Emily, come upstairs, and I'll show you."

Kate took the young woman she loved so much like a daughter and led her upstairs to a loft that overlooked the great room below.

"This is so neat. I would stay up here all the time if this were my room." Emily leaned over and peered at the holiday festivities below.

"It's a great cabin. Coleman and I, we plan to live here full-time. Maybe next year. It's taking him a little bit longer to retire than he thought. The wheels of justice do grind slowly." Kate smiled.

"How long since you've seen your family?"

Emily looked sad suddenly, and Kate was sorry she'd brought up the topic.

"It's over a year. I haven't been back since that day in Coleman's office. I just never fit in with them, Aunt Kate. I know that sounds terrible. They're my family. They're just different. I did get a letter from Dad. He hasn't had a drink in over a year. I'm proud of him."

"And you should be. He didn't always have an easy row to hoe." Kate felt bad for Don, but was glad he'd gotten the help he needed.

"They're still not divorced. Dad doesn't know why Mom won't sign the papers, but he said he was moving on. He likes living in New York again. I guess he's working at a new engineering firm. He seems happy.

"The last I heard, Mother had been forced to close her agency, sell the house, and has moved somewhere in Georgia, where she's bought herself a diner. Sara's married to that druggie creep, and no one knows where she's got to.

"What did you want to tell me, Aunt Kate? I know you brought me up here for a reason."

"Yes, I did. Wait here. I'll be right back."

Kate left and came back in a matter of minutes. She carried a small bundle in her arms. "This is what I wanted to show you." Kate fumbled with the bundle in her arms. She pulled the blanket aside to reveal a tiny face.

"Oh my! She's so pretty, Aunt Kate."

"I think so. She's a very good baby, aren't you?" Kate nuzzled the nose of the small infant inside the blankets.

"So who does she belong to? I thought I heard a baby crying when I knocked on the door."

Cooing noises came from the infant. Kate and Emily laughed. "She'll be talking before you know it. Emily, this little girl is mine and Coleman's." Kate paused, giving her time to absorb the news.

"How? You never said you were pregnant in all those letters. Well, you look fantastic! What did you name this little sweet pea?" Emily took the infant from Kate.

"We named her Alexandra Suzanne."

"That's a mouthful, but beautiful." Emily continued to kiss and tickle the baby.

"Emily, I did not give birth to Alexandra. We adopted her."

"Well, that explains your figure. I think that's wonderful. I know you and Uncle Alex always wanted a child of your own.

How old is she?" Emily asked.

"Three months. Her biological mother was the daughter of one of Coleman's clients. The infant was placed for private adoption after the mother died in childbirth. We named her Alexandra Suzanne because Suzanne was Coleman's first wife, and we both thought Alexandra was a good name, sort of in honor of Alex."

"I think this is wonderful, Aunt Kate. Life sometimes throws you lemons, and boy did you ever whip them into lemonade!" When Emily hugged Kate, Alexandra Suzanne cried, and they both laughed.

"We're going to add a very special ornament to the tree in a minute. I'd like for you to do the honors. Follow me."

Downstairs the guests were standing around the tree. Each had an ornament to place. Wedding ornaments, baby ornaments, and silly ornaments were hung all over the tree.

Kate handed the baby to Coleman. She clapped her hands to get everyone's attention.

"I have a very special ornament to place on the tree. It's been many years since it hung from a branch. Tonight is a very special night for me. I've got the child I've always dreamed of and a husband who cooks." Everyone laughed. "And I have Emily, who has always been like a daughter to me. I would like to give you the honor of placing my own very special ornament on the tree."

Kate took a small box and removed the tissue paper in which the ornament was wrapped. Her and Alex's very first Christmas ornament — their wedding picture etched in the crystal star and those memorable words. She handed the ornament to Alex's daughter.

Tears flowed as Emily hung her father's ornament on the tree. When she finished, there was slow applause, then everyone shouting "Merry Christmas" to one another.

"There is one more thing." Kate took a present the size of a shirt box and gave it to Emily. "This is for you. From Alex."

There wasn't a dry eye in the room as they watched Emily open her present.

She removed the paper slowly, taking her time so as not to tear it. She took out a stack of papers held together with a red ribbon. She removed the ribbon, then scanned the papers.

"This is the deed to the kennel!"

"Merry Christmas, Emily!" Kate whispered.

Later, after all the guests had left and the

night was quiet, Kate stepped outside into the cold winter air.

She removed the top of the container she carried. She stood high on the mountain, on land that she loved. With tears in her eyes, she released the ashes that she'd carried for so long.

"You're home now, Alex. Truly home."

ABOUT THE AUTHOR

Fern Michaels is the *USA Today* and *New York Times* bestselling author of *Home Free, Southern Comfort, Deadly Deals, Exclusive: The Godmothers,* and dozens of other novels and novellas. There are over seventy million copies of her books in print.

Fern Michaels has built and funded several large daycare centers in her hometown, and is a passionate animal lover who has outfitted police dogs across the country with special bulletproof vests. She shares her home in South Carolina with her five dogs and a resident ghost named Mary Margaret. Visit her website at www.fernmichaels.com.

The employees of Thorndike Press hope you have enjoyed this Large Print book. All our Thorndike, Wheeler, and Kennebec Large Print titles are designed for easy reading, and all our books are made to last. Other Thorndike Press Large Print books are available at your library, through selected bookstores, or directly from us.

For information about titles, please call:
(800) 223-1244

or visit our Web site at:
http://gale.cengage.com/thorndike

To share your comments, please write:
Publisher
Thorndike Press
10 Water St., Suite 310
Waterville, ME 04901